ACCIDENTAL HERO
A MARRIAGE MISTAKE ROMANCE

❦

NICOLE SNOW

ICE LIPS PRESS

Content copyright © Nicole Snow. All rights reserved.
Published in the United States of America.
First published in May, 2018.

Disclaimer: The following book is a work of fiction. Any resemblance characters in this story may have to real people is only coincidental.

Please respect this author's hard work! No section of this book may be reproduced or copied without permission. Exception for brief quotations used in reviews or promotions. This book is licensed for your personal enjoyment only. Thanks!

Cover Design – CoverLuv. Photo by Wander Aguiar Photography.

Website: Nicolesnowbooks.com

DESCRIPTION

Accidentally engaged. Then he dared me to make it real.

It was one freaking kiss with a stranger.

I wasn't looking for a hero the day Brent Eden charged into my life.

He saw a damsel in distress facing humiliation.

We played pretend. Swore I was his. Baited sweet chaos.

Blew apart *everything*.

My dating disaster? Gone.

Our kiss? Electric. Divine. Toe-curling.

His mistake? Oh, boy.

Dropping the ultimate F-bomb: fiancé.

Especially when my gossipy cousin tells the whole family.

Forget how he's badass personified.

    The ink. The leather. The abs. The smirk.

    The lightning eyes and the growl I can't resist.

    Nothing changes the fact that he's my favorite student's father.

    I'm risking it all for this charade. And I'm losing.

The closer we get, the deeper I fall.

    The louder he vows to protect me.

    The more we come undone.

    Even my questions have questions.

    What if I'm not the only one who needs saving?

    What if our marriage mistake gets way too real?

I: WALKING MASTERPIECE (IZZY)

I have to bite my lip at how the silence excites me.

This is *exactly* what I've dreamed about for years. A room full of talent. Bright eyes and young souls eager to impress, bleeding creativity.

Every student deep in concentration, glancing towards the drawing on the easel next to my desk only long enough to confirm the next swoosh of their pencil. I hadn't known what to expect when I accepted this position, other than it would bring me one step closer to my goal. Plus a little more money.

Oh, and it's the perfect escape from the weekly family dinners. Losing those gossip-fests is worth more than the income boost any job brings.

Working with this room full of remarkable young artists is way more fun than listening to mom's tongue-in-cheek 'encouragement.'

Or entertaining cousin Clara's dire warnings about

how I'm destined to wind up with a house full of cats and die in my eighties, still a virgin.

That's my future. Isabella Derby. AKA crazy cat lady.

The fact that my family believes that's the path I'm on and insists on reminding me so often never fails to piss me off. No matter how many times I hear it.

This is the twenty-first century. Supposedly. I don't even own a cat, and I'm twenty-three.

Twenty. Three.

Not fifty-three, and pining about what might have been. I have *years* before I need to worry about getting married. I have ambitions. Always have.

If only everyone else in my life would see that and leave me the hell alone.

If only they'd notice accomplishments besides landing men and wracking up babies.

"Ms. Derby?"

I rise from my chair and walk around my desk, happy to have something else to focus on besides my sad, nosy relatives.

Stopping next to her, I look down at the girl and smile. "Yes, Natalie?"

She's what some would call a child prodigy. Only ten, she has the talent of some people five times her age. Not just in fine arts either.

Her enrollment papers says she's in eighth grade. Most kids her age are still fourth graders. I kneel next to her. "What's up?"

She gestures to my drawing at the front of the room. "Um, I just noticed...the dog you drew doesn't have any eyelashes." Her shy voice comes out in a whisper. "Is it all right if I add some on mine?"

"Of course! Your personal muse is always welcome in this class." I look at the drawing on her easel, picturing exaggerated Minnie Mouse eyelashes.

Wrong idea.

My breath literally stalls in my lungs at the detail in her creation. This little girl wouldn't be caught dead making anything unrealistic. The collie she's drawn looks like it's ready to leap into the room. Just like everything she does.

It's more like a black and white photo than a drawing. Especially one done by a child.

Every feathery line she's sketched brings the dog to life in ways I can't even describe.

Hell, it's almost better than *mine*. And it took me a Master's degree and years practicing to get where I am.

I glance between her dog and mine. Forget *almost*.

Hers is far better. A masterpiece.

I choke up as I watch the eyes on her dog come to life as she carefully pencils in a few soft lashes. "Keep going. You're doing a great job!"

"Thank you," she whispers.

The way she's biting the tip of her tongue demonstrates how fully she's concentrating. I smile again, then stand, making a round of the whole room.

Only six students here this evening. The others are all high school kids. Natalie's dad had to pull some strings to get her into this class, meant for kids at least in their freshmen year.

That's what I was told. Since this is my first year with the district, I'm as unfamiliar with the students and their families as I am with the staff. That'll change in time, I'm sure. We're only three weeks into the school year.

The other five drawings look much like I expect. They demonstrate passion and promise, but honestly, there isn't another one that comes anywhere close to Natalie's.

I wonder if her talent comes from her father. The man I try *hard* not to think about every time she steps foot in my class.

If the last two weeks are anything to go by, he'll be here soon. A good twenty minutes before class ends. He'll stand in the back of the room with a spiral notebook, open it up, and let his big, rough hands touch the paper.

The first night, I thought he was making a list or notes. But last week, I had a strong feeling he was drawing. Sketching right along with his daughter and the rest of the class.

We'd started the dog last week, drawing the base after I'd gone over my quick anatomy lesson for animals. Tonight, I showed the students how to make the fur have shades of white, black, and gray.

A small, senseless part of me wonders if Natalie's dad will join in without even hearing my lesson. An even crazier part wants to see his drawing.

It could be a masterpiece like hers.

He certainly is. And that's the problem.

Mr. Tall-Dark-and-Brooding is every forbidden male archetype stuffed into one ripped package.

Mysteriously sexy by default. Imposing by gravity. Protective by virtue.

He's the kind of man I'd love to bring to a family dinner.

Just once.

That's all it would take. He'd render Clara speechless

and end mom's needless sympathy looks in one blow. He'd shut them down and then some.

Every Derby woman would be too busy gasping for breath and fanning themselves to give me any crap.

Honestly, I know the feeling. It was my reaction the first time he walked in. And the second.

At least I hid it well.

The military patches on his black leather jacket were no surprise. He has that air.

Straight back, chest forward, chin up. Disciplined. Hard.

Every move he makes, every glance, has a purpose.

Remember what I said? Every *forbidden* archetype.

The ones good girls are warned about, but never stay away from.

God. I shouldn't be having these thoughts.

Not about a student's father. He's probably married. And if he isn't, *why the hell not?*

But I didn't see a mother listed on Natalie's emergency contacts. That makes me feel slightly less guilty about the impure thoughts stirring in my head. It also concerns me.

I hope she isn't being pushed beyond her limits. Flogged on to greatness by a headstrong father who believes his child should succeed in everything, no matter the cost.

I know the burden.

Just as I arrive back at my desk, the hair on the back of my neck tingles. It's almost like there's a sixth sense before the Walking Masterpiece shows up. I close my eyes briefly, preparing myself for the sight I'll see after the door creaks open.

My heart jackhammers by the time I turn around, air stalling in my lungs.

Right on time. Sure as shit.

It's him.

Brent Eden. His hair is the same wavy black as his daughter's. Natalie has his eyes, too.

Emerald green.

His are colder, though. More seasoned. More cautious.

His features add to his presence. A tiny faded scar here, an inked muscle there, a calloused hand. Things a normal person wouldn't notice unless they're gawking at him like me.

Beautifully rough finishes for a man cut from Heaven's most twisted fabric.

The thick trimmed beard circling his jaw must feel as dangerous as it looks. Delicious torture on any woman's skin. Especially mine since it's as virgin as the rest of me.

Fucking-A. Last week's after-dinner talk with Clara clearly messed with my mind.

Left me focused on things I've never worried over before. Namely, finding a man to take home to mother. And maybe to bed while we're at it.

What the hell am I doing? I pinch my thigh. Ogling a man who's nothing but trouble, apparently.

He eases the door shut and quietly moves along the back wall, taking the exact same spot where he's stood the past two weeks. Leaning against a desk, he unclips a pen from his notebook's cover and then flips it open.

Look away, Izzy.

I sense he'll look up any second. Naturally, I can't. It's like someone telling you to not think about a pink elephant.

There's too much gorgeous mystery in front of me. Too much temptation.

The heat rushing to my cheeks tells me I've been caught staring even before my eyes travel all the way up to meet his. *Damn!*

"Ms. Derby?"

Tad Gomez calls my name, one of the older students, but a snail could beat me turning around.

Brent's gaze is intense. Heated. Almost like he's challenging me not to look away.

I'm not a daring person. I just don't want to lose this staring contest. But duty calls.

Lifting a brow, I rip my gaze off his, and scuttle towards Tad's seat.

I'm grateful for the few seconds I have to find my voice. "Having trouble?"

"Yes, ma'am. I can't get the nose to look 3-D. Not like yours."

I point towards Tad's drawing, which is good, but as he said, a little flat. "It's the angle. Here, let me show you."

He nods, handing me his pencil. I lightly outline how to angle the nose downward in order to give it depth. "See? One little change works like magic."

"Yes, Ms. Derby. Yes, I do. Thanks!" He takes his pencil back and continues filling in the outline.

"Light strokes, remember. They'll flesh it out even more."

Barely touching the paper with the edge of his pencil, he nods bashfully. "Thanks."

"You're welcome, Tad. Keep it up. You're off to an awesome start."

He pushes his thick glasses up his nose. "I really like this class, Ms. Derby."

Such a sweet boy. How could I do anything but smile? "We all do."

The door squeaks again. This time, it's Ester Oden's mother. She works as a custodian at the school and stays late in order to drive Ester home after class. I smile at her as I make my way around the room, checking on the progress of each student, offering a helpful hint and words of encouragement.

It feels good to do my job. And to find a perfect distraction from the man I shouldn't be staring at.

"Five more minutes," I say, once I'm back at my desk.

There are no audible groans, but I can sense each student's disappointment, knowing this week's class is almost over. I'm honored they don't want to leave.

This, right here, is the reason I sunk a lot of time and money into getting my credentials. It's why I spent years doing every part time job in the known universe. It's what I've dreamed about, working at the most prestigious academy in the Phoenix area.

"Ms. Derby?"

"Yeah, Ben?" I reply. Ben Pritchard is a typical teenager. Tall, thin, and a bad case of acne.

"Is it all right if I snap a picture of your drawing at the end of class so I can work on mine later?" he asks, holding up his cell phone.

"Go for it! But no Snapchat filters on me, and you'd better believe I'm watching. Only warning I'll give." I bite my lip and shake my finger, making them laugh.

I nod towards the others in the class and step out of the way, assuring them they can all take pictures. I hear the digital *click-click-click* of their phones and a few snickers.

Then my gaze, all on its own, drifts to the back of the room. Brent's head is down this time, thankfully.

He's sketching again. Furiously.

I have a different reason to bite my lip. This time, not so playfully.

There's something admirable in his focus. Something sexy.

I'm waiting for him to look up, after the older kids are done taking pics. At ten, I doubt Natalie has a cell phone. I assume he'll want to get a picture for her.

He never looks up, though. Never throws his eyes my way. Even though I sense him wanting to behind his determined, subtle smirk.

I suck a deep breath and hold it, hoping it eases the heat coursing through my system. I glance at the clock and then smile at my students. "Okay, guys and gals! Time to start putting your stuff away. Please bring your completed drawing back to class next week."

Every student, except Natalie, finishes taking pictures of my drawing, either before or after they've packed up their belongings. While saying goodbye to each of them, I start gathering my things, too, but leave the drawing on the easel.

What gives? Why isn't Brent getting her a picture?

He's still lost in his own world. Sketching quickly. Frantically. Like he's desperate to finish something before leaving. My curiosity turns into pure adrenaline.

I can't stop myself. "Mr. Eden? Would you like a picture?"

When he looks up, his gaze is so intense my heart nearly stops mid-beat.

"Oh, I'd like that! Please, can you, Daddy?" Natalie asks, turning to him.

I'm glad she doesn't witness me melting into a puddle of nerves.

His bright eyes shift. The smile transforming Brent's face is for his daughter, but it steals my breath.

I've watched lots of men smile. I've seen it, sketched it, noted how a thin quirk of the lips can change a full appearance.

But this man, this beast, goes from hardcore army badass to giant teddy bear in the blink of an eye.

He can't hide the adoration lighting up his eyes the second Natalie calls him Daddy.

At least I've learned one thing tonight: this man lives for his daughter.

Guilt twists in my guts again when I remember my earlier worries about him being overbearing. Not now. It just doesn't seem likely.

"Sure, sweets. One second," he says, closing his notebook.

My heart starts working again. It beats harder with every step he takes toward the front of the room.

I've been this close to him before. Once. The first night, when he'd dropped Natalie off and introduced himself.

I tried like crazy not to freeze up, and failed miserably, barely muttering my name.

Can't let that happen again. I won't embarrass myself a second time, no matter how many feels this handsome enigma shoots through me.

Pretending I'm unfazed by his presence, I say goodbye to Ester and her mother before they walk out the side door. Then, in my scattered state of mind, I accidentally knock a stack of papers off the corner of my desk.

"Oh, f – fiddlesticks!" I say, catching myself.

God. I'd nearly dropped an f-bomb in my flustered state. My tongue is my biggest vice sometimes. I'm still sanding away the rough language I picked up too much of in college.

Natalie shoots forward. "I'll help, Ms. Derby!"

I kneel down beside her and start gathering the papers. "Thanks, Natalie. I certainly can be clumsy sometimes. Must be getting late."

Must be. Or else I'd totally have to admit I've been drooling over her father for the better part of the last ten minutes.

"We all have accidents," she says. "Don't stress."

I smile, nodding slowly. This girl sounds far too old for her age, which causes me to glance up at her father.

He's raised her to be polite. Kind. Intelligent.

He shrugs when he sees there isn't room to step in and help, walking over to pick up the backpack she's left on the floor.

I take the papers Natalie collects and stack them on top of the pile I've formed. "Thanks for your help again, Natalie. You're too awesome."

"Ready, sweets?" Brent asks.

"Coming!" Natalie flashes a big grin. "See you next week, Ms. Derby. Can't wait to finish my drawing."

"Looking forward to it," I answer, flinching slightly at not being able to come up with something more original.

Brent nods at me while laying a hand on Natalie's shoulder and guiding her towards the door.

I nod back. I think. I'm too embarrassed to say for sure.

Woof. I'm so ready to slump into my chair before I leave the building.

I need five or ten. Just a few precious minutes to let my body, mind, and pulse find their baseline.

I doubt there's any time. This is the only evening class near closing time. Oscar Winters, the janitor, who doubles as our evening security guard, is already waiting for me to leave so he can lock up and go home.

Sighing, I set the stack of papers on the corner, hoping the regular teacher in this room, Mrs. Wayne's substitute, isn't overly upset tomorrow morning that they aren't in the same order. Then I start packing my things in my carry-all. I'm so busy trying to get out of here I don't even see him enter.

"Finally! Why the hell have you been ignoring my calls and texts?"

The voice vibrating in my ears makes me shudder like a spider crawling up my spine. A huge, unwanted, hairy one.

Crap. Not this guy again.

I huff out a breath of air before glancing up. "What are you doing here, Preston?"

All five feet and nine inches of Preston Graves stands just a few feet away like he owns the place. He probably thinks he does.

He's that arrogant. If you could take a picture of a blind date gone bad, it would look like this man.

Bleached blond hair, blue eyes, and obscenely rich.

He's also the biggest prick I've ever met.

He looked better in the pics he'd uploaded to the matchmaker app. I was actually excited when it said we were compatible, mainly because I knew mom would approve. Well, and because he didn't look quite as phony with a good filter.

Then we met, and he opened his dumb mouth.

"Isabella, don't play coy. You know why I'm here: you haven't responded to a single one of my messages. You're ignoring me." He leans a hand on the corner of the desk. "For your information, Preston Graves does not like being ignored."

That's how he talks. Third person. It's overly unnecessary and fucking annoying.

Correction: he's overly fucking annoying.

"I've been busy," I say.

I mentally wonder how crazy my intruder is. Could he stop me from reaching for my phone if push comes to shove?

"Excuses, excuses. Who do you think you're dealing with, dear? No one's ever too busy for me. What's the real deal keeping you away?"

Gag me with a fucking spoon. "The school year just started."

I force a weak smile. It does nothing. Call me an idiot for letting the dating app scan my real employer. I'm an even bigger fool if I think it'll help get me out of this madness.

"And?" Preston taps his polished shoe impatiently, scratching his head.

Ugh. Is he dense or just insufferable?

I'd told him when I cut our date short that I didn't

have time to see him again, but he obviously thought I was lying. Why he'd want to chase a liar, who knows.

Time to take a different route. "Preston, look, you shouldn't be here. It's a secure environment, this academy, whether it's school hours or not. We have rules."

"Nonsense. Nothing's too secure for Preston Graves. My Uncle Theo sits on the board of the largest banking chain in Maricopa county. Security's practically my middle name. It's lovely you follow the rules, Isabella, but you've got nothing to worry about as long as –"

Oh, please, *shut up,* Gaston. It's too much like my favorite fairy tale with none of the charm. I stop listening.

It's time to end this right now.

"Do you have a pass, Preston? Did you show it to the guard in the hall?"

"The janitor, you mean? The man who's vacuuming a few classrooms away?" He turns his nose up, walking around the desk, dragging a manicured hand along the edge. "Very funny, Isabella. You're on fire tonight. Why would I waste the time? When Preston finds something he wants, *nothing* stands in his way." He stops right in front of me. "Nothing and no one."

My heart leaps into my throat. This puffed up joke of a man is getting old and weird fast. I don't like the glint in his eye. He's a mega-creep, too. Not just socially clueless.

I think I know a psychotic asshole who was born with a silver spoon in his mouth when I see one. Knew it from the night I was dumb enough to go out with him.

I just didn't think he'd go to these lengths for another chance. Never imagined he'd bother me here.

I freeze, trying to think without making it too obvious. I don't dare glance around.

That would be the worst thing: letting him think he has me scared.

But he does.

This looney tune has my heart crawling up my throat.

"Are we done playing now?" He steps closer, an eerie warmth on his face. "I know you like Preston, Isabella. Everyone does. You just have a rather curious way of showing it."

A shiver ripples through my entire body. I have nothing to defend myself, and shoot a sideways glance at the desk, scanning for something that might work.

Nothing. Not even a sharp pencil.

I'm screwed. Estimating how loud I can scream when everything changes.

Preston falls backwards, grabbing the edge of the desk so hard it moves, scraping the floor. Then I see Brent Eden. Nostrils flaring, he has a hand on the back of Preston's starched shirt collar.

Preston twists his neck, taking in the man holding onto him. "W-Who are you?"

"Nothing and no one," Brent says, echoing his earlier words.

Though I never condone violence, right now I wouldn't mind seeing Preston knocked on his ass.

He tries shaking off Brent's iron grip. "You're making a big mistake! I'm Preston Graves the third and –"

"I don't give a fuck," Brent growls, tightening his hold.

Wow.

Preston squirms, panic in his eyes. "But...this is crazy! Isabella and I are dating."

Brent's green eyes settle on me. My heart's still in my throat, but I manage to shake my head for a split second.

This courtship ended after the first and only date Preston Graves will ever get from me. One date too many.

"I don't think so," Brent says, eyeing me suspiciously.

"Yes, we are," Preston insists. "Tell him Isabella!"

Even if I could find my tongue, that's the last thing I'd admit to.

A mischievous glint flashes in Brent's eyes. "She can't be dating you. She's dating me."

Wait. What?!

I nearly choke on my own breath.

Preston tries harder to get loose. "Impossible!"

Brent spins Preston around so they're face to face. "Then you probably also believe it's impossible we're engaged. And that I'll beat the fuck out of any man who comes within twenty feet of my fiancée."

I'm no stranger to F-words, but that one, on his lips, makes me want to pass out.

He gives Preston another shove and before I know it, Brent grabs me, one hand on the back of my head, and smashes his lips against mine.

I'm gone.

Heat consumes me so swiftly the world melts. His lips are all fire. The blood surging through my veins might be lava.

My lips part – they never have a chance – and his tongue sweeps into my mouth.

Hot. Bold. Amazing.

Brent's other arm wraps around me, holding my body tight against the length of him. It's like an ice cream cone up against a space heater. My entire body melts down from the inside out.

Holy hell. This is the kind of kiss every girl dreams

about. The take-me-out-of-this-world kind.

I'm so engrossed several moments flit by before I remember he shouldn't be kissing me.

We aren't alone. I barely know him. He's my student's father.

A dozen other realizations bum-rush my dizzy brain, including Preston's voice.

I pull out of the kiss – regretfully. Still too worked up to stand on my own, I lean against Brent, taking a few seconds to let the real world return.

"No one dumps Preston Graves!" He says numbly, his anger slowly returning. "And that stupid app guaranteed *three* dates. Three!" He holds up his fingers, as if I don't know how to count.

Hell, after that kiss, maybe I don't.

"I can sue. Sue them, and you. Both of you!" He prattles on, stomping a foot like a child not getting his way. "You've made a big mistake, Isabella Derby. You and your thug boyfriend. I'll take every penny you have and – and her teacher's license. Just watch me. Preston Graves can do that!"

Brent's upper lip curls slightly as he shakes his head. "Preston Graves better get the fuck out of here before he needs to sue for medical expenses, too."

"Hey! Is there a problem here?"

I push away from Brent's side as Oscar Winters and Natalie walk through the door. The poor girl looks bewildered, probably wondering what the hold up is with her dad.

"Yeah. Big problem," Brent replies, pointing at Preston. "Did you let his man in the building?"

"No." Oscar's face falls, realizing the seriousness. He

might not have Brent's rogue good looks, but he's a big man. Over six feet tall and two hundred intimidating pounds, Oscar walks towards Preston. "How did you get in here, sir?"

"Dear God, are you *all* clueless? Preston Graves can go anywhere he damn well –"

"No, he can't," Brent interjects. "I don't know how he got in the building, but I saw him sneaking out of the men's room. Didn't like the look on his face. I followed."

"You're in the wrong place. Let's go." Oscar grabs Preston's arm. "I'm truly sorry for this, Ms. Derby. It won't happen again."

"I hope not," Brent says seriously. "Safety's in your hands." He nods towards Natalie. "That shouldn't be taken lightly."

"Never, Mr. Eden. You're absolutely right. Believe me, I'll find out how Mr. Graves found his way in. It won't happen a second time." Oscar tugs Preston towards the door, none too gently.

Preston appears to have lost some of his arrogance as he crosses the room, at the mercy of two powerful men. But he's still wearing a this-isn't-over glare I don't like one bit. I roll my shoulders, pretending to stretch. Really, I'm hiding the shiver.

Brent's hand slides off my shoulder and down my back. Amazingly comforting.

"Get your things," he says quietly. "I'll walk you out."

"I'll take your sketchpad!" Natalie says cheerfully, ready to chip in.

Her smile suggests she saw plenty, probably through the small glass window in the classroom door. It also says what just happened hasn't bothered her in the least.

My cheeks go bright red. I'm more thankful than ever she's mature for her age. At least I don't have to worry about any gossip that could get me in deep, deep doo-doo.

Still fighting off a nervous tremble, I say, "Thank you." Then I look at Brent. "That's not necessary, but thanks. Again. I can find my own way out, Mr. Eden."

"No. You're coming to your car with me," he insists, grabbing my carry-all off the desk. "This everything?"

He's no nonsense through and through. The hint of irony in his glare tells me not to argue. So I don't.

"Everything," I echo, stepping forward and taking my sketchpad from Natalie. "Thank you."

"You're welcome, Ms. Derby." With another large grin, she leans in and whispers, "Thank you, too. Dad likes being a hero. Doesn't get to do the whole white knight thing as often as he'd like."

"Nat." There's a hint of a warning in Brent's tone.

Natalie shakes her head slightly while her green eyes twinkle. "He's a good knight, too."

Unable to disagree, I nod.

"Where's your backpack, baby girl?" Brent asks.

"Oh! I think I left it in the hallway when you told me to go get Mr. Winters," Natalie answers.

"Go get it. We'll wait right here."

"Okay, Daddy!" There's a skip in her step as she hurries towards the door.

Once again, I'm searching for my tongue as I walk towards the door with Brent by my side. I need to tell him thank you, but I'm afraid I'll sound like a bubbling idiot.

"One question: what made you go out with a man who calls himself by his own name?" Brent asks once Natalie's out of earshot.

Kill me. He's trying to lighten this insanity, I'm sure. Still, full-fledged embarrassment burns my cheeks. "Fuck if I know." I flinch then and bite my tongue.

That's *not* how a teacher speaks. Especially a preschool teacher who does evening art classes for older kids.

For a second, he cocks his head. Then, to my utter amazement, he laughs. It's a nice sound. And it breaks the invisible ice surrounding me. "That's a damn good answer, Ms. Derby."

"Well...thank you," I say sheepishly. "I knew I made a mistake. I thought we were done. Tried to let him down easy. Never, in my wildest dreams, did I think he'd show up here."

He lifts a brow as we step into the hallway. "Is Preston Graves in your wildest dreams?"

"Hell no!" I flinch again at my own language. "I mean, *no*. Gross. He was a match-up from a dating site. One I won't mention because I'm *very* dissatisfied."

"How many times did you date him?"

"Once." I shake my head. "Actually, it was more like a half-date. I didn't even make it through reading the menu at the place in Scottsdale before I knew I had to cut things short. It had already been too long."

My comment reminds him we're probably wasting time, too. He starts walking and I follow.

Natalie is waiting by the main entrance door with Oscar. It's a long corridor. Brent sees them, but doesn't seem to be in a hurry.

"What did you do?" he asks.

"I laid a twenty on the table to pay for my glass of wine, gave the waitress a big tip, which she highly deserved, and lied."

"Lied?"

"Yes. Lied. I told him it was nice to meet him, which it wasn't, and then I said I was sorry, but I simply don't have time to date right now."

"When was that?"

"Almost three weeks ago. He stopped texting me last week when I didn't respond, so I'd hoped it was finally over." It's embarrassing telling him all this, but it's the truth, and he deserves that much after coming to my rescue.

Preston's creepy encounter shook me up more than I want to admit.

"I have no idea how he got inside, Mr. Eden," Oscar says as we approach him and Natalie. "The doors were locked. I let everyone in and out and didn't see him once. I always double check. I'm sure of it!" Oscar looks at me, frustration lining his brow. "He's gone now, Ms. Derby. I escorted him to his car and watched him drive away. I'll gladly do the same for you."

"We're good, Oscar. I'm her escort," Brent says. "Did you search him for a key fob?"

Oscar's face falls as he shakes his head. "No, sir, but I'll make a full report of the security breach. As you know, the academy takes security very seriously."

Brent turns to me. "Could he have gotten your key fob?"

"No. It's right here." I pull the badge around my neck out of the top of my shirt. My I.D. card and the key fob dangle off the end. "It hasn't been out of my sight since I got it two weeks ago. Jesus. This doesn't make any sense..."

Brent nods, turning back to Oscar. "I suggest you find out who lost a key fob recently and make everyone aware what Preston Graves looks like. Make sure they understand he's not allowed on the premises."

Oscar nods. "Of course, sir, I'll do that. I'll stay late. Get the report in the system before I leave."

A million questions race through my mind, but I hold them until after we walk outside. The heat still coming off the nighttime pavement makes me want to fan myself. We're off high summer, the hottest time of year, but not to the point where the nights are really comfortable.

Once we're walking down the long concrete walkway leading to the parking lot, I ask another question I've been holding in. "So, uh, Mr. Eden...are you a detective? A cop, maybe?"

"No."

"He works with cops all the time," Natalie says. "He owns his own company."

I wait for either one of them to add more, but they don't, and I'm too tongue tied to keep probing. Or too scared.

Though he came to my rescue, gave me the hottest, most memorable kiss of my life, there are red flags popping up all over. This whole thing is bad news.

He's a student's father. The academy has rules against teacher-family relationships. Pages upon pages of iron-clad rules. As the most elite private academy in the county, the wait list to become a student, or to get a job here, is as long as Route 66.

Landing this preschool position was pure luck. Same as the very part-time accelerated art class I'm filling in for.

I can't fuck it up. Cannot. Will not.

Not even for drop dead sexy men with beast eyes and beards who kiss like they mean business.

"That your car?" Brent asks.

Lost in thought, I glance up, nodding. Classic Mustang convertible. Old. Not at all what anyone would expect a teacher to drive. "It was my dad's."

He doesn't respond physically or verbally, just keeps walking. At the car, he opens the door and looks inside before stepping aside.

"You should lock your doors."

"I usually do." I'd been running late, trying to get back in time for the evening class and hadn't, but won't make that mistake again. I take my bag from him and pull out the keys, then put the carry-all and my sketchpad in the backseat. I make sure to include Natalie as I say, "Thank you both. For everything."

"Nah, it was our pleasure, Ms. Derby!" Natalie talks like she's forty instead of ten. I smile like mad. She steps forward and wraps her arms around my middle. "Please don't be embarrassed. We were really happy to help tonight."

Something inside me flutters as I hug her back. It's not everyday you run into good people.

Our hug ends, and as she steps away, she twists to look at her father. "Weren't we, Daddy? Happy to help Ms. Derby?"

The transformation on his face happens again. "Yes, baby girl," he says. "Thrilled." His smile fades as he looks at me. "Our truck's right over there. We'll wait until you drive away. Unless you want us to follow you home?"

"No!" I flinch at my immediate response. "I mean, that's totally okay. You've already done more than enough. Much more. Thank you."

Completely unsure what to do, I take a step forward,

but pause, not sure if I should shake his hand, or, well, hug him. Some crazy part of me shouts *hug.*

Fine. I step forward and give him a quick thank you squeeze.

His statue stiffness tells me I should've went with hand shake.

Crap.

I really am an idiot. But it's not like I have experience handling gorgeous men who pretend-kiss like it's the end of the world.

"Goodnight, guys!" I spin around and jump in my car, slamming the door shut, before I make this more awkward.

I wait until they turn around to walk across the three parking spaces between his truck and my car before leaning my forehead against the steering wheel. Mortification overwhelms me.

Heat does, too. Inside and out. It's been a brutal summer. Hot and windy, the autumn break can't come soon enough. Southern Arizona isn't a humid place, but the dry, hundred degree plus days wear on a body and soul.

I crank the window for fresh air and glance out the opening. There's a car rumbling up beside mine. Not Brent and Natalie's.

My heart leaps in my throat, but then slides back down where it belongs when I realize who it is.

Clara. *Damn!*

After everything went haywire tonight, I spaced on our plans to meet here so she could drop off one of her famous pies.

It's too late to stop the chain reaction. I see Brent

gesturing furiously at Natalie to get in his truck as he starts walking back towards me. Opening the door, I climb out, hands in front of me. "Whoa, whoa, it's okay! Nothing scary. This is just my cousin, Clara."

Clara doesn't miss a beat. If she was a curious cat, she'd have lost about all nine lives by now. "Isabella Derby!" She's already shaking her head.

Oh, God. Here it comes.

Holding out her hand, she walks straight toward Brent. "Who on Earth is this fine specimen?"

I run. Around the back end of her car, to her side.

I'm too late to stop anything. Natalie is already answering, "He's our hero tonight!"

Seriously. Where's the hole in the ground? The kind that can swallow a person whole, when we need one?

"Hero?" Both of Clara's eyes are wider than an owl's as she looks at me and blinks. "Isabella *Derby!*"

Forget the hole in the ground. The brutal smile on her face makes me wish I had one in my head.

This night truly can't get any worse.

I love Clara, but she's the biggest gossip in the family. And I'm not sure Derby blood was ever compatible with privacy.

"He's just...the father of one of my students. Nothing to worry about," I say, adding so much emphasis it hurts my tongue.

Her smile turns coy as she turns back to Brent. Sticking out her hand even further, she says, "Well, well, it's truly a pleasure. Clara Derby, Big Daddy. How do you do?"

Brent shakes her hand with an uneasy smile. I just close my eyes and pray for this day to be over. It's cursed. From the very second my alarm went off this morning.

"Nice to meet you, Ms. Derby." I hear him say. Then, "I'm afraid I have to run. Good seeing Isabella with a friend."

He gives me a knowing glance. I die once under his striking eyes, and again when I hear how my name sounds on his lips.

"Brent," I whisper. His name, rather than Mr. Eden, tastes wonderful in my mouth, too.

"Goodnight, Ladies."

My eyes snap open and I watch him walk to the truck. Clara's mouth drops.

I want to laugh. As painful as this is, it's so ridiculous it's kinda surreal.

Nerves. Has to be. Yet, in my defense, the way he didn't give Clara what she wanted, a name to Google, is comical.

He climbs into his truck and starts the engine.

Clara turns to me, mouth still hanging open and eyes wide. Her silence only lasts a nano-second.

"OMG!" she hisses. "He's to die for, Izzy!"

I can't agree. Well, I can, but I won't.

I still can't believe I forgot about her stupid pie.

Fuck. This is turning out to be the night of unwanted company to the nth degree.

Clara's long dark hair whips in the wind as she turns to his truck and then back to me. "Where? How? How long? Is he your dating site match-up guy? Why didn't you tell me you'd matched a ten out of ten hunk, lady?"

"What? No, no, no, and no!" I try to wipe out all her rapid fire questions at once.

"You're terrible for holding out on me. I thought we were family! You never said how your date turned out – mighty good by the looks of him. I mean, *it*."

I shake my head. "Clara, it's late. I should be getting home."

"I brought you a pie! Coconut cream." Clara winks, reaching in the door she'd left open, her car still running. "Your favorite. I made a couple for dinner, and everyone agreed I should drop one off since you missed out. You're welcome, cuz."

Just great. I don't even like coconut cream pie that much.

Like most everything about the family dinners, I pretend I do to keep the peace. Then, a solid escape opportunity dawns on me. "Awesome!" I snatch the pie from her hand, feigning joy. "Better go before this melts. Have a nice night, Clara!"

"You really need a new car, Izzy. One with modern air conditioning."

"Someday, when I can afford it." I hold up the pie and smile as if I can't wait to bite into it. "Mmmm, supper! Thanks again."

I'm half way to my car, when her question stops me.

"Does your mama know about Big Daddy?"

I spin around as my stomach hits the ground. "Nope. And that's the way it's gonna stay because there isn't *anything* to know."

"He's still sitting there. Watching." She smiles, nods toward their truck, and does a small wave.

"He's just being polite." I start walking again. "And we're being rude, Clara. He has a little girl to get home to put to bed. He's waiting for us to leave. Making sure we're safe." I leave it there so I don't have to mention, much less think about Preston again.

"So...no mother? No wife? I mean, if you've got to deal with her, there are always ways around the drama. You can't let that stop you!"

"Clara."

"Okay, okay! I'm just curious."

"Nosy, you mean," I mumble, climbing in my car. As the engine purrs to life, I wave. "Thanks again for the pie."

She gets in her car and pulls away. I follow. Brent follows me. I try to let out a huff of relief, but there's none in me. I follow Clara's tail lights to the highway.

Thank God.

I cringe. Hoping he doesn't plan on following me all the way to my place in Tempe. Knowing Clara, she's already considering how to turn around and follow him home. My mind starts spinning faster than the nighttime traffic whipping down the four-lane highway.

A small sense of relief seeps out of me when I look in my mirrors again. Brent takes an exit. And I don't see a car that looks like Clara's anymore.

Then reality hits home.

Jesus! This night could've been an even bigger disaster.

If Clara ever hears what Brent said to Preston, about us being engaged, I'm toast.

And so is he.

There's no drama in the known universe like Derby drama.

And me, being a single crazy cat lady for the rest of my life, has been the main family tragedy for months.

Who knew the fix could be even worse?

II: PAINT IT ALL BLUE (BRENT)

It's hotter than blue blazes, but not even the sweat pouring down my back can kill my focus.

What the hell was I thinking? Kissing that shy little teacher last night?

I know what I'd been thinking: that I'd like to fuck her.

Thinking with my dick. Thinking like a sex starved maniac who's been too busy working his ass off to haul any woman into bed for far too long.

That's what I try to tell myself. Anything to dismiss the lust fogging my head.

If only it were as simple as sex alone.

Seeing that slick-dick bastard sneaking out of the bathroom pissed me off royal. Got under my skin like a rattlesnake bite before I even got wind of the nasty way he spoke to Blue.

I can't stop the grin forming. *Blue.*

I've come to call her that because of the bright blue streaks in her dirty blonde hair. It's just one side, and just a few strands. More like the emo girls a decade ago than full on punk rock.

They make her look rare. Magical. Damnably hard to resist.

I remember walking her out into the parking lot, the lights glowing overhead. When they caught her face just right, her gray eyes nearly matched the soft ocean stripe in her hair.

Maybe a shade lighter.

Almost like they're speckled with blue diamonds. Like she's blue to the soul, even when she was standing in front of me with her motor mouth cousin, cheeks flushing hellfire red.

That woman was something, all right.

Something unique. Something sexy. Something beautiful.

I've made a point to meet every one of Natalie's teachers. I'll keep doing it, too, right up to her college professors. Until last night, no teacher of hers ever left me hanging by my own blue balls.

Beyond hanging. More like consumed. Strung up.

Blue's been in my wet dreams for the past couple weeks, even before last night. Ever since Nat's art enrichment class started, and I first laid eyes on her, I've lost my frigging mind.

Something that can't keep happening if it leads to madness like last night.

Hell, *especially* if it's like last night. Getting up close and way too personal for our own good.

Slamming the truck door, I hit the key and flip on the air conditioning. It'll take a minute to cool everything down, and then one more to make the sweat stop pouring off me.

This job has been a sonofabitch. Most asbestos removal gigs are.

They also make bank. I hadn't even imagined the amount of money there was to be made in hazmat cleanup five years ago, when I had little more than a tool belt and a will to work long dreary hours.

It's paid off, and will continue to for years.

As the temperature inside the truck drops, I reach over and pull my notebook out of the glove box. After meeting Ms. Derby that first night of art class, I'd gone out to the truck and made a quick sketch of her while Nat wasn't looking, still getting her stuff together.

That's when I'd started calling her Blue, too, in my own twisted mind.

I flip through the pages. Stare at my creations. Each sketch I've drawn since the first night has gotten more detailed.

They all started out with her wearing clothes. The off white blouse and black skirt I've seen on her several times.

Amazing how every sketch winds up with her naked. And in some interesting positions.

Fuck.

That kiss last night, the heat of her lips, the way she pressed up against me, keeps replaying in my mind. She'd tasted as good as I'd imagined. Felt even better.

A dangerously fine young woman. A siren for a man who hasn't had a good solid fuck in eons.

Things could've quickly gotten out of hand last night. Had we been someplace else. Had Nat not been there. Or the pissant who got us up on each other in the first place, Preston Asshole Graves.

A faint shadow has me looking up, shoving the notebook back in the glovebox. I'm barely able to hide my dirty secret before the job site manager, Juan Lopez, pulls open the passenger door.

"Removal's done, Boss. We're just about free and clear." Juan takes off his hat and wipes the sweat off his forehead with the back of his hand. "We'll have the rest wrapped up within the hour."

"Good. That's what I just told the owners." I shake my head. "Why some people think they can cross the yellow tape's beyond me." The two owners who'd just driven away had tried every excuse in the book to get inside the plastic shrouded area of the building my crew worked all day.

"Thanks for coming down," Juan says. "I told them they couldn't come in, but all that did was make them insist on speaking to you."

"Never a problem, Juan. Some people just don't understand the danger. I was in the area, anyway, bidding on another job."

Juan grins. I can practically see money in his eyes. "It's been a good summer."

"And it'll be a better fall. Especially now that we're the number one crime scene cleanup company in the area."

Juan puts his hat back on. "You'll never hear me complain about working too much."

"I know, and I appreciate that."

"These fat paychecks are thanks enough." Juan slaps the seat. "Gotta get back in there. See you later, Brent."

"Stay cool," I say as he shuts the door. Noting the time on the radio, I glance up and watch Juan walk away.

I'm happy to pay him top dollar. Because of him, I can afford to be the kind of father Nat deserves. Not just money wise, but time wise, too. I'm able to drive her to school every morning and pick her up each afternoon.

Shifting into reverse, I back out of the parking lot and head for the highway. Blue should be too busy this evening for more run-ins.

This isn't just about her. I need to speak to the Principal and make sure the key fob that Graves asshole somehow snatched gets found and deactivated.

Natalie's safety always comes first.

I'll pull her out of school in a heartbeat if they can't guarantee this fuckery never happens again. It may be one of the most prestigious schools in the state, but their rankings don't mean shit if safety isn't sacrosanct.

There are bad people in this world.

Bastard Phil, for one.

The thought of that bald headed monster breathing down my neck for the hundredth time fills me with rage, but I can't fret over him. Nothing good will come from a trip down memory lane, either, or stepping on the many landmines lingering in the present.

I call the school to set up a meeting with Bob Jacobs. Fifteen minutes.

Whatever.

Being a father has taught me plenty. In the past, I would've taken care of Preston Graves myself. Gladly.

Probably would have run him out of town. But for Natalie, I follow the rules.

For her, I'm a good man.

Most of the time.

* * *

TRAFFIC IS MINIMAL, and I arrive with time to spare. I circle the parking lot once, looking for a faded blue Mustang convertible.

It's parked on the far side of the lot. I have half a mind to check if her doors are locked.

Personal safety, security, is another thing that was never an issue until Natalie was born. The events of the past couple years have blown it up tenfold.

I drive back to the visitor parking area and find a spot. Despite the evening heat, I grab my leather jacket and slip it on. I'm not ashamed of the ink on my arms, but out of respect for Nat, I cover my tattoos at certain times.

People can be judgmental. Kids can be downright nasty. As a father, it's my responsibility to never let judgments about me taint her.

At the door, I buzz the intercom system and state my name before being let in. The office is around the corner to the left. A dark-haired woman behind the desk points to the door on the right and tells me Mr. Jacobs is ready.

He's an older man, mid-fifties or so, round and balding, but smart. I recognized that the first time I met him. I got a good sense about him at our first meeting, too, but that has little bearing on the reason for my meeting today.

"Welcome back, Mr. Eden," Jacobs says as I enter the room. He's standing behind his big wooden desk covered with framed family photos. "I'm glad you called so we can discuss what happened last night."

Not seeing any reason for pleasantries, I yank the door

shut behind me. "And make sure it isn't repeated, you mean."

"Of course." He points to a chair. "Please, have a seat."

While stepping towards the chair, I ask, "How'd Graves get in the building? Anybody figured it out yet?"

He nods, as if accepting my straight to the point question. "Most of Mr. Graves' family are academy alumni, I'm afraid."

Taking a seat, I give him a look that says that's no answer. "Bull. Don't tell me alumni have key fobs."

"No, no, certainly not." He sits in his well-padded leather chair. "Mr. Graves' cousin, Grace Wilkens, works here. She wasn't aware her key fob was missing until arriving at work this morning. When she heard about the breach last night, she came to me and said Preston stopped by her house yesterday. He must have taken her fob then. He's been questioned, but denies ever having it."

"Sure he does," I bite off, trying like hell not to roll my eyes.

"Please, you needn't be alarmed. I personally made sure the fob was deactivated. So, wherever it is, it's no good here anymore. Also, we've informed Mr. Graves he isn't welcome anywhere near our premises."

"And his cousin? If she can't keep track of a damn fob..." I let my words trail off, knowing he catches my drift.

"Grace Wilkens has worked here for over fifteen years. Practically a model employee with no prior disciplinary incidents. She eagerly cooperated to the fullest in our investigation this morning. Said Mr. Graves has some...dire psychological issues."

I blink my agreement.

"Regardless, Ms. Wilkens feels terrible about the whole thing. I have no concern her new fob ever goes missing again." He squirms slightly in his chair. "I'll be speaking with Ms. Derby as well. Just as soon as her afternoon classes end."

My spine stiffens, but I make sure he doesn't notice. "Ms. Derby? Why?"

"I know she's fully aware of the rules, but perhaps you're not."

"Rules?" *What fucking rules?* I wonder, shaking my head slightly.

His jowls wiggle as he pulls up an imitation smile. "Well, Mr. Graves indicated that although he's been dating Ms. Derby for some time...she might also be dating you."

Shit!

What in the hell was I on last night? What insanity possessed me to kiss a stranger and call her my fiancée?

Besides the fact I've thought about fucking Blue since meeting her, I mean. I read every publication the school sends home, including the new teacher bios. The little black and white photo they'd had of her in their newsletter hadn't done her justice.

Jacobs is still waiting for an answer. I shrug. "Even if that were true, I can't see why it'd be anyone else's business."

He shakes his head. "It would, I fear. We have *very* strict rules at this academy, Mr. Eden. Every employee agrees to conduct themselves to the highest standard at their time of hire. That includes maintaining nothing more than a purely professional relationship with our students, their families, and other employees."

Fuck. I should have known.

I may have buried myself on this one. Just hope I haven't dug Blue's grave, too. "You just went to bat for that Wilkens lady. Tell me, how well do you know Ms. Derby?"

"I must admit, not very well," Jacobs answers. "She's a new teacher this year for our preschool expansion. As you know, she began filling the evening art classes for Mrs. Wayne, the regular art teacher. Like all of our instructors, Ms. Derby came highly recommended. Her presence on our payroll vouches for her character, I'd like to believe. However –"

No. Fuck 'however.'

Nothing he's telling me is new information. "And how long have you known Preston Graves?" I ask.

His chin wobbles as a frown forms. "I was Vice Principal while he was a student."

His expression says it all. Preston Graves was a flaming asshole then, too. To drive my point home, I ask, "And how long have you known me?"

"I believe it's been roughly five years since you first enrolled Natalie, correct?"

I nod before saying, "Given the history you just indicated, and the experience you have from working here for so many years, let's think. Do *you* believe a woman like Ms. Derby would be dating a man like Preston Graves?"

He places both hands on his desk and leans forward, his eyebrows flicking up. "I was certainly surprised by Preston's claims."

"All of them?" I ask.

"Yes, all of them."

Not admitting anything is my best tool right now, and I use it. "Natalie and I were leaving last night when I saw Graves sneaking out of the bathroom. Then I heard the way he spoke to Ms. Derby. He tried to scare her. Intimidate her. I stepped in like any man would. Had to get him off her."

"Your assistance is very much appreciated. The safety of our students and faculty always comes first." Jacobs shoots a nervous glance around the room before asking, "Did you know Ms. Derby before she started teaching here? Before Natalie was enrolled in the art enrichment class she took over?"

"No. Not till three weeks ago, when I dropped Nat off for her first art lesson. First time I met Ms. Derby. Last night was the first time we said more than hello." By this point, I'm ready for this entire situation to become little more than my word against Preston Graves.

If push comes to shove, that bastard won't stand a chance.

The bell rings loudly then, interrupting us. Classes dismissed. I stand.

Jacobs gets up as well and extends his hand across the desk. "I appreciate you clarifying details, Mr. Eden. I give you my promise there won't be any further security breaches here."

"I'll hold you to it." I shake his hand tight and bid him farewell, but by the time I reach the door, my conscience gets the best of me. I can't leave yet. I turn. "None of last night was Ms. Derby's fault, Principal. Reprimanding her would be out of line."

He walks to the edge of his desk, a small sigh escaping his throat. "I'm of similar opinion, Mr. Eden. Thanks again for your input."

I leave, nod to the receptionist, and walk into the hall where dozens of kids are rushing for the door.

* * *

NAT SPIES me as she rounds the corner. My heart swells at how her eyes light up.

I'd never known how deeply one human being can care for another until I'd met this little girl ten years ago. That moment changed my life.

There are times I still wonder what Cindy would think. She'd sworn I'd never be able to think about anyone but myself.

The sad part is, she was right. Once upon a time.

Not anymore.

"Hi, Daddy!" Her arms wrap around my waist.

"Hey, baby girl." I kiss the top of her head before letting go. "How was your day?"

"Aced my English test! So, pretty good."

There's a smile on her face, but no shine in her eyes. I wait until we're outside where it's not as noisy before asking, "But?"

She shrugs. Whatever it is, she's holding it in.

Damn.

The desire to kick the hell out of whoever's alienating her hits hard. It takes effort to squelch it. Some days, I wonder if I should have agreed to let her skip whole grade levels.

She's only ten.

The other kids in her eighth grade classes are older, some by four years. There's a huge difference between kids at those ages, which makes her light on friends. The separate classes don't give her much opportunity to play with kids her own age. I've offered to talk to the school about that, but she doesn't want me to.

I get it. The school can't force kids to make friends, but I hate the idea of her not having anybody close. No one except me. I fucking loathe it. She deserves *better*.

"Are we going straight home?" she asks.

"Yeah. Unless there's something you need?" I tickle the back of her neck, under her ponytail where I know it'll make her giggle. "Like ice cream."

She scrunches up her shoulders against my tickles. "We have ice cream sandwiches at home. And I really want to work on my dog drawing. I'll need to borrow your phone to see the picture."

"Maybe we should get you your own phone? I think the day's come," I suggest, thinking that might put a spark in her eyes.

She gnaws her cheek, considering it, but then shakes her head. "Nah. There's no one I'd call."

My gut churns as if I've just been sucker punched. "There's always Grandma," I suggest.

"Why? We already video chat on the computer," she answers, climbing in the truck. "Plus we'll see her in a couple months anyway, whenever they move back down for winter."

I nod, hiding my uncertainty.

My parents, who'd cared for Nat when she first came home from the hospital and I was still in the army, live their summers on a lake in North Dakota. Then spend winters in a townhome not too far from our house, in the older section of Scottsdale. At least, that *was* the norm until recently.

They haven't come down for more than a week or two in the past few years. Not since Davey died.

A tragedy in more ways than one. They're practically

the only people Natalie associates with besides me and a few of my close friends.

"All right then," I say, giving up. "Home it is, and no phone for now. Let me know if you change your mind."

She nods, buckling her seat belt. "Yep. We're good."

"You're a pretty easy kid. You know that, baby girl?"

"Because you're a pretty easy daddy."

Her smile makes me feel better. I should give it more time. Let her figure this out. She's a brilliant kid, and sooner or later the rest of the world will figure it out.

"We make a good team, just the two of us," she says.

"Sure do." I start the truck and we head for home.

As I'm turning into the driveway, I ask, "Any requests for supper?"

"Spaghetti!" she answers immediately. "With garlic toast. I know there's some in the freezer because I asked Julia to add it to our grocery list."

"Whatever you want." I hit the garage door opener and pull the truck inside. I'm grateful our cleaning lady does most of the grocery runs so I don't have to.

I'd bought the big house five years ago and had it remodeled shortly afterward, including the pool out back. At the time, I imagined Natalie having friends over, and focused on fun things for them to do. That still hasn't happened.

Someday, I tell myself. *Give her fucking time.*

As soon as the hamburger meat and garlic bread are set on the counter to thaw, Natalie takes my phone and heads up to her bedroom to get cracking on her sketch. I go to my office to create some bids and process billings.

My mind has a hard time staying focused lately. Especially when half the damn evening keeps coming back to Isabella Derby.

All sorts of questions creep in. I shove them aside, but they're relentless.

It's bullshit. Everything about this.

Not just how cute she is, with her honey-blonde hair bouncing off her shoulders and those gray eyes shimmering in the pale light.

She's too hot to stay single. That part confuses me. She'd only gone on one date with Preston. He's too annoying for any woman to date twice.

What I can't figure out is why she'd be so hard up for dates in the first place.

In my mind, those match-up sites are scams. Not a fair assumption, maybe, but fuck fair.

I know people who've found their spouses online. However, their final outcomes are yet to come.

That's where the real scam comes in. Not even marriage guarantees a life together.

People change. Sometimes that works for everyone. Sometimes it doesn't.

Sometimes people die before the change ever happens.

I push away from my desk and walk to the window. It's a beautiful, clear evening out there, but inside, it might as well be monsoon season.

I remember what happened to Cindy. She'd wanted the Happily Ever After when we hooked up. I was in it for here and now.

That taught me a lesson. One I'll never forget.

"Two goddamned weeks," I mutter, resting my fist against the glass. If I'd just been discharged two weeks earlier, Cindy might still be alive. Natalie would have a mother, someone else to love her, even if things were never meant to be between us.

Bitter fucking irony. Sometimes, it makes me sick.

"Dad?"

I spin around, dashing the sadness on my face. "Present," I joke numbly.

Natalie walks into my office beaming. "It's time to start supper."

Though she has my eyes and the better parts of my attitude, she's got a lot of her mother, too. Cindy liked everything on time and in order. That was only one of the many things that drew us apart, and one of the things I've changed since.

Purposefully. Children need structure. So do hazmat crews.

"I'll be up soon." I walk to my desk to shut down the computer. "Go wash up."

As we do most nights, we cook supper together.

My mind wanders to Blue again while our Bolognese sauce simmers. The school has rules, which is fine. I have no interest in dating her.

I just want to take her to bed. Relieve some of this tension kissing her had kicked up last night.

Of course, dating and fucking are equally forbidden. Both spell trouble with a screaming capital T.

"I wish I had art class tonight."

I spin around, half wondering if I'd mentioned the class out loud. "Why's that?"

"Because I love it!" Natalie says, dumping a bag of salad in a bowl. "I like Ms. Derby and can't wait for her to see my dog drawing."

I turn back to the stove and stir the sauce. "I'm not

sure I'd get too attached, Nat. She's only a substitute for the regular art teacher," I say, not wanting her to get her hopes up of having Ms. Derby all year.

I don't need that kind of hope either. The faster I forget about that little blonde with blue streaks begging for my fingers, the better off I'll be. It'll also save a few bucks in cold showers.

"I know."

The noodles start boiling. As I'm turning down the heat, a crash sounds.

Front door. Which instantly has my nerves on edge.

It better not be that vicious prick again.

Bastard Phil should've heeded my warning. I told him what would happen if he ever showed up on my porch again, and I wasn't fucking bluffing.

"Wow, it's getting late for company! I'll see –"

"No, Nat. Let me." My tone is harsh. I can't help it.

Natalie frowns. "What's wrong?"

"Nothing," I say. "You watch the noodles. Don't let them boil over. Keep an eye on the timer. I'll go see what that was."

She agrees with a nod, but still looks at me cautiously. I rarely tell her no, especially not so rudely. But when it comes to this, I'd rather be clear than polite.

Fuck the Black Pearls. I warned Davey to stay away.

They're one of the biggest crime syndicates in the state.

He didn't listen. And now, his problem is mine.

On my way to the front door, I make a quick detour to my office. Grab the nine millimeter I keep in the safe behind a picture on the wall, and slide in the clip while making my way back into the hall.

I listen carefully, making sure Nat's still in the kitchen. I don't want her to catch me sneaking around with a gun in our own damn house if I can avoid it.

In the foyer, I tuck the weapon into my waistband and stand off to the side, peeking through the half-moon window in the top of the door.

I can't see anything. Anyone. Not even a shadow.

Can't wait forever.

I yank open the front door and step out, glancing around.

That's when I spy her.

Her!

Blue.

Actually, she's red faced, sweeping black dirt into a pile with her hand.

"I'm so sorry," she says, barely glancing up. "I accidentally knocked the plant off the table by the door. The pot broke. I'll replace it."

Not Bastard Phil. Thank Christ he's taken my warning seriously for now.

Seeing her pisses me off almost as much for a different reason. Mainly because she's the last person I need right now. The hard-on I've fought all day reminds me why.

"I'm truly sorry, again. Just tell me where you got the pot and –"

"Julia bought it." I stand over her. "Cleaning lady," I add watching how the tension on her face smooths out.

Congratulations. You're boned, I hear a voice in the back of my mind say, laughing the whole time. Not if I have anything to say about it.

She pats the pile of dirt, green leaves, and broken

pottery, she'd created on the porch. "Oh, um, do you know where she bought it?"

"No."

Nodding, she stands. "Well...could you ask her?"

"No." I'm harsher than I need to be. The depressed look on her face gets to me. "Lady, I don't give a shit about a broken pot. But I *do* need to know what you're doing here."

"Oh, of course, I, well, I –"

Even her stutter is adorable. I watch her lips moving too long.

Pure torture. I huff a breath, waiting for her to untie that sweet tongue and get the words out.

"Natalie. I brought some supplies for Natalie to use," she says at last. "For her dog picture, I mean. It was the best in the class. I just wanted to make sure she had the right stuff."

"What kind of 'stuff,' Ms. Derby?"

I whip around at the sound of Natalie's voice.

"You *really* think my picture's best in the class?" Her green eyes sparkle. "The very best?"

"Yes," Blue answers, kneeling down in front of Natalie. "Here's to you, queen. I brought you some drawing books. They're more advanced material, old ones I used in college, and some colored pencils."

"Really? Wow! Thank you." Laughing, Natalie's eyes are still glowing when she glances up at me. "Ms. Derby can stay for supper, can't she, Dad? Everything's just about ready." She turns back to Blue. "It's spaghetti night. I just took the noodles off the stove."

I easily read the look in Blue's eyes. She's wondering why I would let a ten year old cook.

None of her fucking business.

Who does this woman think she is? Showing up here after last night? Breaking my shit and leaving me with another hard-on I'll be fighting all week?

If it wasn't for the smile on Nat's face...damn it all.

"Thank you, but I can't," she says, clearly reading my mind. "But here." She stands up and hands a cloth bag to Natalie. "There's the stuff I promised. Also," she unzips her purse. "Let me pay you for the pot right now. So clumsy."

Since I rarely use the front door, I have no idea where the pot even came from, but assume Julia put it there. I give her some creative leeway so Nat doesn't have to grow up in a man cave.

"Forget it, Ms. Derby. Your money's no good here."

"Well, then, um –"

"Please, Daddy, can't she stay?" Natalie asks. "There's more than enough food. And it isn't *that* late."

Agony. I can't lie in front of Nat.

There's always more than enough food, unfortunately. Despite every instinct screaming 'don't,' saying no to Nat is as impossible as ever.

She rarely asks for anything. I'm also interested in knowing what's really going on here. Why Blue felt inclined to bring Natalie art supplies when she could just wait until the next class.

"Be my guest." I step aside and wave for Blue to enter the house. Nat beams like the Phoenix sun.

"No, that's all right, really, I just –"

"My Natalie would really love you to stay for dinner, Ms. Derby. Please." I touch her shoulder and give her a soft push forward. "There's more than enough. My ma's sauce recipe."

"Okay! That sounds lovely, but –"

No. No buts. She's not getting out of this if I couldn't.

"I made a salad, too, and garlic bread," Natalie chirps, taking Blue's hand and tugging her inside our house.

III: SPAGHETTI NIGHT (IZZY)

How did I wind up here? He'd had a gun in his pants.

I saw it. A black pistol.

It's not there now, but only because he stepped into a room off the hallway while Natalie led me into the kitchen. Who answers the door with *a gun?*

I should have left. If I hadn't gotten jumpy, hadn't knocked over that plant with my bag, I'd be halfway home by now. No one would've ever known I was here.

I'd never admit it out loud, but Clara isn't the only Derby with the nosy gene. Last night, I spent some time online. There wasn't a lot in search for Brent Eden, other than a very impressive website for his business dealing with hazardous waste clean up.

Hazmat spills, dirty jobs, and crime scene clean ups are his living, true. But do men need a gun for that? I wouldn't think so.

He's not on any social media sites, but his name did come up in an obituary. A brother, David Eden, who died three years ago. He'd been young, only in his late twenties. The obit didn't give a cause of death.

I'm not sure it matters. That mystery isn't the reason I'm here.

"What would you like to drink, Ms. Derby?" Natalie asks sweetly, holding the fridge door open. "We've got milk, OJ, grape juice, or water."

Brent stands on the other side of the large marble topped island, placing serving bowls full of food on the table. I'm trying very hard not to look his way.

Every time I do, my eyes wander to his lips. Heat wells inside me, recalling how amazing, how easy, how natural they felt on mine. Then I remember the gun.

Dear God.

"Um," I clear my throat. "Water will be fine, Natalie. Thank you."

"How 'bout a lemon slice in it?" Natalie smiles, already reaching for a yellow lemon in a small bowl.

Who is this kid? My own freaking mom doesn't offer lemon water. The teacher in me can't help but worry a little. "No thanks. I like mine plain and ice cold."

She smiles and fills a glass with ice, then water from the dispenser on the front of the fridge. "You can go ahead and sit down."

I glance towards Brent, who gestures towards a chair. I help carry the glass of milk that Natalie had already filled, and set it near the plate he points to, then take a seat on the other side of the table. Natalie carries two glasses of water to the table, setting one near his plate and the other near mine.

"This is so fun! It's been forever since we had company," she says.

"Have a seat, baby girl," Brent says.

Considering I skip as many family dinners as possible, and live alone, it's been ages since I sat at a table and ate with other people willingly. "It smells fabulous," I say. At least that part's true. Still makes me more nervous than I recall being in a very long time.

Partly because of the way Brent keeps watching me. He knows I'm not just here to drop off art supplies, and he's right.

He also has my insides tied in knots. I'll never forget last night's kiss.

It's been on my mind all day. Especially while Principal Jacobs questioned me about Preston and then Brent. Preston told Jacobs what Brent said last night, about us dating. There was a good solid hour this afternoon where I thought I'd be fired for sure.

Until Jacobs said he'd heard another story. Brent personally assured him we're not dating.

Hence my reason for being here. To thank him all over again for saving my butt a second time.

Dread storms through my stomach while we slowly pass food around. I fill my plate and eat, telling Natalie how delicious it is between bites.

All the while wondering how I'll ever drop the other bomb.

How do I warn Brent about my family?

After I got home from work this afternoon, I got a phone call from mother. Clara did her homework and then some. Found out who Brent is. The name on the side of his truck gave it away.

Then, like the annoying sister I never had, she told mom about seeing us together in the school parking lot.

Of course, she elaborated. *A lot.*

Said she'd caught us in a passionate embrace. She denied that when I called her, but the damage is done.

It's too late to fall back into a normal life. Not with Derby women hot on the trail, like hounds specially trained to track down every last whiff of cupid. I cringe, imagining the day either mom or Clara herself show up on Brent's doorstep.

Asking his intentions.

Asking when the wedding will be.

Jesus.

Pure humiliation washes over me. I shouldn't have come here, really.

But I can't have him stuck in the middle of a Derby family clusterfuck.

Clara won't be satisfied with just a name and a quick glimpse of my Not Fiancé. She'll dig deep to learn more. And she'll succeed.

Hell, she probably already has his address, phone number, birth date, and, knowing her, his net worth.

"What kind of books did you bring me?"

I snap out of my funk and glance across the table, smiling at Natalie. So young, yet so mature.

I shouldn't have, but I asked her pod teacher about her today. I pretended it had to do with her art, how impressive it is.

Not that I needed an excuse, however true. Mrs. Gates was more than willing to tell all. Natalie Eden is extremely smart, but struggles to keep up emotionally. She's been in the same school since kindergarten. Skipping grades has made it impossible for her to continue friendships, and difficult to build new ones.

My heart goes out to her. Kids, without even realizing it, can be so mean. Rich kids from powerful families can easily feel intimidated by someone with her brains and talent.

I wipe my lips with my napkin before saying, "I'm glad you asked. One's about drawing animals. It covers their anatomy, how to do form for things like birds, whales, turtles, you name it. The other book, that's for drawing people. I also put some charcoal in the bag if you'd like to experiment with it on your dog drawing."

"Of course!" Her green eyes pop. "Wow, thank you! I saw some charcoal drawings online this afternoon. They looked almost three-dimensional."

"That's exactly what charcoal can do when used correctly. Add depth to a picture."

"Awesome! I can't wait to try it."

Brent points to her plate. "You clean your plate, and I'll let you out of dish duty tonight."

"Deal!" She grins, twirling a fork full of spaghetti. "You're the bestest, Dad." She winks at the obvious shift in grammar.

They've got a good thing going, these two. Makes me remember how strong a connection can be between a girl and her father. And miss it.

She asks me several more questions about drawing while eating, and I answer. Brent doesn't say much, but his eyes say he's thinking plenty. He's a master at keeping my nerves on edge.

By the time he excuses Natalie, who nearly bolts away, it feels like I'm sitting on pins and needles.

She's barely out of the room when he sets down his fork. "Ready to tell me why you're really here?"

I almost choke on a lettuce leaf. It takes several sips of water before it goes down and I can breathe.

"I know it's not about fucking art supplies," he rumbles, thunder in his throat.

I nod and sigh, having no idea how, where, to start. "You're right, Brent. It's not. Although your daughter *is* very talented. No exaggeration."

"I know."

"Right. I'm sure you do."

He leans back in his chair and crosses his massive arms across his broad chest. Waiting impatiently. "Did you get fired today or what?"

"Fired? No!" I take a quick gulp of air. "Because of you, no less. Thanks for telling Mr. Jacobs the truth. I really, really appreciate that. This job, teaching at the academy...it's been my dream since I was in the ninth grade and Marlene Scott won State with her landscapes. She went to school at the academy and I was public educated. Her drawing was like nothing I've ever seen. Right then, I decided I wanted to teach art at the academy." Heat leaps into my cheeks. I realize I'm not only babbling, I'm sharing secrets I've never told anyone.

"Teach? Why? At that age, I'd think you'd have dreamed about going to the academy and learning to draw like this Marlene yourself."

Relieved he wasn't put out by my rambling, I shake my head. "You've heard the saying, 'those who can't do, teach?' That's me. I'm not an artist. I love art. Love how it's created, how it pushes buttons on the soul, but I'm not talented enough to ever create beautiful masterpieces. And I'm sure I'd be miserable in LA, New York, Paris...it's too much. I'm an Arizona girl, born and raised. I've known it for years. And I'm okay with it. Watching others create masterpieces is my dream. That's why I took the full time job teaching preschool at the academy. It was a foot in the door. Hopefully someday, when there's an opening in the art department, I'll be first in line."

His brows furrow in thought. A sexier gesture than it should be.

"I know how it sounds: crazy. But it's what I've worked at forever, and for just a little while today, I was afraid I'd lost it all. Then Mr. Jacobs told me you'd assured him we aren't dating. He also said there'll be no repercussions against me for what Preston did." The elation that hit hard in Mr. Jacobs' office this afternoon returns. "I can't thank you enough, Brent. Seriously."

I can't say Brent smiles, but there's a...well, almost a grin. "I'm glad it worked out for you."

I bite my lip, knowing I have to mention the other thing that happened today.

He lifts a brow. "There's more, isn't there?"

I nod pressing a hand against the knot in my stomach.

"Well, spit it out," he says.

"The woman in the parking lot last night, my cousin Clara...this is embarrassing. She sort of told my mother we're dating."

He laughs.

I don't know what I expected, but this isn't it. "It's not funny."

"Yeah, it is."

"Why? This was *your* idea, remember? When you told Preston we were – you know." I can't bring myself to say engaged.

Can't.

The shine leaves his eyes, turning them cold and barren. "I had good reason. The asshole was threatening you. I had to get rid of him. Don't take it so personal. Nothing could be more absurd than you and me dating."

A touch of anger flares inside me. So that's it – I'm not good enough for him?

I'm about to call him out for being a ginormous ass, when I consider the other possibility. The coldness in his tone makes me wonder if the idea hit a sore spot somewhere. I know there's no wife, but a girlfriend is a real possibility. Am I treading on another woman's turf?

Maybe the cleaning lady does more than just sweep his floors?

"Why's that? Because of Julia?"

This time, there's a bitterness in his chuckle. "Julia's twice as old as you, married, and a grandmother of six. She cleans this house twice a week and picks up groceries."

For some stupid reason, that makes me relax. "Oh."

"I have Nat." He stands and picks up his plate. "She's the only girl in my life, and that's how it'll stay. No time for other bullshit."

I jump to my feet, pick up my plate, and carry it to the sink in the center island. "I told both my mother and Clara that we aren't dating, but they don't believe me."

"That's interesting, Isabella." He takes my plate and sets it in the sink. "And totally not my problem."

Ouch.

I spin around, collecting Natalie's dishes. Then the frustration boils over. "I know that, Brent, but I just wanted to let you know. Give you a heads-up in case they contact you."

"How would they contact me? Why? I didn't even tell your cousin my name."

"She Googled the name on the side of your truck."

There's a sneer on his face when he takes the dirty dishes from my hands.

I pull the serving dishes off the table and carry them over. "Look, I'm sorry. I know it's the last thing you need." Although I've never let anyone know the entire truth, I feel inclined to explain. "It's my mother driving this insanity. She's kinda been trying to marry me off for the past couple years. And Clara? Ugh. She's anyone's partner in crime where there's drama involved."

"Why do they care? Don't these people have lives of their own?"

Ignoring the rude edge in his voice, I shake my head. "Don't know for sure. Mom won't admit it, but I think it's because she won't marry her boyfriend until I'm married first. Some weird parental sense of duty and protocol or something like that." I turn back to the table after handing him the spaghetti bowl.

"My father died ten years ago. For the past five years, mom's dated George. He wants to get married, but she says she can't until I'm settled. In her mind, settled means married."

I bite my lip, realizing how ridiculous this sounds. Thank God for family, right?

At least they've helped me get the crazy part down before I even get my first cat.

I walk back to the table for more dishes. He follows, too, but leans down and picks up my purse and then takes my arm.

Whoa. I'm too stunned to do anything besides let him lead me down the hall.

At the front door, he says, "I don't mind getting rid of pricks like Preston. Happy to do that any time, but I'm not a damn stage prop. You'll have to find some other sucker to play your fake boyfriend, Isabella. We're done."

Snapped back to reality, I grab my purse from his hand. "That's not at all what I wanted! Not what I'm asking now. I just wanted you to know in case they contact you. A friendly warning. Nothing more."

I'm almost choking. Appalled he thinks I was after that. After him since he's shown his true colors.

I'm nobody's prop either. Especially not for a man who's treating me like a worn out doormat.

I tap the center of his chest with my fingertip. "Don't flatter yourself, Eden. You'd be the last man I'd ask if I was looking for a boyfriend, fake or any other kind. Besides being arrogant, dating you would get me fired. Trust me, there's no man on planet Earth worth fucking up my dream for. Not now. Not ever. I've worked too long and hard."

His glare shoots right through me. "Are you done?"

He's challenging me, which only pisses me off more. Big time.

"No." I march around him. "I'm going to say goodbye to Natalie and then I'll be overjoyed to get out of your face."

His hand clamps down on my arm, but at the same instant, Natalie appears at the top of the stairway off the foyer.

"Are you leaving, Ms. Derby?"

Even before his fingers slip off my arm, I say, "Good timing! I was just coming up to say bye."

"Oh, good, I want to show you what I've done with the charcoal. It's amazing." I hesitate and she frowns. "I won't keep you long, it'll only take a second?"

I don't bother looking Brent's way at all before moving toward the staircase. I walk up the steps and down the hallway with my chin up. His badass attitude doesn't intimidate me.

I've seen how this little girl's smile transforms him.

The space on the second floor reminds me just how big the house is. It's nice, too. Newly remodeled from the looks of things, and upon walking into Natalie's bedroom, I have to pause long enough to catch my breath.

It's not only huge, it's like a child's dream room. The four-poster bed is up on a platform, topped with a frilly pink canopy, and besides the massive white furniture, complete with mirrored dressing table and shelves full of toys, there's a huge side room. Her easel is set up there, where evening light shines in through several big windows. A reading nook takes up one corner, complete with a padded window seat, lined with pink and white pillows galore. Another corner has a desk, with more shelves, this time full of books, and a computer with a screen bigger than most television sets.

"I shaded the dog with the charcoal," she says, standing on the other side of the wooden easel. "Come see!"

The white carpet feels so plush it's like walking on air. I cross the room to the easel. Once again, my breath stalls. "That's outstanding." It's all I can say.

The dog looks so real, I can't help but touch the paper. "Truly amazing, Natalie. You're a natural."

"Thank you." She glances towards the doorway. "Come see, Daddy."

I step aside as he crosses the room, fighting to ignore the tension.

"That's fantastic, baby girl," he says.

My jaw drops. "Just fantastic? It's utterly amazing. Out of this universe."

Anger flashes in his eyes. "Yes, it is, and you're leaving." He grasps my arm, whispering under his breath. "Say goodbye."

His grip is harsh yet gentle. I can't blame him, I suppose. I crossed a proverbial line, downplaying the praise for his daughter, and even I realize it. "Goodbye, Natalie! See you next class."

She steps forward and wraps her arms around my waist. "I love, love, *love* the supplies. Thanks again, Ms. Derby, and for having supper with us."

He lays a hand on Natalie's shoulder. "Ms. Derby has to leave now, baby girl, and you need to get ready for bed."

Natalie releases me and he gives my arm a hard tug.

By the time we reach the staircase, I manage to break his hold. Increasing the speed of my departure, I hurry down the steps.

"Goodbye, Ms. Derby."

I ignore him, pulling the door shut behind me hard.

In my car, I consider taking a moment to collect myself, but that'll only piss me off more. I need to get away from this place.

What an arrogant asshole. He's the last man I'd ever consider dating. Right up there with Preston.

I back out of the driveway and head up the street, still fuming.

When my cell phone rings, I consider ignoring it, but can't. Plucking it from the outside pocket of my purse, I hit the answer button and then the icon for speaker.

"Hello, dear!"

"Hey, mom," I answer.

"How was your evening with your new man friend?"

"How wha –"

"Clara said she saw your car at his house."

I should've known. Clara has nothing better to do some nights than go on her drives around town. I guess tonight she decided to drop by the place listed on Brent's business registry. "He's *not* my man friend, mom. He's the father of one of my students."

"Well, I can't wait to meet him, whatever he is. I'm *so* happy for you. This is a big step, Isabella."

My sanity is the price of mom's happiness, and it's not something I can deal with right now. "I'll call you back, I can't shift gears and drive at the same time." Without waiting for a response, I hit the end call button.

Hitting the gas, I speed up and change gears, taking some frustration out on the curves leading out of the development faster than I should, but I need this.

I need to be in control of something.

Have power over a road going somewhere I can actually comprehend.

For a few sweet moments, I have it. Control. Until the flashing red lights in the rear-view mirror appear and a siren wails.

"Fuck!"

IV: BLANK CHECK (BRENT)

I don't think I've ever counted the days between one Tuesday to the next like I have the past week. Yesterday, when I picked up Natalie, I had to fight the desire to walk down the opposite hallway to see Blue.

It's art night again. That simple fact makes every hour seem twice as long.

Today's cleanup job doesn't help. It's for law enforcement.

Not a crime scene, but a body nonetheless. An old man who'd lived alone and died. His body was stuck in the house for a week before someone called it in. The stifling heat is sickening, and the smell, well, respirators can only do so much. The coroner had it worse when he turned down our offer to let him borrow one.

Everybody's glad we'll be done within the hour.

My phone vibrates in my pocket. I wave at Juan as I pull off a glove to take the call. I told him I was waiting to hear about the asbestos job we'd finished last week.

Convinced this is it, the nod that the job passed inspection, I step outside and yank off my mask.

I swipe the answer icon and take a breath of fresh air while pressing the phone to my ear. "Brent Eden."

"Hello, Brent. It's Clara. Clara Derby?" Like I don't remember. "I met you last week with Izzy."

"Izzy?" It takes a second before it hits like a ton of bricks.

"Isabella Derby! My lovely cousin."

Blue? Concern instantly grips me. "Has something happened –"

"No, no, nothing's happened. Izzy's fine. Or will be once she stops beating herself up for getting that speeding ticket after leaving your house the other night."

I shouldn't smile, but can't help it.

Blue was hopping mad when she left the house.

Sick man that I am, I was more frustrated than I'd been for sometime. And turned on.

She's had my blood lit neon red since meeting her, true. But the way her eyes sparked when she got all huffy, shit, let's just say there's something damn sexy about a woman who's all riled up.

"That's understandable, though," Clara continues, "considering how worried Izzy is about her mother. A serious diagnosis does that. Listen, I just want you to know how happy we all are that she's found someone. I'm sure you get it, being a father yourself? A parent's greatest desire is to see their kids happy, and when our days become short, that's even more critical."

She pauses. Sighs. "Oh, goodness, I'm rambling. *Please* don't tell Izzy I just told you everything. She'd be upset.

Anywho, I just wanted you to know how much Aunt Cleo wants to meet you. The whole family does, really."

My mind spins in circles. Diagnosis? Shortened days? What the fuck?

Why hadn't Blue told me the truth? Then again, who wants to admit they're desperately looking for a boyfriend to appease their dying mother?

Blaming crazy family drama, that's a lot easier.

At least it explains why she went out with that twisted prick, Preston.

"Brent?"

"I'm here. Go ahead." I run a hand over my face, wondering what's coming next.

"Well, I just called because it might help if you tell Izzy getting a ticket can happen to anyone."

I may have been born at night, but it wasn't *last* night. Cousin Clara's calling for more than a damn speeding ticket.

Too bad I can't help her. If I hadn't already decided to stay away from Blue, as far as possible, I'd definitely draw the line at bait left by nosy cousins.

"You're right. Tickets can happen to anyone." I'm not leaving the door open. I turn around on the rickety old porch at the sound of a car pulling in and stiffen as it parks next to my truck.

Talk about timing. What the fuck is *he* doing here?

"Clara, thanks for calling." I cut her off.

Suddenly, this woman and her gumption, trying to orchestrate more trouble with Blue, is the least of my problems. This is a mess, but it's not pure evil. Not like the demon in front of me.

Tucking the phone in my pocket, I cross the concrete

and then the hard packed dirt of the neglected front yard, never taking my eyes off Bastard Phil as he climbs out of his car.

I round his front bumper, fighting the urge to kick it in. "I told you once, jackass. Remember? Are you out of your mind or are you just fucking stupid?"

"I saw the deputies leave." Phil smiles. "Think what could happen to your reputation if they knew you're in with The Pearls."

"I'm *not* in with you assholes," I growl. That's all I say because I know the worst thing I can do is show any vulnerability.

Every Black Pearls member thinks he's God. They believe they're so powerful the law means nothing. The only thing they understand is money, and they don't care who gets hurt while they're busy collecting it.

"Go the fuck home. We're not in business. No goddamn deals." I cast an eye over his customary black jeans and t-shirt, almost like a uniform. and his fuzzy black chin strip.

"We know, Eden," he sneers. "You aren't sloppy like little Davey."

My teeth clench at the mention of my brother.

"Big brother couldn't save him. That must still keep you up at night. Knowing how he –"

I snap, grab him by the front of the shirt, and slam his back up against my truck. "I've told you before, you sonofabitch. Stay the hell away from me."

"I will, with pleasure, just as soon as you pay Davey's debts. The ones Davey swore up and down big brother would pay."

Sadist bastards. All of them.

This is his latest ploy. Refusing to take his bait is getting harder and harder. I want to pinch my eyes shut so the furious headache settling into my temples stops, but I don't dare take my eyes off this asshole.

Christ. The idea that Davey's last breaths were spent asking for me, begging for me to help him, hits hard every time I think about it.

That's what big brothers do. They get little brothers out of scraps, big and small, and sometimes lethal.

Knowing I couldn't that night guts me with a dull knife.

But I will.

Someday.

Soon.

I yank him forward and throw him toward his car. "Get the fuck out of here! Last warning."

He brushes the front of his shirt like my fingerprints left dust on him. "Can't do that. Not till we make a little deal. Then I'll go away."

The desire to ring the bastard's neck makes my hands itch so hard I curl them into fists. "I'm *not* making any fucking deals with you."

"Aw, you sound so sure, Eden. Won't take much. Not for a smart, well connected businessman like you. And, since I'm such a standup guy, I'm willing to negotiate. A hundred grand of cash laundered through one of your hazmat jobs. Easy. Shit, or maybe you'd be more interested in a shipping arrangement? You've got the wheels. Least a dozen cube trucks that can haul anything without causing a single deputy to blink an eye." Phil winks. "Ain't I right?"

"Fuck. You."

He lets out a glib chuckle. "Shame the Grizzlies have all gone limp. Too damn interested in their kosher businesses these days. Your old Grizz buddies could've helped you make this go quick and smooth." He nods his head towards my truck. "I've seen the patch on the inside of your jacket. The little one you hide behind all the army crap on the front. You were a Grizz in your younger days. Ain't I right again, *Monk?*"

My teeth clench together when he says that name. Some of my best friends are from the days I was a full patch member of the Grizzlies MC. The motorcycle club still operates up and down the West Coast, based out of Redding.

They went through a lot of turmoil cleaning up their act. I saw the writing on the wall and quit before there was no getting out.

Still, once a member, always a member. Especially with good men like Blackjack, their national Prez, in charge of things now.

I haven't tried to erase everything from that part of my life, and never will.

Bastard Phil's also clueless. Doesn't know the Grizzlies haven't gone soft. They've matured and learned to operate on the quiet side since they ran the cartel back over the border. They gave up their drugs and gun running for gambling, bars, and peep shows to keep the money flowing.

I turn to walk away. "Get the fuck out of here!"

"Come on, Eden, not so fast! I'd think you'd be interested in making a deal. Fuck, I was all ready to sit down and discuss one the other night. Then I saw you had company." The bastard lets out a low whistle. "Lucky man! Real shame that cute little blonde with the blue shit in her hair had to go and get herself a ticket, too. Saw her practically on the verge of tears while Dawson had her pulled over, writing it up."

How the hell does he know that? My spine quivers. These assholes usually make themselves scarce when there's a squad car around, especially a police captain I've known for years. I force myself not to turn around and grab him by his throat until his eyes bug out of his head.

"That's a pretty sweet Mustang she drives. Car like that could break down any time." He snaps his fingers. "Just like *that*. On a lonely stretch of road. These Arizona nights get dark quicker, and cold in a few more months. Poor little thing like that could yell and holler and plead, but no one would hear her stranded in the dark. No one." He shows his teeth like a demented chimpanzee.

Enough.

I pivot and take a step, putting my face so close to his I can smell his filthy breath. "You must've been hit in the head with a fucking stupid stick."

He blinks once. Using only my chest, I ram him against his car, snarling like a bear. "Threatening me is the last thing you want to do. Understand?"

His eyes bulge and his upper lip quivers.

Finally, it's sinking in. And we're not done yet.

I reach down and grab the knife out of the sheaf hanging on his side. Shoving the tip hard enough under his chin that the skin indents, I twist it. "Now, get the fuck out of here before I castrate you with your own blade."

His Adam's apple wobbles against my knuckles as he

nods. I step back, giving him room to open the car door and climb in, all the while holding the knife in the air, clearly letting him know I have no intention of giving it back, and every intent to use it as promised.

Dirt and rocks ping the Buick's underside as he hits reverse and guns away. I watch him back out of the driveway. As the tires squeal on pavement, a cold and ugly jolt hits my spine. The last thing – the very last thing – I need is for the Black Pearls to pull Blue into this nightmare.

I'm already worried sick for Nat. It's too fucking close to her, too near to me, and all thanks to an uncle she barely knew.

I throw the knife at the ground. The sharp blade penetrates the hard dirt deep enough to stand straight.

"Son-of-a-bitch!" The curse burns my throat.

Whether I like it or not, it's happening. Those bastards will rope anyone in for leverage, and they know I know it.

They also know I have a headstone to visit, and I'll *never* tolerate adding another. "Fuck!"

I grab the knife out of the ground and throw it in the bed of my pickup before heading back towards the house.

I spend most of the day wishing Davey had listened. Even though I know that's a moot point and a waste of energy, I wish to Heaven, Hell, and everything in between.

* * *

THE DARK THOUGHTS are still with me when I pull into the school lot to pick up Nat.

The bell has already rung and kids are flying out the door like the Hoover Dam just burst behind them.

Nat sees me and starts running down the steps.

Despite the heaviness inside me, warmth wells in my chest. Seeing my daughter does wonders to lighten the storm.

She always has a smile on her face when she sees me, but it's bigger today. Brighter.

"Hey, sunshine," I say as she opens the door.

"Hi, Daddy!" She tosses her bag on the floor. "Finally. I thought the bell would *never* ring."

I wait until she's inside and has the door closed before asking, "Why's that?"

"Art class tonight! Don't tell me you forgot? I can't wait to show Ms. Derby my dog drawing. I know she'll love it. Oh, and supposedly we're trying landscapes tonight!"

If I could take a picture of her right now, I would. I don't know if I've ever seen her so happy. "Landscapes, huh? How'd you find out?"

"I saw Ms. Derby at recess. She let the cat out of the bag." She stretches the seat belt around her waist and buckles. "Watercolors, Dad! I love watercolors." A more serious expression crosses her face. "Hey, um, if it's not too much...could we order pizza? Or maybe even eat out for supper?"

Her request is a rarity. "Sure, baby girl. What's the hurry?"

"Well, I have to be back here by six thirty. I wanna squeeze some time in to Google watercolor paintings and techniques. I've already read up on it, but today, I'm doing it."

"You'll do great, Nat. You're always prepared."

If this girl inherited any of the slacker genes I had at her age, I've never seen a single hint.

I back out of the parking space and pull into the line of vehicles waiting to exit the lot. "You shouldn't be so nervous over what you don't know yet. Remember, part of this class is teaching *you* the techniques."

"Oh, I know, and Ms. Derby will. She's the best ever! But I like to skip ahead. Have a bit of insight beforehand."

That's my girl. An old soul. I think she was born with more knowledge than most eighteen-year-olds. And she has a never ending appetite for more.

I roll past a blue Mustang and have to work to pull my eyes off it. "All right. Which is it then? Pizza or eat out?"

"Pizza!" she says instantly. "I can research while it's being delivered."

This girl. Damn if it doesn't make me smile.

Inching the truck forward while another car pulls onto the busy road, I flick the blinker. "Okay. What kind?"

She's unzipping her backpack. "Surprise me." Digging deep in her bag, she adds, "But no anchovies or sauerkraut, please."

I cock my head. "Have I ever ordered a pizza with anchovies or sauerkraut?"

She's still digging, now in a side pocket. "No, but only because I always remind you not to. I know you, Daddy. Someday you'll give it a try just because I didn't tell you not to."

Little shit. I just might have to do that to her someday for fun.

There's an opening in traffic, so I pull out. "What are you digging for?"

"A friendship bracelet. I can't remember which pocket I put it in."

Even though the term leaves little doubt what it is, I ask anyway. "Friendship bracelet?"

She huffs out a sigh. "It's like...a piece of jewelry one either gives or receives from a friend."

I grin at how she sounds like she's reading right out of Webster's biggest and oldest book. Hope also rises up inside me. "Where'd you get it?"

"We made them during pod today."

What she calls pod is a close second to what was called homeroom when I was in school. My heart also tugs slightly at the idea she's digging it out to give to me.

Damn. I'd be honored, of course, but I wish she'd give it to a real friend from school.

"Here!" She holds up a few pieces of jute twine braided together and decorated with colorful beads.

"That's pretty." I'm rather indifferent to the style, actually, but do my best to support her in everything. "You did quality work."

"I know. I'm quite proud of how evenly I was able to space the beads." She tucks it in her pants pocket. "I want to remember to take it with me tonight."

"Tonight?"

"So I can give it to Ms. Derby, of course." She does a little pout with her lips like she can't believe I didn't know.

Shit.

My heart sinks. I take a deep breath, carefully choosing my words. "Ms. Derby? Wouldn't you rather give it to a friend from school? Someone your age?"

"Ms. Derby *is* from school." She's looking straight ahead, out the windshield. "And I don't really have any friends my age."

Right. I look at her softly, hoping I haven't kicked up too much crap she'd rather not touch.

Still, this issue keeps bothering me more lately. "It's your bracelet to trade with whoever, Nat. Just curious. You must talk with some of the kids at school? Visit with some more than others?"

"I talk with plenty of kids at school, yeah. But it doesn't mean they're friends." She gives me one of her Doctor Know-It-All looks. "Just like you talk to a lot of people who aren't exactly friends."

I continue trying to be diplomatic. "Nat, Ms. Derby's your teacher. That's all I'm saying. I'm not sure what she'll think."

"I thought about that," she says seriously. "But technically, she's not *my* teacher. Not for the day classes. And she's only filling in for Mrs. Wayne for eight weeks because Mrs. Wayne's son, Forrest, got in trouble this summer. Guess he was court ordered to do community service. Mrs. Wayne has to drive him to his assignments every Tuesday night because Mr. Wayne, besides being the chemistry teacher, is the JV football coach and they play on Tuesdays." She shakes her head while continuing, "Us Arizonians love our football! Lord knows Mr. Wayne couldn't drive Forrest around."

Her gossip makes me smile. I knew Blue was only filling in, but hadn't heard the particulars. "Juicy. How'd you find all that out?"

"I just told you, I talk to a lot of people at school." She leans back and crosses her arms. "Which brings up another subject."

Almost afraid to ask, I glance her way. "What's that?"

"How would you feel about hiring Ms. Derby to

privately tutor me? After she's done subbing, I mean. She's way better than Mrs. Wayne. I'd learn so much more, so much faster, with private lessons."

"I've already paid for the accelerated art class you're taking." I try not to bite my tongue.

I'm searching for excuses. It's not the money, honestly, business is great.

It's Blue. Having her in my house. With Nat.

Barely a stone's throw away from teasing my dick seven ways from Sunday.

And a convenient target for Bastard Phil, if the evil prick doesn't listen.

"I know. I don't want to waste your money. I'll do both." She grins coyly. "I'm sure Ms. Derby wouldn't charge like the academy does. You'd probably be saving a few pennies after Mrs. Wayne's class ends."

Fuck. I wish money was the real issue. Then it'd be a hard limit.

Knowing her, she's too well aware it isn't. Looking for some sort of a round-about answer, I say, "What about something else beyond Mrs. Wayne's class? Something creative – music, vocals, guitar? You love country, baby girl. Bet you'd be damn good at it. All work and no play –"

"Art is my play, Dad. It keeps me from getting dull." She shrugs. "Don't stress. You don't have to answer right now. Just think about it. I still have four more classes with Ms. Derby after tonight, so it's not like there's a crazy rush or anything."

Maybe that's the problem. It's like I'm trapped in a slow moving train wreck.

I don't think I've ever had a person hurled at me from

so many directions as Isabella Derby. Need time to process. Figure this crap out. Time to change the subject.

"So, where're we ordering pizza from? Any requests?"

She rolls her eyes. "We both know Mike's is the only place that makes the crust you like."

"But you like that other place better. The one with the cheesy-bacon breadsticks?"

"I don't want any breadsticks tonight. Too many carbs."

I shake my head, clenching my jaw. Why the hell is my ten year old daughter suddenly freaked about carbs? "You don't need to worry about carbs, baby girl. You're only ten and you're beautiful."

My gaze hardens. I wish she'd go on, let me know if somebody's making her self-conscious. So I can hunt them down and have a real fucking friendly heart-to-heart.

"I know. But...you're kinda getting around the age that you should be."

I snort, my anger drifting away. "You saying I'm getting old?"

"Nope, just aging." She smiles at me. "But don't worry. It happens."

I'm not worried about pushing past my mid-thirties or the carbs. I wish life was that dull.

My anxieties are tangled on mean looking assholes toting guns, up in my face, and a woman I like drawing naked far too much. Every sexy, spitfire shade of Blue knocks around in my brain during the rest of the drive home.

* * *

Nat opens her door after I park the truck. "Can we shoot for pizza around five thirty? That'll give us time to eat and get back to school."

"Perfect." I climb out and meet her on the step going into the house, wondering why she's waiting. "Anything else, Nat?"

"No." She wraps her arms around my waist. "Other than I love you."

My heart melts. I return her hug. "Love you, too, sweets."

She heads up to her room, and I go to my office, where I call in the pizza and then start working on the billing for this morning's cleanup. I remember a time, not so long ago, when a dead body was the worst part of the day.

Bastard Phil comes to mind, front and center. His threat against Blue. How close I came to choking him lifeless, leaving him to rot beneath the scorching Arizona sun.

So does Davey, and the last time I'd seen him alive. I grit my teeth, hating it like hell.

* * *

Years Ago

"Come on, big bro, one more game." Davey taps the end of his cue stick on the edge of the table. "I'll go easy on you this time."

I laugh, chugging the last swallow of my beer. "You, go

easy on me? I just won three out of five. I'm kicking your ass up, down, and sideways, brother."

"One more will tie us up." Davey loads coins in the slots in the corner, wiping sweat from his forehead while the mechanical reels spin. No luck. The dimples he'd been known for since birth appear in both cheeks. "Even Steven. Come on," he turns back to me.

"We'll never be Even Steven. We know how this ends."

I mop the floor with my little brother. He gets pissed. Maybe he makes a scene if he's knocked back too many drinks.

We both storm off pissed, brotherly anger eclipsing our personal woes. It's such a predictable distraction we do it every week or two again.

"Quit wasting time. Let's go, Monk. Even fucking Steven," he insists while racking the balls, centering the black eight ball.

I cringe a little, hearing my old name from the Grizzlies. Those days are behind me.

"Not only even in pool. This time next week, our bank accounts will be squared up real nice." He laughs. "Actually, mine will be bigger."

That hits more than a nerve. My new hazmat company's success annoys him.

I don't know why. Ever since the time he was born, he's been trying to out-do me. I've let him at times, little things, hoping it'd knock the chip off his shoulder. So far, it hasn't.

Damn it, Davey. Life's too short for these games.

"What're you talking about? New photo gig?" I ask.

He shrugs and levels his cue stick on the white ball.

"Not quite. My ship's about to come in, though. Just you wait." He shoots. The colored balls smack together, scattering across the table.

Between my business and taking care of Natalie, I don't have a lot of time for gossip.

Still, I've heard the whispers. Davey, hanging around a crew he shouldn't. One that's too damn close to the underground I left behind.

I eyeball my brother, an electric unease needling the back of my neck.

Just this morning, I'd gotten wind of it again, after asking our ma to watch Natalie, and before I called Davey to join me for beers tonight.

Since he finally touched the subject, I say, "What ship's that? A jet-ski?"

He laughs, still plunking colored balls in pockets one after the other. "A yacht, bro."

I wrap a hand around his pool stick, preventing him from shooting again. "And where are you getting this yacht?"

His signature grin appears. "Jealous? I figured you'd want in."

"Fuck no."

Anger snaps in his eyes. "You should be."

"What the fuck are you thinking? The Black Pearls?" I don't even know if it's true, but I drop the name.

The nervous glance he shoots around the room tells me what I've heard aren't rumors. *Shit.*

"Davey –"

"Don't. Don't even get your mouth running. I *know* what I'm doing, Brent."

"Bullshit, you do. You can't."

He pulls his cue stick out of my hold. The look in his eyes makes me think it's already up his ass. "You think you're the only badass in this family? Only guy with friends in low places? The only one who gets to make scratch doing shit he really shouldn't, and then go hiding behind the hero-in-uniform and father-of-the-year act? Sorry to tell you, you're not."

He's been jealous of the Grizzlies for years. Again, for no reason.

For fuck's sake, I gave it up, and I'm glad. I got out because I had a daughter to think about and it was damn good timing, too. If I hadn't, I might be long dead from the club's infighting, or maybe another casualty of their California war with the Mexican cartels.

I plant myself between him and the pool table. "Davey."

"No. It's your turn to listen: you aren't the only one who deserves a good life. I've fought like hell for years just to have my piece, and now, it's coming."

Fuck his bad attitude.

It's gotten out of hand lately. Almost like all his rage and jealousy and quiet venom has hit a perfect storm. I wish I knew why.

I love my little brother. I'm pretty sure he feels the same, but damn it.

Sometimes, I don't know who he is anymore.

"If it's really about money, come work for me. I've told you from the beginning we'd make a good team. There's plenty of work. Plenty of money. Good, clean honest living."

"I don't want your table scraps."

"No leftovers, Davey. I need the help. A partner."

I'm digging my grave, offering Davey a stake in what I've built. Fucking up is in his blood. But I'll do it in a heartbeat, without hesitation, if it reduces the chances of him winding up in a coffin.

He flashes a sarcastic snarl. "Oh. Yeah, sure. *My* help."

Now, I'm pissed. "Dammit, David. What the fuck's your problem? Talk to me!"

"Nothing."

I know better, but I won't get an answer tonight. Instead I go straight to the point. "Whether you believe it or not, I'm trying to help. You don't know what you're getting sucked into. The Black Pearls are the lowest of the low. There's no easy out once they've roped you in. Back out now. While you still can." Growling, I yank my checkbook out of my pocket and slam it on the pool table. "Whatever money you need, you've got it. Right here."

I want to add a stipulation, that he has to guarantee he's cut it off with the Black Pearls, before I give him a cent.

No, not yet. The contemplation in his eyes, the look that he's seriously considering my offer, holds me back.

I hold my breath as he reaches for the checkbook, hoping it's not too fucking late.

There's always more money. It's replaceable. Unlike flesh and blood.

* * *

Present

DISORIENTED BY THE PAST, it takes a moment before I realize the doorbell's ringing, echoing through the house. Pizza time.

Rubbing the tension out of the back of my neck, I stand, walking toward the hallway.

Nat runs down from her room while I'm paying the delivery guy. "I'll set the table," she says, walking past me.

Needing to leave this stupor, I nod. "Thanks, sweets."

She has plates and silverware on the table and is filling two glasses with milk when I carry the pizza into the kitchen.

"Yum! That smells good."

"Yeah," I agree, giving her a serious look. "Must be the anchovies."

"Very funny." Nat giggles, wrinkling her cherub nose.

We both sit and scoop slices straight out of the box.

She bites the tip off her piece before setting it on her plate. "I like it better when it's cut like this, in triangles, rather than squares, you know?"

I nod and finish chewing. "Unless it's a square pizza."

"The only square pizzas are those cheap ones Julia refuses to buy."

"They used to be round," I say. "Your Uncle Davey and I would have them as after school snacks. He'd have pepperoni and I'd have sausage. Those were the days."

Those days are gone.

"You each ate your own pizza?" She blinks in surprise.

The memory makes me chuckle as I take another slice of pizza. "Yeah. Some days it was two each. Growing boys."

"Jeez! Where'd you guys find the room?"

"I honestly don't know. But we did." A memory of my brother and I having friends over and raiding the kitchen flashes in my mind. "Teenagers can eat like a pack of piranhas. Just about anything, and still be hungry. We used to eat cookies as fast as Grandma baked them."

"Poor Grandma."

"Poor Grandpa, you mean. There were never any left for him." I grin, remembering how pissed dad would get over having his sweet tooth denied.

We both laugh.

"If you're talking peanut butter, nobody had a chance." She knows my favorite cookies all too well. "How about Uncle Davey? What did he like?"

"Chocolate chip. He'd eat the batter before it was even baked sometimes." My smile vanishes.

She laughs again, but then her eyes grow serious. "You're missing him today, huh? I'm sorry, Daddy."

I nod. "Yeah."

"I miss him some days, what little I can recall. Then I remember what you told me. How missing him's okay, and so is remembering how lucky we were to have our time with him."

"I did say that, didn't I?" Everything after Davey's funeral is still a fucking wash in my brain.

"Right after he died."

My throat tightens and I reach for my glass of milk. She does, too.

I'm trying to figure out what's different today as I watch her empty her glass. Acting more grownup isn't unusual, but right now she looks more grownup, too.

It's got to be the hair. "What's going on up there, Nat?" I ask, waving a finger around my own hairline.

"It's called a messy bun." She twists so I can see the back of her head, how her hair piles up and sticks out in all directions. "All the female artists online wear their hair like this. I thought I'd try it out. Do you like it?"

Can't hide my frown. "Give it a few more years, baby girl. It's too adult. Brush it out and put it back in a ponytail before we leave, please."

"Aww, seriously?" she asks.

I nod. "You're too young. Not joking."

I'll be the first to admit she's spoiled. She's my only child, and probably always will be, but even she knows the difference between being spoiled and misbehaving.

I've made that clear since she was little. Just as she knows the difference between discipline and punishment. If more adults and children understood that, the world might not be such a dark, fucked up place.

She doesn't say anything more, and though the sadness on her face makes a knot form in my stomach, I remain silent. I hate disappointing her.

Not everything about being a parent is fun, or clean, or easy.

Too bad. I wouldn't trade it for the universe.

We finish eating, shifting gears to lighter subjects. I cleanup and load the dishwasher while she goes upstairs to get ready. By the time I'm done in the bathroom across the hall, she's back in the kitchen, near the door that leads to the garage, a neatly combed ponytail replacing the bun.

"Need me to carry anything?"

She holds up her sketchbook with one hand and the

small backpack she uses for art class with the other. "Nope, I've got it."

"Did you put a bottle of water in your bag? It's been damn hot today and I don't want you getting dehydrated." I've lived in Arizona for ages, but the constant need to guzzle water never ends.

"Yeppers. I'm not gonna turn into a mummy."

I chuckle. "All right then, I'll get the door." I pat her head while reaching for the knob. "I like your hair this way. Thank you."

Her smile says 'no hard feelings.' "You're welcome. I like yours, too."

Considering it's cropped about as short as it can get, I just laugh.

It doesn't take long to get to the school, and because we're early, Blue is just climbing out of her car when I park next to it.

Natalie rolls down her window. "Ms. Derby! Can I walk inside with you?"

"Of course you can, Nat." She doesn't give me a second look.

Before I have the truck shut off, Natalie plants a quick kiss on my cheek. "See you later, Daddy."

The next second, she's out the door, stepping up the sidewalk beside Blue. Instinct has me grabbing the door handle, but watching the way they're chatting, and smiling at each other, has my hand slipping off it.

I've always known that someday, no matter how hard I try, I won't be everything my girl needs. There'll come a day when she needs a woman's guidance. Someone to learn from and model after.

I just never thought it'd be *this* woman. One who gets

me between nail spitting mad and hard as goddamn granite.

They both have their bags slung over one shoulder, carrying their big sketchpads. If I'd let Nat keep the messy bun she'd liked so much, even that would be the same, except for the difference in coloring.

No wonder I had such a gut punch reaction. It reminds me too much of Blue, and with everything else going to hell, that's a distraction I don't need.

I keep watching. My breath lodges in my throat as Natalie digs in her pocket, pulling out the friendship bracelet.

I know what I'd told her about handing it off to a friend her own age, but a part of me silently prays Blue won't deny the gift.

Of course, she doesn't.

The air seeps out of me as she bends down and hugs Natalie, and then holds out her hand for Nat to tie the bracelet around her wrist. They exchange smiles, heading inside.

The class runs for two hours tonight. The past few weeks, I've done errands, coming back just long enough to spend a few minutes sketching Blue in the back of the room. I start the truck, but only for the air conditioning.

I pull the notebook out of the glovebox and flip to an empty page.

All on its own, my hand sketches out the scene I'd just witnessed. The two of them smiling like old friends.

The next two hours, I do little more than think. Mulling over Blue and her family issues. Brooding on what's happening with the Black Pearls. Tossing around what I have to do and how.

I shut off the truck and open the door, fully understanding the time has come to implement the plan I've put into place.

I can't wait forever. Can't let the Pearls chew another piece out of my family. Or a certain blue haired spitfire who's gotten closer than I ever should've let her.

Soon, it'll be high time to put an end to this fucking mess once and for all.

V: THRILL OF THE CHASE (IZZY)

I twist the new bead bracelet on my wrist as I walk around the room, examining the landscapes being created from the soft pastel watercolors.

Once again, I'm amazed by the talent of these kids, and also excited. Their futures are endless, if they don't get lost along the way.

It's a sad reality life happens for a lot of people, and the cost is dreams. But some of them will make it, I know. Some will go on to do great things. Some will be artists in their own way, whether that means working off easels or giving this world a brighter coat of polish.

My eyes wander across the room to Nat.

I probably shouldn't have accepted the bracelet, but nothing shy of an apocalypse would have stopped me. Not after she pulled it out of her pocket, a nervous smile on her face.

The hope in her familiar green eyes was heavy. So was the respect. I'm not used to being anybody's hero, but isn't that what I signed up for? To change lives? To make these kids live, bigger and better and more beautifully than I do.

I'd watched her briefly on the sidelines again today. She sat on a bench next to a landscaped saguaro cactus behind a fence, reading a book during recess today.

The empathy I'd had compounded ten times over.

This girl needs friends, and though I may not be the answer, I can help. *Have* to help.

I'd like to blame it all on her father, and his overprotectiveness, but that's hardly it. I can even empathize with him being a single parent.

That's never easy. I watched my own mom struggle after dad's sudden death. Not just financially, but physically and emotionally.

That doesn't mean I like Brent Eden any more than I did last week. He might be swoon-worthy, but he's also a colossal asshole.

A handsome, demanding, straight up imposing jackass.

Assuming I wanted him to keep playing my boyfriend, my fiancé. *Dick.*

I'd gone to his house to explain that was the last thing I wanted. Or needed, for that matter.

The soft ding coming from my desk tells me I forgot to turn off my phone. I normally wouldn't consider looking at it, but class is almost over. These kids are engrossed in their projects and don't need anything from me right now. They're busy putting their unique twists on the simple landscape I'd painted last night as an example.

Sitting down, I pull the phone out of my bag and swipe the screen. After turning the volume all the way down, I click on the text icon.

Mother. Ugh.

We're still on for the zoo this weekend, aren't we? I'm so looking forward to it, Isabella. One o'clock sharp! Meet you at the front gate.

I nibble my cheek, scrolling through about a billion animal emojis stacked in a messy line after the first text.

Oh yeah! And please PLEASE ask your new man friend and his little girl to join us. I'm dying to meet them.

Nope.

I push the phone to the edge of the desk, having no intention of responding, and press a hand to my forehead. I try like hell to stop Brent's face from forming.

Epic fail. I'm daydreaming muscle, ink, and emerald green a second later. Red-faced as ever.

This has gotten out of hand.

No matter what I say, Clara twists it around. Tells mom what a happy couple we are, and how she just absolutely knows he's *the one* for me.

How she's never seen me this happy.

How it's just a matter of time until wedding bells are ring-a-ding-dinging.

Actually, I think that's the new bead bracelet clicking softly on my wrist as I fight the urge to strangle her.

Brent would be beyond pissed if he discovers how far along my mother believes our 'romance' has become.

The swoosh of a door opening has me glancing up. Sure enough, it's him.

Mr. Eden, in all six foot something of his paradise flesh.

I was hoping he'd stay in his truck for once.

Maybe let me walk Natalie outside later. Without ever having to interact with him.

Without having to feel stripped bare by his piercing looks.

Silly idea.

We still don't have to interact, though. There's nothing that says I have to.

Except my eyes won't behave. Try as I might, I can't pull them off him.

His arms are like tree trunks. His chest could hold the world. His beard could send my body places I don't dare imagine.

Hate, frustration, and shame are no match for this man's insane gravity.

Worse, he's walking forward. Straight to my desk. Never breaking the gaze that loudly, boldly tells me he'd like me up against the nearest wall.

Crap!

My heart thuds somewhere near my chin. My toes curl, tingling. So do my knees, my thighs, my –

No, no, and no. Time to focus. Keep it together.

I wish. Hell, even my hands, which I squeeze together, burn. His eyes are so flipping mesmerizing. Penetrating.

Like he can see straight into my head and know, without a doubt, I've been thinking about him. Nonstop.

Losing my mind. For days. Weeks.

Without saying a word, he slaps a hand on the desk and pushes a slip of paper towards me.

"What –"

He turns crisply before I can get out a single word, so I reach for the paper and jump to my feet. A total mistake because my Jell-O knees make my legs buckle.

I try to keep myself from falling by grabbing the edge of the desk, and manage to knock over the tin can pencil holder, which topples and hits the floor with all the grace of a cannonball.

So does the stapler, tape dispenser, and my cellphone.

Bravo, Ms. Derby. Every kid in this academy will be laughing behind your back tomorrow, guaranteed.

Sighing and slightly frantic, I scramble around the desk and drop to my knees to pick everything up, ignoring the baffled looks several students throw my way.

He's bent down, too. His royal highness. Already has the can upright, pencils clattering back inside as he drops them in one-by-one. "Were you born clumsy? Or is it just that kind of day?"

His husky whisper sends heat through my veins, my cheeks, and another throbbing part of me I won't acknowledge. Which just pisses me off more than his tactless question.

"No!" I hiss.

"Could have fooled me." He shrugs. Like nothing happened.

Bastard.

I grab the pencil holder in one hand and the stapler in the other, lowering my voice to a mouse whisper. "Were you born an asshole? Or is it just *that* kind of day?"

"Some say I was." He's smirking now. Awesome.

"Well, they're absolutely right." I put the can and stapler neatly on the desk. I'll check it over later to see if anything's broken or missing before Mrs. Wayne returns.

He replaces the tape dispenser and my phone, and with a wink that nearly knocks me back down on my knees, turns and walks to the back of the room.

I stand there, trying to disguise just how hard my legs are wobbling. My eyes flick to the clock.

At least tonight's torture is almost over. Shame to think it started so well.

Taking a deep breath, I say, "Ten more minutes, everybody."

Forcing myself not to look at him, I sit back down. In the chaos, the slip of paper had gotten flipped over.

It's a number. A phone number. I glance up.

He gives a single head nod.

I shake my head, having no idea what he expects.

Every second we're in the same room is pure agony. Now, he wants to do it over the phone, too?

"Ms. Derby, can you come here please?"

I stand, making my way over to Ester, and answer her question about dry-blending two colors.

Then I address the class. "Your pictures need a few minutes to dry before you take them off your easels. Does anyone have any last minute questions that weren't covered earlier, or came up while you were painting?"

Tad asks about brush sizes. As soon as I answer him, Rosa wants to know about canvas versus paper. That leads to a conversation lasting until it's time to leave.

"Great job, guys and gals! I'll pass out feedback for each of you about the dog drawings you handed in soon. If you have watercolors at home, you can certainly continue working on your landscapes. Bring them by next week and I'll review them."

"What medium will we be using next time?"

I smile at Natalie, knowing she'll like the answer to her question. "Oil pastels."

A soft mumble of excitement ripples through the room as the students collect their things and dart for the door.

"Daddy, can we wait and walk Ms. Derby to her car?"

I freeze for a millisecond, then shake my head. "That's not necessary, Natalie, but thank you."

"Sure we can, baby girl." Brent's voice is as soft as it is defiant.

Somebody shoot me.

There are still a few students filing out of the room, so I'm careful. Reserved.

Well aware what could very easily slip out of my mouth. Like telling him there's a special underground place to go, with plenty of fire and pitchforks.

I ignore Brent walking up behind me and head for my desk. The piece of paper is there and I snatch it up. Whatever he's playing at won't work with me.

Spinning around, I hold the note in the air. "Did your phone number change from the one on file with the school?"

I might be imagining things or having a moment of wishful thinking, but the skin behind his soft scruff seems to turn slightly red.

"No." He steps forward. Closer.

"You want this one added to her file as an emergency number then? I'll need a name."

A narrowed glare says he's not impressed. "That's my cell."

"Okay. Noted."

He leans in to whisper-growl. "The school already has that number. It's not for them. I want *you* to have it, Blue."

Holy hell. How can one sentence be so tantalizing and maddening all at once?

I circle around my desk and drop the paper in the trash can. "Sorry. Already have all I'll need on my class roster."

He's right behind me and plucks it out. Glancing over his shoulder at Natalie filling her backpack, he whispers, "Come on. I want you to have it personally."

A jolt of heat shoots through me that isn't entirely anger, but I pretend it is and quietly snap, "Personally, I don't need it."

"You might."

"Nah." Shaking my head, I slide the attendance sheets, my classroom notes, and my phone into my bag. "We're good."

"What if you breakdown on the side of the road or something?"

I zip my bag shut, tilting my head. Jesus. Why does he look like the building just started on fire behind me?

"I have road-side assistance for that like a normal person."

"Bull. What if they don't respond, Blue?"

Flipping the bag's strap over my shoulder, I glance over to make sure Natalie stays preoccupied.

Then I shift slightly to step around him. "I sure as hell won't call you, Brent."

He grabs my arm. "This isn't a game. You need help, you'll call."

Although he's taller, broader, and probably three times stronger than Preston, he doesn't unnerve me. The badass persona he wears is only for show. I've seen him melt on sight in front of his daughter.

That may not mean a lot to some, but, oddly, it tells me I have nothing to fear. With him, I know I'll get the teddy bear. Not the grizzly.

"No. I'm a grown woman." I lock eyes with him, a fierce smile pulling at my lips. "Seriously, what's this all about? You sound *ridiculous*. Like you're my chaperone, or something."

"Are you two ready?"

Crap. We both turn to Nat, who's standing near her chair with a grin stretching ear-to-ear.

It's not too late. I could refuse to walk out with them, but that would hurt her far more than him. She doesn't deserve that. "Coming, Natalie. I just have to get my sketchpad."

"I'll get it," Brent says. His voice is ice.

He still has a hold of my arm. I stiffen every muscle I can, so ready to shake him off.

Sure, I'm a lot weaker. He could drag me across the room without breaking a sweat if he chose, but I want him to know I'm not into these hands. Not like this.

Not even if I've imagined them doing devilish things to my body.

With a final glance I can't quite read, he lets go, walking around the desk to collect my sketchpad off the easel.

I walk toward Natalie. "Sooo, how'd you like painting with watercolors?"

"Loved it!" she answers brightly. "I have some at home, but I was never sure how to get it right. Now that I know how to use them, I have a dozen things floating around in my head just begging to be painted."

"Dozens? Busy girl!" I stay next to her and we start for the door. "Tell me a few of your ideas."

"An Arizona sunset, for one." She sighs heavily. "For all we put up with here, the views are incredible. You've seen our house? Well, I can see the desert out the windows for miles some nights. Camelback mountain in the other direction, too. So pretty. I just want to keep it forever." Her face reddens. "That sounds silly, I guess. Right?"

"Not at all," I assure her. I mean it, too. "Spoken like a true artist."

She beams as we walk out the door. Big Daddy's right behind us, making my spine quiver. Regardless, I keep going. "You did a wonderful job on your landscape tonight. I know you'll paint a spectacular sunset."

She and I chat all the way down the hall, pausing only long enough to bid Oscar goodnight as we exit the building. He's a lot more active tonight, redeeming himself after the Preston intruder incident.

At my car, I unlock the driver's door, toss my bag in, and turn to take my sketchpad from him.

He hits a button, unlocking his truck, and then another to start it. "Go climb in, baby girl. Need one more word with Ms. Derby."

Great. Because I have two very choice words for him: fuck off.

Natalie gives me a quick hug and then spins around to open the pickup door. I hold out my hand, but he keeps the pad at his side.

He lays a hand on the hood of my car. "How often do you have this thing serviced?"

Taken aback, I shake my head. "I know how to handle my car. Why?"

"It's old. Could breakdown any time."

He sounds like Clara, and mother. I'm fuming.

"Surely, they pay you enough that you can afford a new one?"

What next? Is he going to ask me what I'm wearing to bed?

I reach over the open car door separating us to grab my pad. "I'm fine. Don't want or need a newer one, thank you very much. Are we done?"

For the record, I don't make enough, but he doesn't need to hear it.

He steps back, just out of my reach. "I could get you a good deal on one over at Rooster's. I've bought a lot of vehicles there. They're good. Affordable. Solid warranties. Stand behind everything they sell."

He's acting so sincere, so genuine, that my anger slowly melts away.

Now, I'm just confused. If he isn't trying to get under my skin or into my pants, what's going on?

"Thanks. I'll keep that in mind when the time comes for a different car." I pat the top of the car door. "This one needs to last a bit longer though. And I really need to get going."

Mainly because I could go soft on his nosy ass, and that can't happen.

He steps around the door, and me, laying the sketchpad in my back seat.

There's a tingle in the air and up my spine. My only escape is to climb in the car and shut the door.

Thank God and all that's Holy, the engine starts right away. Last summer, it tested me by not engaging on the first try. Or the second. I'll have to get that looked at.

He's still standing there. I wave, push in the clutch and shift into reverse.

Though a part of me wants to shift through the gears as fast as possible, I don't. I've learned my lesson there. Driving fast doesn't make for an easier escape, and it costs money if something goes wrong. Captain

Dawson had no mercy when the time came to dole out my ticket.

There's always traffic, and I have to wait for an opening to pull out of the parking lot. I force myself not to check my mirror, to see if he made it onto the road as well.

It's pitch black by the time I get off the highway and onto the roads leading into Tempe, and then to my building. Even though the headlights behind me aren't all the same, there's no way to tell if one set is from his truck or not.

A sense of disappointment washes over me. Which is silly.

No, *beyond silly.*

It's fucking stupid.

I'm being stupid.

He's the father of one of my students. Having any sort of feelings towards him would be the fastest route to getting fired. And if I want to find out how fast I can pulverize my own heart, a reckless night with Eden is the swiftest way to do it.

I pull into the apartment complex, driving around the first building to the back, where my assigned parking spot sits next to the dumpsters. I never know what my car will smell like in the morning. Whoever invented air fresheners needs a medal.

There's a small man made hill with palm trees around it on the other side of the garbage, and a well-used street at the top of it. I swear people toss stuff out as they drive by, trying to hit the dumpsters, but never do.

When I first moved in, I picked up the trash daily.

Now, after discovering that was being taken advantage of, I leave it to the maintenance crew.

Unless something lands on my car, which has happened a time or two.

With my bag over one shoulder, I open the door and climb out. As I'm reaching in to grab the sketchpad, I get the sense I'm being watched. I take it and turn around.

Third floor up the adjacent building, I spy someone on the balcony.

"Good evening, Mrs. Butler," I say with a wave.

She waves back from her chair next to the metal railing. "Hello, dear. How was your day?"

"Good. How was yours?"

"Oh, I'm a bit under the weather." A glowing red tip moves in the darkness, and she lets out a cough. Tobacco smoke rolls up my nose. "It's hard as blazes to breathe in this heat."

I think the two packs she works through each day have more to do with that.

"It'll be October soon," I say hopefully. "And cooler!"

"That'll be nice."

I wave again. "Have a nice night."

"You, too, dear."

At the door, I use the fob on my key chain to let me in, and then climb the three flights of stairs. The air is stifling hot. It's an old building, prone to retaining the daytime heat.

I shift the keychain in my hand, positioning the apartment key, anxious to unlock the door as quickly as possible and step into my air-conditioned cave.

The rush of cool air feels heavenly. I enter, close the door behind me, and embrace the sweet relief.

Letting out a long sigh, I turn on the light, dropping the keys in the dish on the counter and kick off my shoes. "Home sweet home."

I laugh at my own words. It's not much.

A tiny kitchen, separated from the living room, with a counter that's barely big enough for three appliances. One of the doors off the living room leads to the bathroom, and the other, my one and only bedroom.

I can't help but think about Brent's spacious house as I step forward.

Another sigh escapes. This one, longing.

"Make it a goal, Izzy. Not just a dream." I smile. Those words hold weight.

I have no idea when mom first said them to me. Sometime in the chaos after 9/11, and war, and dad dying, probably. They've become my mantra ever since.

As annoying as she is, like any good mother, she's left some golden nuggets.

I drop my bag and sketchpad on the coffee table, then plop down on the couch. Someday, I'll have a house like Brent does. All my own. Without any worries about a subversive, sexy, brooding beast inside.

My eyes settle on the sketchpad and the piece of paper taped to the front of it.

Wait. That wasn't there before...was it?

I carefully remove it, wrinkling my nose.

His phone number. For personal reasons.

Asshole. Sneak. He only let me think I'd won a small skirmish.

I don't even know why I'm smiling. If I do, I definitely don't want to admit it.

I let it drop and grab my phone, finally finding the courage to respond to mom's text.

Yes, of course I'll be at the zoo this weekend.

And yes, Brent and Natalie will be joining us. I barely stop myself from typing it out.

"And come Monday, you'll be fired," I tell myself.

Disgusted, I wad the paper into a ball and toss it on the table.

The only thing worse than bad ideas is making them reality.

VI: SURPRISE, SURPRISE (BRENT)

The past few days have left me feeling lower than that fuck boy, Preston.

Stalking a woman. For her own good. To protect her.

With my daughter in the truck next to me.

Christ. How did I get here again?

Davey's jealousy. Bastard Phil's threats. A thousand heartaches.

They all cascade in my mind so fast, so fierce, it's hard to even focus on the day-to-day.

"Aren't these the same buildings we drove past last night?" Natalie asks, gesturing out the passenger window.

"Yeah," I admit. "Good eye. I'm just checking to see if my crew got started over here today."

It's a white lie. We don't have a job anywhere near Blue's apartment, but I can't stop myself from driving past her place once a day. Every evening. Making sure her Mustang stays where it should be, parked out back.

"Why don't you just call and ask them?" Nat flashes me a confused glance.

Sometimes, I wish she was just a little less whip smart. A tiny bit less observant.

"No need. Just wanted to check with my eyes since it's on our way home."

She yawns. "I hope we don't have any shopping tomorrow night, I've barely had time to paint."

Nat's sick of the busy week and I can't blame her.

I've made up excuses every afternoon when I pick her up from school.

New tires for the truck. New shoes for her. Haircuts for both of us at a new salon. Ice cream twice, and she's bored of it.

Whatever takes us out near Tempe.

I have to make sure she's home, safe and sound, by nightfall.

So far, Bastard Phil hasn't shown up again. He's out there, though. Watching her.

I know it.

I know this can't keep happening either. Dragging Nat around every night until damned near seven or eight o'clock. "Well, I have a surprise for you tomorrow."

"What?"

"Can't tell you."

"Daddy! Why not? You know I hate secrets."

Because I'm not sure how I'm going to pull it off. Since I can't tell her that, I say the obvious, "Because then it won't be a surprise. And I won't get to mess with your pretty little brain."

She bursts out laughing, stomping her shoes softly on the mat under them. "You're so bad sometimes."

I catch a glimpse of Blue's car, next to the dumpsters at the bottom of the hill. Satisfied and relieved, I push my foot a little harder against the gas pedal. "Ready to head home?"

"More than ready," Natalie says, covering another yawn.

Blue hasn't called. Of course not.

I should've swallowed my pride. Apologized for what I'd said about not being a prop. Rather than just giving her my number, I should've said I'd stand in anytime as her fake boyfriend.

It wouldn't have been hard. My way of thanking her for being so good to Natalie.

There's no denying the last part. Every day, Natalie comes home with another Ms. Derby tale.

Seeing her in the hallway or at recess or an assembly. Chatting about Vincent van Gogh and Salvador Dali. Blue gave her some paint brushes, too, which Nat has barely had a chance to use.

Damn. I'm so close to taking care of the Black Pearls, too.

Just need a little more time to get everything in place. I sure as hell don't need this extra hitch. Of them threatening to hurt Blue.

Well, too fucking bad. I won't let them.

Also don't have time for this cat and mouse shit.

"Don't think I'll forget the surprise," Nat says, chin up, folding her little arms.

Mind made up, I tell her. "Tomorrow morning, baby girl. Promise."

I just hope I can convince Blue to go along with it.

* * *

THE SUN ISN'T UP YET when Natalie throws open my bedroom door. "Rise and shine, it's surprise time!"

I laugh and throw a pillow at her. She's got all the zest for life I used to have plus Davey's non-stop energy.

She dodges swiftly and pounces on the foot of the bed like an overgrown cat. "Where, Daddy? Let's see it!"

Her eyes are shining so bright they almost glow in the early light of dawn peeking through the window.

Enjoying her excitement, I yawn and stretch. "Nat, you know the rules: Daddy doesn't talk before coffee."

"Yeahhh, and it's a total lie because you *just* talked. Or spoke. You just spoke, I mean!"

I jump up, grab her, tickling her sides. "Which is it, little lady? Talked or spoke?"

She laughs, squirming to the edge of the bed. "Either or. Doesn't matter! You're just distracting me. What's my surprise?"

I climb out of bed and stretch again, taking my time to walk towards my bathroom.

"Dad!" She lets out a groan. "You're killing me here."

I walk into the bathroom, but spin around before closing the door. "We're going to the zoo today."

"We're – really?!"

"Yes, really." I close the door as her squeals fill the house.

A short time later, showered and dressed, the smell of coffee brewing fills the air as I walk into the kitchen. Natalie's at the island, eating a bowl of cereal. There's a second bowl, the box of cereal, and a gallon of milk sitting in front of another stool.

I wink at her as I collect a cup and fill it with coffee.

Dark, dense, and bold enough to strip paint. Just how I like it.

She sets down her spoon, eyeing me critically as I lean back against the counter to take a drink off my cup. "So, what's up?"

"What's up with what?" I ask.

She crosses her arms. "Well, something, obviously. You don't even like the zoo."

I knew she'd question it. She's smart, and I've never hidden my distaste for gawking at caged animals. "No, I don't. But you do."

"And we've already had our annual visit. July, remember?"

How could I forget? The pavement was hotter than the surface of the sun.

Annual is right, too. Or close enough. I take her once or twice a year because she likes critter watching. I snag the first excuse that crosses my mind. "Figure I owe you, Nat. For being so good about tagging along while I looked for truck tires this week."

"Which you *still* haven't bought."

Because I don't need them. I shrug. "I'll have to order some. No one has the right set. If we ever go up to Flagstaff or Utah for camping later this year, we'll need them for winter."

"Still doesn't explain the sudden zoo trip." She shakes her head. "You'd rather go anywhere else."

I cross the room and ruffle her hair. "Well, kiddo, sometimes we all have to do things we don't want to do. Compromise." I'm not referring to the zoo.

This mess with the Black Pearls is something I'd rather

not have to contend with, but don't have a choice. There's also no negotiating my way out of it.

She's frowning when she looks up at me. "Like not being able to wear a messy bun, you mean?"

I'd forgotten about the hair incident, but since she brought it up, I give her a hug. "You were really good about that, peanut. Sometimes I don't give you enough credit for how well-behaved you are. But I do appreciate it."

Her smile brightens as she hugs me hard. "For you, anything."

I kiss the top of her head and let her go. Taking another sip of coffee, I say, "How about I let you bring a friend with us to the zoo?" Before she can say she doesn't have any friends, I add, "That friendship bracelet you made. Whoever you gave it to, you can bring them along."

She goes stock-still and glances around the room, looking everywhere but me. "Whoever? No matter what?"

The bracelet hasn't come up since the day she showed it to me. She has no clue I know she gave it to Blue. "You heard me."

I take another drink of coffee and play along. "Get me their phone number and I'll call their parents, make sure it's all right."

She climbs off the stool and shoots a nervous glance at the floor, and then the door. "Well...I'll have to get that together. How long do I have?"

I have no idea what Blue's plans are before meeting her mother at the zoo, so we need to get to her place well before then. "I figured we'd leave here around ten, pick up your friend, and grab some lunch. Get to the zoo around one o'clock."

"Gotcha," she says, heading out of the room. "I'll be back."

I refill my cup as I hear her feet racing upstairs. She's off to do the same thing I did.

Google Blue.

There's an address and apartment number listed, but no phone number. Unless my daughter is a better sleuth than I am. Honestly, it's not a complete impossibility.

It's later when she walks into my office. She's dressed in denim shorts and a pink T-shirt and has her hair pulled back in a neat ponytail. "I can't find a number for my friend, but I have her address. Do you think it would be all right if we just stopped by? Maybe asked her to join us?"

I inwardly smile at the shy quiver in her voice. It's always there when she's walking a tightrope with what I'll let her get away with.

I usually don't use people to get what I want, but in this case, I'll take it. "Sure. You ready?"

She nods, and I can tell she's nervous.

I lay a hand on her shoulder. "Don't worry, I'll convince her parents to let her join us."

She nods again before running for the door to the garage.

Once we're in the truck, she hands me a slip of paper with the address I recognize as Blue's. She's quiet on the way, wringing her hands together. I'm not sure if she thinks I'll be mad to learn who she wants joining us, or that she's nervous Blue will say no.

As I turn onto the road leading to the apartment complex, her frown deepens.

"Are we looking to see if your crew started that new job again?"

"No," I answer. "This is the address you gave me." Down the hill I see Blue's car parked in the usual place. A weird thrill zips through me.

"Oh. Um. So this is it?"

"That building right there." I click on the blinker.

She scratches her head, releasing a big sigh. "Dad...I have to tell you something."

"Oh? What's that."

"Well, that friendship bracelet?" She squirms in her seat.

"Go on, sweets."

"I said I was going to give it to Ms. Derby...remember? I know you said I shouldn't, but you didn't say I couldn't, so I did." She tenses, bracing for my reaction.

I bite the inside of my bottom lip to keep from smiling and pull into a visitor parking space in front of the building. "You mean the friend we're here to pick up is Ms. Derby?"

She cringes. "Yes."

I nod, trying to look like I'm seriously contemplating what she just said, rather than wondering if Blue will refuse to go.

I know she'd say no to me, but am pretty confident she won't say no to my girl.

Who could say no to that face? I sure as hell can't.

"Fine. Whatever. Only one thing to do." I pause, letting out a long sigh, leaving her in playful suspense. "Ask if she wants to spend today with us at the zoo."

She beams. "Oh, Daddy, you *are* the best! The absolute best!"

Luck is with us. An older woman leaves just as we enter the building, so we don't need to buzz up to Blue's apartment to be let in.

At her door on the third floor, I stand to the side, where she won't be able to see me through the peephole and tell Natalie to knock. She's short enough that Blue should only be able to see the top of her head.

A moment later the door opens. Just as Blue peeks around the edge, Natalie shouts, "Surprise!"

Surprise is right.

Blue's eyes are wide and her mouth drops open. She's brutally fucking adorable.

The messy bun sits on her head again. Her gray eyes shimmer. She's wearing a bright blue, short, sleeveless sun dress, and no shoes. Even her feet look good. Then they draw my eyes to parts of her I'd love a whole hell of a lot more.

My dick jerks. Suddenly and inappropriately. Just imagining how I could twine this woman around me, run my hands across her, plunge in hard and deep and find out exactly how she sounds when she comes...

Fuck. Stop.

The thought vanishes the second she starts stammering.

"What the...what are you doing here?" she glances up at me. "Jesus. You're both here, aren't you?"

"In the flesh." I hold my arms out, striking a goofy pose that makes Nat laugh.

"We're here to ask you a question!" Nat chirps.

Blue smiles at her, but there's plenty of skepticism in her eyes. "Okay. Let's hear it."

Natalie claps her hands together. "Do you want to go

to the zoo with us today, Ms. Derby? Please? Daddy said I can bring a friend along and you...well, nobody else can talk about how to draw the animals we'll see."

The door across the hall opens and an older man pokes his nose out. The scorn on his face instantly irritates me.

"Hello, Mr. Barrett. Sorry to have bothered you." Blue waves at him and then gestures at Nat and I. "Come in. Hurry."

We step in, and I shut the door behind us. "Friendly neighbor," I growl.

"Fish!" Natalie shouts "You have fish tanks?"

Blue nods. "You can look. Go right ahead."

Natalie rushes forward while Blue levels a nasty glare at me.

"You read my mother's text?" she hisses.

It hurts not to smile. I barely had her phone long enough to do anything in the chaos last Tuesday, but an army man never loses the precision and speed screamed into him by Drill Sergeants.

Pleading the fifth, I say, "Nat loves the zoo." Nodding to where she's enamored by the two large tanks taking up the far wall of the living room, I add, "She loves all kinds of animals."

"How could you do this? Such. A. Dick." Poisonous darts are practically shooting out of her eyes, yet she keeps her voice low. If it wasn't for Nat, I could do a lot with her and the best part of my anatomy. "How could you use your daughter like this?"

"Like what? Taking her to the zoo? A place she loves?" My nostrils flare.

"Don't play stupid. It's no more believable than your bad boy act."

"What bad boy act?"

She rubs her forehead and then throws her hands in the air. "You *know* what I mean. You also have no idea the can of worms that'll open if we go to the zoo together."

She's wrong. The can of shit is already ripped in two, and it doesn't give me a choice. I have to protect her. "Well, find a way to let Nat down easy. I'm *not* going to the zoo with you. Don't care what kind of guilt trip you start."

She frowns, defiant as ever. The raging desire to slam her up against the nearest surface and gag that smart mouth with my tongue howls in my blood. *If only.*

"You're going with us today. We'll have a nice time. You, me, Nat, and Mama Blue."

"Are you for real?" She blinks a few times and then buries her face in a palm.

I shrug. "Am I?"

She takes a step backwards, and not fully sure what she's going to do, I grasp her wrist with one hand. As softly as I can.

I haven't had to swallow my pride in some time, but there's no other option. Not now.

Not if I want to keep her safe.

Want isn't a question either.

This is a fucking need. I *have* to keep this woman safe, secure, and smiling. Even if she wants to slap my face around like a beach ball.

"Look, Izzy, I shouldn't have said what I did the other night. That was rude. No question. You've been so good to Nat. Befriended her. She's happy every afternoon when I pick her up. She's found another person she likes connecting with. That's something." I shrug again. "I know about your ma, your family, how crazy they get over the whole boyfriend thing. It's the least I can do. What harm can come from me pretending to be your date for a day? Getting them off your back?"

She pinches her lips together while shaking her head. "You have balls, I'll give you that."

If only she had any idea what my balls are really like.

"Don't flatter yourself too much. You'd know what I mean about *balls* if you'd met my mother." She slaps her forehead. "Look, even if I wanted to accept, I can't. I worked too hard to land a job at the academy. I won't just blow it, and one pretend date is all it'll take. I'm just digging my grave deeper."

I ignore the grave comment, knowing how real it is.

Fuck, I'd forgotten Principal Jacobs and his silly rules. Although, in the scheme of things, it doesn't mean jack shit. I'm determined.

"No one at the academy has to know. You won't tell them, I won't either, and neither will Natalie if I ask her not to. What're the chances of seeing someone, anyway? And even if we do, there's plausible denial. I'm only your boyfriend, fiancé, whatever, to dear old ma."

"Brent..."

"It's the zoo," I say, growing frustrated. "You're there. We're there. No big deal."

"My freaking *mother* will be there. That's a mammoth deal."

Up until this point, I hadn't realized how serious I am about this. Not just her safety, either. Natalie has her heart set on this, so I have to make it happen. "We'll tell her we have to keep it under wraps because of the school. She'll understand, won't she?"

I see the wheels start turning. She's torn.

The whole 'I should, but shouldn't.'

I know. I've been there, done that.

I'm living it since she came into my life damn near every day.

"Later, make something up. Some reason why it didn't work." The way her cousin Clara talked the other day, her ma's practically on death's doorstep. I morbidly wonder if our fake out will outlast her. "You want to make her happy, don't you?"

Blue rubs her forehead again, then her temples. After a long silence, she lets out a huff. "All right! Whatever. I'll meet you near the gate at one."

"Actually, I promised Nat we'd do lunch first. The three of us. If you'd be so kind."

Right on cue, Nat turns away from the fish tanks. "Are we ready? I'm getting kinda hungry."

Quietly sighing, Blue opens the closet door, slips her feet into a pair of sandals, and closes it. "Ready as I'll ever be."

* * *

WE HEAD out and stop for lunch at a chain restaurant. If this was a real date, none of which I've had since well before Nat was born, I'd have stopped at the local Mom and Pop place I know.

Best burgers in the nation, their sign proclaims. For this place, it's actually true.

But I can't do that today. Word could spread. The place is always packed thanks to how good it is.

Blue doesn't need interlopers any more than I do.

She doesn't want the school to know. I don't want the Pearls to notice.

I just want to find a way to keep her sheltered until this ends. Besides, if those twisted fucks think we're closer than we are, she could become a real liability. The twenty-four hour kind.

We arrive at the zoo shortly before one, and while I search for a parking space, Natalie tells Blue how much I hate zoos.

"You do?"

I find a spot and pull in. "I don't hate them, exactly." I shoot a glare into the back seat, where Nat grins back at me. "I just don't like the whole caged-up aspect."

Blue's face pulls into an adorable thoughtful expression as she looks me straight in the eye. "For you or the animals?"

Damn. She's too good at reading me.

Better than I thought. The army. The tents. The isolation. It was like being a caged animal. "Both."

The service turned me around, despite its harder points. Sandblasted my wilder edges and forced me to fly right. But shit, the years in Iraq were not an experience I'd ever want to repeat.

"Look at that woman!" Nat says. "The one by the gate with the hat on. Is she a movie star or something?"

We all look in the same direction, at the woman wearing a long bright top and matching pants. They're loose and flowing, the exact same shade of red as the big bow on her hat and the frames around her plastic sunglasses. The only thing not red is the big white purse hooked over one shoulder.

"No," Blue says with a sigh. "That's not a movie star."

"How do you know?" Natalie asks.

"Because that's my mom." Blue tenses, exhaling another breath.

Stunned, I ask, *"That's* your mother?"

I'm not sure what I expected. A thinner, frailer woman with a walker or something. This lady looks perfectly healthy and alive.

"That's her. Cleo Derby." She opens the passenger door and glances at me. "Ready to back out yet?"

I laugh. "Hell no."

"Your funeral." She shrugs. "Let's get this over with."

"Get what over?" Natalie asks.

"Introductions," I say, climbing out of the truck.

Cleo Derby is her daughter's total opposite. Her nails are long and painted the same shade of red as her lipstick, and despite my first impression of her flaming red outfit, she wears it with the elegance and poise of an actress. Just like Nat said.

She's graceful, too, and genuinely happy to see Blue. Even though she kisses the air on both sides of Izzy's face rather than her actual cheeks. The joy in her soft face doesn't lie.

The introductions are brief, thankfully. Cleo's head-to-toe scrutiny leaves me feeling like a slab of steak at the meat market being judged on its marbling.

Her response to Natalie is a hit to my ten-year-old daughter.

Cleo places both hands on her knees as she leans low to look Nat in the eye. "Oh, my. You just might be the prettiest little girl I've *ever* seen. You have your daddy's eyes. Green like the hills around Portland. Used to spend my summers there growing up."

"Thank you," Natalie replies. "And you're as beautiful as a movie star."

Cleo presses a hand to her chest and sighs, grabbing Natalie with the other one, hugging her ferociously. "Oh, aren't you a child after my own heart!" With her arm still around Natalie, she twists them both about face. "Come along, dear. You and I are going to get along stupendously today."

I buy tickets for all four of us, and as I'm divvying them out, Cleo points at me.

"In my day, we called those bedroom eyes," she says to Blue.

"Mother!" Blue hisses.

Cleo shrugs. "Just saying."

"So, which way are we going first?" I ask.

"The lions!" Natalie and Cleo say as one, and then laugh, beaming at each another.

"Lions it is." I lay a hand on Blue's back to ease her forward and follow the other two, who are already several feet ahead.

Cleo Derby is so far from what I expected, my question bursts out before I can stop it. "What exactly does your mother have?"

"Have? What do you mean?"

I can't put that cat back in the bag, so I might as well let it loose. "Her condition."

Blue's brows knit together and confusion flashes in her eyes. "Condition? You mean her sleep apnea?"

"Sleep apnea?" I've heard of that, but was thinking

more along the lines of cancer. Heart failure. Something dire.

"That's the only thing she's been diagnosed with, and that was last year." Blue stops and crosses her arm. "It's actually pretty serious if it doesn't get taken care of. Mom claims she sleeps like a baby with her little machine, though."

I watch how Natalie and Cleo march forward, not caring if we're following or not. "Good."

"Spill it, Eden," Blue says. "Who told you about mom's health? When? And why?"

I have no reason to hide it, even if I feel like a jackass for being duped. "Your cousin, Clara, called me last week. I can't remember exactly what she said. Mentioned a serious diagnosis, parents wanting their children to be happy. Days being short."

"Fuck her!" Blue snorts under her breath. "That sounds *exactly* like Clara. Sneaky little drama queen. Well, at least we can drop the act. I get it: because I've been so nice to your daughter, you decided to play my fake boyfriend so my mom can die happy. Clear as day." Her tone grows harsher with each word.

I'm silent.

"Wow." She shakes her head, then nods slowly. "Just wow. Like, I knew your badass persona was just for show, but I didn't know you were *that* much of a sucker."

She spins around.

I grab her wrist. "Blue."

She pulls her arm out of my hold. "Blue what? You really blew it this time? Blew your cover? Or maybe there was nothing to blow to begin with."

I'm hesitant to admit much more, but I can tell she's ashamed. Of her family and me.

Fuck, I'm to blame for this, too. "Blue. That's you, woman."

Her laugh comes out forced and raw. "Nice! Do I look that depressed constantly?"

"No." I run a fingertip along the blue stripe in her hair. "It's this."

She nods. "Another mistake I made."

"Bull. You want to know the truth, I love how it goes against your cheeks when they light up siren red."

Her eyes get a little bigger, and she whispers, "Ready for the real truth?"

I nod.

"Okay. I bought some hair dye at the dollar store. While I was mixing it, the cap flew off. By the time I was done cleaning up the bathroom, I realized I had a big glob in my hair." Her facial features are comical. Just like her hand gestures. "I washed it out, but it was too late."

"Was the dye blue?"

"No. Ash blonde. Must mean something a lot different in the country where it's made. You get what you pay for."

Turning my head, I let out a short cough, quelling the laughter tearing up my throat.

"Oh, it's all right, you can laugh. I did."

I give her a solid stare, eye-to-eye, just to see if she's lying. She's not.

"What else could I do? I wasn't going to pay a fortune to have it fixed." She puts both hands on her hips. "Actually, you're the first person to even mention it. Or notice."

She waves a hand towards where her mother's red outfit stands out among the crowd. "Not even mom said anything. And she spent years in fashion, selling cosmetics for a living."

I release the chuckle torturing my throat.

Damn, she's adorable. And funny. And likeable.

Very likeable.

I'm starting to get hard again. *Fuck me.*

"Well, I like it." I grab her hand. "Come on, Blue, let's catch up to those other two before we're completely left in the dust."

Her fingers wrap around mine. I can feel the tension slipping away from her as I lead us, dodging our way through the crowd. It's been a long time since I've held a woman's hand.

Something about it, the warmth of her palm against mine, maybe, makes me feel alive. My blood goes molten.

"It's about time you two caught up," Cleo says.

She and Nat are near the lion enclosure, but they aren't gazing into the pen.

"Look!" Cleo points to the next exhibit over.

It's the giraffes. A man and woman nearby, dressed in wedding attire, are having their pictures taken with the tall, sleek animals in the background.

"Who the hell gets married at the zoo?" I ask, dumbfounded.

"Oh, it's the latest craze," Cleo says. "You'd be mighty surprised."

"The zoo's the *last place* Dad would get married," Natalie chimes in.

I give her a knowing smile.

Cleo pulls down her big sunglasses and looks at me over the rim. "Well, it's not the location, but the timing, isn't it? There's no time like the present, Romeo." She winks at me before turning to Nat. "Zebras next?"

Natalie does a solid fist pump "Zebras!"

Off they go again. I'm surprised I didn't choke.

I glance at Blue slowly.

She laughs. "Good luck. You'll never keep up with her. After the cosmetic counter, the zoo is mom's favorite place on Earth."

I glance in the direction they've gone. That lady has so much energy it's almost scary. I hope she knows to stop for shade. She might be protected under that crazy hat, but Nat...

"She's harmless. They'll be fine," Blue tells me, as if reading my mind.

"Yeah, I can tell." I take her hand, lacing my fingers between hers as we slowly start walking. "You get that from her."

"What? Craziness?"

"No. Passion. It shines on her face like yours does when you're teaching art on Tuesday nights." I'm usually not so open and honest, but I'm comfortable, because of her.

"Fair point." Taking a sidestep, she bumps my arm with her shoulder. "I suppose now would be a good time for me to apologize for what Clara said. God. I can't *believe* she called you. I'm going to wring her neck one fine day."

"Why bother?"

"Why?" Confusion ripples in her voice.

I lean closer, next to her ear. "If I was you, I'd wait till the moment when it's going to embarrass her the most.

Then remind her how she said your ma was dying. Patience."

She turns slowly and looks up at me, her eyes glittering in the sun. "I like the way you think, Eden. Deviously." Her smile grows wider.

Good word for every wicked thought hitting me like lightning.

The desire to kiss her hits hard and fast. Her lips look too inviting. Too delicate. Too helpless.

I haven't forgotten how sweet they tasted since the first night, when I kissed her with everything I had in front of Jackass Moneybags. How smooth and slick and hot they felt under mine.

I don't realize we've stopped walking until someone jostles her and she stumbles. I grab her around the waist as she collides with my chest. Seeing her head back with those soft gray eyes looking up at me stalls my breath.

I tell myself she's giving me permission.

Permission to kiss her.

I pull her closer, feel the heat of her body against mine.

It feels so fucking good. So right. So taboo it makes me sweat.

I dip forward, the sound of her sigh echoing around me, before I catch myself.

Fuck.

Trouble is, this isn't right. The only reason I'm here is to keep some psycho from hurting her. One far worse than that prick, Preston. Bastard Phil won't stop at just scaring her, begging for another date.

I take a step backward, pretending I don't see disappointment in her eyes. Like I don't feel it either. Disoriented inside and out, I ask, "Which way to the zebras?"

"Right over there."

I don't look at her. The dryness of her tone says more than words.

"Next to the tigers. Bears are on the other side."

"You know this place well." I stick my hands in my pockets as we start walking, needing to put a bit of distance between us. There's too much at stake for me to lose focus now.

"Well, I should." She sighs. "I've come here once a month like clockwork for as long as I can remember."

"Izzy!" Cleo waves a frantic hand. "Izzy, Izzy, come here right this second!"

I glance around, and thankfully, don't see another wedding party. Cleo Derby's none too subtle in her awkward hints. She's holding something.

It's not until we arrive and she shoves it at Blue that I realize it's a cell phone in a flowery case.

"It's Megan!" Cleo yips. "She's *finally* getting married in two weeks. In Flagstaff!" She pats Blue's arm. "Oh, darling, isn't this just perfect timing? You'll have a date for this one. Won't have to go stag like you did all your other cousins' weddings."

I watch Blue's face go from pale to red, and I sense the pressure she's under. The embarrassment, too.

"Don't worry, Brent," Cleo says. "You'll have a delightful time, and so will little Natalie!"

"Flagstaff?" Natalie says. "Daddy, we can stay at the ranch. We haven't been in so long. Please, Daddy, please say we'll go!"

I'm cornered. Goddamn.

The dread and sorrow on Blue's face as she glances up at me tugs at something inside me demanding attention.

Can't dismiss it any more than I can the urge to protect her from Preston and the Pearls.

"You're in luck, baby girl. We'll go."

While Cleo and Natalie squeal and hug, Blue hangs her head. I'm not sure whether she's shocked numb by my quick agreement, or still tangled up in shame.

Grabbing her hand, I don't say anything. Just nod. That wipes the worst of it off her face, and soon, we're walking again.

They say timing's everything. It's never been truer in my life. It's damn sure never fallen into my lap so easily and obviously.

I've needed the perfect excuse to hit the ranch. To finish the scheme there I've started.

One that'll take the Black Pearls down once and for all.

VII: FLIRTING WITH DISASTER
(IZZY)

I can't help but watch the clock.

I've never done that before. Not during art class. The students are busy working with oil pastels. It's free form, whatever they'd like to create. Mainly because I was too out of it to come up with a fresh sample for them last night.

Been out of sorts since Saturday. After mother's nuclear bomb announcement of Megan's wedding, and Brent's attendance shocker, my mind has been mush. Pulverized.

The hundred plus text messages from mom hasn't helped either. I hope – no – I pray, beg, and plead she'll hold true to the promise she made Brent and hasn't told Clara anything.

Any. Thing.

My cousin has called, as usual, jabbering a mile a minute about Megan's wedding details. How they had to move the date up because her fiancé has an internship in Alaska. He's studying to be a doctor, apparently – one more fucking thing I have to contend with – so they'll be moving to Alaska right after the wedding. Cash-only gifts.

Fucking-A.

Fortunately, the only thing Clara worries about for now is the frosting melting on the wedding cake she's baking because it's an outdoor wedding. In Arizona.

Good thing wedding cakes are mostly for show.

I should be thankful for the distraction. With all this going down, she hasn't had time to obsess over who is or isn't attending.

She hasn't mentioned the zoo, either. Fingers crossed it stays that way, and mom doesn't slip a peep about my date.

After the zoo, we'd gone out to eat together. Twice in one day.

That's when Brent told mother that we had to keep our friendship under wraps because of Nat and my job. I wasn't there. I'd helped Natalie to the restroom with an upset tummy and gave her some Pepto, so I don't know exactly what was said.

Worse, I haven't even seen him since he dropped me off that evening.

Maybe that's why I can't peel my eyes off the clock. He should arrive shortly to pick up Nat.

I've thought long and hard. It's time.

I'm going to insist we end this sham. Before it does more damage. There's no reason – none – for him to go to Flagstaff.

Mother may have made it sound like I'm perpetually dateless, and maybe so, but bottom line is, so what?

This thing between us – this jaunt through Heaven and hell – it's a burden. I've lived my whole life without dreaming of some gorgeous man charging into my life and promising me happily ever after.

That's mom. Not Isabella Derby. She's the one who reads a dozen wild romance novels every month.

The familiar click of the door opening has me glancing up.

Brent.

Here we go again.

I could brace myself a thousand times, and it still couldn't stop the instant reaction in my blood. My pulse kicks higher, some kind of crazy flutter mode.

He's really hero material. Like something out of those dirty books with his chiseled looks, inviting scruff, and screaming green eyes. I'll admit it: sometimes I read the novels mother sends home with me.

The ones with shirtless hunks and women who are halfway unraveled hanging on their arms. Brent Eden may be the spitting image of a cover model – possibly the world's hottest – but damn.

This is no romance. And I'm no damsel in distress.

I'm a grown woman who got in too deep, who let her fantasies off their chain, and who desperately needs to end this sweet chaos before it ruins everything.

He shuts the door quietly, but rather than staying at the back of the room, he heads forward. Straight for me. Tension shoots up my neck as his eyes capture mine in an ornery glare.

What the hell now? What has his badass attitude flaring today? I've already told him I see right through it.

Unless...

Crap!

Clara must have called him. Again.

He arrives at my desk around the same time I decide that's just as well. If he's annoyed, sick of this, exhausted with *me*, then maybe it'll be easier. This whole thing ends in the next half hour.

"Where's your car?" His voice is hushed, but harsh. "I drove around the entire building and didn't see it."

That gets my attention.

Then I remember why he didn't spot it. With everything else going on, I'd forgotten the bad news for a short while. "It wouldn't start," I tell him. "Had to get a ride."

He puts both hands on my desk and leans closer. "It was here this afternoon, Blue. When I picked Nat up from school."

I sit back, not impressed by his attitude, even if the growl in his voice touches something primal deep inside me. I shake my head. "So? It started just fine then, but when it was time to come back for class, it wouldn't start."

"How'd you get here?"

This is nuts. I can't imagine why he cares.

Giving a half-snort, I point to my cellphone. "Uber. Duh. What else?"

"Uber?" He chokes off a curse. "You've gotta be more careful, babe. You don't know who those people are. Could be anyone. Why didn't you call?"

Resisting the urge to bite my lip, I stare through him instead. This isn't happening.

I'm *not* about to say I considered it. Even though I did.

Right before I called him an asshole for putting a curse on my car last week by saying it could breakdown anytime. It finally did. And with everything else I've put up with from this man, a girl's entitled to be slightly superstitious.

Pushing away from the desk, I stand. "Why would I call you? I'm not helpless. You just keep thinking I am." Before he can respond, I address the class. "Ten more minutes!"

Knowing how quick he is, I dodge around him, and spend the next ten minutes drifting from student to student. So far, nothing's happening like I planned, and the last thing we need is a scene in front of the kids on top of it. He'll have to cool his heels until class finishes.

He's still standing next to the desk when it's dismissal time. A pissed off wall of muscle.

God. For the first time I wonder if his badassery isn't so much for show as it is a revival of sorts.

A throwback to the time he'd been a hardcore rebel? Or his army days?

Whether by choice or circumstance, and though his life is far tamer now, the aggression was so instilled in him, he can't stop it taking hold.

The students wrap up and I make a few brief closing remarks. I feel bad watching them shuffle out the door. It's the first night I haven't given this my all, no thanks to the frustrated beast stewing in the corner.

This can't keep happening.

Soon, Natalie's the only student left. I have no choice but to return to my desk and pack up my things. Doesn't mean I have to say a word to Mr. Broody. I tap my phone's screen a few times and lay it down, summoning a ride. It'll take at least ten minutes for someone to get here with the academy being tucked back on slower roads.

I don't say anything to Brent.

Until he speaks.

"I'm giving you a ride home, Izzy. I canceled your Uber."

The transformation inside me is instant. From just annoyed to psycho-bitch mad.

"You...what?" I rip my phone from his hand and fight to keep quiet enough so Natalie can't hear.

Sure enough, my ride's canceled. Before the penalty fee even hit. I didn't even see him do it.

He. Can't. Keep. Getting. Away. With. This.

"Eden...just who the fuck do you think you are? Jesus!" I've spent hours of my life with this man and I still don't have a clue. "Look, you might be able to keep your daughter in arm's reach at all times, but that doesn't extend to me. You've got no freaking right to even *attempt* it." My wrists tremble as hot blood pumps through them.

If this man had a season, he'd be Phoenix, high summer. Always.

He's staring, his green eyes weapons, not temptations this time around. The tiger glare says he's beyond pissed. So does the strength in the hand that takes my wrist. It's amazing how swiftly he can do it without actually hurting me.

I really don't give a damn. "Let. Go." I seethe.

He doesn't release me, but his hold eases. "Okay. Whether you hold my hand or not, it won't change the fact you're riding home with us."

"I'm not!" I hiss. To prove my point, I add, "I've told you before I won't lose my job over you. Over this. You're making it too hard. Now, please, let go before I –"

"What? Scream? By the time Oscar walks into this room, you'll be so tongue-tied on my mouth you won't even know he's here." His lips part ever-so-slightly, warm and feral and weirdly inviting.

Insane. That's what this is.

"You wouldn't dare?" I hate how it comes out a question.

He steps closer, his lips barely an inch from mine. I was hot and bothered before, and now it's getting worse for very different reasons. "You know damn well I would. Haven't stopped thinking how good you tasted since the first night you said more than 'hello.' How bad you wanted it last weekend, Blue. Fuck, how bad I needed it."

My eyelids flutter.

I officially hate him. And I hate wanting him ten times more.

His breath mingles with mine, stirring something hot and carnal inside me. Just like at the zoo, when I thought he was going to kiss me.

It's a deep, physical ache. A self-destructive want.

A need to have his body on mine so intense it's every insanity known to man.

Tonight, it's even worse. I wanted it then, Saturday, but I need it now. *Need*, like he said.

Even though I'm furious.

He dips his chin. His bristles barely graze my cheek. They're softer than expected. More delightful, too.

My breath catches in my throat.

"I dare, Isabella Derby. Dare to tell Nat she can squawk to the whole world we went to the zoo together. That you've been to our house for supper. That you've been on my goddamn mind like a wet dream stuck on repeat. Morning, noon, and night."

Holy hell.

Forget insane. This is suicidal. Every last bit of it.

The consequences of anyone hearing about us hits me like a water balloon. His touch becomes kryptonite.

I snap my head backwards so fast I nearly lose my balance. My feet hit the chair. The harder I try to keep from falling, the harder it is not to. My near tumble couldn't have lasted more than a second or two.

Time is no match for him.

Before I can even blink, Brent has my arm and he's grabbed my waist with his other hand, keeping me upright. I'm breathing like I just ran a marathon.

A second later, I realize exactly what part of his body presses against my stomach. *Oh, hell!*

I push at his chest, flailing with my free arm. "Was this your goal since the beginning? Getting me fired?"

"No." He releases my waist and takes a step back before dropping my wrist. "I just want you to see the danger, taking rides from strangers."

Ridiculous. I shove everything into my bag. "In case you don't know, I teach preschool, Brent. Stranger-danger's a key part of the lesson plan."

He grabs my sketchpad. "Then you need to practice what you preach." Turning, he says to Natalie, "Ready, baby girl? We have to give Ms. Derby a ride home tonight. Her car's out of commission."

"Awesome!"

Seriously, what did I ever do? To deserve all this?

I sneer at the grin he flashes my way, but then smile at Nat. Guilt hits like a brick.

It's the same feeling that whacked me yesterday at lunch, when she'd snuck a subtle wave my way after looking to make sure no one was watching. She shouldn't have to keep any secrets. Or worry whether or not she'll look like a teacher's pet.

One more reason to stop this sham. ASAP.

Only, that seems impossible tonight.

The ride to my place is tense. The air seems electric in the front seat. If Natalie senses anything, she's very good at hiding it, chattering away about tonight's oil pastels.

As soon as he pulls into my building's lot, I tell him he can park out front, but of course he doesn't. Instead, he drives around the side, insisting he's looking at my car before leaving.

Apparently, mechanical precision is another one of his many talents.

He quickly determines the starter needs to be replaced, and soon a tow truck arrives to haul my Mustang to the shop.

I don't say much. I'm too strung up on how hard it is to get rid of him when he keeps saving my ass.

Also, because I'm not about to ignite another argument in front of Nat.

Also, also, because it'd be more than another argument. We're a few choice words away from a dynamite explosion.

I wish it ended there.

A pickup with his company name on the side pulls into my parking spot as soon as the Mustang disappears. He says it's mine to borrow tomorrow.

Screw it. I can't hold my tongue.

"You really *are* trying to get me fired, aren't you?"

"Wrong, Blue." He takes the keys from the man who climbs out and holds them to me. "It's not a favor. You either drive that, or I'll drive you to and from school, just like I do Natalie. Your choice."

Some choice.

So ready for this day to be over, I throw up my hands. "Whatever. You win. I'll drive the damn truck."

Grabbing the keys, I tell Nat goodnight and make my escape.

Later at home, try as I might, sleep won't come. Predictable.

It wasn't the fear of someone at school noticing what I drove, or Megan's wedding, or even his caveman attitude that keeps me awake.

It's how frightfully close he came to kissing me.

How badly I wanted that to happen.

How badly I still want it.

Want it. Against every warning and shred of common sense and decency. Against everything I think I am.

* * *

ANOTHER DAY BLURS BY. I'm driving his loaner truck home after a day of finger painting, cutting enough apple slices to feed an army of fifteen four year olds, and singing about tiny spiders and big mouthed frogs.

Paradise. It'll be years before I work my way up to teaching art full time for the older kids, but it's a nice start. It's hardly the reason I'm bothered, impatiently clicking my nails against the steering wheel.

My lips still quiver every time Brent Eden invades my mind.

I need to get over this. Really.

And I need to find a way to get him to back out of Megan's wedding. I don't trust myself in close proximity with him. It's no good. I've only seen what happens a dozen times.

I'm no good in close range with this beast of a man.

Not now, not next week, not ever.

My Mustang sits in my parking space when I pull around my apartment building. I park the truck next to the dumpster as a man climbs out of my car.

It's the employee from last night. Juan, I think. His friendly smile brightens his brown eyes. Knowing it was his cousin's shop my car was towed to, I open the door. "Sorry for the wait! Didn't expect it done so soon. If you tell me how much I owe, I'll cut you a check right now."

He hands me the keys. "You'll have to settle that up with the boss. It's on his tab, I think. I'm just the delivery guy this time." He winks.

Shit. I don't want to settle anything with his boss, yet can't hold that against him.

Sighing, I turn over the truck's keys and thank him. After Juan drives away, I search the inside of my car for a receipt showing the work done.

Of course, there isn't one.

When Brent canceled my Uber last night, he'd also punched his phone number into my phone, but I'm not about to call him.

Or text him.

It takes willpower, but I refrain.

* * *

BY NEXT WEEK'S art night, I've gotten three estimates for

replacing a starter and have the average amount of cash needed for the job in my purse.

Whenever he comes to pick up Nat, it's his. And I have my entire speech laid out. All about how he doesn't need to attend Megan's wedding this weekend.

I'm also a nervous wreck.

Truly can't believe the mess I'm in.

Between mother and Clara and their endless phone calls and texts – nine out of ten mentioning *him* – I'm praying for an onslaught of the flu. Or appendicitis.

Whatever helps prevent me from having to go anywhere this weekend.

Not having a date when everyone thinks I do is guaranteed hell.

The students are painting with oils tonight, the most difficult medium we've used. Because of that, their assignment is abstract, which leaves me too much time to once again watch the clock.

I haven't seen or heard from him in a week, and somewhat expected to, considering I've talked to people about Natalie. I've had her schedule changed slightly. For her own good.

She needs to be around kids her age. I want to encourage it as softly as I can, but the time has come.

That, right there, probably pissed him off, too.

Fuck, the door!

I keep my cool. Don't turn around. Just keep meandering from student to student, commenting on their work. Pretending the devil himself isn't at my back.

My peripheral vision checks to see if he's walking toward the front of the room. So far, no.

Small favors.

"Five more minutes," I say, heading for my desk.

He's still in the back of the room. Lingers there even after I dismiss class.

Natalie packs up her stuff and heads for my desk, rather than her father. "Dad says we'll pick you up right after school on Thursday." Her smile is murder.

I cringe inwardly. The thought of telling her no, it's too much, and I level a glare at him.

After digging out the envelope with the car repair money, I flip the bag over my shoulder. "You should have your dad carry your sketchpad tonight. Oil paints take a long time to dry."

"Oh, you're right! I'm being super-duper careful, Ms. Derby," she says proudly.

"I can see that. Here, let me take your bag. I'll give it to your father."

She hands over the bag and we both walk to the back of the room. I hand him her bag and the envelope.

He takes both, frowning at the offering.

I say nothing as I walk out the door. Not verbally. Silently, I tell myself I'm not lost in his scent.

It's a lie.

His cologne is faint. Subtle. It goes to my head. How can a simple smell make this harder?

Once outside, I take a deep breath, hoping another scent will override his. Of course, it doesn't.

"Four-thirty okay?" he asks.

It takes me a moment to catch my bearings and know what he's referring to.

He shrugs. "I'd like to get to Flagstaff before dark, Blue."

I shake my head. "I'm not leaving until Friday morning, and really, you don't need to..." I pinch my lips together as Nat spins around and looks up at me.

One look. I'm gutted.

"Already told your ma you're riding up Thursday evening with us."

Once again, I cringe, lowering my voice. "Well, my hotel room's locked in for Friday and Saturday night."

"You don't have a hotel room." His eyes narrow.

"I'm sharing one with mom," I lie softly.

Actually, George is sharing her room, but mother wants everyone to think they're just friends. It always amazes me how hard she tries to keep her own drama under wraps.

"No, Blue. Your mom, plus Clara, are staying with your aunt. Janice, I think. Clara and Megan's mom."

My chin drops. "How –"

"Cleo. You're the only one who doesn't call or text."

Frustrated. Mortified.

Enraged.

Right now, they're the same emotion, sending a dull pain to my temples. I rub them swiftly. Now I know why mom and Clara stopped asking about him the last couple days.

They don't have to. They're talking to Brent privately.

Can it get any worse?

Oh, yes.

Riding two and half hours next to him sounds heavenly hellish.

So much for backing out. Or saving face. Or pretending I haven't totally lost my mind to this smirking man-beast, who reads me so well my blood boils.

* * *

He picks me up Thursday at four-thirty sharp, and soon we're heading north out of town. Along the way, Nat describes, in full vivid detail, the dress Brent bought her to wear to the wedding, and then the old ranch that was once his grandfather's.

We arrive near dusk and settle in. I've never been so worried in my life.

This is crazy. *I'm* crazy.

"Isn't it awesome?" Natalie asks, standing on the front porch of an old farmhouse with both arms spread wide. "Finally here! My favorite place in the whole wide world."

"I can see why." The peeling white paint gives the single-story house a rustic look. So do the old fashioned Bermuda shutters that have saved the windows from intense wear and tear by the wind and odd dust storm. Several full-grown trees have also protected it from the elements.

It's easy to see a kid running wild around here.

"Come on!" she says, waving a hand. "I'll show you where you'll sleep."

Sleep. Very funny.

As if I'll ever be able to sleep in this strange little place with Brent freaking Eden one room over.

Speaking of, he's already unlocked the door and stepped inside ahead of us. Lights flicker on in every window.

"I'm ready for the grand tour. Lead the way," I tell Nat.

The inside isn't as rustic as the exterior. The old oak floors creak, but every room seems neat and clean. The kitchen hangs off the back of the living room A good-sized bathroom and two bedrooms round out the other side of the place. One with bunk beds, and another with a double bed.

"You can sleep in this one!" Natalie says as we enter the room with the double bed. She grabs my hand. "That's not the best part, though. Let me show you my *favorite*."

I follow her back through the living room and around the kitchen. She takes me out the backdoor and onto a screened-in porch.

She points towards a play kitchen set. "I've always loved it here. Let's open the windows and it'll cool right off."

Together, we open all the windows. By the time we walk back into the kitchen, Brent is busy unloading a cooler, putting the contents in an old, but sturdy refrigerator.

His grin makes my stomach flutter. "Taking it in?"

"Yes," I answer, bending down to hand him the last couple items from the cooler. "Nat showed me her favorite place."

"The old porch." Nodding, he takes a bottle of mayo and package of lunch meat from me. "It was mine, too, when I was a boy."

Our hands touch. Our eyes meet. I've been here no more than ten or twenty minutes, and I already feel beguiled by some sorcery.

A tingle zips up my arm. Air lingers somewhere in my chest. Not quite caught, but not flowing freely, either. My whole body feels the same way.

Snagged.

Trapped in emerald green.

Searching for a way to break the spell, I ask, "What about now? I see why you like this place."

"He and Uncle Davey used to dream about moving out here and having all kinds of animals like their grandpa did," Nat cuts in, digging into a grocery bag on the table. "But then Dad went in the army and Uncle Davey died."

It's the strangest thing. Almost like watching a shield, a barrier, slide across his eyes, taking the shimmer with it, the second those words are out of her mouth.

He takes a couple last cans from me and puts them in the fridge. He never answers my question.

"Yippie! The stuff for s'mores!" Natalie's squeal echoes off the walls. "Can we make some tonight, Daddy?"

"Yeah, sweets. Hold up a few. Let me get a fire going first." He closes the cooler's lid. "Which can't happen till we get everything put away and organized."

"We'll help," Natalie chirps. "Won't we, Ms. Derby?"

The formality seems completely out of place here. "Of course," I say, "And while we're here, you can call me Izzy."

"Izzy?"

"My nickname. What everyone in my family calls me."

"I have lots of nicknames, too! All from Daddy. Nat. Baby girl. Sweets. Kiddo."

I glance at him. He nods once.

There's something so flipping handsome about a man who treats his daughter like a princess and tries to hide it.

Still, a weird dread I can't quite put my finger on wells inside me at this entire pretense.

Handsome or not, he's not my boyfriend. Never my fiancé.

It's not just duping my family, it's deceiving myself.

I don't want a pretend relationship. I don't want

anything.

Because with him, even one more kiss might leave a smoking ruin.

* * *

Half an hour later, everything's put away and we're outside under a canopy of stars, roasting marshmallows over a fire crackling in a big ring of red stones.

"Dad says s'mores are too sweet." Natalie licks the remnants of her fourth s'more off her fingers. "Can you *believe* that?"

"No." I only had a single big one, but enjoyed it immensely. "No such thing as too sweet in my book."

"Right?!" Natalie says. "That's what I say, too."

We sit back in old metal chairs. Mine creaks as I lean closer to her. "I think that's just a guy thing. Being too hung up on sweet."

"Yeah," she agrees, a crooked smile crossing her face.

Across from us, Brent sits quietly, listening to our chatter. The flames cast shadows across his face, making his eyes brighter. "You two are ganging up on me," he growls jokingly.

Before either of us can respond, a loud meow rings out.

"Shadow?" Natalie freezes for a second, then jumps from her chair. "Dad, it's Shadow!"

She shoots around behind me. "Here kitty, kitty!"

I do a slow turn. We're in the middle of nowhere. I haven't seen another house in the last ten miles. I turn to Brent. "You leave a cat up here? Alone?"

He takes a drink off his metal cup. "You really like

thinking the worst of me, don't you, Blue?" Setting down his cup, he nods towards Nat, who sits on the gravel driveway petting a cat. "Shadow belongs to the neighbors down the road. Always prowls around at night. Usually takes him a day to figure out we're here."

"Oh. Sorry. I didn't mean –" I cut it there, changing the subject. "How often do you come up, anyway?"

"Try to make it once every month or two. Been more like three or four lately. Too busy. Nat loves this place, though." His eyes are on his daughter. The adoration in his eyes is breathtaking.

That was the first thing I'd noticed about him and it's still the same as the first day he walked into my class. How much he cares.

"Daddy, I'm taking Shadow inside to feed him!" Natalie arrives with a huge gray cat in her arms. "Want to pet him first, Izzy? He's so sweet."

I run a hand along his back, recognizing the thick, short blue-gray hair and golden eyes. "Wow, a Chartreux. Kind of a rare breed." I smile softly, memories flooding back.

"The neighbors breed them. Good mousers," Brent says.

"I know. My mother had one years ago."

"Really? What happened?" Natalie asks.

As gently as possible, I say, "Life. She just got old and died."

"That's sad." She kisses the top of the cat's head while the animal paws at her face. "I'm going to feed him now."

Nuzzling him the whole way, she walks into the house. "Daddy bought treats just for you, Shadow. You're gonna be a happy, happy boy."

I smile. One more confirmation Brent's badass persona is just that.

A façade he tries to hide behind. Only a kind soul buys treats for an animal that isn't even his.

It also returns the same question that's been nagging me for weeks.

Why does he try to hide? Pretend he's something he isn't?

Why do I keep going along with the sham?

He's looking at me as I pull my gaze off the house as the door closes behind Natalie. "Tell me something, Brent. Why are you doing this?"

He stretches over the side of his chair, grabs a log, and throws it on the fire. "What?"

A thousand tiny, bright sparks fly into the air, falling back into the pit as the flames spread upward, consuming the new log.

"Oh, I don't know," I say sarcastically. "Buy treats for a cat that's not yours. Pretend to be my boyfriend. Let my mother and cousin text and call you. Act like it doesn't annoy you." That last part should win him an acting award.

He glances at the house. "For her."

Heavy.

I nod. "Okay, the cat treats, I get. But not the rest."

His gaze goes to the fire and he keeps it there. "Nat likes you. Simple."

Not quite. I'm not buying it. "I'm sure she likes all her teachers, but I bet you didn't kiss them and go to their cousin's weddings."

Shrugging, he takes another drink. "Felt sorry for you after Preston, Izzy. That's the long and short of it."

Way to strike a nerve. Sympathy? *Please.*

I might be thankful he helped me out of a jam, but it doesn't explain anything. "Preston hasn't contacted me since." I stand. "And I don't need anyone feeling sorry for me."

He grabs my wrist, before I can stomp away. "Wait. I started the whole thing by telling Preston we're dating. Guess I feel obligated –"

Obligated? Jesus.

He's too good at torpedoing my heart in one word.

I rip my arm away. "Wow. Sorry I asked. I don't want anyone feeling *obligated.* Ever."

He doesn't chase after as I storm off toward the house. None of this should be my fault, yet the burden is there, pressing me down. Leaving me so fucking confused. I feel like I'm caught in a maze that doesn't have an exit, or a map, or an end.

"Isn't he pretty?" Natalie asks as I walk into the kitchen.

She's sitting on the floor petting the cat as he wolfs down treats.

I kneel. "Yes, he is."

"I wish I could live here all the time. Shadow could practically be my cat."

"Maybe you'll get a cat like him? Keep him at your house in Phoenix."

She shakes her head, a frown appearing. "Dad's allergic at home."

"At home?"

"Yeah. Shadow doesn't bother him here because there's enough fresh air."

That makes about as much sense as everything else

that's been happening. I suppress the urge to let out a snort. "Does Shadow come visit every day while you're here?"

"He never goes home. He'll hang around every day until we leave." She scoops the cat who's finally had his fill into her arms. "He even sleeps with me."

Happiness shines on her face. "Every night. It's comforting."

No lie. Within fifteen minutes, she and Shadow are snuggled up in bed, both fast asleep by the time I shut off the light. I enter the other bedroom and stare at the double bed, trying not to wish things were different.

Until the idea of him sleeping in the short and narrow bed above Natalie hits.

I have to apologize for getting pissed so easy.

He's still by the fire, and glances over his shoulder as I walk down the steps.

I sit down in the metal chair beside him. "She's asleep."

"With Shadow?"

"Yep." I pick up a small stick and throw it in the fire. "I'll sleep in that room with her. You can have the guest room."

"Why?"

"It's your house, Brent. You should have the bigger bed."

He leans back in his chair. "No."

"I have to." I level a knowing look his way while saying, "Heard you're *allergic* to cats."

He wipes a hand over his lips but can't fully hide his smile.

I grin, letting him know the truth is out.

"Blue, you tell my daughter that and I'll –"

I laugh. "You'll end up with a cat, is what you'll do. Here and in Phoenix."

"I might at that." He takes a swig of his drink and hands it to me. "Cheers."

It's a peace offering, I realize, so I take it.

There's a challenge, a quiet smirk in his eyes, as I lift the cup to my lips, without even asking what's in it.

Big mistake. The whiskey straight up burns my throat. It's like napalm going down.

I barely have a chance to swallow before a coughing fit explodes in my lungs.

My eyes are watering by the time it's over and I catch my breath.

Laughter lines his voice. "Shit, are you all right? Didn't mean –"

I nod. Furiously. "I...I'm more of a tequila girl, I guess. My dad liked bourbon."

He flips open the lid of the small cooler beside his chair and yanks out a can. I catch it as he tosses it my way, needing something to cool the fire in my throat. Twisting the can to see the label, I ask, "What's this?"

"Margarita in a can."

My lips twist. I blink, surprised. "*You* drink canned margarita?"

"Wrong. Had a feeling you would."

My face heats. Oh, God. Every look he gives me might be divine. Or divine punishment.

"Never tried it, but hey, there's a first time for everything." I pop the tab and take a drink. Strawberry. Surprised, I take a second taste, confirming it's good. "Pretty decent! Thanks."

"You're welcome."

We sit in a companionable silence for a few minutes, slowly sipping our drinks. "This really is a nice place. I'm not just saying it."

"Nat loves it."

"Bet she'd love it even more if there were animals here." The alcohol rush must give me a bit of liquid courage because my next question plops out before I can think twice. "Hey, what happened to your brother? Davey?"

Despite the fire and the heat of the summer night, a chill ripples my arms at the grief that crosses his face.

It wasn't just my imagination earlier. Every mention of his dead brother shuts him down.

"He died, Blue. Nothing else to say."

Damn. Unsure what to say next, I take another sip of margarita.

He tosses a fresh log on the fire. "So did Nat's mother." He glances my way. "That was your next question, wasn't it, Detective Derby?"

I shrug, dropping my face to hide the fierce red on my cheeks. Slowly, I nod. There's no use hiding it. I'm drunk and nosy and we both know it.

"Aneurism during child birth did her in. She never knew if Nat was a girl or boy."

"God, I'm sorry. No ultrasound?" I want to slap myself over the stupid question. Blame it on the canned tequila and slushy strawberry mix.

"Don't know if she ever did one or not outside what's required to check for health issues. Always said she wanted the gender under wraps till the baby came. I was in the army. Overseas. We'd dated on and off for a couple of years."

I'm still looking at him. Slowly, he sucks a mouthful of whiskey, and swallows loudly.

"Cindy didn't approve of the shit in my younger years. Running around with a motorcycle club. Said turning into anybody's old lady didn't appeal to her, and I can't say I blame her. It's a rough life. Club had its problems, too – big fucking problems it's taken years to straighten out. I saw the writing on the wall and joined the army. Things were still shit between her and me. When I found out I was going to Iraq, I broke it off for good. Then I was home on leave a year or more later. We were both lonely. Nat was conceived. Told her we'd figure it out after my tour was over. That we'd get married." He takes another swallow off his glass. "Nat was born two weeks before I put in for my discharge papers."

I'm shocked he's spilled so much, and don't want him to regret it. "She's a very lucky girl to have you. My dad was in the army, too. Overseas. Could've gotten out before things really ramped up, after 9/11, but he said he owed them another term. He couldn't walk away in a crisis. Wound up in the wrong place, wrong time. He didn't come home after a Taliban ambush. I was in my early teens. My mother was a wreck, but eventually, we adjusted."

Brent's eyes burn right through me. It's an equal trade, at least, confession for confession.

I shrug. "We survived. Somewhat, anyway. I think what happened to dad, to her, is the real reason she wants me to find Mr. Right so bad and get married." I shake my head and finish my drink. "To know the love of a man. A husband. Before it's too late."

"You don't want that?" He takes my empty can and

hands me a full one.

I open it and take a long pull. "Maybe someday. Right now, I just want to teach."

"Art."

"Art. That's what kept me sane after dad died. I could lose myself in it. Pretend I was somewhere else. Forget everything."

"We all need to do that sometimes."

"Right." I pretend to scratch the bridge of my nose so he doesn't see the tears.

Brent holds his cup towards me, offering solidarity. I click my can against it.

"To the struggle. And fuck tragedy, too," he rumbles.

I nod. "Fuck tragedy."

I take another long swallow and then look at my can. "These are really good."

"Wouldn't know, Blue. I'm a whiskey man. Sometimes beer."

"Oh, come on. Here, try a sip." I hold it out to him. He's incredulous. "Our little secret. One taste. Nobody ever knows."

I lean over to hand him my can. Brent just smiles.

My head feels a little woozy, but it's the uneven ground that catches me off guard. The chair tilts and I'm not fast enough to stop it.

He's quick. Keeps it from falling all the way over and I jump to my feet. My can slips out of my hold, and I kneel down to grab it. The contents splash all over a notebook, which I instantly recognize as the one he's always had in the back of the class.

Too curious not to, I flip it open, before he can snatch it away. My breath catches at the images he's drawn.

A woman's body. Naked. Fabulously detailed.

I'm in the midst of appreciating his skill when I see what's printed across the top in big blocky man letters.

BLUE.

That's when I notice the woman's face.

Holy flaming hell.

Pure fire rushes my cheeks. I flip the page. And the next.

There are several more nudes.

All of me. I flip one more page and a new sense of warmth fills me.

It's me again, but this time I'm dressed, hugging Natalie. I recognize the scene. The day she gave me the friendship bracelet.

Growling, he rips his notebook away. "You weren't supposed to see that!" He tosses it on his chair.

No longer content with being his secret model, I look up at him. "Why? They're good."

Good, if I ignore the fact they're living proof this man has been undressing me with his eyes in screaming detail since day one.

He traces the side of my face with one hand, his eyes locked on mine. Every thought I'd warned myself to avoid rushes forward.

Him kissing me. Me, returning his kisses. His caresses.

Touching. Kissing. Giving. Getting.

"You, Blue. You're what's good. Not those damn drawings."

My heart kicks into high gear and my chest goes tight. I've never wanted to be kissed so badly, to be touched like now.

"Don't be silly." The air between us crackles.

Electric. Charged. Intense.

I want to beg. Plead for him to just put his lips against mine.

One. More. Time.

He nods, never looking away. "Too good," he echoes, forcing his point.

"Hardly." I step closer, laying a hand on his chest. The beat of his heart thuds against my palm.

"You're wrong, Eden," I whisper. A crazy warmth folds around me, sinks through my skin, inside me, swift and ever growing. "I'm done being good." I take one more step, so our bodies are almost touching. "Tell me I'm bad. Tonight. Just this once."

"Blue."

I've lost it. And it's too late.

"No. Kiss me, Eden. Just fucking kiss me already."

The animal glint in his eye swells.

In a flash, he grabs my hips, pulling me forward, closing the gap between us. My nipples harden, pressed against his hard chest. I tilt my hips, rejoicing at the feel of his hard cock, deliciously close.

When his lips seize mine, all thoughts abandon me, except for one word.

Yes.

Maybe two words.

God, yes!

I wrap my arms around his neck and let desires that have kept me awake for weeks flow. His lips are softer, his tongue hotter, wilder than anything I've imagined. My pussy aches. So wet, so tense, if he doesn't give me something soon I might die.

There's no more space between us, but we're not close

enough.

I want more. Crave it.

His hands roam under my shirt, up my back. Heaven. I rub against him, arching upwards, as his hands grasp my butt, pulling me against his cock all the more firmly.

Fantasies don't compare to the desires leaping forward when he kisses a trail down my neck. He pulls my T-shirt up and kisses my breasts, tonguing inside the top of my bra.

I gasp at the pleasure and squeeze my thighs together.

Throbbing heat. Soaked. Frantic.

Confused when he stops, I freeze, unable to move as he pulls my shirt back in place.

"This is fake, Blue," he says. "Fake and fucking dangerous. Remember that."

He releases me and turns away.

"Go to bed, Blue. Go now. Before I fuck you right here on the ground."

There's a crack in my desire.

Just enough to send all the conflicted feelings streaming back. Wiping my very red face, I turn.

I get up and stumble backwards. Have to blink back the tears of frustration needling the backs of my eyes. Recalling how my knees work, I head for the house.

In the bedroom, I close the door, still breathing too hard.

Still wanting more.

Asshole or not, he's right. It's *fake.*

Fake and dangerous.

I grab my overnight bag and head for the bathroom, but as I undress, all I can think about is him.

His hands. His mouth.

Every glorious inch of him.

Heat swells my pussy again, begging for more. I turn on the water and step in the shower. Leaning back, I let the warm water flow over my breasts, imagining it's his lips. I run my hands over myself, rubbing my nipples and then down lower.

Lower.

Tentatively, I slide my fingers between my folds and settle on my clit. The pressure makes my breath catch. I never bring myself off this hard and fast.

Maybe because I'm imagining it's not my hand working my sweet spot, but Brent's.

I find a rhythm and pick up speed, pretending I'm not alone. I'm getting good at that.

Getting good at this.

I plant my other hand on the wall, letting hot water cascade down my back as I throw myself over the edge.

Coming!

And all I can see is him.

Between my legs. Pinning me down with his hands, fucking me with those tiger eyes, taking half my soul as he plunges in deep again and again and –

Oh, hell.

I'm breathing so hard. Shaking. My thighs hurt. I keep Brent's image in my mind as I slide my finger deep inside me a few more times, sweet relief fading to numb.

The rush hits like a monsoon. Sudden, fierce, mysterious. An explosion that leaves me limp, leaning heavily against the wall.

It keeps me sane, but strangely unsatisfied. Unfulfilled. And too horny.

It also leaves me lonelier than ever.

VIII: SHOW AND TELL (BRENT)

The sweat dripping off my brows makes my eyes sting. I wipe my forehead with the back of my hand and finish screwing the final wire onto the detonator.

It's not the reason I'm sweating. The detonator isn't connected to anything.

Not yet.

Can't just blame it on the heat, either, even though this windowless old shack is hotter than the devil's diner.

It's her.

Blue.

I've sweat bullets since sending her into the house last night. Ever since she left my dick harder than the flag pole at Iwo Jima.

I wanted her like I haven't wanted any woman in years.

Wanted it worse because I knew I couldn't have her, too. Even though she'd wanted it just as bad.

Pure torture.

Both of us are drowning in our own flesh and there's nothing we can do about it.

I go to sleep hard. Wake up harder. Brain, body, and soul tangled up in Blue.

Fuck, I couldn't even face her this morning. So I woke up before dawn and left while she and Nat were still sound asleep.

Assembling this very illegal, high powered weapon of death is preferable to spending another morning staring at those lips. Fixing my eyes on her ass when she's turned around. Pushing every growl down with coffee, paint-stripping strong, hoping it'll keep me from thinking how bad I want that ass under me for two fucking seconds.

My lip curls back in a snarl. I shouldn't be doing this. And neither should she.

"Damn it, Davey!"

My shout echoes off the building's walls and worn rafters. Very fucking worn. Should've collapsed years ago.

I set the screwdriver down and pick up the detonator to give it a closer look. This little remote will take lives. Set off a blast that could clear a city block.

End this shit once and for all.

Rubbing my face, I choke back an apology. I'm not even sure who it's for.

It's easy to blame Davey. To wish he'd listened and stayed the hell away from the Pearls, but it won't bring him back. Won't change anything.

Honestly, I'm just as pissed off at myself as him.

I'd vowed to change. To become everything Natalie would need in a father. And I have.

Had, rather.

Until the Pearls poked their evil fucking noses in my

life. That left me with no choice but to return to the man I'd left in the past. Turn into something I don't want to be.

I'll pay off Davey's debt, all right. Just not with cash.

By the time I'm done with the Black Pearls, there won't be enough left of them to bury.

Justice *will* be served.

I set the detonator in an old army ammunition box and stash it in the far corner, along with the rest of the supplies I'd bought, bartered, and damn-near stole from salvage yards and skeezy looking gun runners from here to Tucson. Trained by some of the best, the years I spent being a tactical and explosive expert in the army has its benefits.

After strategically layering the old lumber to look like a misshapen pile of driftwood, rather than a hiding spot, I put the tools in the toolbox and carry it out to my truck.

Bastard Phil knows I was in the army. Believes I was in disposal and clean up – skills I built my business on post-Iraq. Luckily, he's just like everybody else. Doesn't know that in order to clean up a mess, you have to know how it was made in the first place.

There are parts of this mess I don't understand.

Like Davey. Why and how he got snarled in a web woven deep and tight by the Pearls.

I might never know all of it, true, but I've accepted that because the how or why doesn't matter. Not as much as it ending.

All of it.

I let the air conditioner cool off the cab before I put the truck in gear. The trap is set, or close to it. Actually planting the explosives can't happen till I figure out how to lure the Black Pearls out here. There's an old road that runs along this side of the small mountain separating the ranch from the decaying shed.

It's the perfect set up. I just have to figure out the enticement to get them here.

Everyone. The head honchos and their minions.

Having not been used for years, the trail that leads back to the ranch is rough, and I take it slow. Which gives me ample time to contemplate my other issue.

Blue.

Damn it. I've never been attracted to someone like I am her. From the moment we met.

Never wanted anyone so bad. Not even Cindy.

I don't even know how to pursue someone like Blue without destroying her.

She's clean. Honest. Innocent.

I sense that in her every waking moment we're together. Innocence.

Shit, I've never had to pursue anyone. These looks plus the patches I've worn, Grizzlies MC and US Army alike, pull pussy like no tomorrow.

Cindy was the one who chased me down, and I let her catch me. It was fun. Good at times. That's what we were both after. A good time. For the moment.

When she told me she was pregnant, we both took it seriously, figured we had to find a way to make it work.

She would have held up her end of the bargain. Deep down, she was a good person.

Just wasn't good for me.

Never got into my head. Under my skin. Not like a little teacher I've spent far too many hours pissing off, and too many more drawing naked.

I crack the window, needing a breath of fresh air. I'd nearly flipped my shit when she found my sketches. Thought for sure I had a slap or two coming, after she had proof what an obsessed pig I can be, but fuck...it's like they just made her want me more.

Fuck.

I don't know what this is. Can't comprehend it.

I've had other women. Before Cindy and in between our on-again off-again relationship. Life made sense then. Had no need for a full-time woman lodged too deep in my life.

It's the one familiar thing I wish I could bring back with everything else going to hell.

The Black Pearls may have forced me to become the man I'd left behind. One whose only focus is on the here and now, but I can't let that spill into the rest of my life.

Can't let two maddening problems fuse together. Can't let them multiply.

The last thing Nat needs is me dragging women into her life, only to have her watch them leave.

Exactly what I'm doing to her with Blue. Her fucking teacher, no less.

A fireball of anger rolls across my stomach. I squeeze the steering wheel harder.

Fuck the Black Pearls. They've gone too far. Threatening Blue, bringing us face to face with our demons, that's the final straw.

The truck's Bluetooth system firing up breaks my concentration. It's Blue calling. Concerned, I hit the answer button. "What's up?"

"Hey, Dad!"

I may be mad at the world, but the sound of Natalie's voice still makes me grin. "Hey, baby girl."

"Where are you?"

Remembering the hike I'd promised her, I say, "I drove out to check the hills to see how far we can go this morning. On my way back now."

"I was hoping you remembered!"

"Course I did."

"Well, Izzy and I have pancake batter ready to fry. The bacon's done and the scrambled eggs are ready to go in the pan, so we're wondering when you'll be back."

A hard bump rattles the truck before the trail evens out as it starts to run along parallel to the old fence. "I can see the ranch," I tell her.

The screen door creaks in the background before she says, "I see your dust plume. Great timing! We'll start the pancakes and eggs."

"Sounds good. I'm hungry."

"We are too. Love you."

"Love you, baby girl."

She clicks off, ending the call, and I let out a long sigh.

I've fucked up too many times lately. Have to put a stop to this before it goes any further.

* * *

I ARRIVE at the house a few minutes later and smell the bacon and pancakes the second I get out.

Unfortunately, it all tastes as good as it smells. Had it been burnt, I would have had more reasons why Blue can't spend another night at the ranch with us.

Natalie isn't going to like that no matter what, so delicious food really doesn't hold credence.

Natalie talks non-stop about the hike while eating. She already has on her boots and jeans, and practically gobbles down her food. "Izzy can come with us, can't she, Dad? I already told her she could."

"And I already said no thank you," Blue answers.

She's barely looked at me since I walked in the house.

I shouldn't have kissed her last night.

I knew that, and it took all I had to stop it from becoming more than a kiss. Even later, when I found her sleeping in the top bunk, I was aching hard. Dick practically begging to get wet.

"I'm going to clean up the kitchen while you two go hiking," she says.

"And then you have some paperwork to do," Natalie says solemnly.

"Sure do," Blue says, smiling softly at Nat. "The academy being closed for the long weekend gives all you kids a four-day weekend. But teachers still have work so everything's ready when you return on Tuesday."

Nat shakes her head. "I don't want to be a teacher when I grow up. You never get a day off." She smiles at me. "I like Daddy's job better. It might be stinky and gross, but he gets free time."

"That's the trade off," I say, standing. "Ready to hit the hill?"

A hint of guilt rolls through my stomach at leaving before the kitchen is clean. Natalie and I have been on our own from the beginning. We're used to cleaning up after ourselves. But I also sense Blue wants us gone. Me, especially.

"Have fun," she says. "Don't forget to take plenty of water."

I don't have to reply. Nat speaks for both of us, assuring Blue she's packed nearly a gallon's worth of bottles in her backpack, along with a bowl for Shadow, who always tags along on our hikes for the first leg or two.

We're barely off the steps when she says, "Isn't Izzy the best, Dad? Those pancakes were delish!"

I hold my tongue. 'Best' isn't the word I'd use for the black magic around this woman, turning every damn drop of my blood molten.

Blue's still inside, well within earshot, and I'm struggling not to turn around, hoping to get another glimpse at her. She has on a flowered dress that leaves a good portion of her sleek legs bare, as well as her sun-kissed shoulders. There's not a single part of her body that isn't stare worthy. Not a square inch of her I don't want to tame with my tongue.

"I know you thought so, too," Nat says. "You ate four. I've never seen you eat four pancakes before!"

Guilty. "I was hungry. Long morning," I mutter, which is an excuse and the honest truth.

"She's fun, too." Nat steps around a big boulder and watches as Shadow jumps onto the rock. "I know you like her, Dad. I've seen you looking at her when she's not looking at you."

Nat turns, a wicked smile on her face, reaching up to stroke the purring animal's chin.

Shit. Like this can't get any worse.

My breath sticks in my throat.

I'd been careful about that. Extremely careful. Hiding.

"There's nothing to be embarrassed about."

"I'm not embarrassed, Nat. This isn't something you should be talking about." I take a hold of her upper arm as she steps over a wide rut. "Bl-Ms. Derby is your teacher."

"Well, yeah!" She jumps over the next rut. "And I know the academy has rules about teachers fraternizing with students and their families."

I live with this kid, have her entire life, and know she's extremely intelligent. Still, her matter-of-fact tone catches me off guard now. She's my baby girl, and growing up way too damn fast. "How do you know? Do you even know what fraternizing means?"

She rolls her eyes. "It means socializing outside school, Dad. Jeez." With one hand on her hip, she asks, "Would you like me to spell it, too?"

That's not like her. "Are you being smart with me?"

Her chin falls. She turns and starts walking again. "No. I just don't understand why you don't want me to like her. What's the big deal? It's not like Principal Jacobs is here eavesdropping."

Parenting is the toughest assignment I've ever had. Ever will. "Nat, that's not the point. I'm not saying we can't like her. Just trying to save you from being upset. We're helping her out this weekend, a one time favor, but after..." Having no clear explanation, I shrug. "The only place you'll see her is in school."

She stops walking and stares up at me with a quiet anger I rarely see.

"Why? I won't tell anyone." She spins around and stomps forward.

Flustered, I follow, trying to come up with an answer she'll accept. She might be smart as a whip, but she's got a lot to learn about the world's many fucked up complexities.

Without looking back at me, she says "You're always telling me I need friends, Dad. Well, you need them too, you know."

"I *have* friends."

"You mean Juan? Collin? The people you work with are employees, Daddy. They aren't your friends, just like the kids in my class aren't my friends."

My heart takes a hard tumble. Damn it, that's not the same. "Nat."

"I like Izzy, Dad." She plops down on a rock. Elbows on her knees, she sets her chin in her palms, gazing up at me. "She's fun. Easy to talk to. You get along with her better than you admit, too. And I can talk to her about stuff I can't with anybody else."

Stuff? I sit down beside her and take a deep breath.

I'm not ready for this.

Not now.

"We have our fun, and you can talk to me about anything."

She picks up a pebble and throws it. "No, I can't."

Although I'm scared shitless as to what the answer might be, I ask, "Like what?"

"Like how old a girl is when they start wearing a bra, or using deodorant, or –"

"You can ask grandma all that," I say, a shock rolling through my blood.

"No, I can't." She throws another rock. "She'll start blubbering and tell me I'm growing up too fast."

That hits the nail on the head. But, I'm sure if I talk to

my mother first, she'll be able to approach the subject less emotionally. When the time comes.

It certainly hasn't. Right? "Nat, listen, you're only ten and –"

"And in eighth grade. Four years from now I'll be fourteen and graduating high school. Then what? College? Trying to get my driver's license while the other girls are old enough to drink?"

The shimmer in her eyes as she looks up at me stops my heart.

"Kinda scares me, Dad. It *really* scares me."

I wrap an arm around her, hug her tight, and tell her the truth. "That scares me too, baby girl. Doesn't matter, though. We'll figure it out like we always do."

Always. I'd crawl over broken glass in Chernobyl for this girl to keep her smiling.

Shadow jumps up on her lap and she twists to snuggle the cat close. "Just so you know...I haven't asked Izzy any of those things, but I know she'll have the answers if I do. She's already helped me so much."

"Helped you with what?"

"Things."

Needing to know, I push her harder, "What things?"

"She saw me at recess one day, reading, and then talked to my pod teacher. So now I have fitness with the fifth grade instead of the eighth. It's fun. I like it, and I like how I have the same lunch period as those kids, too. Izzy gave me some books girls in that grade are reading, so I have things to talk to them about."

It doesn't sound like much, but I can tell how much they mean to her. "That was nice of her."

Her eyes hold unshed tears when she looks up at me. "Please let her be my friend, Dad. Let her be yours, too."

I'd give this girl the world if I could, but I also have to be cautious what I promise. "I can't make anyone be your friend, Natalie, or mine."

"I know." She sighs heavily and leans against me again. "I know."

Having no idea what more I can do, or say, I let silence do its work.

Before long, Nat lets Shadow go and gives me a final hug before jumping to her feet. "If we're going as far as the notch tree, we'd best get going."

The notch tree is just that. A dead old tree that we put a notch in every time we hike this trail.

I'm still raw on the inside and torn over what to do. Being a father's the one thing that doesn't get easier with experience.

I can take the pressures of the army, of running my own business, of the Black Pearls breathing down my neck, but this...being a preteen's dad, outweighs all the other issues. Easy.

Natalie reverts back to her usual smiling self when we arrive at the house. Blue sits in a chair on the porch with a stack of papers on the table beside her. Shadow lounging lazily by her feet.

"How was the hike?"

The shine in Blue's eyes as they settle on Nat scares me as much as I appreciate it. Might not know what the hell to think about this woman, or what to do with her, but I do value what she does for my daughter.

"Awesome!" Nat says. "We made another notch in our tree. Number fifty eight."

"Good for you." Blue gestures towards the kitchen. "I made some lemonade. It's in the fridge if you're thirsty."

"Thanks. I'll get some. You want a glass, Dad?"

"Sure." I sit down in the chair opposite Blue. "What are you working on?"

She gathers the papers into a neat stack. "Lesson plans."

Hearing Nat in the kitchen, talking to Shadow about getting the cat some treats and water, I lean closer. "The other day, when you accused me of keeping Natalie within arm's reach, what did you mean?"

She frowns and glances towards the kitchen. "Just that...you seem to have control over everything she does."

"I have to, she's my daughter."

Blue nods, keeping her voice hushed. "She certainly is, but she's also her own person. A few opportunities for her to interact with other children her age, without an adult around, could really benefit her."

I can tell how carefully she's treading. "Like a different gym class or lunch period, you mean?"

She bites her bottom lip and nods. "Yes. I apologize if I overstepped, but she's lonely. Very lonely. She's smart. Brilliant. But emotionally, she's ten, and needs to be around other ten year olds in order to learn how to cope with things better."

Again, she's stepping lightly. Carefully.

If it was anyone else, I'd probably be so pissed off I'd send them packing, but whatever Blue did for Natalie, it was totally to help her. I respect that.

An excited squeal comes from the kitchen. "Cookies!"

Blue cringes slightly. "You had a visitor while you were gone. Mrs. Wingard. Shadow didn't come home last night, so she figured you were here and brought over a platter of cookies."

I hold my breath for a second. The harder I try to crawl out, the deeper this shit gets.

Old Lady Wingard is as nosy as her cat. "She ask who you are?"

"Yes." Her cheeks redden. "I said I'm Natalie's tutor."

That was a better answer than I could have come up with.

Hell of a lot better than a fake fiancé, like I'd told Preston. I still hate that guy. Hate the idea that he had a real date with Blue. Whether he'd fucked it up or not, she'd actually agreed to go out with him.

I don't like the idea of her agreeing to go out with anyone. Also don't give a damn how insane that sounds.

Nat returns carrying lemonade and cookies. After eating a few, and enjoying how intently Blue listens to everything we say about our hike, I need a way to release the tension.

That's all it takes. Five minutes with her and I'm hard as stone. Thinking thoughts that I shouldn't be thinking and wanting things that I shouldn't be wanting.

"Think I'll go take care of that dead tree behind the barn." I down the last of my lemonade and stand.

"We'll help," Natalie says. "I'll get Izzy a pair of your old gloves."

"She'll need more than gloves," I say, referring to her dress and sandals as I head for the door.

Lady Luck isn't on my side. In fact, she's decided to give me the bird today.

Blue has jeans. A pair that molds to her sweet ass perfectly.

Fuck.

The next several hours of cutting the tree into logs and splitting each one into smaller bits is close to hell. I can't take my eyes off her as she carries the wood to the barn and stacks it in a pile. The tight tank top and jeans leave little to my imagination, besides imagining how bad I'd like to rip that tank top off with my teeth, suck on those perfect tits, and bury my throbbing cock deep in her.

I'm so fucking hard it hurts.

Have been the entire time. There are few things worse than being so close, yet still not able to get your rocks off. Every part of me stays on edge, screaming for a release it's not getting.

I pull my t-shirt off and toss it on the ground. Fuck it all.

I have to stop getting so worked up over her. "That's it."

Blue turns towards me, tilting her head. A soft sheen of sweat makes her skin glisten, and her nipples couldn't be more noticeable. "What's it?"

"The wood. You're done. I'll finish up."

"But I can –"

"No."

She's staring at me. Frowning.

I know I sound pissed. I am.

Fully frustrated. Need a few minutes of reprieve. "You and Nat should go inside. Start getting ready for the rehearsal dinner." I send the axe into another log so hard my shoulders pulse.

Now, I'm imagining her in the shower. Cleaning up. Naked. Fuck!

I can't fathom how this ends, but my gut tells me one way, and one way only.

One of us gets fucked. The other, completely destroyed.

* * *

Hours later, after an ice cold shower, partially because the hot water heater needs to be replaced, and not allowing myself to do more than glance her way, we pull into the Mexican restaurant for the rehearsal dinner.

A crowd of people will help. It has to.

There's a crowd, all right, and a hushed silence fills the banquet room as all eyes turn to us. Dread fills her eyes as Blue glances up at me.

Despite all the misery I've put myself through the past twenty four hours, I put my hand in the small of her back and guide her forward. It's too late to do anything else.

Dressed in another flowing red outfit including a floppy hat, Cleo rushes towards us. If I was hoping she'd act as some sort of shield, I'd thought wrong.

"Finally, the man of the hour! Everyone's bursting at the seams to meet you, Mr. Eden." She lowers her voice to add, "They all thought I was lying. Even though Clara insisted she'd met you, too."

I catch the way Blue's breasts rise as she draws in a deep breath and holds it. She's wearing another short dress. Dark blue with a low-cut neckline. Her hair hangs loose, past her shoulders, and flutters slightly as she bows her head and presses a hand to her forehead.

"Come with me, darling," Cleo says, taking Natalie's hand. "I'll introduce you to the other children. I've told them all about you and our trip to the zoo. There's a kid's table set up so you youngsters can all eat together when the food is served and won't be bored by all the silly adults."

Silly is right. Every adult in the room stares at us, whispering. Nat looks up at me, and unlike Blue, excitement shines in her eyes. I give her a nod and she hurries off with Cleo.

"Ready?" I ask Blue.

She lets out a long sigh and glances up at me. "To leave? Heck yes."

Hoping to ease her anxiety, I laugh, loud enough so others hear, and then lean closer, "Just say the word and we're out of here."

"I wish!" she answers. "But we have to stay long enough to eat. Common courtesy."

"I'm sure they make a good margarita."

She shakes her head. "I had enough last night."

"We've all been waiting for you," Clara says, approaching with a group of others. "Izzy, make the rounds with our man of honor! Everybody's waiting for Brent."

Blue does just that with a worn smirk on her face. Onward we go, and I make an effort to remember specific people and their names.

Particularly the ones who cast the most scornful, jealous glares.

I don't know what sort of joy these people get out of embarrassing her, but they do, and a few of their remarks do more than irritate me.

"He doesn't mean any harm," Clara says, after a cousin makes a snide remark. "Izzy's been a member of the lonely-hearts club for so long, a few people took bets you were an imaginary friend. Thought she'd *still* show up all by her lonesome. Joke's on them!" She elbows Blue, grinning.

I slide my arm around to Blue's side and tug her closer. "I'm not imaginary and she's not alone. Won't be tomorrow, either."

Clara smiles and bats her eyelashes. "You'll have tongues wagging, talking about another wedding happening soon."

The bride and groom arrive then, along with the rest of their small wedding party. I'm thankful as hell the focus of the room shifts to them, until Clara says one more thing.

"Don't worry, your secret's safe with me. I haven't even told Cleo I ran into Preston Graves. Or that he mentioned your engagement."

Blue smothers her gasp only because she quickly covers her mouth with one hand.

I escort her to the table and order us each a margarita.

She offers a shaky smile. "Thanks."

I nod, but have to ask, "Didn't you say you met Preston on a dating site?"

"Yes."

"Then how does Clara know him?"

Her shoulders slump. "Fuck if I know. Right now, I can't say I care."

I don't say anything. No need to give that little bastard a second more of thought than he deserves.

There are bigger sharks in my pond right now. Far more dangerous ones.

Others arrive at the table. Small talk trails from one

end to the other. I join in with those nearby, especially Cleo's boyfriend, George, sitting across from me.

Of all the people here, he was the only one who greeted Blue with sincerity, and his expression held respect when he shook my hand. I get the sense he doesn't care as much as the rest of the family if Blue and I are really dating. Only that she's not here alone. I can appreciate that.

Halfway through the meal, I glance around the table and say to Blue, "Isn't the rehearsal dinner usually just for the wedding party and immediate family?"

She huffs out a breath while nodding.

George laughs. "You've been recruited. Congratulations."

"Recruited?"

"Sure," he says, "after the meal ends, we're all expected to go over to Janice and Joe's house. Bride's parents. There, we'll set up tents, tables, chairs, and anything else they need strong, abled-bodies to complete."

I look at Blue. She takes a sip off her margarita. "We can leave. I've already told mother."

Sitting across from Blue, Cleo gives me a pleading look.

It's a test. Or, in my eyes, a challenge. Something I can never back away from.

This family is harsh, but only on Blue, which rubs me the wrong way. And continues to as people keep glancing our way. They don't even try hiding their doubts, or how they whisper to each other.

Later, as I pull in the wide driveway and park behind George and Cleo, Blue insists we don't need to help. Under her breath because Nat seems excited, hoping to play longer with the girls she was introduced to at the restaurant.

Natalie flies out the back door of the truck as soon as I cut the engine. She slams the door and runs straight toward the minivan where the other girls are climbing out.

"You can leave, I'll watch Nat while she plays for a while," Blue says.

"Nowhere I need to go." I climb out.

She meets me at the front of the truck. "Really. You don't have to stay." Shooting a nervous glance, she says, "Go back to the ranch. I can borrow mom's car and bring Natalie home later."

Others are pulling in. No doubt they're watching us.

Enough of this fuckery. I grab her by the hips and yank her forward.

She plants her hands on my chest. "What are you doing?"

"Giving them the show they're waiting for." I brush my lips over hers.

Pinched tight, her lips don't respond against mine. Not at first.

Then I pull her closer, running my hand over the silky material covering her ass. "Come on, you can do better than that," I whisper against her mouth. "I know you can."

The heels she's wearing make her a bit taller, but still, she has to tilt her head back slightly in order to look up at me. "We shouldn't do this, Eden. You shouldn't. It's –"

She's trying too hard not to smile, to hide the flash of excitement in her eyes. "I want to," I growl, grabbing her ass.

Taking advantage of her lips parting, I lock my mouth

on hers and give some solid tongue action. Her response, her tongue twisting around mine, shoots a thrill through me. Within seconds, I'm as hard as I'd been this afternoon, aching like hell. I'm willing to take the pain.

She's worth it. So's giving her family something to stare at.

The heat between us intensifies. Her hands go up my neck, her fingers in my hair. I feel every curve of her body as she presses it harder against mine, and it's fucking amazing. Intoxicating.

I drag my mouth away from hers and do my damnedest to act like I'm perfectly fine. "I'll be staying till it's time for all of us to leave." I plant another kiss on her forehead and then spin her about. Wrapping my arms around her waist, I press my hard bulge against her backside.

She gasps, pressing into me. "Now, you get it. I've got you, Isabella Derby. And I don't want to hear another word about it."

She steps forward, and so do I, keeping us tight together and flattening my hand over her stomach. The pressure of my dick against her ass is an extra stimulation I don't need, but love. It's like pushing on a wound, how the pain makes it feel better.

"Stop being silly," she hisses, twisting her hips.

I nip the lobe of her ear. "This isn't."

I thrust my hips forward.

She jolts. "Whatever it is, stop! Before you make us a spectacle."

I laugh, stepping out from behind her. "Too late for that." I grab her hand to lead her to the front door the others are walking through, glancing back at us.

The beasts are quickly separated from the beauties by a thin gray-haired man in the front foyer who directs the men to the backyard and the women into the living room. For good measure, I give Blue a quick parting kiss and head out to help set up tents, chairs, and tables, just like George said.

The thin man is Joe Derby, Megan and Clara's father. Apparently, brother of Blue's dead father. He has two other daughters, older, and already married. The mothers of the girls playing with Nat.

Megan is Joe's youngest, and if throwing together a wedding in two weeks has him frazzled, it doesn't show. He's friendly and jovial and continuously passing out beers in payment for the work.

I finish pounding the final tie-down stake in the ground for the big tent and stand up as he walks closer, a bottle of beer in each hand.

"Ready for a fresh one?" he asks.

"Sure." I set the sledgehammer down and take a bottle. Swallowing a long drink, I nod towards the huge back yard that also hosts a swimming pool. "Nice place you've got here."

"Thanks. We built it years ago while raising our girls." He takes a pull off his beer. "I'm sure you don't remember, but we spoke on the phone a few years back. One of my sandwich shops had a fire in the kitchen. Called your company for a clean-up quote."

I point out the obvious. "I didn't get the job."

"You'd come highly recommended, and even though I tried coaxing you to reconsider, you said you were too booked to take on another job in the time span I had to get things done. Especially a gig up here." He holds up his beer. "No hard feelings. The guys you recommended did a fine job."

"Wes Raine out of Flagstaff?" I ask.

"Yep. I've used him since, too."

I've known Wes for years. Always happy to recommend him. "He's good. We've worked together on several big projects around the state." My attention shifts to the patio door opening. Blue steps outside, following a few other women.

"Aw, hell," Joe says. "Looks like they're ready to decorate the arch and it's not up yet."

I empty my beer and hand him the bottle. "Where's it at?"

He points towards the house. "Box in the garage."

"Let's go grab it," I say, clapping his shoulder.

'Some assembly required' involves so many tiny screws I could have built the damn thing from scratch faster than it takes us to throw it together. Except, then I wouldn't have needed all the assistance from Blue.

Of all the women here, she's by far the prettiest. Every time I look at her, my eyes land on her lips, remembering how soft and lush they get under mine.

"Looks perfect," she says, admiring the archway.

"Marvelous!" Cleo holds up a mess of flimsy fabric. "Now, Brent, could you be a dear and help us get this tulle wrapped around the top?"

"I can do it, Mother." Blue walks over and picks up one of the folding chairs.

"You can't stand on that!" Cleo says.

I take the fabric from Cleo. "I'll help her."

"Thank you." Cleo waves at both of us as she walks away.

Blue sets the chair next to the archway. "I can do this."

"Not without my help. Not standing by while you roll off that thing and crack your neck." I plant a swift kiss on her lips, enjoying how her cheeks go cherry red. "Let me hold the chair. Help you balance. It'll collapse if I try standing on it."

She kicks off her shoes. "All right."

I grasp the back of the chair and take her hand to help her step up onto the seat.

"The quicker we get this done, the quicker we'll be able to leave," she says.

"Whaaat? You're leaving us already, Izzy?"

The question comes from a young woman walking past. One who's not nearly as pretty as she thinks she is, and has made a habit of walking past me several times tonight, casting looks any fool could read.

Some fools might take her up on her offer, too.

She doesn't get it.

Ever since the day Isabella Derby walked into my life, I'm no fucking fool.

Ignoring the question, I cup one of Blue's butt cheeks. Standing on the chair, she's taller than me, and has to bend down, just as expected. Before she can speak, I kiss her.

"What're you doing?" she asks, breaking the kiss.

"Marking territory. Letting everybody know you're taken."

"Oh, please! No one's concerned about that."

I lean back so I can see her face, the sheepish expression forming as she stands straight again. "I've convinced them, you mean? Glad that was fast." I say, happy to have been of service.

"Convinced them? You can say that, I suppose." She holds her hand out for the fabric.

I hand it to her. "That upset you?"

"I'm past being upset by what any of them have to say."

First, I'm irritated, then my thoughts go in a different direction. One I should've thought of before. "Even if they say you're too good for me?"

"Hardly, Eden!" She rolls the material over the top of the archway. "Quite the opposite. Between nearly every woman drooling over you with their tongues out, I've been told constantly how hard I'll have to work to keep a man like you satisfied."

My irritation at her family returns, turning to anger in two-seconds flat. "Bullshit. All of it."

"It's true." She evens out the fabric flowing over both sides of the archway to the ground.

I let go of the chair and grab her waist, lifting her into my arms. Then I let her body slide down the front of mine.

"What are you doing? I'm not done yet."

Isn't it obvious?

Or is she just playing hard to get like a pro?

I hold her against me with her feet barely dangling off the ground and capture her lips. Heaven.

This kiss holds nothing back. It's long and hard and hot.

Doesn't stop till she's slumped against me, moaning softly, holding onto my neck and gasping for air.

I must be getting used to the fact that I have no control over my body when she's near.

Maybe I just don't care.

I'm hard. I'm ready. Eager to fuck her all night long,

past sunup, but it's not the only reason I'm running down her lips like a starving lion.

It's the desire to teach her entire family a lesson.

When they pick on Blue, they pick on me, and I retaliate.

IX: SHOW ME (IZZY)

I watch the ranch come into view with a nervousness I've never felt.

It would be easier if Natalie was with us. She's not.

Though I believe allowing her to spend the night with Paige and Hannah, Janice's granddaughters, is a good thing, she's the shield I need right now.

Not against him. Me. Brent's kiss earlier rocketed my libido to Jupiter and it hasn't come down yet.

His kisses are fake, I know. He's playing a role. My bogus boyfriend. My not fiancé.

But hell, who would've thought he was such a great actor? I'm half-believing we're real.

Which we're not. And can't be. And that can never change.

Damn, I should've stayed with Uncle Joe and Aunt Janice, too. Slept on the floor, maybe.

Which would have proven to everyone how false this is, leaving him for the vultures among my many single cousins. If that one bridesmaid, Pamela something or another, made *one more* comment about Brent's God abs, I swear I would've ripped her bleached blonde hair out by its black roots.

Every time I turned around that little bitch was outside, strutting past him.

Presenting. Pleading. Filling me with a jealousy there's no rational reason for me to have.

"Home," he whispers, parking the truck.

I take a deep breath as he shuts off the engine. Staring out the windshield, I see Shadow on the front porch, his big gold eyes catching moonlight. "Natalie will be fine, if you're worried. Mom loves company. She'll keep a close eye on her."

He opens his door. "Yeah. Wouldn't have allowed her to stay if I didn't already know it."

Of course. I knew that, too, but I'm stalling.

It feels like I'm on some sort of rickety bridge. I've made it too far to turn around, yet, if I go forward, all the way across, I know I can never go back.

Forward it is. Like there's another choice.

I have to see what's waiting for me, even crave it deep inside, and that frightens me.

What if I reach the other side and find out I'll want more? *More.* And then maybe the wanting never ends.

It just swallows me whole, chews me up, and spits me back out piece by mangled piece.

"You gonna sit there all night, or what?" He's smiling, despite the teasing edge in his voice.

I glance across, to where he's standing, door open. Moonlight shrouds him, blending into darkness. Deep green man eyes shine brighter than Shadow's.

Brighter than they've been all day, even. And they were damn bright.

This afternoon, when he'd taken his shirt off, I'd nearly fainted. Pamela Bitchface wasn't kidding about God abs.

Putting Brent Eden and ripped in the same sentence doesn't do him justice. Neither does assigning him a mere six pack.

Seeing him shirtless stopped my heart. I had to tell myself to breathe.

He's beyond good-looking. He's art. Sculpted to perfection by life. The tattoos he keeps hidden are magnificent, too.

They're huge and dark and meaningful and just the slightest bit scary.

I wish they were scarier. Then I wouldn't want to examine each and every one of them. Up close.

Each and every inch of him.

"Blue?"

I grab the door handle, open the passenger door, and climb out.

Taking another step to the proverbial bridge. Toward the other side, the unknown, and possibly my self-destruction.

Brent runs out of patience. He steps up next to me and takes my hand.

I should say something, but what? I had a nice time tonight? Thanks for being so nice to my family, who all want to fuck you? You know, like I do?

Dread bubbles up in my stomach. *What am I thinking?*

It's Pretend with a capital P. He was pretending to like me.

Kissing me to make things look good. To make it look like neither one of us was lying.

He lets go of my hand and opens the front door. I step past him, into the living room. My breath catches in my lungs, hanging heavy in my chest. I swallow and turn around.

"Thanks for, um..." God, he looks so good.

His button up pale green shirt still looks fresh and neat even after all the work he did setting up the tent, the chairs, the tables. And the archway.

How could I ever forget?

That kiss, when he lifted me off the chair, swung me around, and attacked my mouth, still has my blood smoking. "Everything," I say, the air rushing out of me. "Thanks again."

He steps closer.

My heart races.

"My pleasure, Blue." He tucks a lock of my hair behind my ear. "Everything," he growls, throwing my strained word back at me.

Heat swirls deep inside me. A whirlpool of fire.

I'll never forget the first time I saw that face. He walked into the classroom, looking all grumpy and formative.

I thought he was the sexiest man I'd ever seen. Still do.

Even after everything we've been through.

"You're a good actor," I say.

Lame.

His grin nearly knocks me off my feet. Literally.

I have to press my heels into the floor to stay upright. God.

"I'll share the Oscar, Blue," he says. "You weren't half bad yourself. Not half anything."

His eyes swoop downward, and back up, slowly. My nipples tingle when they settle there, as if he can see right through my clothes.

I swallow hard and flip around, needing to breathe. "I wasn't acting. Not the whole time, I mean."

"No?" he raises an eyebrow.

Crap.

I shake my head, still trying to convince myself not to turn around, rather than answering his question. "No. I –"

He twists me around before I finish. Runs both hands down my arms, sending shivers clear to my toes. "Fuck the acting, Blue. I'm just as sick of it as you are."

His voice is so husky. So sexy.

Fuck me.

In a flash, he pulls me against him. "I want you, Blue. Honestly. Right the hell now."

My mind is gone. All I can do is nod.

"Right now," he growls again, running his hips into mine.

He's too hard.

I'm too wet.

This is too insane.

Then it finally happens.

My lips land on his while my arms wrap around his neck. Hallelujah!

He spins me around and around, plants me against the wall, kisses me until I can't breathe.

I pull away, sucking at the air, and then go back for more. His hands are under my dress, free marauders, running up my thighs. Whatever surges through me –

some adrenaline I've never experienced – gives me courage.

Freedom.

I hook one foot around his leg, giving him more access.

His fingers slip under my panties. I arch into him and press my head against the wall as his lips leave mine and trail downwards. Lower than ever. So low there's a soft weight in my panties from how drenched I am.

My breasts throb, nipples aching as his tongue leaves a burning path from my neck to my cleavage.

I'm not sure how it happens, but the next thing I know, he's carrying me like one of the heroes in my mom's dirty novels. I throw my head back and laugh. "Are you for real, Eden?"

"Very real, Blue. Very, very real." He kisses me again. "You'll see how fucking real I get just as soon as we reach the bedroom."

Reality comes crashing down like a cold shower. I have to tell him I have no idea what to do.

I know the gist of it, have read all about it, but actual experience...with sex?

Nope. None.

Shit.

Maybe I can just pretend. That's what we've been dancing around forever, right? Act like I know more than I do.

If only it weren't for my face.

He sets me on the bed, kneels in front of me, and lets me know I've blown it with one question. "What's wrong?"

Trying to quell the nerves overtaking me, I shrug. "Nothing."

He lifts a brow. "Blue?"

My heart pounds. My body pulses. I've never been the sole focus of a man at this level, and I want it.

Want it beyond all else.

I close my eyes and give it up, "I'm a virgin, Brent."

"Like I don't know."

My eyes snap open. "You do? What? How?" The horror. "That bad?"

He chuckles, running his hands up my thighs. "No. That good, Blue. That tense. That ready. That eager to be fucked for the very first time."

Fire shoots up my legs, hitting the crux between my thighs so hard I gasp. We haven't even gotten started and the pleasure comes in waves.

"Want you, Blue." He leans forward and kisses the tip of my nose. "Want you fully. Completely. The thought of being your first thrills me, but it has to be what you want, too."

His sincerity excites me, but also fills me with wary embarrassment. "I do, but what if I disappoint you?" The very idea makes me cringe.

"Not a chance in hell of that happening."

He sounds like he means it, too. Wow.

He kisses me long and passionately, until my mind can't stop spinning. His thumbs press deep into my inner thighs, slowly working their way up, inciting a wild intensity to swirl deep inside me. Like an inner thunder disappearing the rest of the world.

When he breaks the kiss, we're on the bed, side by side, both gasping.

He combs my hair away from my face. "We'll take it slow and easy."

I'm so close to coming, I'm fighting to catch my breath. Twisting onto my side, I squeeze my thighs together, trying to ease the commotion down there, just long enough to get his shirt off, button by button. "Not too slow, I hope. Don't know how much longer I can last."

"Not long, Blue," he growls, slipping a hand inside the v-cut neckline of my dress, cupping one breast.

Oh, God. *Not long* is painfully accurate.

The heat of his palm, his pressure, against my tender nipple is perfection.

Whimpering, I squirm against him, silently pleading.

His brows make a v as he frowns. "Too fucking hot, Blue. I thought –"

"I've had orgasms. Self-inflicted." Heat burns my cheeks. I have no idea why I felt the need to share.

"Really?" He nips at my earlobe.

"Everybody does it." Don't they? I spread his shirt open, exploring the hard curves of his chest with my hand. It's as amazing as I imagined.

"Yeah, they do. Always wondered about you coming, thinking about me..." His lips are just in time before I die. They take control of mine for another long, luxurious kiss. Then he lifts my chin, looks straight at me. "Show me."

Evil excitement shimmers in his eyes. Part of me loves knowing I put it there. But I also have to squeeze my thighs together, harder to keep from peaking.

He rolls my nipple between his thumb and finger. "Show me, Blue. Show me how bad you want this."

Flushed, I'm nodding.

He jumps off the bed and pulls on my arms. "I'll help you get ready."

A mischievous grin covers his face as he pulls off my shoes, one with each hand. "Let go, woman. I've got you."

I'm nervous, and a bit unsure. It's one thing to do it alone, in the shower.

Something else to have an audience, but I'm committed. *Fully.*

I shimmy to the edge of the bed, and he helps me stand. After taking off his shirt, he grasps the hem of my dress.

His eyes ask permission. I nod, biting my lip, lifting my arms. He pulls my dress over my head in one swift jerk and tosses it aside. Never taking his eyes off me.

Holy.

"You're so beautiful." He runs both hands down my side. "So perfect. So damn mine tonight."

I could say the same about him.

If I could find my voice.

Or stop my eyes from roaming down his torso to where the dark crop of hair disappears into the top of his jeans.

"We don't need this, either, do we?" he asks, plucking at my bra straps. "Now, Blue. Show me."

Brazen encouragement flares inside me at the idea of bringing myself off for him. Suddenly, rather than worrying about holding back my climax, I'm excited to bring it, and not just for the release.

I want it to be his.

"Okay," I whisper, pointing to the wooden chest behind him. "You watch."

Growling, he nods. I watch him cross the room, imagining how hard he'll thrust into me soon when I catch an inviting glimpse at his powerful backside.

He sits. I unhook the back of my bra, glad I'd bought the dark blue silk bra and panty set. I lean forward, letting the straps slide off my shoulders, and then down my arms.

The bra drops to the floor. There's definitely a smolder in his eyes when his gaze meets mine. Eager to please – maybe *too* eager – I slide my hands inside my waistband.

I'm not sure if it's him I hear sucking breath, or me.

I'm no longer nervous, but on edge. Eager to put on a show for this man who's driven me insane for weeks.

A sexy show. A tease that'll make him want more.

I push my panties down, slowly, my pussy helplessly tingling as it touches the air. He watches as the panties slide all the way down to my feet, and then meets my gaze again.

"Blue, Show me."

Again, the same mantra. Every time he says it, my body burns a little more. Fire lashes the tips of my fingers, urging them inside me.

With his eyes locked on mine, he unbuttons his jeans, and pushes down his zipper.

That kicks off new chain reactions inside me. I want to see what's hiding there, but this is my show.

I lift a leg, exposing my pussy fully. His eyes lock on, and I wonder if he can see how wet I am. How hard I'm throbbing.

He draws in an audible breath, then lets out a low groan. "Fucking. Show. Me."

The vicious smirk on his face, the way he lifts a brow,

thrills me. I've never been bold about anything. Until now.

"Usually, I do this in the shower," I say.

He cocks his head, never saying a word.

"So my hands are wet." I stick one index finger in my mouth and slowly pull it out. "I'll have to improvise."

His lids lower halfway and the muscles in his neck become more prominent. "Yeah. Improvise."

I slide my fingertip down my torso, between my breasts and lower, getting more of a thrill out of the way he watches the downward movement than from touching myself. Passing through my trimmed bush, I run my fingertip along one side of my pussy. "I start like this...work my way back and forth...then a little side to side."

His hands are on his knees. I watch as his fingers spread out and grip them tighter.

I've never experienced the pleasure erupting inside me. Hot. Wild. Uninhibited.

Hell, I've barely even started.

"Then what, Blue?" Sex fuel. That's what his low, husky growl is.

"More...like this...several times." I brush my clit, heat overloading my core. "Then I find my clit. I press." I have to swallow a gasp before I can add, "Hard."

"Legs wider, babe. Let me see it all."

"Wider," I echo softly. Trying not to burst into flames.

How my voice sounds normal is beyond me. I can barely breathe. I'm sure my movement up the bed is anything but graceful. It doesn't stop me for a second.

I push my bottom as close to the edge as possible while

still being able to plant my heels on the mattress, giving him a full-on view.

Propping myself up with one hand so I can keep watching him, I find my clit again. "Sweet spot. Here," I say, teasing myself, firmly twirling my fingertip. "I work it over. Once in a while, slide my finger inside. Right here." I raise my hips for him to see. "In. Out. Again." I go slowly at first, but the rhythm quickly finds itself.

So does the pleasure.

It comes quicker and hotter than ever. My hips rise and fall against my hand, desperate for friction.

"Talk to me, Blue." I just know he's suppressing a devilish smile.

"Back out, to the clit. Again," I whimper. My breathing is fast, uneven, and words are too difficult.

Oh, God. My head falls back as my climax rushes in. Totally off guard.

"And? Blue?"

I squeeze my eyes shut, fighting to gain enough control to answer. "And – oh!"

A moan overtakes my words. There's no stopping it.

I drop to my elbows, unable to speak as he jumps to his feet. "Since you're done talking, I am, too. Got something better to do with this mouth."

My hand gets pushed aside, replaced by a concentrated heat.

Brent's mouth.

I dig my hand into his hair, then spread my legs wider, giving him full access and loving every fricking nanosecond.

The rush. The fire. Pleasure so intense it almost hurts.

Lifting my hips off the bed, I scream ecstasy as he sucks my clit, lashing it with his tongue again and again.

Drawing me out to the fullest.

Pushing me rudely, sweetly, furiously over.

My thighs shudder. My pussy tightens. A moment later, I hit the climax of climaxes.

Dear fuck – I'm coming!

It consumes my entire body. Unlike usual, when I'm alone, it doesn't end.

Brent keeps going. Licking and sucking and taking me on a ride so wild, so amazing, I'm begging him not to stop.

He keeps his mouth glued to me. His beard grazes my thighs, presses into tender flesh, and his growl echoes up my body. It's too much. Too intense. Too good.

Muscles I didn't know I had seize. Electrified.

I flop against the mattress, convulsing, riding out the ripples of the best O ever.

"Holy. Shit." I mumble two distinct words.

Finally, he lets my thighs drop away from his face.

He gives me a final lick, then pokes his head up between my legs, still running his tongue slowly along his lips. "That was fucking amazing, Blue. Never tasted pussy so sweet."

The heat roars back, this time in my cheeks. I'm drowning in feels.

Happy. Ecstatic. Spent.

I can't do anything except roll my head from side to side, trying to come home. My senses return slowly. He's on the bed. Beside me. Grinning.

"Hope I didn't ruin the show," he says. "And if I did, well fuck, I don't regret it."

I laugh. More of a happy purr, but it gets the point across. I'm too exhausted to do more.

"No choice, Blue. It was either taste you or blow off in my pants like a kid on prom night." He kisses my forehead.

It dawns on me that I'm satisfied, but he's not. *Is he?*

Unsure what to do, I ask, "What now?"

"Now, we fuck," he whispers in my ear while his palm makes large circles on my stomach. "While you're wet and ready. My mouth was just the beginning."

My body leaps to life as his hand works between my legs. His finger slips inside me.

Amazing.

I can feel myself tightening around him as it goes in further, past the knuckle, tantalizing some strange, marvelous spot inside me I can't pin down.

"I'll probably fuck you till sunup, Blue." He twirls his tongue over one of my nipples.

My hips arch. I'm chewing my lip.

Bastard.

He's going to make me come again. And I want to. This time, I'm ready.

I reach between our bodies, finding his hard-on, squeezing through his pants. "Better get your pants off before I finish again."

He laughs and sucks my tit. Finger-fucking me harder.

"I mean it, Eden," I growl this time, a split second before the bliss chokes my tongue quiet.

Heat swirls hard and fast, deep inside me again. It won't take long before I'm gone. I slide my hand inside his boxers, folding my fingers around his cock.

It's velvety soft on the outside, hard underneath.

Naturally, it's huge. What else?

Big and wide and vowing to split me in two.

"Careful, darlin'," he whispers. "I've been ready to bust since we met."

"I know the feeling." I pump his cock. "But I'm one up on you."

He grasps my wrist and pulls my hand off him, then rolls over and slides out of his jeans and boxers with one swift movement. "Have you ever put on a condom before?"

"No."

"Do you want to?"

I sit up and grab a packet out of his hand. "Yes. You're always this prepared?"

"Bought a few at the gas station when I fueled up on our way home."

I laugh, overly pleased. "That was pretty confident of you."

"Optimistic, Blue. That's the right word."

I tear the foil packet open. It's not the first condom I've seen, but comparing the tiny circle of latex to his erect, impressive cock, I question exactly how this works.

His entire body is art. A walking masterpiece, just like I thought that first fateful night in art class.

A perfect palate of sculpted muscle, glistening skin, and dark patches of hair.

All adorned with several mingling tattoos.

Dark eagles and lines of cursive script that look like they're straight from a spell book. I recognize NATALIE near his shoulder, stamped next to a date that has to be her birthday. There's a tangle of barbed wire lower, snaking toward his gorgeous abs, along his side. There's a word anchored in it I'm just able to make out: DAVID. And a date next to it that's more recent.

I don't dare ruin the sexy times by asking pointed questions. Another time.

Once again, I glance between the condom and him. "Show me, maybe. Just this once."

He sits up, kisses me. "Just put it on the head of my cock and roll the edges down."

"Will it fit?"

His laugh comes out so sexy my pussy aches.

"Too good, Blue. You're too fucking good to be true." There's no doubt in his eyes as he guides my hand to his cock, though.

With ease, the latex stretches, covering him fully as I do exactly what he suggests. "That's impressive."

He grabs my shoulders and lowers me back down on the bed. "No, Blue. That's this."

My face heats. Impressive is right.

He's too skilled. He's stolen my ability to think of anything but him.

The way he's touched me. Fingered me. Kissed me all over.

My mouth and neck and breasts.

The heat inside me pulses beyond description. I spread my legs wide.

"Now, Eden," I'm begging. "Please. It's your turn: show me."

Smiling, he reaches between us, guiding the tip of him to my folds. I arch, desperate for a satisfaction I've never known, but want so badly every nerve-ending goes up in flames.

His gaze locks on mine as he slowly eases his way in. First a small amount, and then back out.

The muscles in his neck, his shoulders, are tight. His jaw clenched. But it's the passion in his eyes that captures me fully.

I grip his sides, pulling him forward, pushing backwards as he continues to work his way inside me. I know he's holding back. Being gentle. Allowing my body to conform to his size and rhythm, but I've waited too long.

We've already done it slow.

"Give it to me, Eden. No playing nice. Give. It. All." I arch into his thrust, urging him deeper. The sensation rocks my world.

Growling, he lets go. Pushes into me so fast, so hard, my pussy glides against his cock. Something tears sharply for a split second. Then there's just new heat, pleasure and pain blurring, colliding, owning every piece of me.

Holy hell. I never knew what I was missing.

Being full of him expands my whole universe.

I don't just lay there and let him work. Tightening my hold, I meet every one of his thrusts, digging my nails in his back as our momentum grows. The pace quickens by the second, his hips pounding into mine, frantic and deliciously rough.

Every pummel pushes me deeper into the mattress and gives me the buoyancy to rise up to meet the next.

This is our rhythm.

Hearts and bodies and one raging fire.

Wild and wanton pleasure shuts my eyelids, but I tear them back open, intent on watching him. The wave is coming closer, threatening to swallow both of us. I just know it.

Next time I come, it won't be alone. And the thought makes coming that much quicker.

Witnessing his pleasure is powerful. Captivating. So fucking hot.

"Blue, fuck," he growls, throwing himself into me.

His pubic bone drifts against my clit each time he goes deep. My pussy tightens a little more every time I feel the soft smack of his balls against my flesh.

I'm falling for this cock and it's happening too fast. Much like the man attached to it.

Every thrust sends us closer and closer to a zone I've only dreamed of.

I don't want any of this to end.

Brent captures my mouth with another demanding kiss that shoots me across the point of no return. I go rigid. Cry out. Sign my body over to ecstasy with a squeal, and my pussy clamps down on his cock so hard he loses himself in one long growl.

His body goes rock hard as he slams deep inside me, holds himself there, and something swells deep. "Blue! Come!"

And I do.

I come beyond words. Beyond my wildest imagination.

Somewhere in the inferno, I *feel* his release, his cock pulsing deep inside me.

I'm coming so hard I see stars. And feel them, too. Everything is light and heat.

My toes curl and my fingers pinch his skin. Pure liberation. Spreading through my all.

He grinds against me, milking our climax until there's nothing left to give.

Trying to conquer.

Trying to mark me.

Trying to give and take every single bit of us.

As my delirium slowly subsides, he stamps a parting kiss on my lips and pulls out. I whimper at the sudden emptiness. He laughs, climbing off the bed.

"That good, huh?" There's a smug look in his eye I can't even fight. I just nod.

A moment later, he returns to the bedroom. The condom, gone.

I sigh. "Too bad they're only single use."

He plops on the bed next to me. We're both laying spread eagle. He takes my hand and threads his fingers through mine. "You think I only brought one?"

"Four. I counted," I say, deadpan, trying to act disappointed.

"That's not enough?" His eyes go wide, and then he laughs. "Shit, Blue. We'll pick up more first thing in the morning."

X: WHILE IT LASTS (BRENT)

The sunlight filling the room almost seems as bright as the light in Blue's pale eyes.

Fuck. It wasn't just a dream.

I plant a quick kiss on her lips. It's been ages since I had a night like we'd just experienced. Actually, I've never had one quite like it. Not like this.

Fucking her doesn't leave me wanting to get up and leave the next morning. Doesn't make me want to get on with my life. This woman, in my bed, naked and glorious, is it.

"Morning, Sunshine," I growl, watching her eyelids flutter open.

Her giggle includes a little sigh.

I run a hand across her silky stomach. "How you feeling? Sore?"

I'm still on cloud nine knowing I'm the first man to touch her.

First to show her peaks she never even knew existed in her own skin.

First to make her call my name, coming loud, raking her nails down my back.

Fuck again.

I'd never even thought about stuff like this before, but she's got my brain stuck on it. She also brought me to some heights I'd never seen before – primal satisfaction like no other.

Hell, I blew three times inside her and a fourth time in my hand, spattering her tits. I'm still ready to go again. But I don't want to wear her out.

"What are you going to do if I say yes? To being sore?"

Damn, but she makes me happy. "Kiss you, Crazy. Then go make us some breakfast."

She runs a single fingernail across my chest, which makes my morning wood throb like mad.

"And if I say no?" she asks.

"I'll kiss you." I run my fingers through that strip of hair tucked above her sweet cunt. "Fuck you, and then go make us breakfast."

Smiling, she thrusts a knee between my legs, rubbing my hard-on against her thigh. "Only one condom left."

I slide a finger inside her. "Maybe we'll go to town for breakfast. And grab more."

"I love eating out." Her tongue slides across my bottom lip. "And no, I'm not too sore."

Best damn words I've ever woken up to.

We use up our last condom. I put her down in front of me, on her belly, then draw her hands behind her back. I mount her from behind and fuck like a bull in rut.

She screams after a minute or two of me crashing into her, holding her wrists together, moving my free hand to her hair. Tugging that blue-blonde mess in my fist brings me over after a couple more minutes of rodeo tier thrusting.

I come right in her tight little pussy clenching for dear life. Through the condom, at least, but fuck, of course I imagine what it'd be like to go bare. My seed has an animal need to be inside her.

Someday.

For now, I just come. Come hard, still fucking, not wanting to let up even when my dick softens.

Finally, we take a shower together to save on hot water. Which is all gone by the time we're done. She's still riled up, the little minx. Can't keep her paws to herself. I've never had a woman jack me off before, but hell, I'm more than willing to let her try it.

Anytime.

Breakfast is an old place I remember in Flagstaff. We have big omelets with all the fixings and sausage gravy before popping by the drugstore. With a full box of condoms, we head back to the ranch, and christen the new pack with a hot roll on a blanket in the screened in part of the porch.

For once, I'm thankful the cat isn't around. The sun peaks in the sky and starts drifting lower.

"Shit, it's afternoon. What time's the wedding?" I ask, my chest still heaving after another extremely intense fuck. I don't even have the strength to get up and take care of the condom yet.

"Three o'clock," she says, breathing as hard as me. "But we'll have to get there early enough for Natalie to change into the dress you bought her."

"You're right." It's already after one. "Shit."

She giggles.

I groan.

Snuggling closer, she lays her head on my shoulder. "Will you ever move out here? Full time?"

A flash of darkness overcomes me. "Someday."

Maybe. When the Pearls are finished forever. Can't even think about it till then.

I hold her closer to my side, rubbing her arm. Not wanting to expose her to how dark my thoughts could become if I let them, I kiss her. "When my business can run itself, anything's possible." I smack her sweet ass lightly, loving how it bounces against my hand. "Come on. Up. Gotta get showered and dressed."

"Again?" Blue gives me a knowing wink.

I should be beyond satisfied, but I swear I could take her one more time. Two more. Easily.

Not actually doing it, that's hard. I kiss her forehead. "You go first."

A little pout forms on her lips. "Alone?"

"Blue." I laugh and roll over, pushing myself up. Taking both her hands, I pull her to her feet. "Alone. Or we'll *never* get to that wedding."

She laughs, then plants a quick kiss on my lips, spinning around. I admire her back. That shapely, perfect ass, as she walks into the kitchen and then disappears around the corner.

It's different with her, the admiration. Not like anybody else.

It goes deep. Gets inside me like venom. Like nothing really has.

She's too good, just like I said last night. Too damn unique and then some.

I realize it again later, after I'm showered and dressed,

putting a bowl of cat food outside the door in case Shadow shows up.

"You really are a sweet man."

I turn around at the sound of her voice, nearly losing my ability to speak. Her dress is royal blue, silky, and loose fitting, yet hugs her in all the right places.

The lacy white sweater is unbuttoned and stops above her waist. Her hair hangs in waves over her shoulders. All in all, she looks demure. Innocent.

And once again, I'm struck knowing I'm the only man who's discovered what a wild cat she is underneath that school teacher mirage.

I take a step toward her. It's almost as if I have a split second ripple in my knees.

Crazy.

I've seen hundreds of good-looking women naked in the contraband passed around in the motorcycle club and the army. Bedded dozens in the flesh. But she mops the floor with them. "You're the most beautiful woman I've ever seen."

She dips her chin shyly while shaking her head. "You've already charmed me, Eden." A teasing glint forms in her eyes. "Enough. What more do you want?"

Several sexual innuendos come to mind, but I keep them to myself. They'll only make us late.

Besides, what I'm feeling goes deeper than sex, as fucking ludicrous as it seems. That makes me nervous.

I can't have *deeper*. Not with her. Not with anyone. Not right now.

She holds up a bag with one hand. "I have Nat's things. We better get going."

I take the bag and open the truck door for her, stealing a kiss before closing it.

* * *

ON THE WAY TO TOWN, she fills me in about more family members I'll meet today. I listen, mainly between the lines, noting her tone so I'll know the ones to keep an eye on. The ones who've given her the most grief in the past.

She has no idea I'm picking up on it, taking mental notes.

She apologizes, too. About how I've been caught up in this. If she knew the truth about why I'm here, I'd be the asshole down on my hands and knees, asking her forgiveness.

I want to tell her that the grief is overdone. Under my protection, she's got nothing to worry about, if it were just her family.

But the truth is, her family's antics are nothing compared to the Pearls. I've put her in more danger by keeping her close.

I glance her way. "If you remember right, I'm the one who started all this."

She lets out a sigh. "And never thought it would go this far."

I find a place to park the truck near Joe and Janice's house. After shutting off the engine, I reach over and take her hand. "I'm not sorry it's gone this far."

"You haven't met everyone yet. Just wait. Even mom said it took her years to settle into this family. Now, she fits like a glove."

"Blue," I tug her into me as I lean across the console.

Nose to nose, I say, "I'm a grown boy. I can handle it." I give her a quick, possessive kiss. "Stop worrying."

If only I could take my own advice.

Out of the corner of my eye, I see Nat running up the sidewalk. "Looks like Natalie was watching for us."

Blue spins her head around and I laugh at her reddening cheeks, opening my door. "Hey, baby girl."

"Hi, Daddy! Did you bring my dress?" Two of the girls she'd been playing with last night are with her, dressed in their best.

"Sure did."

"It's right here," Blue says, holding out the bag she's packed. "And I brought along my hair ties so I can French-braid your hair like we talked about."

"Yay! Thanks, Izzy," Nat says. "I told everyone you were going to braid my hair."

Blue glances up at me as I arrive at her side. I knew nothing about the hair braiding and smile at the apology in her eyes. "Go," I say. "I'll save us some seats."

"I already saved them, Daddy," Natalie says. "And Joe says you can join him in the garage for a pre-ceremony beverage."

"Perfect." A drink sounds awfully good right now, honestly.

We walk to the house together, but the girls pull Blue onto the porch and through the door before either of us can say a word.

I walk to the garage, where I recognize a few faces from last night, including Joe, who invites me over to a bar that's been set up for the big day. He introduces me to several other guys.

There are a few lifted brows when Joe says I'm Izzy's

friend. I bite my tongue to keep from saying I'm more than a friend. Totally for their benefit. Let them know straight off I won't stand for a single word spoken against her.

I soon discover the men aren't as hard on her as the women. When she and Nat show up in the garage and the three of us have walked into the back yard to take our seats, the gossip mongers strike.

Whispering and pointing. Blue's ability to ignore them surpasses mine. I don't give them any attention, but they have the hair on my neck standing on end.

When the usher holds out his arm to Blue, I point to Natalie.

He nods and holds his arm out to her. I hook Blue's hand around my arm as we follow the teenager and Nat up the center aisle, between the dozens of chairs we'd set up last night.

It seems much longer ago. Mainly because of the amazing time we had after leaving yesterday.

Nat put our seats next to her newfound friends. She sits beside them. Blue sits next to Nat, and I take the last seat in the row, near the aisle. I drape an arm around her shoulders, hoping this doesn't take long. My mind drifts back to the ranch, last night, this morning. With Blue.

It's typically hot out here. Not as bad as summer, but damn if the daytime heat wants to give up its grip before late October. There's barely a breeze.

I consider rolling up the sleeves of my shirt, but that won't help much. A good portion of the heat overtaking me is internal, too. Last night was hotter than the balmiest 120 degree day in Phoenix.

The little sideways glances beneath her lashes that

Blue keeps sending my way increases the anticipation pumping in my veins. I run my hand over her shoulder and down her back, beneath her silky hair, and lean close to whisper in her ear. "Should we stop for another box of condoms on the way home?"

Her head snaps my way as she puts a finger against her lips. There's also an excited shine in her eyes.

I lean close again. "Should we?"

She puts a hand on my thigh. "Hush."

"I just want to be prepared." I nuzzle her ear.

"Stop," she hisses, smiling anyway.

I kiss her earlobe. "Let me know when you decide."

She shakes her head, but also squeezes my thigh.

The shimmer in her eyes makes me wish we were anywhere but the middle of a wedding. Brutal, insistent ideas of what we'd be doing fill my head and keep on filling it as we sit through dinner later.

I'm counting the minutes till we can leave, knowing we've got hours to go.

The sun sinks lower in the western sky when the dancing begins. The desire to feel Blue's body against mine has been eating at me all afternoon. I lead her onto the dance floor and pull her close. Holding someone in my arms never felt so good. *So right.*

"You certainly are set on keeping tongues wagging, aren't you?" she whispers in my ear.

No shit. Keeping my hands wandering all over her reflects what's been in my head all day. "Can't say I've noticed." I tug her closer, pressing her hips firmly against mine as we sway to the music. "Tell me who said what and I'll take care of them for you."

She buries her face in my shoulder while giggling, and then leans back to look at me.

I kiss her lips. Gently, but long enough for her to know what later promises.

Our lips barely part when someone taps her shoulder. It's the bridesmaid from last night.

"May I cut in?"

Blue's hand slips off my shoulder as she attempts to step back. I see the disappointment in her eyes and tighten my hold, keeping her planted against me. "No," I say.

Blue has more manners. "Sorry, Pam," she says to the other woman.

The bridesmaid walks away and Blue shakes her head. "I don't think that's what she expected."

I couldn't care less. "Too bad. Only got one date I'm interested in tonight." Running my hand up and down her back, I nip at her earlobe. "I didn't want to shock her, anyway."

She leans back again to look me in the face. "Shock her?"

"Yeah." I thrust harder against her. "Tell me you don't feel how hard I am right now."

"Oh!" Her brows lift. "Not surprised. Considering all the things you've been whispering in my ear all day."

"Would you rather I drew pictures? I can, and you know it. Show you exactly what we'll do when we get home." I grind against her. "What we're going to do." I grasp a handful of her ass. "In vivid detail."

She kisses the side of my neck. "I've seen your drawings. I *know* the details you like to include."

"But you'd rather have the real thing."

"So real."

Fuck, her voice. I'm so hard it's torture. "When can we leave?"

The music ends and Blue glances across the room. "Once Nat's ready, I guess."

Since the day she was born, I've always put my daughter first, but right now, seeing how much fun she's having, and knowing she wouldn't want that to end anytime soon, I clamp my teeth together to hold in a growl.

A moment later, as I lead Blue back to our table, Cleo's smile gives me hope. And an idea.

Within fifteen minutes, Blue and I are heading for my truck. Alone. Both Cleo and Natalie were happy with the thought of Nat spending another night at the house. So am I.

As soon as we arrive at the ranch, I walk around the house and start piling kindling in the fire pit.

"What are you doing?"

I smile at the confusion in Blue's voice. Although I'm helpless how my body begs for release, my cock screaming for me to fuck her hard and fast, I'm holding out.

I've got no clue when we'll be alone together again and I'll make the absolute most of the next few hours.

Running a hand down her arm, I say, "I thought we could sit out here for a while."

The bewilderment crossing her face looks adorable. "Why?"

I kiss the tip of her nose and turn back to the fire pit. "Why not?"

Biting my jaw tight at how she mutters, 'Why not?' I

set flame to the wood, and once the fire's going, add a couple larger logs.

She's sitting in one of the chairs. I pat her shoulder as I walk past. "Wait here. I'll be right back."

Excitement of what's to come puts a beat in my step as I head inside the house and collect several items. Back at the fire, I hand her one of the canned margaritas I'd taken out of the fridge, then spread the blanket on the ground and drop the pillows.

"Plan on being out here a while, do you?" She pops open the top of her can and takes a swallow.

I sit down on the blanket and open a can of beer. "You ever slept beneath the stars, Blue?"

"No."

"That's one of the things out here that makes putting up with the Arizona heat worth it. Clear skies." I pat the blanket beside me. "Come the hell here."

She kicks off her shoes before stepping onto the blanket and then sits down next to me. "You plan on sleeping out here, too?"

I shrug. "Maybe." Anticipation is winning. I suck a few gulps from my beer, set it aside, and kick off my boots. "That'll depend on if we're interested in sleep or not."

She flicks her tongue over her bottom lip, watching me unbutton my shirt. Blue sets her can on the ground. "Need some help?"

"Would you like to help?"

She nods and scoots closer. "You know I would."

I love how open she is with me, how trusting and uninhibited. I pull my hands off my shirt and hold them up in the air. "Be my guest. Undress me."

She laughs. "Is that an invite to do whatever I please?"

My dick lets me know how it feels about that. "Sure," I say. "Whatever you please, Blue. Long as it gets me hard."

Her grin turns mischievous as she finishes undoing my shirt and tugs it wide open. "Let's see," she says. "I think it'll please me to see you shirtless, so I can examine each of those glorious tattoos." She pushes the shirt off my shoulders. "And kiss them."

Her breath is hot and damp against my skin. My cock throbs harder with every little kiss she plants on my chest. Fuck.

This woman will be the end of me. And maybe the beginning, too.

Her weight moves me up the blanket. My lungs catch as her kisses twist down my stomach. I'm hard enough to cut diamond.

"Oh, my," she says, rubbing her hand down the front of my jeans. "It'll please me, Brent, to see what's gotten so hard under here."

Fuck yeah. She's right.

It'll please me to the moon.

My jaw tightens at how hard I have to fight to maintain control as she unbuckles my belt, and then unzips my jeans. The throb of my cock matches the pounding echo in my ears.

"I knew it," she whispers, pushing down my boxers, freeing my cock to spring upright. "They're too tight for something so big."

A growl bubbles up my throat as she grasps hold of my dick, stroking softly. My balls go nuclear.

"Don't you like it?" she whispers, eyeing me sideways.

Before I growl agreement, she bends, moving lower.

"Maybe *this* is better."

Her lips, hot and heavenly, suck the head of my cock before she pulls me fully into her mouth. My hips rise, thrusting my length deeper through her lips.

I love how her sweet heat engulfs inch after throbbing inch.

Blue tugs down the waistband of my jeans, grasping my ass as she proceeds to suck. It's some kind of sex miracle. First time she's done this – I think – and it's the best fucking blow job known to man.

It's so stunningly good I'm about to lose it, but don't want to. Tonight's for both of us. Grabbing both sides of her head, I force her to stop. "Enough."

Her lips smack as they release my cock. "You don't want more?"

"More, yes." The pressure behind my cock is practically killing me. "I want to fuck you, Blue. My dick inside your pussy. Fast and hard. Now."

"Please," she whispers, helping me pull her dress over her head. "Hope you remembered the condoms."

My jeans are down around my thighs. "In my pants pocket."

She finds one, and as she rips it open, I unhook her bra. Her nipples are dark pink, shadows dancing across them in the fire's light.

Like they're calling me. I pull her forward to suck on one, flicking the hard nub with my tongue.

"I can't put this on while you're doing that!" she says.

I stop long enough to ask, "You can't?"

"No-ohhh!"

Her answer becomes a moan as I take her other tit in my mouth. No stopping now.

I stick my hands inside her panties and push them

over that perfect ass of hers. She shifts enough to get one leg free. All I need to work my fingers inside her. Her pussy is slick, wet, and my cock jolts instantly. It's killing me not to shred what's left of her panties and push the fuck in her.

Still, I work her folds, press her clit, twirl two fingers deep inside her. Love the way she groans, huskily calls me Eden, begs me to continue.

Too bad she's able to form too many words. I fix that, running my fingers deeper, finding the spot against her wall that makes her whole body arc like a cat in heat.

Ground zero. My fingers go wild, frigging her to Heaven.

Her breath comes faster and she pumps against my hand. Much as I'd love to make her cum right now, the pressure building at the base of my spine is too strong to ignore.

I give her nipple a final nibble before growling, "Now, Blue. Put that condom on."

She's nearly an old hand at rolling the condom over my cock, and a moment later, she's straddling me, lowering her hot wet pussy over me.

It's almost so good I lose it. I've never fought back a climax this hard in my life.

Damn if it stops me from taking what's mine. Vigorously.

We both let out satisfying groans as I completely fill her, and then start moving. The friction shreds my soul. I grasp her hips, pulling her down, against every upwards thrust.

Faster and faster and faster and fuck!

We're both so fucking close it's painful.

She has her head thrown back, blue hair flying. Her body quakes. Lips frozen in a half-open pout as she shouts my name.

I thrust upwards, hard, and let out a bearish groan as her pussy clenches. Her body shudders as her climax lets loose.

My own hits so savagely I'm stunned.

Gloriously senseless as her pussy locks tight, sucking every last come jet out of my balls.

It's so fucking good I'm lost to anything but her.

But *this*.

She collapses on top of me later, gasping for air. As breathless as she is, I hold her tight, my dick still buried inside her, until we're able to breathe again.

"Holy crap," she says. "Eden, you beast."

I laugh, kissing the top of her head, running my teeth playfully through a strand of hair.

She pushes off and kisses me as our bodies separate. I help her roll onto her back and then toss the condom in the fire.

"Won't the bugs bite us out here?" she asks.

"Fire should keep most of them at bay. No ants. Only seen scorpions three or four times in all the years I've been here." I roll over to lean across her. "If your worried, I'll take top next round."

She loops one arm around my neck and meets my lips for a slow kiss. "Okay."

Each night with her gets better than the last. Something I'd never have believed possible if I hadn't actually experienced it. We don't spend the whole night outside after all because a brief rain blows through.

Just enough to wake us so we move inside. The double

bed encourages a quickie before we both drift away again. Exhausted.

* * *

"What are you grinning about?"

I set the cooler in the back of the truck. "Memories from last night."

Her blush makes me laugh. This crazy, beautiful woman has two sides: kitten in the light of day and wild cat at night.

Wouldn't have it any other way.

"This it?" I ask, taking the bag from her.

"Yeah, looks like everything."

I shut the tailgate and tug her close for a kiss. "I try to get up here once a month." Not sure exactly how to let her know I want her to join me, I ask, "Interested in coming up again sometime?"

She smiles before dropping her eyes to the ground. Fuck. The second the question left my mouth, I knew we had a problem. "Brent, we should talk about..."

"Us?"

She nods. "There can't be an us. Not back home, anyway."

I knew that's been on her mind the past few hours. The rules of the academy. Been like lead on mine, too. I take her hand and lead her back to the house for a final walk-through before locking the doors.

"Let's not tempt trouble," I say.

Lord knows I have enough of that waiting for me. Damned sure don't need any more. Even though I know I'll have to face my trouble, in full, head-on one day soon.

So will she if anyone at the school learns we've spent the weekend together. That's the part that bothers me.

Her having to face career consequences – ridiculous. Whether she's Nat's teacher or not, it shouldn't have anything to do with who she chooses to date.

And it's not like we're dating, but after this weekend, I won't be able to go long without seeing her.

I'm still cursing inwardly as I make the final rounds. The house is in order, right down to the freshly made beds. We'd washed the linens while eating lunch.

"Ready?"

She nods and walks out the front door. I follow, locking the door, then take a hold of her hand as we head for the pickup.

It's a solemn ride home. We talk, but not about anything serious.

I know she's worried, but refrain from telling her to stop.

"You can just drop me off at my apartment." Blue looks at me as we enter the outskirts of Phoenix.

"You don't want to see your ma when she drops Nat off?" Cleo and I made that our plan last night, that she'd drop my daughter off at my house at five this evening.

"I'll talk to her," Blue says. "But then you'll have to give me a ride home later and Natalie will probably be ready for bed."

She's right, damn it. I'm just not ready to be done yet. "I'm sure she won't mind riding with to give you a ride home."

Her gaze remains out the side window as she answers, "Probably not, but she's had a busy weekend and needs a good night's rest before school. She has art class tomorrow night, so it'll be a long day for her. And me."

She's right about that part, too. I take the exit towards her apartment. Her car is in her parking space, and I pull up behind it since there aren't any other open spaces.

"I'll get your bag."

"No need." She opens her door. "I'm on it."

I grab her arm as she's climbing out. "I'm walking you up to your apartment, so there's no use trying to stop me."

She's trying hard not to smile. "Fine."

Because it's still daylight and I have no idea who might be watching, I release her and open my door. I grab her bag out of the back and follow her to the door. Then up the stairs.

The hallway feels balmy as ever and I catch a whiff of something sour. Her nose wrinkles, too. "Christ, what is that?"

"Don't know, never smelled it before," she says. "But it stinks."

"Almost smells like...rotten fish," I say, as she's unlocking her door.

The instant her door swings open, the stench assaults us full blast. Holy Moses.

We both cough, covering our mouths and noses with one hand. I push her aside to step in first, wondering what, or who, died in here.

Shit. It's not just a joke.

Both her large fish tanks are shattered. Shriveled and dead, fish and plants are scattered across the light-colored carpet.

Fuck. The Pearls.

I spin around at her gasp, then at the wall behind me

because that's where she's staring, her eyes practically glued to it. A picture hangs above the couch, her and her mother.

Someone wrote TEASE, BITCH, WHORE on the wall, with arrows pointing towards Blue.

I fight the urge to put my fist through it.

"Jesus. You...you told me there was something dead in here," she whimpers, still in shock.

"Dead's right," another voice says.

I step forward and pull Blue against my chest before turning to the door. The old man from across the hall stands there, looking as ornery as before, as well as a younger guy, staring straight at Blue.

He steps forward. "Ms. Derby, are you all right?"

As I tighten my hold on Blue, a stab of jealousy hits me like no other. There's way too much concern, too much want on this man's face for my liking. "Who the fuck are you?" I snarl.

Blue stiffens and pushes against my chest while taking a single step backwards. "He's the building manager. Scott Riker."

"I told you something was dead in here, Riker," the old man repeats. "Been stinking like a damn latrine for the last two days."

"Go back to your apartment, Mr. Barrett," Riker says, but his gaze never leaves me. "Who are you?"

Keeping Blue close to my side, I say it loud and clear, "Her fiancé."

Her eyes widen, but not in surprise.

More like they want to say *not again.*

Riker eyeballs me suspiciously, until he catches a glimpse of the wall behind me. "Whoa. What happened?"

"Obviously, the place was broken into." With a gesture towards the door, I add, "Those ten dollar locks on the doors in this place can be shimmied open with a credit card."

"Have you called the police?" Riker asks.

"We just walked in," I point out.

"I'm calling them right now," the old man says with a phone at his ear.

Riker spins around and grabs the man's phone. "Give me that, please." A moment later, he steps in the hall, "Yes, I need to report a break-in..."

"Did you hear anything? See anything?" I ask the old man.

"No, just got a whiff of something dead a few nights ago." The old man points a thumb over his shoulder. "Called Riker. He said he'd check on it, but never did."

Blue keeps trembling hard. I spin her around and escort her into the bedroom, away from the hell-stench. I give the room a solid once over before I lead her to the bed. The room looks untouched, so I sit her down, kneeling in front of her. "Breathe, Izzy. Just breathe."

She nods, then shakes her head. "Who would do such a thing? My poor fish..."

I squeeze her hands. "The police will find out. I'll stay on them till they have answers."

She closes her eyes and swallows hard. "There's only one person I can think of: Preston."

I nod grimly, but wonder if it was really him, or the Pearls trying to get my full attention.

There's a knock on the wall beside the open door. It's Riker.

"Police are on their way. I'm going down a floor to see

if there's any ceiling damage in that apartment, but I'll be right back."

"Thank you," Blue says with a meek smile.

I still don't like how he looks at her, so remain silent until he leaves. Then, I nod towards her closet. "Pack your things."

"What things?"

"Whatever you need," I say, just as my phone rings. "You aren't staying here." Glancing at the phone, I tell her, "It's your mother."

"Don't tell her!" Blue jumps to her feet. "Nothing, Brent. Not a thing. I'll never hear the end of it."

I answer the phone and listen to Cleo explain they're running late and won't have Natalie to my house until after six. I tell her that's fine and hang up.

I gesture towards the closet again, certain Blue isn't done putting up a fight about where she's staying. "You either stay with me, or your mother. Your choice."

She opens her mouth, but a shout from the other room interrupts her.

"You in there, the fiancé?" the old man says from the living room. "Come take a look at this."

"Coming." I tell her, "Start packing."

"You can't tell me what –"

"Blue?"

"Brent, it isn't –"

"Pack, babe. Now."

She turns around in a huff.

"I'm only saying what the police will tell you." Having already witnessed her hard-headedness, I add, "For your own safety, they'll suggest you stay somewhere else for a few days. Common procedure."

I walk out of the bedroom. In the living room, the old man stops near the remnants of the broken fish tanks. "Don't touch anything," I tell him.

"Yeah, yeah, I know better." He points to the floor. "Look at the hammer laying there. Bet that's what was used to smash the tanks. Pretty dumb to leave it behind, don't you think?"

"That's *my* hammer," Blue says stepping up beside me. "Weird. It's usually in the kitchen drawer."

I grab her arm as she starts walking forward. "We can't touch anything in here until the police arrive." Glancing around, I notice the lamps are on. Even weirder.

I hadn't flipped any switches. I'm sure of it. And I walked in before her, so she hadn't either, which means whoever did this, did it at night.

My stomach knots at the thought of what may have happened had she been home. Last week, after realizing I couldn't keep following her, I'd paid one of Juan's cousins to, but only until she'd arrived home for the night.

"I have to clean up this mess," she says. "The entire building will start stinking."

"I'll send over a crew first thing in the morning," I say. Looking her in the eye, I ask, "So, which is it, Blue? Your mother's place or mine?"

XI: ELEPHANT IN THE ROOM (IZZY)

I keep my trembling hands in my lap beneath the table while mother paces Brent's kitchen.

"Who on earth would do such a thing?" she says again. "Destroy someone's property like that? Kill their fish?"

"The police are looking into it," Brent says. "Probably just vandals."

Thankfully, he's only told her someone broke into my apartment and smashed the fish tanks. The loss of the fish didn't scare me as badly as the writing on the walls. I see those devil words every time I close my eyes.

TEASE. BITCH. WHORE.

"Well, I'm so glad that you'll be staying here, darling," Mother says. "I hate the idea of you being alone. I can stay home, too, if you'd prefer. If you need a hand with –"

"No," I say sharply. "You go to Vegas with George, Mom. There's nothing you can do here."

Brent's phone rings. After glancing at the screen, he walks out the sliding door, closing it tight before answering.

Mom sighs and the look on her face tells the world what she thinks of Brent. "Such a wonderful man, Izzy. I'm so glad he was with you this evening. He's exactly what you need. Strong. Solid. Caring. Handsome..."

I stop listening to her long litany celebrating my Not Fiancé, however true.

Brent is all those things. But this is a clusterfuck.

It's living a lie. One that can't continue.

I was set to go to mother's house, even though I knew it'd be hellish, until she said she and George are heading up to Vegas tomorrow for a car show. I really don't want to be alone, but I can't stay here. I'll lose my job for sure. And though Brent and I had some amazing sex the past couple of days, that doesn't mean we're meant to live together. Even if there's a new reason.

Brent walks back in and I curse my heart. It jumps way too noticeably when he's near.

Ridiculous. I don't need that any more than I need the rest of this insanity.

If only I'd known what a mess signing up for an online dating site and having one date with a first class douchebag could cause...

I stand to give mom a hug and assure her I'll be fine. Brent walks her to the front door and yells upstairs for Natalie to come down and say goodbye.

Fine. I wait in the kitchen.

Brent and mother are talking, saying I'll be okay. I will be. As far as the break-in goes.

I walk to the patio door, stare out into the darkness that's settled over the desert.

What scares me, what really shakes me up, is being here.

At his house.

After what happened this weekend.

I could fall in love. I'm more than halfway there, honestly, and I can't be.

I've worked too hard to get what I want. A job at the academy.

I can't throw it all away for a man I barely know.

My heart skips a beat, telling me he's near even before I see his reflection in the glass. I close my eyes to his smile. If only it was so easy to shut out everything else.

His warm hands gently settle on my arms, and then he caresses my skin so softly my insides melt. What should be sweetness hurts.

I take a step away. "We can't do this."

"You can't stay alone, Blue."

"If the school finds out, I'll be fired. You know that."

He shrugs. "No job's worth your life. You're a smart lady. You've got to know that."

There's frustration in his voice. I'm frustrated, too. And pissed.

I spin around to face him. "Haven't you ever wanted something, Brent? Wanted it so bad you worked day and night?"

"It's a job." He shakes his head. "A fucking teaching job. There has to be a thousand others. Jobs come and go. Can't replace your life, Blue."

"To *you*. To me, it's the job. A dream that actually came true." I twist away from him, as flustered with myself as I am with his lecture.

No one else has ever understood, so there's no reason he should either, I suppose. Art was the only thing I could focus on after dad died. The only thing no one could take away.

Brent's arms fold around me from behind, and as badly as I want the comfort, I can't accept it.

Not from him. If only he was anyone else. Someone who didn't have a connection to the academy.

"I'll talk to Jacobs."

I shake my head. "And tell him what? That you're my fiancé? That seems to be your standard answer and what got us in trouble in the first place." I step out of his hold and turn around. "Besides…I don't want to be your pretend fiancée. Don't want to be anyone's pretend anything."

He stares at me. "I get it, Blue. But you have to know, I wasn't pretending this weekend, and I don't believe you were either."

I wasn't, but can't admit it. "This weekend has nothing to do with any of this."

His glare grows icy. "You're right. It doesn't." He gestures down the hallway. "Your things are in the bedroom across from Nat's and your car will be here by the time you need to leave in the morning."

He walks out of the room. I slump against the counter. What the fuck is wrong with me?

Seriously? I just spent the last four days with this man, loving every minute, and now, when I want nothing more than to feel his arms around me again, I push him away.

He's right and wrong. Both simultaneously.

It's just a job. But it's also my everything, just like I told him. A chance to put me on the fast track to the goal I set many tumultuous years ago.

I push myself off the counter and head upstairs.

Natalie comes out of her room just as I arrive at the door across the hall.

"I'm sorry someone broke into your apartment, Izzy," she says, "but I'm happy you're staying here with us."

I give her a hug. "Thank you." Not wanting to get her hopes up, I say, "My apartment should be ready for me to move back in just a couple days. I shouldn't be here long."

"I know. Dad told me. I just want you to know I'm happy that you're here."

My heart takes a tumble. Of course, he told her.

This isn't what he wants either.

Maybe his reasons are different – they must be – but he knows how crazy this is.

I tell Nat goodnight and spend a restless night trying to figure out why Brent keeps letting things go as far as they have. I don't mean the sex. I mean agreeing to be my pretend boyfriend. Vowing to protect me. Practically telling me he won't take no for an answer.

He might be a nice guy, with the background to make good on his strongman promises, but no one's *that* nice.

What the hell?

Sure, he loves his daughter, but I can't believe he's doing all this just for her sake, either. There has to be more behind it.

But what?

* * *

HE'S in the kitchen the next morning, looking far too handsome this early. He's wearing nothing more than a pair of pajama pants. Their tight cut makes me remember the weekend mornings all too well.

"Coffee?"

I shake my head. "I'll get some on the way to school."

He sets down his cup. "I'm not blind, Blue. I get this has gone farther than we ever anticipated, but –"

"No, buts," I say. "I'll go straight to my mom's after work tonight."

"No, you won't. That call I took last night was from a captain in the sheriff's department. He's bringing the papers by tonight for an Order For Protection against Preston Graves. I told him to be here at five. So you'll still make it to your art class this evening."

I'm full of protests, but know they'll be a waste of breath and time. "Are the keys in my car?" I'd given them to Riker last night, for Juan to collect, and deliver my car to Brent's.

He digs in his pocket and sets them on the counter.

I pick them up and leave the house. The gut sense that came to me last night, that there's more going on, is stronger than ever this morning. I just can't make sense of it now.

Later, I will.

The day is a total circus. Four days of vacation this early in the year disrupts the routine I'd spent weeks instilling in the preschoolers. There are tears, bathroom accidents and temper tantrums that leave me euphoric when 2:30 finally rolls around.

I've just finished saying goodbye to the last student when the phone on the wall rings. Intuition hits hard, telling me who it is even before I hold the receiver to my ear.

"Ms. Derby?" Sally Jones says. "Mr. Jacobs would like to see you in his office."

ACCIDENTAL HERO

"I'll be there soon. Thanks." Amazing how calm I sound. Dread pricks my entire body.

I collect my things and leave the classroom. I've never been fired before, so don't know exactly how it happens.

Natalie sits in the front office when I get there, tears in her eyes. "I didn't want to tell him we went to the wedding with you, but Mr. Jacobs made me. I'm sorry."

Anger boils inside me as I wrap my arms around her. Whatever I expected from the principal, it isn't this. "You didn't do anything to be sorry about," I whisper. "Nothing at all."

Behind her desk, Sally Jones gives me a nod and then glances towards Mr. Jacobs' office. I'm beyond pissed that he made Natalie cry. "I'll be back shortly," I tell her.

I enter the Principal's office, and as I'm closing the door, I say the first thing that comes to mind, "Brent Eden is going to be furious when he finds out you interrogated his daughter."

He nods slowly, as if unaffected by what I'd just said. "Then perhaps Mr. Eden, and you, should have been honest with me from the beginning, Ms. Derby." Sitting down, he points towards the chair in front of his desk. "Have a seat. I'll get to it. You came so highly recommended. I'd be extremely disappointed to have to let you go, so I suggest we consider this a warning in the strongest possible terms –"

If his office door opening with a bang doesn't interrupt him, Brent's angrily distorted face does.

No denying it. That badass attitude I thought was a grand charade exists.

The door slams shut and in two steps Brent slaps a hand on the desk hard enough to knock over a photo.

"Who the fuck do you think you are? What I do, what my daughter does, outside of this school, is no business of yours."

"Now, Mr. Eden, listen here, I –"

"No, you listen. If you and your fucking academy cared more about your teachers and students than you do your rules and regulations, you'd have had Preston Graves charged for breaking and entering." Brent slams a hand on the desk again. "But you didn't. So, that slimy little bastard breaks into Ms. Derby's apartment, destroys her stuff, kills her fish, and leaves her no choice but to file a restraining order against the bastard. And what are you worried about? If she's fraternizing with a student and her old man outside of school? How fucked up is that?"

Jacobs looks shocked. "He-he broke in to –"

"Yeah. Just a couple days ago," Brent answers. "Tore the place up."

"Well, this is a new development, I hadn't heard –"

It's hard not to smile, watching Jacobs go pale with a thousand ugly legal implications invading his head.

"Then listen good. Right now." Brent waves a hand towards me. "If Ms. Derby can't be friends with my family outside of school because Nat's a student, then I'll pull her out. I'll raise hell for a refund. And I'll make sure everybody knows this place puts red tape over real safety. There are plenty of other schools just as good as this one."

I jump to my feet. "You can't do that!"

"No, there aren't!" Jacobs says at the same time.

"I can," Brent says to me before turning to Jacobs. "And there are." Brent sets both hands on the desk and leans towards Jacobs. "Last chance, bub. You'd better get a handle on what you're trying to cover up with this rules bullshit, or I'll expose your dirty laundry. Every damn bit of it."

The air goes so still a shiver tickles my spine.

Jacobs goes bone white as he slowly lowers himself onto his chair.

Brent straightens. "I'm sure you'll have a change of heart. Agree Ms. Derby's done nothing to put her employment here in jeopardy. And once you've apologized to her, you owe my daughter one, too."

Jacobs nods.

The next few minutes, which include the apologies Brent demanded, are subdued. I can't help but question what sort of cover up Brent kept referring to.

If it was just rules, which every parent agrees to when they enroll their kids, the academy would have the upper hand. Jacobs wouldn't be scared out of his skin. I don't ask until after we're all at his place, later.

"I have no idea," Brent says. "It was the only thing that made sense. Calling the bastard's bluff with one of my own. It worked. Probably a few laws on the books that would've landed him in hot water over you and Graves, the break-in, giving a predator access to the school. Hell of a lot worse than his dumbass rules with you and me."

We're in the kitchen and Natalie's upstairs. I'm still suspicious. "All schools have rules about teacher and student relationships."

"Which they need to, but Jacobs blew this one out of proportion."

I step closer to the kitchen island separating us. "And what about you? Didn't you blow up, too? Threatening to send her elsewhere?"

"No." He leans across the island, laying a hand on

mine. "I was telling the truth. Don't know why you love that school so much, but you do, and if it means you losing your job, then fuck yes, I'll send Nat to another school."

I try to pull my hand out from under his, but he grasps it tight.

"That's what Natalie would want, too," he says softly. "No lie."

I shake my head, heart sinking to depths of confusion I never knew existed. "No. I'd never allow that to happen."

He keeps his tense hold on my fingers as he walks around the edge of the island. Stopping in front of me, he takes my other hand. "Just like I won't allow Jacobs to bully you."

Damn!

The question I'd asked myself all night comes out. I can't hold it in any longer.

"Why?" I shake my head. "Why are you doing all this, Brent? It doesn't make sense."

I can't pull my eyes off him, and also realize just how over my head I am in all of this. Pure instinct is what kept me going last weekend. Instinct and pleasure. *Unbelievable* pleasure.

It was a game. Mindless fun.

Back here, in Phoenix, it's real life, and it's far from carefree. I've never done anything like this, and don't know what to do. If there are rules for this sort of thing, or not.

"Does this make better sense?" he asks, moments before his lips meet mine.

The kiss is so soft, so sweet and gentle, my insides melt at the same time a fire sparks.

He does that.

Makes me forget everything except how perfect we can be.

It can't keep happening. It's not the answer to any of this.

It takes all my effort to pull away. "No. None of this makes sense. You didn't want to be my prop, my pretend boyfriend. You said –"

"I *know* what I said, Blue." He frames my face with both hands. "And I thought you knew I meant it at the time."

"Thought?"

"I was attracted to you before." His fingers comb my hair. "You saw the pictures I drew. From the moment I met you, I couldn't get you out of my head. Still can't. Shit happened. Drew us together. Still happening."

That's true, but it's no answer. "Okay, fine, but –"

"Quiet. You're putting too much thought into this, Blue." He kisses my forehead. "You no longer have any worries over losing your job. So let's just go slow and see what happens."

Again, he's right, but I'm still not convinced. Maybe because I've always been wary of relationships. Seen too many broken hearts.

Maybe the job at the academy wasn't my ultimate goal. Or maybe it was just an excuse to not have to be in a relationship of any kind.

"It's too much," I say loudly. "All of this. It's just too, well...complicated."

He slides his hands down to my shoulders. There's a simple answer in his touch that makes my blood seethe. "Doesn't have to be. Quit thinking. Stop doubting. Saying we're impossible before we're even anything."

"Jesus, it's not like that. How can we be? The school. My family." I shake my head, battling back tears. "It's gone too far, too fast."

"We'll slow down then," he says. "Set boundaries."

"Boundaries?"

He nods. He's trying so hard. "You name them."

"Well." I step back so I can think. It's harder than it should be while he's touching me. My mind becomes focused on only one thing then. "No more charging into the Principal's office and pounding his desk like a Neanderthal, for one."

"Okay." He shrugs.

He agrees so fast I haven't had time to think of anything else, other than how badly I want him to kiss me again, and then do a few other choice things. This *is* impossible, however he wants me to think otherwise. Staying here with him. "And no kissing," I say.

He lifts a single brow. "Bull."

"Not in front of Natalie, I mean." I bite my tongue softly, but it's too late. I can't stop a strained smile.

"Whatever, fair enough," he says. "Anything else?"

Nothing comes to me. How could it when he's staring. Knowing I want more than kisses. "I'll let you know when I think of something else."

He steps forward and touches the end of my nose with one finger. "Got it."

Walking toward the hall, he gives me a wink. "I'll order a pizza for supper while you do your thinking. That shit always makes me hungry enough to eat a water buffalo."

Flustered because I'm not sure I gained any ground, I yell after him, "No anchovies!"

He laughs.

I spin around and consider banging my head against the countertop. The marble countertop.

Despite all this tension and heart-to-heart madness, I'm no closer to finding out the truth. The missing piece that's hanging in the air between us. Invisible and omnipresent like dark matter.

There *has* to be more than meets the eye here. I feel it in my bones. Deep down.

Has to be more for him wanting to be my boyfriend so bad. Pretend or not. Attraction aside.

It's not like I've had guys lined up out the door. The only reason I signed up for that dating app was because I knew Megan's wedding was just around the corner.

No, I hadn't known *which* corner, but they'd been looking at rings since Christmas, so it was inevitable. I'd just wanted a man by then. A 'man friend,' as mom would say.

Nothing more than that.

Instead, I accidentally ordered up a fucking psycho. Preston.

Who I'm rescued from by a dream come true. A complicated, overprotective beast with a heart of gold under his fuck-the-world exterior. A man who also might have the best dick on the planet, which I'm now telling myself I can't play with.

Fucking idiot. Crazy. That's what I am.

That's what he does to me.

That's what this is.

I'm still in the depths of chiding myself when the doorbell rings. A moment later, voices and footsteps sound in the hallway. It's too soon to be the pizza man.

I step away from the counter and try to busy myself at

the sink, getting a glass of water. Which I damn near choke on when I recognize the stocky cop standing beside Brent.

"Izzy, this is Captain Bob Dawson from the sheriff's department," Brent says. "He's brought the paperwork for you to sign for the OFP."

Oh, we've met.

He's the one who gave me a ticket weeks ago. And was extremely rude about it.

I'm hoping the captain doesn't remember my face, but considering my car in the driveway, there really isn't much hope.

"Hello, Captain Dawson," I say, trying not to grit my teeth.

"Ms. Derby." He gives a shallow nod. Then he sets some papers on the counter and pulls a pen out of his shirt pocket. "If you'll just complete these forms, and sign them, I'll have them sent to the judge promptly."

"Thank you." I take the pen and slide the papers closer.

Brent and the Captain talk while I read the instructions and check the appropriate boxes. I'm in the midst of explaining what happened at my apartment in as few words as possible when the doorbell rings again.

Brent excuses himself to go get the pizza.

The captain steps over and leans against the island. My nerves are already shot, and his closeness makes my spine ice up.

I really don't like this man. Something weird about him. Police officers are supposed to make you feel safe. With him, it's the opposite.

"How long have you known Brent Eden?" he asks, glancing at the lines I've completed.

It's hard not to turn and look him in the eye. I don't think that's anyone's business and keep my attention on the papers. "A while."

"Did you know his brother? David?"

I don't glance up. "No."

"Ah. Just curious. Brent's done a lot of work for the department, and I've known him for years. It's too bad what happened to Dave."

I'm curious, but don't dare ask. Not with that strange, soft edge in his voice.

I sign the last page and slide them all over to him. "Done, officer. Anything else you need from me?"

Brent and Nat enter the room, chattering away. Thank God. Natalie sets the pizza box on the counter.

"Got all I need right here, Brent," the captain says. "I'll head out now. Better get at that pizza before it gets cold."

Brent walks him outside while Natalie and I set the table.

She's still a bit subdued, so I turn the subject to the pizza, pretending I've never had Mike's before. Her demeanor changes instantly, and by the time Brent returns, we're laughing and comparing local pizza joints.

After we eat, Brent insists on driving us both to the school and sits in the back of the room the entire time. By the time we get home, the stress of the last two days is dragging on me.

I go upstairs, take a bath, and then crawl into bed. I hear Brent come upstairs. I don't want to imagine how comforting it would be to flop down next to him, feel those strong arms wrap around me. But tonight's not the night or the place for it.

I shouldn't be so selfish. This isn't easy on him, either.

He's as stressed as I am. I can tell.

Even though I'm tired, I know I won't be able to sleep, so I pull out my tablet to read. I don't get far. None of the books I've downloaded hold my attention tonight, so I open up my web browser, and before I even realize it, I'm typing David Eden into the search bar.

There are plenty of people by that name, and I only need to pay nine dollars and ninety-nine cents to shady background sites to learn all about them.

Snorting, I narrow my search. Including Brent's name in quotes helps, but the only things that come up are Davey's obituary on several different websites.

That creepy cop is why I'm more curious now than before. Why in God's name did he ask me about Brent's dead brother?

It makes no sense and it's eerie as hell. I don't just dislike Captain Dawson. He freaks me out.

I sigh, shutting off the tablet. "You don't like him because he gave you a ticket," I whisper to myself. It's not very reassuring. "Just go to sleep. Stop trying to make a mountain out of every molehill..."

An hour later, I'm still wide awake, and seriously contemplating sneaking down the hall to Brent's bedroom, apologizing for being so foolish earlier, and begging him to let me crawl into his bed. Preferably naked.

It's wrong, but there are a few walls between his room and Nat's. If we're careful, there isn't a chance we'll wake her.

The click of the door opening has me sitting up, and the dark silhouette that appears in the doorway a second later sends my heart soaring.

He walks in and closes the door behind him. "Nat's sound asleep."

"Oh?" It's all I can think to say.

He steps closer to the bed. "I'm not, Blue. Wide awake."

"Same," I whisper, slowly flipping back the covers, exposing the wide-open space beside me.

He's not even completely on the bed before we're kissing. Seriously and deliciously. Tongues fused, thrashing, hot omens of things to come.

Pulling his mouth away, he says, "I suggest no boundaries once she's sleeping." He cups one of my breasts firmly, rolling the nipple between his fingers. "None whatsoever."

I slide my hands under his T-shirt. "Sold."

XII: DARK FORMULA (BRENT)

I pull the door shut on Blue's apartment and lock it. Her place is as good as new.

Better, really, than when she'd first moved in. That's for sure. The job took longer than it needed to, replacing the carpet and sub-floor. I usually leave that to someone else.

Clean it and get out is the motto for most of the jobs I contract. This one wasn't contracted, though, and I wanted it to take as long as possible.

I've gotten used to Blue being in my place. Warming my bed. Sneaking into hers.

Fucking her brains out after we've both had a long, hard day. Usually keep my hand pressed over her mouth or stuff her face in the pillow so the little screamer doesn't make too much noise.

I'm too damn used to the new routine. Like it too much. Don't want it changing.

Too bad I'll have to let her know the place is done, though. Riker, the manager, just did the walk through with me. So did the nosy neighbor, Mr. Barrett. Both kept asking when Blue would be coming back.

Not for a little while, I told them. Now, I just have to make sure she agrees to it.

There hasn't been a word from that asshole, Preston, but I'm still not totally convinced he's the one who trashed her place. That keeps my nerves on edge. There's no peace. More like the calm before a storm.

Bastard Phil hasn't shown up either. Not since I threatened him with his own knife.

It's not like any fuckers in the Pearls to give up so easy. He'd been hounding me for weeks, and now, nothing?

Doesn't make sense. Stinks worse than the rotten carpet we just ripped out.

Then again, none of this ever did. No sense. Going all the way back to Davey getting tangled up with them in the first place.

I push open the double glass doors of Blue's apartment lobby and walk to my truck.

Davey got greedy, but he liked his job with the newspaper and was a damn good photographer. When he said he'd quit, neither my parents or I believed it. He floundered around then, taking odd jobs, spent months at the ranch. Kept saying he was fixing the place up, but never actually did any fixing.

I climb in the truck and turn on the ignition.

I slap the steering wheel. Can't fucking help it.

"Damn. If only he'd taken my offer that night." My business wasn't as successful then as it is now, when I'd offered my brother money, but I'd have given him every dime I had.

***

Years Ago

"Whatever money you need, you've got it. Right here."

Davey laughs as he picks up my checkbook and tosses it back at me. "This isn't about money, big bro. It's bigger."

"Bigger danger, you mean. You're going to get yourself killed."

He shrugs. "Same shit they said about you. As I recall, you could've gotten killed in the Army, but that didn't stop you, did it? Didn't stop you from wheeling drugs and guns and fucking God only knows how many sluts when you were a Grizz." An angry glare appears in his eyes. Jealousy.

Christ. Doesn't he see how I hang my head when he mentions my past? The club was dirty in those days, but the worst of it never snowballed into Arizona. It still nearly cost me my life, and my soul.

"The only reason you left," he says, "only reason you came home for good, is because Cindy died."

He's done that before, the prick. Acting like Cindy's death was my fucking fault.

It wasn't. An act of God took her away before her time. I step closer to him, balling my hands into fists to keep from grabbing at his shirt, and shaking some sense into him.

I'd tried that once. It doesn't work. Just makes him more determined to fuck up his life.

"Davey, don't you think I wish she was alive? That Natalie could know her ma?"

"You kept Cindy on a yo-yo string for years. On again, off again. Left her wondering. Had everybody scratching their heads."

Keeping my anger in check grows harder. "This isn't about Cindy, dammit. It's about you, and how you're a chin hair away from fucking up your life. Throwing it away."

He shrugs. "Mine to fuck up, bro."

"You're right about that," I say. "But what about Mom and Dad? Don't you care about them? About how they'd feel knowing you're mixed up with the mob?"

He laughs. "There you go again. It was fine for you to be part of the Grizzlies, but not me. Oh, no. Never little Davey. I'm the good brother. Can't measure up to big brother's success or his disasters." He shoves a finger in my chest.

"No, Brent. This time, it's different. I'll be the one everyone's talking about. The one everyone's so proud of." He tosses his pool stick on the table. "It's been a long time coming, but it'll be worth it. Just wait."

* * *

Present

MY EYES ARE STINGING and my throat burns like hell, remembering how I'd stood there and watched him walk out the door. That was the last time I'd seen him alive.

Two days later, I was identifying his body at the morgue. A job I didn't want to hand off to either of my parents. A sight I couldn't stand them to see.

I reverse the truck and drive out of the parking lot.

Cross-fire. That's what the police said. That Davey was caught up in the cross-fire of a drug deal gone wrong. That he was simply in the wrong place at the wrong time.

Like hell.

He'd been shot in the head at point blank range and then put in his car. His keys were in his pocket. I wanted to know more, but my parents believed the story. They wanted to believe and I couldn't ruin Davey's memory by insisting it was a lie.

Even now. That's why I have to be careful.

My phone rings at the same time the speaker tells me Blue's calling. I glance at the clock while tapping the answer button. Nat had ridden to school with her today and she'd sent a text a short time ago, saying they were home and going swimming in the pool.

"Hello," I say.

"Hey."

She doesn't sound right. That instantly heightens my instincts. "What's wrong?"

"Are you on your way home?"

Blue's voice trembles. Urgency has me stepping harder on the gas. "Right this second. Why?"

"Captain Dawson...he s-said they found Preston Graves. He's dead, Brent."

Fuck.

I suck in my breath. "I'm on my way. Be there soon, babe, don't go anywhere." Although I have a ton of questions, now's not the time. "There's nothing to worry about. Is Dawson still there?"

"Y-yes. He asked when you'd be home."

I wish I was there. To comfort her and tell Dawson he should've called me first. Dropping this on Blue...it's too damn much.

He shouldn't have knocked on the door with this kind of bomb. What the fuck was he thinking? "I'll be home in a few."

"Okay."

Her voice sounds so meek, so drained, my pulse kicks higher. "It'll be all right, babe. Everything."

Concern for Blue, how she sounded, stays first and foremost as I speed toward home. Meanwhile, I curse Dawson.

The man's not an idiot, so what gives?

He's hired me for a large number of jobs the past couple of years. Has to know I don't appreciate him telling Blue that type of news alone.

His squad car sits in the driveway. I park behind Blue's car and jump out of the truck.

Dawson steps through the front door just as I step on the porch.

"Ms. Derby's fine, Brent," he says, blocking me from going around him. "We need to talk."

"Why?" I play dumb.

He rubs a hand over his stiff mustache. "Preston Graves was beaten before he was dumped in the desert. Left to die."

A chill rips up my spine. "Yeah, what else? What are you insinuating?"

Folding his arms across his chest, he raises a brow.

"Hope you won't take this the wrong way, however...it's no secret you had some rough friends, Eden."

"The Grizzlies?" I'm instantly pissed, but hide it by shaking my head. "Fuck, you know I haven't been a member for a long time. But even if I was, that wouldn't have anything to do with this. Besides, their national Prez, Blackjack, keeps the uglier elements on a tight leash these days. Local chapter flies right from everything I've heard. All the straight up scum long purged. The MC doesn't do shit like that anymore. Not in Arizona, or anywhere."

"Standard procedure. Nothing personal," he says quietly. "Surely, you can't blame me, considering how it looks. An old boyfriend breaking into your girlfriend's apartment? Who winds up dead a couple weeks later?"

"You're barking up the wrong tree, Dawson." I look him dead in the eye. "Tell me one thing: do I need a lawyer?"

He says nothing. "Just want you to know you'll be looked at long and hard. Friendly warning. If you have anything to say, you'd be better off telling me privately. We've worked together a lot recently. That could work in your favor."

He's overseen the L.E. cleanups I've been hired to do, and he's referred me to others, but it's not as if we're drinking buddies. "I don't need any favors," I say. "No one's above the law. If I've got to clear my name, I will. Didn't have anything to do with Preston Graves."

He shrugs. "The investigators will think differently, given all the evidence."

Evidence? The fuck is he on about?

"What evidence? I've only ever seen the guy once. The night he was in Izzy's face, trying to strong-arm her into a second date she wanted nothing to do with." I stop right there. I've got to be damn careful what I say next, however true.

He slaps my shoulder as he walks past. "We'll talk tomorrow."

I spin around, watch him walk to his car, then let it go.

He's just doing his job. Right?

Now, I have to do mine.

I walk into the house and find Blue in the kitchen. The moment she sees me, she squeezes her eyes shut. The recent tears are obvious, and so is her fighting to hide more. I walk over and pull her into my arms.

"I didn't like him, but I didn't want him dead," she sobs quietly into my shirt. "Just wanted him to go away and leave me alone!"

I kiss the top of her head. "Course you did, Blue. You don't have a mean bone in your body."

Preston was a little prick. Not a stretch to believe he pissed off the wrong person. I cringe slightly at the thought. I *had* threatened him, once.

He could have told others. Fuck.

I could get in some scalding hot water over this shit. I can't have that. Not with the Pearls already breathing down my neck.

I need to know more. Releasing her, I keep one arm around her while leading her to a stool. "What else did Dawson say?"

She sniffs, wiping her eyes. "He wanted to know when the last time I saw Preston was. I told him I haven't seen him since that night at the school. Two times, ever."

Shit. I'm not expecting her to have lied, but if she'd told him word-for-word what happened, I'm fucked.

"What's wrong?"

I shake my head. "Nothing. Preston must have pissed off the wrong person. Maybe he's been harassing another woman from that dating site."

Her phone rings. The screen says Mom.

Glad for the interruption, I slide it across the counter. "Good distraction. You should take it."

Blue shakes her head.

"You'll have to talk to her sooner or later," I say. "Clara knew Preston, she said. Fundraiser or something, like she told us at the wedding."

"Shit. You're right." She picks up the phone. "Hey, Mom. How's Vegas? Oh, you're home already..."

My mind weighs a hundred pounds and it's spinning out of control.

The way Davey's death was handled, no one in Phoenix investigations was overly worried about discovering the truth. I know the workload of those detectives. The quickest and easiest route to a resolution is the one they usually follow. Especially when the signs of foul play aren't ironclad.

"Hey, Dad." Natalie opens the sliding glass door and steps into the kitchen with a towel wrapped around her wet body. "Did Izzy tell you we're making tacos for supper? Hatch chilis with 'em!"

"Sounds good. How's the pool?"

"Perfect." She nods towards Blue. "We were just heading out the door when the sheriff showed up."

I hadn't noticed Blue has a swimming suit on because it's covered with a long shirt. Needing a way to release the tension that's overwhelming me, I say, "I'll go get my suit on. We can all take a swim before supper."

"Awesome," Natalie exclaims. "I told Izzy you'd probably join us once you got home." She lowers her voice. "Is everything okay? Did they find out who broke into Izzy's apartment?"

"They're still working on that," I say, recalling the bikini I'd packed up at Blue's last week and brought here, along with most of her other personal items. "I'll meet you outside in five or ten."

She heads back out the door and I go upstairs to change. A few minutes later, we're all in the pool.

I've always appreciated my daughter, but do even more right now. There's nothing like a child to put life back in perspective. And watching Blue glide through the water in her skimpy pink and blue bikini has me determined to hire the best fucking lawyer in Arizona if necessary to prove I had nothing to do with Preston's death.

Which will screw up my chances of paying the Pearls back for Davey's death. But not forever.

It'll still happen. Even if it takes a bit longer than I'd planned.

* * *

AFTER OUR TACO DINNER, Blue and Nat do some homework in the living room while I watch a movie. It's a new one, five star review, but it doesn't hold my attention.

Blue's captured too much already. She's changed into a pair of shorts and a T-shirt after swimming, but I keep seeing her in that bikini. Actually, I keep thinking about taking that little swimsuit off her.

Something about the stress makes my dick hard. Relentless.

Nat kisses me goodnight and heads upstairs. I switch the channel to the local news. Blue gets glued to the TV and I know she's waiting to hear the same thing I am.

That a body was found in the desert.

Nothing's reported. That doesn't totally surprise me. They'll have to notify family before releasing information. Sometimes, the media will sit on investigations for a little while by police request, too.

Done worrying about the dead prick, Preston, I click off the TV and set the remote on the table. "Be right back."

Blue nods and piles up the scraps of construction paper left over from all the shapes she'd cut out for her day class. I check on Nat first, who's sound asleep, and then use the bathroom.

I find Blue in the kitchen, filling the coffee pot for morning. "I have an idea," I say, grasping her hips and pulling her back against me.

"You *always* have that idea." She smiles, wriggling her ass against my cock.

"Nah, babe, this one's even better," I whisper in her ear. "You'll like it. Trust me."

She spins around and loops her arms around my neck. "I'll try."

Her kiss comes fast, barely happens before she asks, "Is Natalie sleeping?"

"Yeah." I take her hand, grabbing the towels I'd just set on the counter. "And we're going swimming."

"Just hung up my suit."

"You won't need one," I growl, opening the sliding door.

"Skinny dipping?" Her eyes go big and a familiar blush heats her cheeks.

I nod seriously. Before stepping out, I turn off the outdoor lights. They all have motion detectors that I don't want tripped.

"Did you read my mind earlier?" Her eyes have more stars in them than the sky.

Man, I love how honest she is. How ready and willing, how eager.

She's like a fantasy come true. I kiss her. "Maybe."

"Maybe?"

I drop the towel and pull my shirt over my head. "Can't say who was first. Maybe you're the mind reader digging into mine. Same wavelength, babe."

She follows my lead, undressing, and then unhooks her bra, freeing those glorious tits. I lick my lips, imagining sucking on their dark circles. Feeling those nipples turning into hard little nubs beneath my hungry tongue.

A moment later, she disappears with a giggle. The splash is quiet, subdued. I spin toward the pool, knowing she just dove in like a dolphin. She's so graceful and sleek there's barely a ripple in the water.

I get rid of my shorts and follow. The cool, refreshing water takes me light years away from the evil fuckery hanging over our heads.

I've been swimming since I was old enough to walk, and consider myself good at it, but she could swim circles around me. And does. I feel the movement in the water, but she stays just out of my reach.

She giggles softly each time her head pops out of the water and gives me a catch-me-if-you-can look. The one thing I'm very, very good at, is holding my breath.

I go beneath the water, and rather than swim towards

her, sink to the bottom, knowing she'll come to investigate.

My lungs are rigid by the time I snag her waist and shove off the pool's floor. We break the surface at the same time.

"Ass!" she says, slapping my chest. "You scared me."

The water's chest deep. I take advantage of that and nibble the tip of her nipple. The water laps against my chin as I tell her, "Only way I could catch you, Blue. You swim like a fish."

Her fingers wrap around the base of my cock and she gives it a long, perfect stroke. "Well, maybe you weren't dangling the right bait."

"There's no dangling here, darlin'." I give her nipple another bite. "I'm hard as a rock."

"I feel that," she says.

The way she strokes me feels like fucking Heaven. Better than any hand job in the universe.

I stifle a groan as she increases the rhythm. It's damn near brutal the way she turns me on, instantly brings me to the brink, the very edge where I can't last long.

She knows it, too. And loves it. Her eyes shine sheer excitement.

I reach between her legs, find her clit, and pinch it while working another finger inside her. The vibration of her breath, a pleasure gasp, steals my ability to breathe.

I love this shit.

Pleasuring her, owning her, with all the time in the world.

"We're two of a kind," I whisper against her lips.

"Yeah." Her tongue delves into my mouth.

I catch it with mine and kiss till we both have to throw our heads back and gulp in air.

"Condom?" she whimpers.

I'm still gasping, too, and the pressure building at my spine is almost to maximum. "With the towels," I growl.

Perfect timing. I'm so fucking close to coming from her hand, I can barely stand it. I shove another finger inside her and tease her clit with my thumb. "This what's got you bothered? My hard cock in your tight wet pussy?"

She gasps as the walls of her cunt spasm against my fingers. "I – Oh!" She groans, pressing down against my hand.

"Go for it, baby," I whisper, too close to stop.

I find her clit, shift my fingers deeper, finger-fuck her to completion. She presses her mouth against my chest, muffling her cry.

Warmth oozes around my fingers. Despite the fact she's in the middle of an O, she never stops pumping my cock in her hand. Not once. Her fulfillment rips through me. My cock jolts.

Wave after wave of pleasure rocks through me as she keeps stroking, stretching my climax for what damn well might be forever. I pulse between her fingers, out of my mind and then some.

It's some kind of black magic when a woman can drive me batshit off a hand job.

When we're both spent and slumped against each other, she giggles softly. I wrap my arms around her, utterly amazed. Never before have I been brought to the depth of an orgasm. Not before her.

I've never been so ready for an encore fuck either.

Can't get enough of this woman. Not tonight. Not ever.

"Want that condom now?"

She laughs shyly again, a sound I love. Lifting her head, she looks up at me. Eyes shimmering in the moonlight. "Let's take it inside the house. Upstairs. Somewhere we won't have to move after."

I chuckle, knowing exactly what she means. A few minutes ago I wouldn't have been able to walk if my life depended on it.

The encore's worth the wait. I haul her upstairs and tip-toe past Nat's room, holding her in my arms, bringing us into the bedroom.

She goes under me on the bed, ass up. I push deep inside her, plant my arms against her shoulders, binding her hair in one fist. I give it to her hard.

And when I say hard, I mean fuck-quake *hard.*

My dick drives fast and deep. Hits the spot that makes her little body seize. She whimpers sweetly under me, her O coming fast. Her pussy clenches me like silk madness, wringing come up from my balls, but damn if there isn't something else.

A warmth like never before. All over.

Her clit throbs against my balls as I fuck us both over. I empty myself inside her groaning, drowning Blue's screams in my hand. They rush out between her teeth against my palm. Her eyes roll, practically shaking the rest of her, and I give it back just as fierce.

I'm coming so hard it's barely human. And I think she just squirted for the first time.

Running my hand over the wet spot on the sheets underneath her tells me it's true. I suppress a wicked smile, proud of another first, knowing there's many, many more to come before I've fully branded my flesh on hers.

I crawl back into the bed after getting up to toss the condom. She welcomes me with a gentle smile and soft sigh as her head settles on my chest. "Brent, what was that?"

"That was you at your finest, babe. And me there, joining you, thanking my lucky stars. Fucking this good used to be rare. Before you." I take her lips in mine again.

When I pull away, her smile fades. "I don't just mean the sex, Romeo."

I give her a serious look.

"He might be your friend," she says quietly. "But I don't like him."

I run a hand down the length of her back, loving the silky feel of her skin against my palm. "Who?"

"Captain Dawson." She sighs. "I know it's probably just because he gave me that speeding ticket. The only one I've ever had."

I kiss the top of her head, but can't stop a frown from forming. "Dawson gave you the ticket you got leaving here that day?"

"Yes."

"Really?" Venom drifts through my veins.

She lifts her head. "Yes, really. I won't forget him." Sitting up, her brows knit together. "You don't believe me?"

"Not that." I shake my head. "I believe you, Blue. It's just that he works for the sheriff's department. County level. This is city limits. He can issue citations, but this area's out of his jurisdiction for that sort of thing."

"Not that night. It was him." She lays back down and

runs her nails softly across on my chest. "You've known him a long time."

"Not that long," I say.

"But he knew your brother, too."

"Davey?"

She nods.

Stupid question. I only have one brother. *Had* one.

But Dawson hadn't started working for the force in this area until after he'd died. "He never mentioned that to me. Knowing him."

She sits up again. "What? Weird."

I nod. "You act like you're not that surprised?"

"I am. I mean, he's asked me about Davey each time he's been here. When he brought out the OFP, and then today." She crosses her arms. "Which, by the way, he never even filed."

What the fuck?

Confused why Dawson would ever ask her about Davey, I shake my head to catch what she's talking about. "Filed what?"

"The OFP. Restraining order. I asked him what I should do when I get the signed copy back from the judge. He said not to worry about it, that he hadn't had time to file it yet."

"That was almost two weeks ago," I say.

"I know. I thought that's why he was here at first. To deliver my copy. From what I read, it usually only takes like forty eight hours or so."

My mind runs a hundred miles an hour in very dark directions, but I can't let her know it.

It's like we're staring down some dark, fucked up formula designed to produce nothing but bad answers.

I just pull her back down and run my fingers through her hair as her head settles on my chest.

This whole situation's too fucking odd. Too wrong. That scares me in a way I haven't ever felt before. Maybe because I have more to lose than ever before.

After I'm sure she's asleep, I ease off the bed and slip on my shorts. Down in my office, I dial a number I haven't called in years.

When the gruff voice on the other end answers, I say, "It's Eden. Monk. We need to talk."

XIII: MIXED UP (IZZY)

I can't stay focused. Partly because I expect Mr. Jacobs to call me into his office any second. I'll be fired this time for sure. Once he hears about Preston.

Weirdly, being fired doesn't have the same reaction as before. This job – the entire aspect of a job meaning more than the people in my life – no longer holds a choke-chain over my life.

Sure, I want to keep it. But I also want more.

I can't pinpoint when that became apparent, but it has.

That's only part of why I can't focus. Brent was acting odd this morning.

Jumpy. Distracted. I don't know.

Also couldn't guess how long he'd been gone when I woke up and realized he wasn't next to me. That wasn't unusual. He always goes to his own bed before morning, but it wasn't morning today.

Not even close.

I found him outside. At the table near the pool. He said

he couldn't sleep, and told me to go back up to bed. I can't say he was trying to get rid of me, exactly.

Just had a feeling he didn't want me out there right then.

There was a faint scent of cigarette smoke in the air. Even stranger. I've never seen him smoke, not even once. Never saw any indication that he does, but my father smoked and the scent of it always brings back memories.

Maybe it's the stress. Old habits coming back. I've heard of that, people who quit seeking comfort in old familiar tobacco when times get tough.

I can forgive him. The memories, with dad, maybe not so much.

There's too much there. Good and bad.

The good ones are of him. Of us. The bad ones are of missing him. Losing him. The day several neatly dressed officers showed up on our doorstep with bad news. Those are the bitter, ice cold memories lingering inside me.

They stoke very present fears.

Of losing Brent. And Nat. And everything.

"Ms. Derby, Ginger's eating paint again!" A small voice yells.

Speaking of the present...I hurry to the finger paint station, where little Ginger sucks on the bristles of a paint brush. Kneeling down beside her, I take the brush from her hand. "No, no, little lady. We don't want to eat paint," I say, shaking my head.

Her curly black pigtails flip and flop as she shakes her head. All the while licking the blue paint off her lips.

"Let's get you cleaned up." I take her hand and lead her to the sink, where I drop the brush in the plastic bucket of soapy water and wet a paper towel to wipe her face.

With big brown eyes and golden-brown skin, she's absolutely adorable, and the tiniest four year old I've ever seen.

Probably because she doesn't eat much except for things she's not suppose to. Paint. Glue. Crayons.

"Five more minutes until clean up time!" I tell the rest of the class, giving Ginger a paper cup full of water to rinse out her mouth.

I hear my phone buzz as a text comes in. Normally, I leave it in my purse in the closet all day, but not today.

It's on my desk.

Brent has already sent several messages. Asking how things are going and saying that he misses me. Which is sweet, but also odd. That's not like him. He's always saved his love for us in-person.

Something's going on. Something bigger than I'd first imagined.

More than Preston's body being found. I truly don't know how I feel about that. Sad, shocked, but also scared. Like there's another shoe ready to drop, and it may just be an ass-kicker.

I get Ginger interested in a puzzle and then put away the rest of the paint before I go to my desk. It's Brent again.

How are you doing?

Fine. I type back. *And you?*

Good, babe. See you in a couple of hours.

I set the phone down, but then pick it back up and type, *Did you get a new phone or something?*

You've just never sent this many messages.

His reply comes in. Weirdly off. *Nah. Missing you.*

I swipe to the emoji screen, but only have time to tap

on a heart and hit send because the crash of building blocks needs my attention.

* * *

Class finally ends by the time I get a chance to look at the phone again. No more messages, but I have to admit that I'd enjoyed knowing he was thinking about me all day.

"Do you ever go to football games?"

"No," I say to Nat, who walks into my classroom. I've never been a big sports fan, but enjoyed going to high school games with friends years ago. "Why? Do you want to go to the game tonight?"

"No." She starts helping me set the chairs on the tables so the janitor can clean the floor. "Just curious. The kids in my class were talking about it."

The entire school's been buzzing about how well the team is doing this year. "Well, if you do want to go, just let me know," I say, not wanting to push, but certainly wanting to encourage. "I'll take you. Your dad probably would, too. I've seen a Cardinals logo or two in his office."

"Okay! I'll think about it. Thanks, Ms. Derby."

I grab my purse out of the closet and walk over to the desk to collect my phone. "Ever asked him to take you before?"

She shakes her head. "I'd rather go to the ranch. Or hike up Camelback. Hey, you think Dad would want to go this weekend? It's finally cooling off!"

Everyone leaves early on Friday afternoons. It's barely three when she walks out the door. Following her, I click off the light. "We'll see. No idea what his plans are for the weekend, I'm afraid. You're right about the weather, though."

I smile, noticing I no longer feel the urge to instantly bust into flames stepping into the sun.

Her eyes sparkle as she grins. "If we both ask, really nicely, I bet he'll say yes!"

I can't help but smile. I love a good scheme. "Are you suggesting we gang up on him?"

She shrugs, but her smile never falters.

The more I'm around this kid, the more I like her. She has a light about her that never dims. Grasping her shoulder, I pull her to my side for a quick hug. "Let's feel him out. I've got your back if you give him a few words of encouragement."

Brent is home when we arrive, outside lounging near the pool, and on the phone. He spins around as he sees me, changing his expression, but I'd already seen the look on his face.

Something's wrong. Seriously wrong.

He's in full badass mode.

I feel the change in the air as much as I see it in him. That doesn't scare me, but at the same time, it's unnerving how tormented he looks. Like it's taking everything he has to figure something out.

"Hey, kiddo," I say to Natalie. She'd been talking about the chocolate cake we'd had at lunch today, so I use that as an excuse. "Will you go search chocolate cake recipes? Print out a couple and then we can see if we have all the ingredients. I bet we can improve on what the cafeteria serves up."

She lifts a brow, having also seen her father out the window. "Sure!" With a nod towards Brent, she says,

"He'll be fine after he hangs up. It's just work stress. I tell him he should hire a manager for some things."

I laugh, loving how she's so ready to advise him on business. Still, I wish she was right about this just being work-related. A sick vortex in the pit of my stomach says it's anything but.

"Nat, go Google those recipes."

"On it!"

I wait until she leaves the room before I open the sliding glass door. Brent shoves his phone in his pocket as soon as I step outside. He turns and walks towards me.

"Hey. How was your day?"

His smile is as false as Santa Claus. "What's wrong?" I ask. "You look –"

He kisses my forehead. "Nothing, Blue."

I step back and hold up my hands to keep him at arm's length. "Don't lie to me, Eden. A moment ago, you'd transformed into your badass papa bear self. I saw it."

"Blue –"

A mixture of fear and frustration boils inside me. "I know what I saw! Jesus. You've been acting strange all day. Either tell me what's going on, or..." I can't think of a threat he'll take seriously.

He grasps my wrists, pulling me closer. "You'll what?"

"Leave." I'm serious, because I know something bad is happening. He might think he's hiding it, but he's not. It's still on his face. Whatever it is. "I'll leave."

"Leave? And go where?"

The challenge in his voice makes me more determined. "My apartment's done. Riker called. I don't have to stay here a minute longer if there's no good reason."

"When?"

"Wednesday. Said he'd already done a walk through with you, too, and squared the work away with the city code."

He releases my wrists and steps away. "You can't go back there."

"Why? Preston's no threat."

Running a hand through his hair, he shakes his head. "No body yet."

He'd lowered his voice to little more than a whisper. Not sure I heard correctly, I ask, slowly, "What do you mean? No body?"

"Preston Graves," he growls. "They haven't got his body. The police have no record of it."

"But Dawson –"

"I know," he growls. "He didn't file your OFP, either. Heard it straight from the horse's mouth today."

A shiver darts up my spine. So does the gravity in his voice. Fear and anger race to curdle my stomach first. "God, what's going on, Brent? There's been something happening behind the scenes for weeks, something you don't want me to know about. What is it?"

He glances around and shakes his head. "Nothing, Blue. Nothing you need to worry over."

"Bullshit!" It just explodes out. "It's too late. Too late for games. I'm worried *sick*."

"Don't be. I'll keep you safe."

"Safe. From. What?"

"Nothing."

This is nuts.

I study him, wondering why he's fighting so hard to lie to me. His jaw is tight, his neck muscles showing. I lurch forward and shove at his chest with both hands. "You sonofabitch! I just asked you *not* to lie to me. And here you are." My anger turns raw and painful as the truth reveals itself. "You've been lying to me since the beginning, haven't you?"

He stays stock-still.

Searching for a way to break through that hard fucking shell of his, I shove his chest again. It's like trying to move solid steel. "Who the hell answers their front door with a gun? You, that's who. The first time I came here you answered the door with a freaking handgun. And never said a word."

He shoves my hands aside. "Yeah, and I wish you'd never come here that night."

My jaw drops. Whoever said words will never hurt is a fucking liar.

It's like my heart was just sliced in two. "Fine. Fuck you. And your fucking creepy cop friend."

He grabs my hand as I spin around. "Blue –"

"Shut up!" I break his hold on me and step away. "You know what, I don't want to know. Whatever you're mixed up with, it's bad. I don't want to know, and I don't want to be a part of it, either. I'm such an idiot."

I'm two steps away when he says, "I wish like hell you weren't part of it. I didn't want you to be. Still fucking don't. But it's too late."

Another cold chill. Another flash of anger. I hold my breath for a moment, trying to decide my options. The hurt, the pain inside, making it hard to see reason. To see any choices.

"And I need your help."

I turn to see his face. His emerald eyes. And the sincerity in them.

Wow. I know him. Asking anyone for help would gut him. "My help?"

He nods.

"Brent, you better not be –"

"I'm not," he says. "I don't know what's coming, Blue. Not all of it. But I have to stop it. I can't lose you."

"Stop what?"

"I'm not exactly sure."

I want to ask how he can stop something when he doesn't know what it is, but refrain. He's not lying. He doesn't know. And that's what's tormenting him. I step closer. "What *do* you know?"

"Not much."

"Then tell me not much." I lay a hand on his chest. "I deserve to know. Whatever it is, if I'm mixed up in it, I need the full truth."

He huffs out a breath and then pulls me into his arms. "You're right."

As much as I love being in his arms, I don't lean against him. That would be too easy and make me forget the anger that had my blood boiling only seconds ago. He knows what his touch does to me, and I have to prevent that from happening. From forgetting everything except what it feels like to be held in those heavily inked arms. "Then tell me."

"Where's Nat?"

"In her room."

He nods and leads me over to the table he was sitting at early this morning when I'd smelled cigarette smoke.

"Who was here this morning?" I ask.

"Did you hear someone?"

I shake my head. "But someone was here. I know it."

He nods slowly. Gestures for me to sit while he drops into another chair. "A friend. Old acquaintance."

"There's a difference," I point out.

"Yeah, there is." He leans forward, puts his elbows on the table. "There's always a fine line between the right side and the wrong side of the law, Blue. Some people weave across that line for the good of the law. Others, for ill."

Not about to be buffaloed I say, "Don't beat around the bush, Brent. This isn't a movie."

He cracks a slight grin. "Sometimes you're too smart for your own good."

"What the hell does that mean?"

He shakes his head and takes my hand. "There's a crime syndicate in Phoenix called the Black Pearls. If it's illegal, they've got their paws in it, usually heading it up. Drugs. Smuggling. Trafficking."

The name wasn't familiar to me, but the crimes were. With the border so close, the unexplained disappearances on the reservations, the bad news is never ending. I don't want to believe it, but have to ask, "Are you mixed up with them?"

"My brother Davey was." Pain fills his eyes. "I tried to stop him. Tried like hell to make him understand he was on the road to nowhere, to death, but he wouldn't listen."

I squeeze the fingers he's wrapped around my hand. "What happened?"

"He was shot. Police said he was in the wrong place at the wrong time. Driving past a drug deal that went to shit, but his keys were in his pocket. Someone shot him and put him in his car after he was dead."

Jesus. I feel the color drain from my face.

"Surely an investigation –"

"Wasn't one. Not a thorough one." He shakes his head and slams a hand on the table. "They arrested two young kids from Mexico, claimed they were responsible, and shipped them back across the border, but it wasn't them."

"Why do you say that?"

"Because it was too easy. Too clean cut. But because my parents had already been through enough losing their son, I didn't push it. I'd almost learned to live with it myself, until a few months ago when one of the Pearls contacted me. Said Davey died owing the bastards a large debt, and that I needed to make it right."

"Did you go to the police?"

His chuckle sounds fake and bitter. "No. Think I'd probably have had an accident if I had." Scorn twists his face as he seethes, "Shot by two young kids from the wrong side of the tracks."

A shiver ripples my skin.

"I told the Pearls I've got no interest paying off the debt. Yet, every few months, Phil shows up again. Each time what they wanted was different. I could launder some money for them, they said, or deliver some cargo."

He shakes his head before letting out a sigh and glances around, as if he isn't sure what to say next.

"But you didn't?"

"No. Fuck no."

He's torn, and angry, that much is obvious. My heart sinks, wanting to help him with all I have. "Why did your brother hook up with them?"

"I don't know. It came out of the blue. I didn't even believe it when I first heard, but then Davey confirmed it." He shrugs. "Two days later he was dead."

My heart goes out to him. Blinking at the tears

stinging my eyes because of his pain, I ask, "What do you mean out of the blue?"

"Well, wasn't a complete shock," he says. "Davey had worked for the newspaper for several years. A photographer. He wrote a few articles too, but mostly took pictures. Then he quit. Took odd jobs now and then. Spent a lot of time out at the ranch. At first I thought it was a woman, but he never had a steady girlfriend. He was just friends with everyone. A likeable guy. My ma once said some girl smashed his heart to pieces while I was in the army, and that it was going to take him time to get over it." He scratches his head. "I'd been home from the army for years, so he should have been long over it. I don't know."

I hold my tongue to keep from telling him some people never mend a broken heart.

He doesn't need to hear it right now, and having never experienced it, he wouldn't understand. Focusing on the rest of what he's said, I ask, "So, what did he say when you tried to stop him? Told him he was on the road to nowhere?"

"Some stupid shit. That it wasn't about money. Not entirely. He told me everyone would be proud of him soon and his ship would come in. Riches. Fame. Power. Whatever."

"Why do you say it was stupid?"

"Because it was. Davey was..." He pinches his lips together for a moment. "He wasn't much bigger than you. In height or weight. And he wore pop-bottle glasses before he switched to contacts. As a kid, he got picked on all the time and –"

"And you protected him," I say, sensing the obvious.

"Made the assholes picking on him stop." Tears press harder on my eyes at how it's torturing him.

He wasn't able to save his little brother that one time, and there'd never be a second chance. "Brent, it's not your fault."

"Like hell it's not. He didn't know what he was getting into. My words didn't work. I should've clubbed him over the head and dragged him back to my place. Made him see sense."

His pain just makes him angrier, which won't help either of us. My insides are trembling. I have no idea what to do to help him. And I'm no closer to understanding what's going on. "Who told you the police have no record of a body being found? These Pearl people?"

Some of the pain leaves his face as he shakes his head. "No. I have a friend, a guy who has an in with the city police."

"What sort of friend? A police officer?"

"Not exactly. He's...a member of a motorcycle club I used to belong to." He stands up and rubs the back of his neck. "I think Dawson's trying to pin Preston's death on me."

I jump to my feet. "You? Why? How?" My mind lurches all directions. I rush to his side and grab his arm. "He can't! No way. I'll tell him you were with me. Twenty-four hours a day."

He pulls me against him. I wrap my arms around his waist and hold on for dear life.

"I don't know why, but I have to find out. That's where I need your help."

I lean back to look up at him. "Anything, Eden. Name it."

"I need to go meet some people and need you to stay with Nat. Just for a little while." He brushes my hair back with one hand. "There's no one else I trust to take care of her."

"Of course I will, but there has to be more I can do than that."

He shakes his head slowly. "There's nothing more important than knowing you two stay here. Safe."

His kiss is long and slow and full of emotion. He presses my head into his chest after. "I wish you weren't involved, but I'll never regret you coming to the house that night," he says. "Never regret having you in my life. You're the sunshine I needed. That Nat needed. I won't lose you over this bullshit."

Tears needle my eyes again. "You won't lose me."

His hold tightens even more.

I understand why and though I don't want to know, I have to. "When are you leaving?" I ask. "When will you be back?"

"As soon as I get the call. I'm not sure how long it'll take. Could be all night."

He's too elusive. "I need to know more," I say. "If something happens –"

"Nothing's happening, Blue." His jaw goes tight. "Not to you or me. I'll do my business and come right home."

Before I can come up with a response, his phone rings.

He lets go of me, grabs his phone out of his pocket, and walks into the grass. "Eden."

I hold my breath, but it doesn't help. I can't hear anything the other person says. When he turns around and meets my gaze, an overwhelming fear washes over me.

"You're leaving now?"

He nods. "Have to, babe. Take care."

Two hours later, I'm still scared. Still pacing the floor. Still doing my damnedest not to let Natalie see me freaked out.

I've tried hard not to let anything show as we make supper and then bake our chocolate cake.

As I take the cake out of the oven, she points at the hook by the door, a frown on her face. The keys to the ranch are gone. I always remember the little turtle he keeps fastened to the chain, how its silver and turquoise catch the light.

A chill sinks through my bones. This isn't working, trying to stay calm.

Pacing, chewing my lip, won't bring him home any sooner.

So, I pick up my phone and dial while walking into the hall. As soon as there's an answer on the other end, I pop the question, "Hey, Mom, I need a favor...could Natalie come stay with you for the night?"

XIV: CROSS-BONES (BRENT)

That motherfucker's trying to set me up.

Think I know why too. That asshole, Dawson, is in with the Pearls. Has been for years.

I should've caught on sooner. He stopped by every clean up gig I did for the Sheriff's department. Those nasty, grim jobs, where he always said who he thought was responsible.

Never said the Pearls, but I'd known who he was referring to. He'd wanted me to see how they got rid of anyone in their way. In *his* way.

He'd made comments about Davey, too. Disguised them, claimed he'd heard I had a brother who died, and how hard some of those violent scenes had to be for me.

His remarks weren't so often I caught on, but I sure as hell should have. And he never mentioned knowing Davey once.

Only thing I can't figure out is what the bastard wants from me. Or what Preston, dead or MIA, has to do with any of this. Dawson has to know I'd never sink to the level of working with the Pearls.

Fuck. That's exactly what I've sank to.

But only to catch them.

To put an end to this.

The ranch is where it has to happen. That's always been the plan. Out of Dawson's jurisdiction.

It's no wonder the Pearls have the power they do with a captain of the sheriff's department on their side. Well, I have backup, too. The Grizzlies have come through for me.

A call to Blackjack, their national Prez, put me in touch with the new reorganized chapter in Phoenix. I never thought an old biker dude with long gray hair and a bad hip could leave me choked up, but fuck, there it is.

Remembering his words tears at my throat. *Anytime, son. Any damn time. Whether you hung up the patch or not, you're family.*

Some people blaze through your life for a few bright seconds. Others remain, even in the shadows, and no matter how infrequently you see them, they're there when the going gets tough.

Someday, I'll repay that old man. He saved my skin once, helped me get out when Fang, the dirty old President, didn't make that easy. Now, he might be saving my ass again.

Same with Blue.

Without her, I don't know what I'd have done with Nat. It's more than that, though. I'd wanted all this put behind me for years, for Davey's sake, but now it's stronger.

It's for her sake, too. I can't have a future while I'm focused on the past. A future including her.

By tomorrow this time, I'll be well on my way to carving that future with sweat and fire.

This will be behind me.

If I'm careful, strong, and most of all, lucky.

My hands sweat when I steer the truck into the final fuel stop near Flagstaff. A Harley, black and sleek, turns off the road from the other direction. It parks on the other side of the pump.

The rider doesn't take off his helmet, but I recognize him. Not too many men are that wide or tall. Civilians wouldn't be caught wearing the patch with the roaring bear. Or the blood red one-percenter patch near his collar.

We both make our selection. He jams one nozzle in his fuel tank while I do the same with mine.

"Good to see you, Monk. Been a long fucking time," he says.

"Yeah. Too long."

He flips up his shield and my throat gets hard. "Cross-Bones," I growl.

He nods. It's a face I'll never forget. Half his teeth are still just as silver as I remember. A long scar lines his right cheek, merging into the end of his missing earlobe.

A long time ago, I'd trusted my life to this man. Followed him into danger on the road and in the worst corners of Phoenix. Besides Blackjack, he's the only reason I left the club with my life.

He worked his way up to Vice President in our chapter, back when times were bad. These days, he's top dog in

Arizona, ever since the club cleaned up its act. Blackjack doesn't let dirty players rank in any chapter.

Once upon a time, old Cross-Bones was like a second father.

Before the army. Before I'd made the choice to change the path I'd been on. Before I had to leave the craziness behind.

"You sure you're ready?" he asks.

I want to ask him the same thing. Shit, I want to ask him why he's doing this, but I already know.

Family.

I could be walking into a larger trap than the one I've set up. Swallowing, I nod.

He lifts the nozzle out of his bike's tank and swipes his card. "The bait's been taken. Three o'clock a.m."

"You have the coordinates?" I ask.

His partial grin is sarcastic. All silver. I take his crap. He wouldn't be here if he didn't know every last in and out.

"I'll have everything in place." My back teeth clench as I squelch any fear trying to rise up inside me. It's been years since I've put everything aside except for the mission at hand.

And it's harder than it's ever been. I didn't have Nat in those days. But now, I have to. "Everything."

He starts his Harley and rides off. I finish fueling the truck and walk inside to pay. I also pick up a couple of snacks, mostly beef jerky, and bottles of water before getting back in the the driver's seat and heading north.

I can't help but think about the last trip to the ranch, with Blue in the front beside me and Natalie chatting like a magpie in the backseat.

The memories of that weekend are too good. I have to bury them and concentrate on the plan.

The sun's already sinking low in the sky. I won't have much daylight to get everything left in place. Urgency has me stepping harder on the gas pedal, hoping to turn the normal two hour trip into half that time.

I don't dare sigh a breath of relief as I pull into the ranch. Grabbing the bag of snacks, I head to the house. Out of habit, I give the place a quick search before I grab the backpack from the top shelf in the closet.

Tossing it on the bed, I pull out two nines and ammo. After putting on the double shoulder holster, I insert the magazines into the guns and slide them into place.

I put my coat back on to cover the harness and check the other contents of the backpack before heading back out to my truck. The road to the shack is rough. I focus on driving rather than all the other thoughts that keep trying to steal my attention.

Ten years. That's how long I've lived for my daughter.

Now, when I think about living, think about the future, Blue gives me a brand new reason.

Same reason I need this shit with the Pearls done and over.

A deep rut makes the truck bounce so hard my head smacks the roof. I can't act on the urge to rub it, or my knee from where it bashes the steering column. There's more to go. I have to keep both hands on the wheel to maneuver around the treacherous switchbacks that take me to the other side of the hill.

I arrive at the shack, and as I shut the truck off, I glance at the key chain. "Shit." A sense of regret fills me as I look at the silver turtle.

Once, it was Davey's. I'd given it to him for his sixteenth birthday. The turtle's back was a piece of turquoise. Or had been. The stone must have fallen out when I hit that rut and slammed my knee against the column.

He'd had this in his pocket when he'd died. It was the one thing of his I'd kept. Usually, I only keep the ranch keys on this ring, but today, for some reason, I felt the need to clip it to my day-to-day chain.

Now, it's broke, like a bad fucking omen.

I glance to the floor mat, looking for the stone. It's there. I pick it up and try to stick it back into the tiny prongs. It won't go, so I push harder.

Then the back pops open. I'm stunned. Never knew it was hollow inside.

I'm baffled at what I see in the tiny compartment. It's a memory chip. One from a camera. Lodged against the edges, still, never giving off a rattle.

The fuck? Davey had too many cameras to count, but why would a chip be in here?

I snap the turtle shut and unclip it from my keyring before putting it in my pocket with the stone. Then I head inside the shack to gather the explosives.

The sun's practically gone by the time I have the bombs and detonators in place. I'm almost back to the house when I notice headlights on the road leading into the yard.

My lights are off, but I double check just to make sure. I slow the truck in order to pull up behind a cluster of rocks.

It's not long before the vehicle comes close enough for me to recognize.

Classic Mustang.

Blue.

Dark dread overshadows the excitement I normally feel, which flickers out way too fast. "Fuck. What's she doing here?"

I told her not to come. Told her to stay with Nat. Anger and worry storm through my veins.

I pull back on to the dirt path and arrive at the house, just as she's climbing out of her car.

Blue holds up a hand as I jump out of the truck, sensing I'm about to give her an earful. "You said you needed my help."

"Yeah," I growl back. "To watch Natalie." I gesture towards the car. "Where is she?"

"With my mother."

I'd be even more worried if she'd brought my daughter.

I'm not as mad at her as I am the entire world. For years, I've focused on being a good father, a good man, yet the past just won't let go. It's like I'm chained to it, and so's everybody else who walks into my life.

"How'd you even know where to find me?"

"Natalie pointed out you'd taken the keys to this place." Blue steps closer, holding her hand out. "I have no idea what's going on, but whatever it is, we're in this together. From beginning to end. You asked for my help, Brent."

I don't want to take her hand. She wasn't in this at the beginning and I don't want her involved now. Don't want her hurt. Or worse.

"You need to leave, Blue. Right the fuck now."

She drops her hand to her side and walks toward the house. "Not happening, Eden."

I follow, and though the urge to grab her is strong, I resist. Knowing as soon as I touch her, I'll want to hold on. Tight. "No fooling. It's too dangerous for you to be here."

"Why?" she asks while we walk into the house. "There's going to be a shoot out or something?"

She's being flippant. I'm not.

I close the door behind me and pull open my coat. "Close enough. You can't stay."

Her eyes lock on the guns in my holsters. She realizes I'm not joking.

Fear flashes in her eyes as they meet mine. So does tenacity. "Whatever. It's too late. Tell me what I can do."

I admire her grit, but shake my head. "Leave. Leave now."

"That's *not* happening." She walks into the center of the room and looks around before asking, "Is this where your brother met with the Pearls?"

"No." I shrug then. "I don't know, really. Don't know where he met them. What went down between them. I just know they're the reason he died, and now they want something from me."

She's here, goddamn it. I might as well accept that because she's too stubborn to leave. And there isn't enough time or energy to fight her on top of everything else. It's also too dangerous. Both the Pearls and the Grizzlies are on their way.

"Who told you Davey was involved with the Pearls?"

"Someone."

"Another acquaintance?"

"You could say that."

She throws her hands in the air. "Quit being so allusive. If you can't trust me, why'd you ask for my help?"

"I asked you to take care of Nat."

"She's with mom and she's perfectly fine. Safer than with me." She steps closer. "Listen, I want to help. I want this over. I really, really do. But I've never done anything illegal so you need to give me a reason why that's the only choice besides –"

She snaps her mouth shut and closes her eyes. I put a finger under her chin and lift her face to look at me again. The need to know what she'd been about to say hits stronger than anything else I've felt tonight, and that's saying a lot. "Besides what?"

Something akin to anger flashes in her eyes. "Besides the truth. I love you, Eden. I trust you."

Fuck me.

If I live to be a hundred, I'll never be able to describe what rocks my insides right then. It's like a hydrogen bomb. Fire and lightning, out of control, filling me in a way I'd never been full before.

Like every empty spot, every hole inside me, suddenly goes solid. Real. Warm and alive.

I gather her against my chest and bury my face in her hair, anchoring my nose in her trademark blue stripe. "I love you, too, Blue. Love you like no woman I've ever had."

I could have stood there forever, just holding her. She pulls back first.

"Okay," she says, smiling. "Now that we have that out of the way." Her smile fades. "What's happening tonight? Who are you here to shoot?"

Leave it to me to find a woman smarter and more forward than I am. I did. And don't want it any other way.

"I'm not helpless, you know. I have my conceal and carry permit," she says.

"You do?"

She nods. "I've just never gotten around to buying a gun."

"You don't need a permit in Arizona," I say, amazed but not shocked by what she's said.

"I know, they taught us that in the class. I took basic safety because I thought if I ever decided to buy a gun and carry it, I should know what I'm doing."

She's too serious for me to laugh at, though I am amused.

"I've taken self-defense classes, too."

"You have?"

"Yes. I just get sort of clumsy when I'm nervous."

"Don't I know it," I say, remembering when we first met.

She holds out both hands and shrugs. "So, who are you here to shoot?"

Considering all that, it's safer for her to know the truth. Not that I have any plans to let her within thirty feet of any live guns and the assholes behind them.

"Told you, I used to belong to a motorcycle club. One that didn't always operate on the right side of the law. It's full of men, many former military. They're the reason I joined the army. I thought I'd do my tours of duty and come home, make a life with the patch, but Cindy got pregnant. Natalie was born. I broke my ties with them when I got back in civilian life. It was hard, but a couple good guys understood. Helped me get out. We never spoke much after."

"Until now."

I nod. "I need their help to get this settled with the Pearls."

"Why?"

"Because of Davey."

"Why really?"

Christ. It's almost like she's forcing me to break through the fog that's been filling my head for years. "It was a Grizzly, Cross-Bones, who told me Davey was putting his nose in things he shouldn't. That he was going to get himself hurt. Or worse." I don't want the memories, I realize.

That's why there's fog. I'd been here before, with Nat, at the ranch, when Cross-Bones Haggerty had shown up. I close my eyes and open them again, ready to give her one last missing piece.

* * *

Years Ago

"WHAT ARE YOU DOING HERE?" I ask even before he climbs off his bike. Natalie's playing in the screened in porch with her kitchen set. Only five years old and she's already memorizing English teas. I told her to stay there as soon as I'd heard the familiar sound of a Harley.

"Need to talk to you, Monk," he says, using a nickname I haven't heard in eons.

"Not interested," I growl. "I'm out. Remember?"

The past few years haven't been easy, transforming myself into the sort of father Natalie needs. Sure, there were times when I'd craved the old days. Partying. Running wild. Women. Taking what I wanted. The army had been a lot like that, too, when I wasn't in a war zone. The whole now or never attitude. The constant reminders of death.

"Won't say you wouldn't be welcomed back, but I'm not here to recruit you. Relax." Haggerty lights a cigarette and takes a long draw between his silver teeth. "It's about your little brother. He's not you, Monk, and he's gonna get his ass stung. Bad."

"Davey?" I shake my head and laugh. "You don't know what you're talking about."

"Wrong, boy. I do. The Pearls are playing serious eight-ball these days, and don't think twice about clearing the table. Pulling people in, bright-eyed and bushy tailed. Expanding like a fuckin' plague."

My nerve-endings tingle. He's not talking about a game of pool, but about the Pearls discarding anyone in their way. Using anyone and anything to make blood money. I've seen their latest scraps in the news, too. The ugly aftermath.

Haggerty squishes his cig with the toe of one boot, then swings his leg over the seat of his bike. "I came as a friend, Monk. All I've ever been. Your old Veep. Not an enemy. But that's all I can do. Send you a message. We both know what it's like, looking out for family."

* * *

Present

"Brent?"

I shake my head, clearing the memories.

Blue frowns as she asks, "What was Davey doing?"

"I never found out," I say, pissed at myself for not digging deeper then.

If I had, this wouldn't be happening, and Davey could still be alive. I can't change that. "Whatever it was, the Pearls want me to pay for it. Last night, I called a club member. There's no proof, but it's thought that Dawson was in with the Pearls all along. I believe he's trying to pin Preston's death on me. Payback for not giving into the Pearls." This was my only option, but I'm not sure she'll see it.

"I called a meeting with the Pearls. Here. Tonight. Made 'em believe I'm ready to bury the hatchet, filling up their coffers." I gesture in the direction of the kitchen behind her. "Beyond that hill you see from the back porch, there's a small valley that can only be accessed by an old mining road off the highway. I told the Pearls I'd meet them there tonight."

"Alone?" Her soft eyes widen.

I nod. "Close. The Grizzlies will be there, too. Out of sight until needed."

"Needed? For what?"

I shake my head, not wanting to reveal the rest, but the look in her eyes has me relenting. "I need to cut off the head. The masterminds behind it all. That's the only way this ends. My plan isn't to listen to what the Pearls want, but to set up a rumble between the Pearls and my old MC."

"A rumble? You mean a fight." She points to my holsters. "One with guns."

"Ideally, it won't get that far." I plan on using more than guns, but that much I'll keep hidden from her. "If all goes well, they'll be done before they slink away to fire any shots."

"When?"

"Three o'clock a.m."

"There has to be a better way," she says. "The police, the –"

"Wrong. If Dawson's involved, others could be, too. That's why it has to be here. Out of his district. Away from any eyes and ears who'll warn them."

XV: CHASING GHOSTS (IZZY)

I can't let this happen.
He could be shot. Killed.

There *has* to be something I can do to make him see reason. Not knowing what else to say, to do, I shake my head. "None of this will bring Davey back."

"I know that, Blue, but it *will* end it. Before I lose anybody else."

I'm trying to see the whole picture here. All the ins and outs, understand how he came to the conclusion that this was the only sane resolution.

"End what?" I ask. "Dawson trying to frame you for Preston's death? I don't see how this does that. What you need is *proof* that Dawson's involved. Then take that to the authorities."

"That's what I'm going for, Blue. He's gotten word of the rumble and will be here. Made sure of that before leaving Phoenix. I'll get all the proof I need."

He walks past me, into the kitchen, and takes a bottle

of water out of a bag on the table. I shake my head when he holds it out to me. I'm too nervous to drink anything.

After taking a long swallow, he sets the bottle on the table and then pulls something out of his pocket. He's looking at it intently. I move closer, recognizing the turtle on the keychain Natalie knew was missing.

"That was Davey's?" I say. "The one you keep the keys to this place on."

He nods. "It broke. Hit a hard bump in the road up on the hills."

The turquoise stone had fallen off. "I'm sure a jeweler can put it back in."

He squeezes the side with his other hand. "Not what I'm worried about. Found out it opens."

The back had popped off. There's something small, black, and metallic inside.

"Is that an SD card?" I ask.

"Sure looks like it. Must have been an extra for one of his cameras. He had dozens."

He goes to close the lid and I stop him. The hairs on the back of my neck stand up as scenarios play out in my mind. "Wait. What if Davey was telling you the truth? That his involvement wasn't about money. Wasn't what it seems?"

"What are you talking about?"

I pick up the SD card. It's only a hunch, but I feel it clear to my bones. "What if Davey wasn't working with the Pearls, but *against* them? Hoping to bring them down and make a name for himself that way? What if he had proof? Pictures?"

Brent glances at the keychain. "This was in his pocket

when he died. No camera in his car. Which was odd because he never went anywhere without one."

"We have to see what's on this," I say. "Is there a camera here? Something we can put this in?"

"In the trunk. Bedroom." Brent grabs my hand. "It's full of Davey's stuff. I never felt like going through it."

My heart races. Makes my chest burn by the time we open the lid of the old metal trunk. I tell myself not to jump to any conclusions, but I can't help it.

It's only nine o'clock. With solid proof we can go to the authorities before the battle ever begins.

There are half a dozen cameras in the trunk, but not a single one has batteries. Lovely.

"You don't have any double A's in the entire house?" I ask for a second time. There must be batteries somewhere.

"No. Don't need them for anything."

"Well, keep digging," I say, pulling out a stack of newspapers and magazines. "Maybe there's some in here, or a charger."

He keeps digging. A birthday card slips out of one of the magazines and hits the floor. I can't stop myself from opening it, or reading what's written inside.

"Holy shit..." I whisper it to myself, barely out of his earshot.

I can't believe my eyes.

I KNOW I'm the last person you want a card from, but we'll be a family soon. Are already.

And I'm sorry. I've said it before, and I'm saying it again.

We both know the baby is Brent's.

What happened between us shouldn't have happened at all. I was lonely. Missing him. So were you.

I'm sorry about saying you don't want his leftovers. I didn't mean it the way it sounded. You're a good man. A kind man. You'll make the world a better place one day.

Happy Birthday, *Davey.*

Love, *Cindy*

"What's that?" he asks, standing behind me.

I close the card and consider tucking it back inside the magazine, pretending I never saw anything, but it's too late. Brent's already reaching for it.

I hand it over and reach back inside the trunk, not wanting to see his reaction to the card.

Still, I can't help myself.

He reads it, more than once by the way he's studying it. My stomach gurgles, not knowing what to say. Cowardly, I pull out another stack of newspapers. This time, it's the headline that catches my eye.

Hard Evidence Proves the Cameras Are Working.

I skim the article about the Border Enforcement Task Force installing Buckeye cameras along the border. It talks about how the motion activated sensors send pictures straight to the sheriff's office, then onto Homeland Security and the DEA.

The article goes on, showing how the task force can respond to the pictures within minutes. Within the first few months of operation, thousands of pounds of drugs were seized, dozens of smugglers arrested, and several human trafficking operations busted.

Last, it mentions how the local sheriff's department declined commenting on the issue. I glanced at the pictures then, of the task force and of Captain Dawson refusing to talk to a reporter.

The photos were taken by Dave Eden.

I hand the newspaper to Brent. "We have to see what's on that SD card. Now." An epiphany hits. "Hold up. I think...we can put it in my cellphone."

"Phones don't use SD cards anymore," he says, scanning the newspaper.

"Your brand doesn't. Mine still does. Jesus, I'd forgotten that little slot..." I've already pulled my phone out of my pocket and pry off the back.

I collect the card from where I'd set it on the window sill, and carefully slide it in. I pop the back on again and power up the phone.

Brent's putting everything back in the trunk. I try not to notice he's still holding the birthday card.

I can't imagine what he must be thinking. Or if he already knew Davey and Cindy had what I'm assuming was an affair while he was in the army.

When the screen appears on my phone, I tap the photo icon. "Look, it says SD card."

Brent finally tosses the birthday card back inside and shuts the trunk lid. We both sit on it as I click on the icon again.

The first few pictures make my heart sink. Nothing but black.

The next few have some odd shapes and shades of gray, but nothing I can make out. I keep scrolling.

There's a truck and a building of sorts, but the colors are off.

"He must have been using a thermal imaging camera. Maybe a setting for that," Brent says, his eyebrows inching up.

I scroll some more. Brent grabs the phone from my hand. "Fuck. I know that place. It's one of the first cleanup jobs I did for the sheriff's department. That house had been used for human trafficking. Those poor girls had a bad end."

That tells me I don't want to see the pictures. "Was Davey still alive then?"

"No, I didn't start doing cleanup jobs for them until after his death." He's scrolling faster. "It's him, Blue." He turns the phone towards me. "That's Dawson."

"You can't see his face," I say.

"That's him. His size and shape."

He keeps scrolling. Faster than I can focus in on anything. Until one picture stands out.

"Stop. Go back one."

When he does, I point towards the close-up picture of a hand. "Jesus. I've seen that ring before. Zoom in if you can." My heart skips several sorely needed beats as he zooms in on the ring. "That's Mother-Of-Pearl behind the turquoise."

"Seen it? Where?"

I swallow hard before saying, "On Dawson's finger. I'm sure of it. When I was filling out the OFP."

He swipes to the next picture and I have to look away. The hand with the ring is holding a knife to someone's throat. Brent curses beneath his breath as he swipes through several other pictures. "I've seen enough," he says, clicking out of the photos.

I take the phone. "Davey took those pictures, didn't he?"

"Yeah. Had to. Fuck, he must have had enough time to stash the card in his key chain before they took his camera. Before they killed him." He puts his elbows on his knees and rubs his head with both hands. "You were right. Davey must've tried to prove Dawson was in on the trafficking. That house was hell on Earth. *Awful,* Blue." He huffs out a long breath. "Must have had my crew out there roughly six months after Davey died." He shakes his head.

A wild flicker enters his deep green eyes. "Dawson was testing me. Trying to see if I knew anything."

I'm rubbing his back with one hand, but can't think of anything to say when he jumps to his feet.

"Someone's here."

"Your motorcycle friends?"

"No. Too early." He spins around. "Stay here."

I don't have time to utter a response before he's across the room, clicking off the light, shutting the door behind him.

Crossing the room, I tuck the phone in my back pocket, but then pull it out again.

Not sure what to do with it, I tuck it under the mattress, and then walk to the door. Carefully, I turn the knob and open the door, just enough to hear –

Nothing. Dead silence. *Or was that a car door?*

"What are you doing here?" Brent asks, an edge in his voice.

There's a faint sound of laughter. Repulsive laughter.

I sneak out the door and down the hallway, my heart drumming in my ears so loud I can barely hear. I can't make out the words, but know the voice.

Asshole Dawson.

I peek around the living room doorway. Brent's outside, standing on the front steps.

"Disappointed," I hear Dawson say. Then something about "my boys" and "out here."

"I don't know what you're talking about," Brent says.

"Let me explain, numbnuts." Dawson must have walked closer, because I hear him clearer. "Your little meeting tonight with the Pearls and the Grizzlies won't be happening. Not the way you planned, anyway. After we're done here, we're blowing those bears to shit. Good news is, there *will* be a meeting. You. Me. That little girlfriend you have inside, and my other guests."

Brent's mumbled curse is only part of what I hear.

"Let go of her, you heathen!" My mother's voice.

I race across the room and push open the door.

"I told you to stay inside," Brent snarls, whirling around.

"I'm sorry," is all I can think to say. "So sorry."

No words in the universe can do justice to the nightmare in front of me.

Mother stands next to a car, her arms wrapped around Natalie. There's a burly man behind them, a smug demon look on his face.

Dawson, who's just a few feet in front of us, laughs again. "Don't be thinking about pulling one of those guns out, Eden." He waves a hand in the air. Two men step out of the driver's doors of the two cars parked behind the first. "I have backup. Plenty of it. You can't outsmart me,

Brent. I'll always be one step ahead of you. Got the best of both worlds. My badge and my Pearls."

"Cut the shit, Dawson. What do you want?"

Brent sounds unaffected. Furious, really. But I can hear his breathing. It's quick and shallow. His eyes never leave Nat.

"Regret how it's come to this. Truly, I do. I've given you plenty of lovely opportunities for you to fess up what you know about your brother," Dawson says. "You've ignored them."

"I don't know anything. Never have."

"I find that hard to believe." Dawson takes a step closer. "I know he took pictures that night. They weren't in his camera. Where are they?"

"Pictures of what?" Brent shakes his head, a cool deception in his eyes.

Dawson's eyes nearly glow red as he glares at Brent, then me.

Eventually he turns his neck, glancing around. He lets out a laugh and rubs his chin. His ring shines as it catches the moonlight.

"You know, fuck it. This might be better than my other plan." He waves a hand. "They'll find Graves' body over there in the barn, where you killed him in a jealous rage. Then you went on a rampage, killing the girlfriend, your very own daughter, and of course, the future mother-in-law."

I don't know how I'm still standing. My stomach churns, way past ready to be violently, violently sick. I'm shaking so hard there's no feeling left in my legs.

He laughs again. "The staging will be easy. Your guns

are already loaded. Plenty of prints. Ballistics will prove it all."

"You win, Dawson," Brent says. "I'll give you what I have. Just let us go."

No! I scream it in my head, but my lips won't work. Neither does my throat.

I grab Brent's arm. He can't give them the SD card.

His body feels stiff. Hard as stone while he shakes his head.

I want to say Dawson will still kill us. Kill us all. But he already knows that.

"They're not here," Brent says.

"Really?" Dawson says. "I don't believe that shit for a second. You're a bad fucking liar."

"They're on the other side of the property. There's a shack. Anything Davey ever had is tucked away there. Hidden."

Dawson casts a doubtful gaze at Brent before he turns slightly, the wheels turning in his evil head. "Natalie, you got a shack on this property?"

Don't answer, Nat. Please don't answer. Please, please, please, I say over and over in my head.

"Yeah," she whispers.

Fuck!

"Do you know how to get there?" Dawson asks.

I find my voice. "What?"

I find my feet, too, and leap forward. Brent grabs my arm, but I continue to speak. "You're dragging a child into your selfish, miserable life? Can't you find anyone bigger to pick on, Captain Dawson? You're officially the most useless, twisted, choked up shit-worm I've ever laid eyes on."

"Blue, stop it!" Brent says.

"No, Eden, let her go on," Dawson steps closer. "Would you prefer I pick on you, Ms. Derby? Seems you're asking for it." He lifts his brow. "Better yet, would you like to be the one who goes on a rampage? Killing Graves, then Eden, then his kid and your mom before doing yourself in? That'd make a fuck of a story! Blue the Cold Blooded Killer. They'll love it!"

Brent holds me back from stepping closer, but I let Dawson know what I think. "Fuck you."

He lifts a brow.

I glare. "How do you even know if Preston's dead?"

"Oh, he's dead all right. Just on ice till I decide where I want him found." Dawson's beady eyes scan me from head to toe. "Graves found out exactly how I take to other people trespassing on my territory. That fucker's family tried to strong-arm a few choice real estate deals way too close to my liking. Then I found out he was tangled up with you, with Eden. Can we say 'match made in Heaven?'"

Demon laughter. Again.

My blood runs cold for real. "You're one sick puppy, aren't you?"

"I'll take you to the shack," Brent says. "The women and Natalie stay here."

"Have you forgotten, Eden, that you don't have any bargaining chips?" Dawson steps forward and holds out his hand. "I'll take those guns now."

Brent pulls me backwards and steps in front of me. The glance he gives me over his shoulder tells me to stay put. I'm not that stupid.

Shame washes over me. Stupid is exactly what I was earlier.

It's my fault mom and Natalie are here. If I'd just stayed home like he asked, they'd be safe.

And Brent would be alone. He wouldn't know what Dawson was after, either.

At least I gave him that. Closure.

Small price for our lives.

But I can't get hung up on defeat. I have to keep thinking. Have to figure out what we can do next.

I close my eyes in order to swallow the lump in my throat, refusing to admit we're cooked.

"Everyone won't fit in my truck," Brent says. "The trail's rough. Your cars won't make it."

"Don't tell me what my cars can and can't do, asshole," Dawson says, sticking one of the guns Brent handed him in his waistband. The other one, he points at us, while talking to his men. "Phil, load those two back in the car. Kessler, you take Ms. Derby, and Albright, you ride with Eden."

I can feel the fury radiating off Brent. It might just be the scariest thing here.

I lay a hand on his back and stretch up on my toes to whisper in his ear, "I love you."

It's all I can think to say. The truth.

The full no-holds-barred truth. I never imagined that love, when I found it, would take precedence over all else. But it does. It's stronger than life and death.

"Come on, girlie," Dawson says.

Brent squeezes my wrist as I step up beside him. I nod, real subtle, silently telling him we're in this together and that I won't let him down. Whatever happens.

Then, I step down off the stoop, wrenching my arm out of Dawson's reach when he tries to grab it.

This psycho *will* pay. One way or another. If it's the last thing we do.

"Cuff her, Kessler," he says.

"Dawson!" Brent growls.

"Get in your truck, Eden, and stop bitching," Dawson orders. "And remember: one wrong move and somebody dies. That's an easy rule even a dumb shit like you can understand."

The man called Kessler grabs my arm, spins me around, and slaps a zip-tie on my wrists. I wish I was a hundred pounds heavier, or a hundred times stronger. Either one would come in handy right about now.

A piece of my self-defense training pops into my head. "Are you a cop too?" I ask, trying to draw his attention off how I'm keeping my wrists crossed while he tightens the tie.

Rather than answering, he shoves me towards the car he'd stepped out of earlier.

I don't know if others are in there or not. I'm mildly relieved the front and back seats are empty when he opens the passenger door. The man who'd driven the other car climbs in Brent's truck and Dawson gets in the passenger seat of the car carrying mother and Nat.

Brent's truck darts off through the field I'd watched him drive across while I'd driven up the driveway. The car with Dawson in it goes next and we follow.

I don't know if I'm so scared I can no longer feel it, or what, but I've gone numb inside.

Completely numb.

I don't have a fucking clue what to do next. Which

thoroughly pisses me off.

Without even thinking about doing so, I kick the dash. The glovebox falls open and I kick it again, slamming it shut.

"Hey, knock that off!" the driver shouts.

"Fuck you!" I kick the dash again, keeping my foot against the box. I thought I glimpsed a gun in there, but I'm not sure.

I keep tapping it with my foot, rage taking over, trying to make the latch let loose again so I can get a better look.

"Stop, bitch. I won't think twice about shooting you!"

"You don't think twice," I say. "That's for sure. If you did, you wouldn't be working with Dawson. But go ahead, shoot me. I'm sure he'll be impressed."

The car bounces over ruts and he's squeezing the steering wheel with both hands. He's nervous. There's sweat dripping down the side of his face. He doesn't look that old, either.

Close to my age, I'd guess. A new recruit in the Pearls, maybe. Young and unseasoned.

I press the advantage. "Is this your full-time job? Or are you a cop, too? Cop by day, thug by night?"

He doesn't answer.

Brent's four-wheel drive truck climbs the terrain better than the cars, but we're still traveling faster than we should. I hear rocks scraping the undercarriage. We hit a rut so hard, the entire vehicle jumps.

"Should have buckled up!" I let out a false laugh. "Don't want to die prematurely, do we?"

He flashes a glare my way.

I don't mind irritating him. Not in the least. "I'm a preschool teacher. And an art teacher." I kick the dash again, watching as the glovebox pops open, then kick it shut.

Yep, it's a gun.

"This kind of shit doesn't happen to preschool teachers, you know. I'd never even had a *ticket* until your lovely boss pulled me over. Perfect driving record, gone, just like that! You got any kids? Think this sort of thing ever happened to their teachers?"

"Shut. Up!"

"I bet it hasn't. How old are they? They know what you do? What about your parents? Do they know you're making them oh-so-proud?"

"Shut the fuck up!" He's roaring.

"What's that saying they used to have on all those police ride along rescue shows?" I'm working at getting a fingernail inside the clip of the zip-tie. Self-defense classes showed us how to do that, how to snap off the little tab inside, at just the right angle. "Crime doesn't pay, right? Remember?"

His jaw clenches as tight as his hands grip the wheel. We're losing ground on the car ahead of us. That's flustering him almost as much as my constant chatter.

"Better step on it, brah. Don't want to piss off your boss, do you?"

"Shut up, shut up, shut up, you fucking evil bitch!"

"Evil? Yeah, fuck you." The zip-tie loosens. "How long have you been working for him? Does he have Preston's body stored in your freezer? Bet your wife loves that."

We stop so fast we both fly forward. My leg on the dash stops me from hitting it, but he smacks the steering wheel hard.

"See what you did now, you whore?"

Pain explodes on the side of my face. It's a hot moment before I realize he's slapped me.

I was pissed before. Pissed and scared.

Now, I'm livid, and know I don't have much to lose.

Dawson isn't going to let any of us out alive. "I wasn't the one driving, you stupid SOB. It's no wonder Dawson put you bringing up the rear. He knew you wouldn't keep up."

He's laying on the gas, but we're hung up. Stuck. I hear the tires spinning, rocks flying everywhere.

Brent's truck rounds a bend at the bottom of the hill, slipping out of sight, and the other car is about to enter the bend, too.

"You better see what we're caught on." I nod toward the disappearing car. "Or you'll never know where to go. Won't have anyone to follow soon."

He slaps the steering wheel. "Fuck!"

Throwing open his door, he leans out, looking beneath the car before hitting the gas again. He curses again and then slams the car in park before climbing out.

I wait until he's at the back of the vehicle before I pull my hands out of the zip-tie and grab the gun.

The car rocks like a seesaw from the way he's pushing it from behind.

"Poor bastard, should have put it in neutral. Not park," I mumble, quickly sliding over into the driver's seat. I pull the door shut and hit the lock button.

He sees that and comes running up to the side of the car. Praying for the biggest break of my life, I drop the car into drive, slam my foot down on the gas pedal, and close my eyes against the gun he's pulled out.

The explosion of his shot is deafening.

XVI: FIRES ABOVE AND BELOW
(BRENT)

The sound of a gunshot has me slamming the brakes. I can see one car behind me, the one with Dawson in it, but the other hasn't made it around the first switchback.

"Keep driving," the motherfucker beside me says.

His gun never moves from the side of my head, and I want to break the bastard's arm like a dry stick.

I hit the gas, shaking my head.

It's been poisoned. My mind.

The idea of Blue being shot. Hurt. Begging for help.

Makes it hard to breathe. My lungs blaze. So does my rage.

I take the next switchback so fast the truck skids, back-steering it straight. Knowing I only have a few seconds before the other car's headlights will round the corner, I have to act.

Right the fuck now.

The cliff is on the passenger side. Keeping one hand on

the wheel, I grab hold of the hand he has wrapped around the butt of his gun and use it to smack him in the face.

The weapon goes off, blowing out the passenger's window.

I smack him with it again.

Again.

Fucking again.

Warmth, his blood, splatters my hand. I ram metal into his face three more times, all the while keeping the truck hugging the hill side of the road.

When his grip loosens, I take the gun away. Drop it in my lap, then stretch across him and grab the door handle.

Fuck. It won't open. Locked.

I use my knee to steer in order to hit the unlock button. The door opens, and I give his shoulder a push.

He screams, tries reaching for the door. I stomp the gas like a madman, swerving toward the cliff. My tires slide on the loose gravel. I swerve back at the very last second.

The door knocks him against the truck. I make the truck go jagged again, as close to the edge as possible, without throwing us open.

It's enough. The door flings wide open and this time, when it flies back, it slams shut.

Empty. Asshole, gone.

I check the the rear-view mirror, and side mirrors, but don't see a body.

One down, three to go.

If that shot I heard hurt Blue – if it was even aimed at her – I won't leave a single Pearl alive in the entire fucking state.

She's not dead, though.

I know she's not. My heart wouldn't still be beating if she was.

I have to press on, get to the shack, eliminate the others before I can go back for her.

My eyes are scalding hot. My chest about to explode.

Blue's smart. Real smart.

A survivor. Like me.

That's why we're so good together. Two of a kind. In some ways.

In others, we're complete opposites, which makes us good for each other.

The truck bounces and skids as I take the last corner. The hill's downward slope is smoother, and I lay on the gas for the short straightaway.

Look behind me before taking the next corner. One set of headlights. Has to be Dawson.

Natalie has to be terrified. I shouldn't be thankful to have pulled Cleo into this, but I'm glad she's with her. That has to help.

Dawson has so much to pay for, threatening my baby girl.

So fucking much.

Stay focused, I tell myself. Focus on what has to happen, what has to be done.

I take the last corner and then bounce over another pit in the road. Stomping on the gas, I make a beeline for the shack, thankful I've left one bomb under the lumber and boxes in the shed. It's a last ditch measure I'll have to use tonight.

Its detonator is hidden on the top of the door frame. The other triggers, the ones for the bombs I'd buried along the road in the valley, are in the backpack.

The road can't be seen from the shack, so I go over the placement of each bomb in my head, knowing I'm on my own. The Grizzlies won't be here yet, but the Pearls are already down there. Possibly dozens of them. A small army of cold blooded killers coming to save their friend, Officer Prick, and destroy the evidence that might flay them all alive.

Dawson wouldn't be here if they weren't close behind. He counts on backup.

He's where my focus has to stay. On him. On elimination.

The trees that shelter the shack come into view and I hit my bright lights, scanning the area for vehicles or movement. Nothing.

I park on the north side of the shed, so Dawson will only see the tailgate, and then jump out.

Time to run. There's barely a minute left.

Snatching the detonator off the door frame, I circle back, grabbing the backpack. After pulling out my last gun, I stuff it in my holster, keeping the one from Dawson's man in my pocket, and then I run out to the trees and hide the backpack.

When the time comes, I'll have to make it to the top of the little knoll at the end of the tree grove to see the road. I'll know when to trigger the explosions. My jaw tightens.

Headlights wind closer as I run for the shed. I glance up the hill, searching for a second set.

Something's up there, glistening in the moonlight. But it's not moving, and there aren't any lights.

I don't know what to make of that. What to think, except that Blue's still alive.

I refuse to think anything less.

Can't think otherwise.

I camp just inside the door, where I can watch the car roll to a stop, but Dawson can't see me.

Come on, you fucking demon shit. I'm waiting.

The passenger door opens. Finally, he steps out. "Albright!"

Silence echoes. He's calling the dead man's name.

"Albright!" A moment later, Dawson says, "Shit. Get them out of the back!"

I watch as the driver gets out and opens the back door. Cleo climbs out first and then helps Natalie out. Wrapping her arms around Nat, Cleo keeps her tight against her as she sidesteps away from the car.

"Eden!" Dawson shouts.

I step into the doorway. "Here."

"Where's Albright, you fuck?"

I shrug. "No lights in here. Got lost, maybe."

"Get in the car," he tells the driver, Bastard Phil. "Pull it up to the doorway."

I don't dare move, but I glance at Cleo.

She whispers to Natalie, who nods.

There's really no place for them to run. The trees aren't that thick, mostly overgrown brush. Rocks everywhere. Plus there could be snakes inside. Spiders, scorpions, stinging ants.

But I need them as far away from the shed as possible when I hit the detonator.

As the driver pulls the car forward, Dawson swings around, pointing his gun at Cleo and Nat. "You two stay right where you're at."

Cleo's head snaps up, and in that moment, I see where Blue gets her grit.

"And just exactly where do you expect us to go, Captain Dawson?" Cleo says. "Take a little jaunt up here in the hills? And please, stop waving that thing at us! You should be ashamed of yourself. Pointing a gun at a defenseless child." She steps in front of Nat. "Have you no pride? None whatsoever? You call yourself a man?"

Dawson sneers at her before turning back to me. "Now, where's Albright? Where?!"

"I don't know," I say. "Maybe he's taking a leak."

"For a man who's about to die, you're awfully calm."

No, I'm not, but I'm playing the part well.

I used to have to play it often. Zen-like calm masking an urge to hurt. That's how I got the nickname Monk, and that's who takes over now. "I could say the same about you, Dawson."

"Bullshit," he says, stepping closer. "I'm not the one dying tonight."

I nod. "Yeah. Dying would be too good for a fucking limpdick prick like you. You'll get what you deserve. Prison time. Sleeping next to convicts you put there. Some who used to be on your payroll." I hold up a hand. "I know you killed anyone who saw your face. Slit their throats."

Dawson's eyes widen.

"I've seen the pictures, Dawson. Grisly shit. All the men you promised to pay for hauling those young girls out of Mexico. Instead of money, they got their throat's cut. Bled to death right there at your feet." I shake my head, mainly to keep his attention on me as Natalie and Cleo inch their way backwards. "Did you think I'd just turn them over to you, idiot?" I let out a sarcastic laugh.

Now, his eyes are huge.

"There'd be no fun in that. No chess match. No kings. No queens. No pawns. No fun."

The gun in his hand shakes like a rattle.

I smile. "It's been five long years since Davey died. Pictures can be copied a lot of times. Sent many places."

Dawson shakes his head. "Enough! Don't fucking try me, Eden. You're a dead man. And if anyone but you has copies, I'd have caught wind of it by now. Just like I'd have heard about you snooping around to see if I'd filed the OFP, or if Graves' body was really found. There's *nothing* that happens in Phoenix I don't know about."

"Whatever. Just wanted you to know I've been snooping around." Movement catches the corner of my eye. At first, I think it's Bastard Phil, but he's still behind the wheel.

I keep my eyes on Dawson while trying to make out what's moving. "Wanted you to wonder where Davey put those pictures he took." My heart slams into my throat as I realize it's Blue. Sneaking up the road. She's crouched low, apparently unhurt. Thank God almighty.

"Other than the one on the front page of the paper, I mean. Where you declined to talk about the cameras you had installed on the border. Why was that? Afraid you might be recognized? That's when you had to move your crossing points. Found a new place to cross where there were no cameras not under your control."

I pretend to glance over my shoulder while I'm really getting a better look at Blue, just to make sure it's her. Cleo must notice, too, because she and Natalie are slowly inching backward.

Further and further. A little bit more and they'll be in the clear of debris.

Thank God again.

"Everything Davey left behind is in this shed," I say. "I boxed it up real neat. Put it out here. Of course, at the time, I didn't recognize you. Didn't know you till you hired me to start cleaning up your messes." I lower my voice. "Bloody, filthy, evil fucking messes. But your signature was on every one of them."

"Phil!" Dawson shouts. "What the fuck are you still doing in that car? Get inside that shed! Tell me what's in there."

The driver jumps out and storms past me. I regret not running Bastard Phil through the throat with his knife the day I decided to tell him to fuck off. Maybe we wouldn't be standing here.

"Watch for snakes," I tell him. "Nasty way to go."

"Fuck you," he snarls. "You're not so tough when you're outgunned, Monk."

Just wait, asshole, I think to myself.

I step out of the doorway and around the opposite side of the car from Dawson.

"Hold it right there, Eden," he says, swinging his gun at me.

I hold up my hands. "I was just giving him more light."

"What's in there, Phil?" Dawson asks.

"Can't tell for sure, but it looks like...a stack of boxes? Lots of 'em."

"Check them. Now!"

I glance through the doorway, see how close to the pile Phil is while sticking my hand into my coat pocket. I wrap my hand around the detonator and then count to three before I yell towards Cleo and Nat.

"Get down! For God's sake, keep your heads covered!"

Four lives.

Three seconds.

Two screams.

One chance.

Punching the button, I hit the ground. Barely start crawling under the car trunk before there's a noise like the end of the world.

The explosion rocks the mountain. From where I'm at, I can see where Cleo and Nat took cover behind a boulder, and how Cleo's body has completely covered Nat. Blue's on the ground too, closer now.

While the debris falls, I roll out from under the car. Though I'd love nothing more than to kill the bastard with my bare hands, I take aim at Dawson running for the trees, and shoot him in the knee.

Down he goes. *Now.*

I jump up and run. Getting to him before he has a chance to roll over, I kick the gun out of his hands.

Jerking both his arms, I twist them behind his back. "Shut the fuck up," I tell him.

"Yeah, you fucking cry-baby!"

The sound of her voice has me looking over my shoulder, where I see the most beautiful sight of my life. Blue.

She's smiling. "Hold him! I'm sure there's a few spare zip-ties in his car. I'll get them."

"Sure are!" Cleo shouts. "Right in the back seat. They thought they'd put one on me, but let me tell you, I told them Cleo Derby doesn't chafe her wrists for anything."

Blue returns within seconds. It just seems like hours. So does the time it takes her to zip-tie him. She not only binds his wrists, she ties his fingers, too. Making sure there's zero chance the evil fuck ever slips out.

"Are you about done?" I finally have to ask.

"Almost. He won't have a chance in hell of getting loose when I'm through."

Cleo and Nat arrive while Blue stays busy – she's moved on to using a zip-tie to hold a rag in Dawson's mouth.

"Daddy!" her little voice sets me off all over again.

I lift Natalie into my arms and hug her so tight.

So. So tight.

"You okay, baby girl? Did they hurt you? Tell me!"

"Yes, Daddy, I'm fine. Cleo didn't let them touch me." She kisses my cheek and then points to Dawson. "That man told us you were hurt and that we had to come with him to see you. I thought he was a cop. He showed us his badge."

"He is, baby girl. Unfortunately, sometimes bad people hide behind good things."

"That's what I told her, too."

I put Nat down and hug Cleo. "I'll never be able to thank you enough for tonight." I kiss her cheek before taking a step back and asking, "How do you manage to look like you just stepped out of a magazine even after hours of being held hostage?"

It's true. Her clothes don't have a wrinkle, and there isn't a single hair out of place on her head.

"A woman never tells all her secrets, Eden." She winks and then puts a hand on Natalie's shoulder as they both step back. They're clearing a path.

Blue steps forward.

There's dirt on her face. Her hair is a mess. Her shirt, torn. There's a gun stuck in the front of her jeans.

All in all, she's absolutely gorgeous.

My throat swells. I try, but words won't come. My eyes burn, this time with something besides maniac rage.

I shake my head, clearing my throat. "Blue, I heard a gun go off." I have to clear my throat again.

"That was Kessler." She shrugs. "Shooting at me. Idiot missed."

"Where is he?"

"I'm not sure, but I think I hit him with the back of the car. I never saw him in the mirror after I took off, but it sorta felt like I hit something. Could've been whatever the car hung up on, though." She shrugs again. "Or not." Glancing over my shoulder, she asks, "Is that the only way out of here?"

She's pointing up the road. "Yes," I answer. "Why?"

"Because there's a car hanging off a cliff up there, and I'm not sure where it'll land. But it could be on the road."

I grab her by the upper arms. "What?"

Fuck, when does it end? That had to be what I saw glistening in the moonlight.

"I shut off the headlights so no one would see me following and sort of misjudged that one really sharp turn." She steps closer to me. "Only two wheels went over the edge, but the other, the back one, was skidding over when I climbed out."

My heart stops. I pull her close.

Hug her. Kiss her. Kiss her some more.

She's the one who finally stops the kiss I want to last forever.

Holding up a finger, she says, "Hold that thought because this –" She makes a circle in the air with one finger. "Isn't over. I saw a *ton* of headlights down in the valley, Brent. And after that explosion, they'll be heading this way. Pronto."

Fuck. "Wait here!"

I run to the trees and snatch the backpack off the ground. At the top of the knoll, I see Blue's right.

A shitload of headlights the size of a small army rolls on, coming this way. It can't be close to three in the morning, so the Grizzlies aren't here yet.

I don't have much choice. I'll set off the bombs I've buried, and then we'll have to make a run for it. Hopefully, the blasts will take out enough to give us a fucking chance. Panic the ones who survive into running.

I pull out the detonators and hit the first trigger. Suck a breath and hold it in.

There's a slight delay before the first bomb down in the valley explodes. Then the second.

By the time the third one goes, I'm in jaw-hanging awe. The hills around us light up. None are close enough to make out completely, but I imagine there are dirt bikes, four-wheelers, dune buggies, and damn near every kind of all terrain vehicle.

As the sixth and final bomb goes off, the lights start descending down the hills. Harleys send their deep growls through the valley, and tracer fire rains down on the smoldering wreckage below.

"Your friends?" she asks.

"Yeah," I say, wrapping an arm around Blue. "They've got the high ground. Cross-Bones came early. They'll clean up real nice."

She wraps her arm around my waist and we watch the lights for a moment. Then she sighs. "Do you think all those bikers will want to come to a wedding?"

I turn, twisting her about so we're facing each other. "Wedding?"

She nods and grimaces. "My mother expects you to marry me after..." She shrugs. "All this. And she likes big weddings. Won't care one bit if half the guys are wearing leather and tattoos."

"What do you want?" I ask.

She shakes her head.

My heart takes a tumble. I would've sworn she'd say yes in a heartbeat. "You don't want to get married?"

She shakes her head and then nods. Bites her little lip.

"Blue, talk to me? Which is it? Yes or no?"

She presses both hands to her lips and shakes her head again.

"What? You can't talk?"

Shrugging, she nods. Then she shakes her head at me again.

Damn.

She closes her eyes and holds up a finger as if saying 'give me a minute.'

I get it. She's been through a lot the past few hours. I was speechless not that long ago myself. Grateful to be alive.

I don't have a ring, just the remains of Davey's turtle stuffed into my pocket.

Fuck if I care. All she has to do is say the word.

Letting out a long breath, she says, "I want...whatever you do."

"That's not an answer."

"It's the only one you're going to get until you tell me first."

I smile. That's my girl. Willing to give up whatever she might want for someone else.

Selfless. Sweet. Beautiful. Infuriating.

Blue. Red. Pink. And mine.

There's only one thing missing from that list, which I'm not waiting another minute to add.

God, do I love her.

This small, blue-haired, gun-toting preschool teacher. I've never been more sure of loving her. Tonight, after hearing that gunshot and fearing it was her, I knew exactly what I wanted.

A future. With her. All *ours.*

She's shown me that with her, I don't have to change. Be one thing or the other. I can be me.

Hard-ass when I need to be, or family man. Eden, Brent, or Monk. It doesn't matter.

She's there.

She's here with me right now. Staring nervously with the same pale gray-blue eyes I fell for what seems like an eternity ago. She's the angel for the devil inside me. The voice of reason. The love of my life.

The one I have to – fucking *have to* – call my wife.

"You already know what I want, babe." I stand up, kiss the tip of her nose, reaching into my pocket. Then I'm down on one knee again, grasping her hand in mine, pressing that silver turtle against her palm. "I've been your fiancé for over a month now. I'm ready for the wedding the second you say yes. Marry me, Blue. Give me all of it. All of you. Let me love you like I've never loved anyone else."

"Brent..."

I nod. "Tell me, babe. Gotta hear it. Straight from your

lips to my soul. Say yes."

"Yes!" It's barely a hiss. But it's enough.

I jump up, throw her back in my arms, hold on tight, and kiss her longer than it'd take to count the lights dancing all around us, above and below.

It's the strangest kind of fireworks between the stars and the flames crackling in the valley, smoking debris, but it's ours. It's fitting. It's chaotic and scary and exhilarating all at once.

It's everything I've wanted since the second we locked eyes in her class. And it's everything I'll keep till my dying day, smiling like a wrinkled old fool, remembering how our love blew the world apart and outshined Heaven itself for one crazy, unforgettable, heart-stopping night.

"I love you, Blue. Give me a week. I'll take part of Davey's turtle, whatever I can't repair, and have it made into a proper ring."

She pulls back before kissing me again, the tears in her eyes falling out. "Jesus. You're sure?"

I give her the most solemn nod of my life.

It's one last homage to my little brother, wherever he is, and it's also continuity. Without his sacrifice, I might not be here. There wouldn't be an us. I wouldn't be free from the oppressive weight on my back.

Free and clear to focus on making this woman the happiest on planet Earth.

"Blue, I'm positive."

She wraps her arms around my neck, bringing her lips close to my ear, speaking straight to my soul. "I love you, too, Eden. You and your everything."

* * *

Two Months Later

"Kiss the bride."

There's nothing more exciting than hearing those words.

Nothing better than tasting her lips.

Nothing better than pulling my newly-married Blue into my grasp and fusing us with a kiss that promises forever tenfold.

It seems like a whole eternity passes in a kiss.

I can't hear the laughter, the screams of joy, all the friends and family and even a few bawdy bikers roaring in the distance.

Right here, right now, it's me, her, and nothing else.

My feisty, blue beautiful all. My passion, wrapped in her ivory white dress with a fresh blue stripe in her hair.

My temptation. It's hard as hell not to rip off the veil I've just thrown back to own her lips.

Fuck, it's hard not to just pull her out of the whole ensemble and put her where she belongs: under me.

I've never wanted to be in this woman more than I do now.

Every waking second since she became Mrs. Eden.

"God!" She whispers one word, turning away, just as reluctant as me to break the kiss. "We'd better get going. We've got a reception to get to."

"Yeah. That thing," I tell her with a wink.

Her hand pulses several times in mine. I lead her down the aisle and we walk through the confetti shower. Nat stands on a chair next to my parents, hurling it everywhere. Country music blasts from the elaborate sound system.

Never been completely my style, but today, it works. It's us, after all our highs and lows and near-death somersaults to this very moment, when forever isn't just theoretical anymore.

I've married the woman of my dreams. I'm walking with her hand-in-hand, past my grinning daughter, my family, a hysterically sobbing new mother-in-law, and big men with Grizzlies MC and US Army patches alike.

It takes almost a million years to make our way through the many handshakes, back slaps, hugs, and congratulations coming from all sides.

Finally, we're in the limo. Blue barely has time to pour herself a glass of champagne before I tug her on my lap, storming kisses up her neck. "Easy, babe. I promised you four hours. My limit. Then we've got ourselves a date with a bed and a closed door."

"You're lucky I agreed to a short reception. If mom had her way, there'd be karaoke blasting until dawn."

I grin, loving how she shudders the longer my beard grazes her throat. Encouragement. I plant several more kisses, marking on my territory before I say, "Like I don't already know I'm the luckiest man between here and Pluto. Four hours, babe. I'm pushing it so hard because it's all I can take."

"Oh?"

Growling, I play with the frilly collar of her dress. One little rip is all it'd take. I'm able to reign in my inner caveman just enough to keep her gown intact. "Need to fuck my wife, Blue. All night. Very hard."

She bats her hands playfully at my chest, laughing. I

show her how serious I am, palming her cheek, bringing her in for another kiss. Her champagne lips taste sweeter than usual.

Good way to get started this evening, too. I'll need a few stiff drinks at the reception just to keep my dick in line.

Let the four hour countdown begin.

* * *

"Brent, what's wrong?"

I can't take my eyes off the scene in front of me. We're lucky we had the dance floor to ourselves for our first waltz, or we damn well might have been upstaged by a very drunk Clara dancing like mad with Scarecrow.

I hadn't seen him for years since. Not since leaving the Grizzlies. The mean, lean young man with the long tawny beard became an even more jacked thirty year old with an even longer beard in the meantime. Possibly the only man on earth capable of shutting Clara's big mouth.

Hand on my face, I turn back to see Blue laughing. "Oh, that? She's having fun doing something besides wagging her tongue. Proves this wedding's *really* something special!"

"There's your chance, Blue."

"Chance?"

I swing her around as another song starts, bringing us closer to the odd couple. "You. Her. Gossip. Payback."

"Eden!" She pinches my cheek.

I close off her gasp, smothering her lips with another feral kiss.

"What? You're telling me you really can't stand kicking

up a little mischief?"

"Not *here*. Sure, she annoyed me, but our guests should be immune from –"

"All right," I growl, pulling out my phone. "We'll do it your way, then."

Her jaw drops as I snap a pic. Then several more in quick succession, just as Scarecrow dips Clara low and she runs a clumsy hand through his scruff. "Brent, hey –"

"I'll be sure our photographer cleans it up and posts it front and center all over social media. That'll get some Derbys clucking, yeah?"

Blue's eyes go big. Then she's smiling, wrinkling her nose, trying to suppress a snicker.

"Sometimes, I think you're trying to give the devil a run for his money."

I shrug. "Yeah, Blue. Except I'm better looking. You knew that long before we said 'I do.'"

She slaps me playfully again. I turn away from the bizarre mating dance between my old biker bud and her cousin, giving her lips my full attention again.

They're more than happy till a small voice behind me hits my ears. "Daddy? Izzy? Can I cut in?"

"For you, baby girl, anytime. Come here!" I bend down low to take Nat's hands and spin her slowly to Johnny Cash.

Blue gives me a knowing look and saunters aside, casting one last sexy glance my way before she trots off to mingle with her relatives. The night couldn't get more perfect.

I'm left smiling. Teasing my daughter constantly about how the next time we're dancing at a wedding, it might be her own.

Later, I rejoin Blue. We spend another hour talking up our guests. A whole slew of folks from her ma's side I hadn't met at Megan's wedding, Derbys I already know, then men on my payroll, vets from my unit, and guys from the club I used to call home.

Cross-Bones reluctantly takes the huge bear hug I lay on him before we head out. I don't care. "Thanks again, Veep. For everything. Wouldn't be here today if you hadn't sent the cavalry that night. Give my best to Blackjack when you see him again."

"You're damn welcome anytime. I will. Drop us a line sometime, Monk. Even if it's just for beers."

"Will do."

Our limo's waiting outside. Cross-Bones whistles to the guys. I'm a made man, plenty of money to go around, but I'm not sure I'll ever get used to this high class shit.

I'm not Knox Carlisle, the Phoenix billionaire who owns the Black Rhino jewelry company, where I had her ring made using bits of Davey's old turtle. Knox heard about the blowout with the Pearls and personally ordered it done free of charge.

And I'm perfectly okay with that.

Life is good. Especially when we're in the limo again, on a one way trip to our fancy hotel near the airport. Tonight only. Tomorrow, we're bound for Zurich. A city steeped in history, beauty, and art Blue's always wanted to see. I'll be perfectly happy to load up on fresh air and good Swiss beer.

"I hope Nat won't miss us too long," Blue says.

Makes me smile. She can't help it.

Even on our wedding night, she's got my little girl in mind. I didn't go into this looking to find her a mama, but damn it, I did. There's no one else I'd rather have in Nat's life than me and Isabella Eden.

"My parents will keep her plenty busy, Blue. Probably buy her pizza and tacos every night they're in town, holding down the house, after dragging her to every art museum between here and Tucson."

"You're right, I suppose."

"Totally," I say, pulling her closer onto my lap. "Now, Mrs. Eden, we're close to the four hour mark. We both have some *very* pressing business."

I grind my hips into hers, shifting up slightly. She smiles, feeling my hard-on.

So full, so ready, and so wild. Aching like hell to claim my wife's sweet cunt for the very first time.

* * *

LESS THAN A HALF HOUR LATER, we're stumbling into our honeymoon suite. She tugs on my tie, muttering a few words about how she's sorry to see my tux go. Not sorry enough to resist my hands when they start pulling her out of that dress.

We crash down on the bed after we're free. Naked. Frantic.

She sucks me with a vigor I haven't seen for weeks. Maybe it's because we swore off fucking for the past seven days, something she wanted, telling me it'd make tonight that much sweeter.

I put up a fight at the time.

Damn if she isn't right, though. Her little mouth takes me so good, so deep, it's hard not to pop off in the first couple minutes.

Good thing I've got stamina. I'm not the only one looking my finest this wedding night either. Her hair looks damn good.

Feels good in my fist as I gently tug several blue-blonde locks, lifting her away.

Then, I push her back on the bed, spread her legs, and hear the word that makes my cock tingle. "Oh, Brent!"

Oh.

O.

That's what I'm here to deliver. Wedged between her legs, tongue going, lapping at her folds like the sex starved maniac I've become.

Her clit goes between my teeth. I suck until she whimpers.

Hello, Heaven.

But it's nothing like every beautiful inch of Blue quaking as she goes off on my tongue. Her thighs catch my face. I don't fucking stop for anything. She rides my mouth, my beard, my tongue – which leaves nothing to the imagination about how hard we'll be fucking soon.

She's still clenching the sheets when I come up for air, wiping her sweetness off my fingers. "Babe," I whisper, hovering over her.

Blue's already trying to twist onto her belly. Hot and bothered, ready to put her ass up for me.

Growling, I pin her down, loving how desire flashes in her eyes as they roll.

"Up," I say, taking her hand, leading her across the room.

I love fucking her from behind. There'll be plenty of that to come.

Right now, I've got something different in mind.

I booked this place months ago. It's a Presidential suite which has probably had a few real Presidents and reams of royals and CEOs calling it home during their stay in Phoenix. These fancy ass rooms need a draw, and the big one here's obvious.

The mirror up against the wall in the bathroom is *huge.*

Like something damn near out of the seventeenth century. I have to spread her arms wide to flatten her hands along the edges. Love how she huffs a small, uncertain breath as my hand drifts lower, spreading her thighs.

I fist a long lock of her hair before speaking again. "First of many wedding presents, Blue. Soon as I saw the pics of this place online, I knew it'd be perfect."

"Perfect...why?" Her eyes narrow as I rub my swollen tip against her aching pussy lips.

Fuck, so wet. So ready.

"For this." I push dead into her with a growl, going balls deep in one stroke. Her voice hitches and the adrenaline hits my system. "Wanted to fuck you first in our favorite position. But I also wanted to look into my wife's eyes the first time she comes on my dick."

"Oh, God. Oh, Eden."

I thrust. Slowly, firmly, fiercely at first, picking up speed. My lips graze her shoulder each time she leans into me, and then my teeth come out to play.

No more words. Not anymore.

We're both too lost in the frenzy. In each other. In this crazy sweet chaos we've decided to weave a life from, drunk on every molecule of us.

"Oh. Brent. Oh. Shit!" She's practically screaming.

It's nice to hear her let it all out for once.

Here, there's no worries about Nat waking up down the hall if we're too loud. It urges me on, and I lay into her. Wanting her to scream like a banshee.

We go hard.

Give it so hard my ass clenches each time I drive deep, balls slapping madly on her clit.

She needs to come. Right the fuck now. Because watching her tits bounce wild in the mirror while she's bent over with her ass against my abs is too much.

"Blue!"

"Brent, I'm –"

Fuck! Make that both of us.

Coming so savagely it could shear us in two, if we weren't already *one.*

I see her eyes flutter shut the very second it hits. Then I feel her heat, her silk, her O clenching my cock.

One more thrust and I'm done.

If there's anything else on this earth better than coming deep in my woman without a rubber, I haven't found it. Don't fucking want to.

My seed wants to claim her at a primal level. The fire ripping through my cock reminds me of that, turning my spine into one long torch running up my brain.

Bliss.

Sweet bliss. Knowing it's just a matter of time before I own her completely, and give Nat a little brother or sister.

Won't be for a few years, probably. We've talked about kids and decided they're at least a year out, maybe two. But fuck, when she's ready, I'll be waiting with every aphrodisiac known to man.

My cock gives a few last fiery jolts. I force my balls to empty inside her and I barely go soft. If I didn't have to spin her around to lay a proper kiss on those lips, I might've just stayed in her and kept going straight into round two.

"That. Was. Incredible."

I smile at her breathing more than her words. Kiss her with a fierceness that says I'm glad I've done my job, stealing the air from her lungs, rendering her speechless.

"Incredible, yeah. Only the best for Mrs. Eden," I say, running my fingers through her hair.

"Baby, don't rush. We've got our whole lives ahead." Her eyes are huge, beautiful, sparkling. "Also, we *have* to get some sleep by two or three. Our flight's at eight o'clock."

"Plenty of time to sleep on our way to Europe."

"Eden –"

"Blue," I whisper, taking her lips again. The next kiss lets her know I'm not messing around. So does how I squeeze her shoulders. "Let's move this to bed. Got a couple hours to ourselves to find out if Mrs. Eden does a better job than Ms. Derby did at tiring out her husband on their wedding night."

"Ass!" Oh, but she's laughing.

I lift her up, carrying her across the makeshift threshold, before throwing her down on the mattress.

This, right here, is where we belong. She isn't wrong.

We've got our whole lives ahead to refine, to explore, to do what we do best over and over and over.

And tonight, I know, that's all of it. From the way we kiss with everything in our bones, to how she looks at my little girl.

It's right. It's mine. And it'll always be Blue.

XVII: EXTENDED EPILOGUE (IZZY)

Three Years Later

"Rome?" Mouth open, Natalie looks at Brent and I.

We nod together.

"Rome! Rome! Holy crap, I'm going to Rome!" She jumps up and down and hugs her birthday card to her chest. "To study art."

Her high-pitched squeal fills the room. "Mom, Dad, I can't believe this! It's going to be the best three months of my life!"

Brent goes stiff beside me. I lay a hand on his thigh. Although he's totally agreeable with the idea, he's worried. So am I.

Natalie is mature as ever for her age, but she's only thirteen, and no matter how old she'll ever become, she will always be his baby girl. And my daughter.

Some days, I truly can't believe I have the privilege of being her mother.

"Thank you. Thank you!" she exclaims, running across the room to hug us both.

"You did all the work," I say, kissing her cheek. "Good things come to those who earn them."

"We just get to pay for it," Brent flashes a grin. He winks at her and kisses her forehead. "You're worth it, baby girl. Every damn penny."

"We're all so proud of your accomplishments, Nat," Mother says. "Grandpa George and I will fly over with you and spend two weeks while you're getting all settled in. It's been *years* since I had a decent rabbit ragu. Oh, I can't wait!"

George reaches over and squeezes mom's hand. "We're ready. And we're all very proud indeed, Nat."

I smile, wondering where the time goes.

Seems like yesterday when Mother and George snuck off to Vegas and got married. Less than a week after Brent and I tied the knot. They may have done it sooner, but mother was too busy organizing my wedding.

I let her plan the entire thing. She and Natalie didn't miss a single detail. All I had to do was put on the dress they'd picked out and show up.

Which was fine with me because I didn't care about the when, where, or what. All that mattered to me was *who*.

Mom claims it was the biggest wedding our family's ever seen, and people still can't stop talking about it. So far, she's right.

It's been three years. Not a family event goes by where

someone doesn't mention the fleet of motorcycles that filled the parking lot of the reception hall.

"We're so happy for you, Natalie," Brent's mother, Rose, says. "Grandpa Tom and I will fly over for your last two weeks, and then fly home with you, too."

I smile, thanking her. Ever since the truth came out about Davey's death, both of Brent's parents have started living again. That's how he describes it.

Those hellish years, between Davey's death and Dawson's arrest, they'd only been shells of themselves. Brent's happy for them, and his happiness is more than enough to make me tap dance on cloud nine.

Natalie runs from one set of grandparents to the next, hugging them tight, declaring she's the luckiest girl ever.

I feel pretty darn lucky myself and lean against Brent as he puts his arm around me. "Your dad and I will fly over anytime you want," I say. "All you have to do is call."

"Wait until the family hears about this!" Mom glances toward us. "You *will* be at the family dinner this week, won't you? Clara's trying her new French Silk recipe. I didn't know a pie could send a person to Heaven and back, but this one...dear God."

"Yes, Cleo," Brent replies. "We'll be there."

I no longer dread family dinner night. We barely miss one, yet Mother still calls every week to make sure we're coming. I don't blame her. She's proud of her family.

So am I.

We each have our own version of what happened that night. Brent claims Davey and I were the heroes. That without his pictures, the head of the biggest crime syndicate in the state would've never gone down, and that without me, those pictures would've never turned up.

I know the real hero was him. He set it all up. Orchestrated perfectly.

By the time red lights started rolling in, the Grizzlies had all dispersed, leaving the police to believe Brent had indeed taken down the Pearls single-handedly.

Then there's Mother's version. I tell her she should write books rather than read them.

By the time she's done telling what happened that night, she has people believing she was digging her own grave in the middle of the desert, surrounded by dozens of gun-toting madmen, when Brent started detonating the bombs he'd strategically placed. Just like he read their minds.

The real truth came out under oath, during the trial against Dawson. Captain Asshole is now experiencing Hell on Earth, sharing prison cells with men he'd put there. Many of them former Pearls, arrested the morning after in sting operations across Maricopa and beyond.

Everybody gets what they deserve in life. Sometimes.

A soft cry coming through the baby monitor has everyone in the room standing up.

"That's DJ. I'll go check!" both my mother and Rose say at the same time.

They laugh then. The rest of us exchange looks, smiling.

Since the day he was born, David Jacob Eden, named after his uncle and my dad, has been as big a charmer as his father. He's stolen countless hearts with his forest green eyes plus the adorable little curl in his hair.

"You go ahead," Rose says.

"No, *you*, my dear," Mom says.

"For crying out loud, not this again!" Tom says. "Why

don't you both just go? One can wipe his nose while the other wipes his butt."

Rose hooks her arm through Mother's. "Well, maybe we will."

They march out of the room.

George glances at Tom. "Kid's been asleep since we arrived. New record?"

Tom nods and grins. "And I swear he grows two inches a week."

"Maybe we should see if they need some help," George suggests.

"Good idea."

The two men walk out of the room.

Natalie sighs and shakes her head as she follows them. "I'll go make sure there's no fighting."

Brent and I look at each other and laugh as we sit back down on the couch. I lean my head on his shoulder, completely content and happy.

My eyes settle on the drawing I've framed and hung on the wall. Brent and Natalie drew it together and gave it to me on our wedding day.

It's the three of us: Brent, Nat, and me. But we're older, what they surmised we'd look like in the future – twenty years from our wedding day. Their attention to detail is amazing. I can believe that's exactly what we'll look like, and that we'll be just as happy as the picture shows us.

Brent must see what I'm looking at because he pulls me even closer. "Nat and I are working on a new one that has DJ."

I lift my head to glance up at him. "How do you know what he'll look like? He's only six months old."

He kisses my forehead. "He'll be big and strong. Just like his old man. Smart like his ma."

I smile and lay my head back on his shoulder. "You're right. The best of us."

"I *did* draw something else for you to take a look at, Mrs. Eden. All by myself. I'd really love your opinion."

I bite at the smile forming. "Oh?"

"Yeah. Right here." He shifts slightly, pulling a piece of notebook paper out of his pocket.

My heart starts thudding. He does this a lot.

Draws rather lewd pictures of the two of us.

I'll never tire of them.

I fold open the paper and sigh. "Hmmm."

It's the two of us. He's so predictable, but that doesn't mean it isn't hot. We're naked, of course, and in the midst of performing a rather interesting sexual encounter. "Have we tried this before?"

He nibbles on my ear. "Last night."

"Aw," I say, as if just now remembering a night I'll never forget. Which is most every night. "I do recall something similar...but I think your hands were over a bit. And mine were lower, more like here."

He slides a hand under my shirt, under my bra. "I don't remember," he says, attempting to sound serious.

"Really?" I cup his bulge, thrilled by the hardness. "Maybe I'm thinking of someone else then."

Growling, he acts so fast, it's less than a second.

I'm on my back. On the couch. And he's on top of me.

"Let me show you so you'll remember correctly," he says, thumbing my nipples.

Happiness explodes inside me as my body goes electric. I'm more than willing, but feel inclined to point out the obvious. "Careful, Eden. Your parents and mine are upstairs with our children. All *six* of them could come running down here at any given moment." I wrap my arms around his neck and brush my lips over his. "So jealous. There'll never be anyone else. You fill me completely."

"I know," he whispers. "And if you ever do so much as stare at another man too long, I'll fuck you straight, Blue. For hours. Till you can't walk for the next week."

Holy hell.

Even after hundreds, maybe thousands, of times, he's still able to find just the right words to make me ache. After a long and thorough kiss that has me wishing for night time, he jumps to his feet and pulls me off the couch.

"Where are we going?" I ask as he leads me across the room.

"My office," he says. "We've got time for a quickie."

I laugh, yet have to act like I'm concerned. "Seriously? The house is full of people," I say, hurrying down the hallway beside him.

"Distracted people. They won't come sniffing around for at least another hour." He shuts the office door, locks it, and unzips his jeans. "After they change DJ, they'll each need a turn to hold him. Then they'll have to decide who's going to get his bottle ready. They'll want to sit and tell stories after that. You know how my old man is. He'll talk your ear off once he gets going. Plenty of time, Blue."

He isn't wrong. And for once, I'm thankful Tom Eden can be so long-winded.

I'm already pulling down my shorts and panties. "That's true, but plenty of time for what?"

He grabs me, hoists me in the air, and then spins us around, planting my back against the door.

My breath catches as he eases me to him.

"Time for this," he whispers. "Every inch of me deep inside you, Blue."

I can't stop the pleasure groan that rumbles up my throat as his hard shaft sinks deep. Wrapping my legs around his waist, I grab his shoulders as he starts pumping.

In no time, we find our rhythm, as fast and furious as our kisses.

"I love this," I say between gasps, my O coming faster than it should.

Today, I don't care. I may not be capable of caring about anything while he's in me, thrusting like mad, his breath coming in faster, shallower waves.

"Quickies?" he asks.

"Everything!" I say. My pussy tightens, heat surges, and it's hard to form words. "Absolutely everything. Every part of being Mrs. Brent Eden."

"You're in luck, Blue. I love the hell out of everything Mrs. Brent Eden does, too." His eyes narrow. His thrusts quicken. Our bodies shake. "Now, come for me, babe."

Like I have a choice.

His last thrust sends us both over the edge, where we know how deep, how true, how beautifully we can fall.

THANKS!

Want more Nicole Snow? Sign up for my newsletter to hear about new releases, exclusive subscriber giveaways, and more fun stuff!

JOIN THE NICOLE SNOW NEWSLETTER! - http://eepurl.com/HwFW1

Thank you so much for buying this book. I hope my romances sweeten your days with pleasure, drama, and all the feels! I tell the stories you want to hear.

If you liked this book, please consider leaving a review and checking out my other romance tales.

THANKS!

Got a comment on my work? Email me at nicole@nicolesnowbooks.com. I love hearing from fans!

Nicole Snow

More Intense Romance by Nicole Snow

CINDERELLA UNDONE

MAN ENOUGH

SURPRISE DADDY

LAST TIME WE KISSED

PRINCE WITH BENEFITS: A BILLIONAIRE ROYAL ROMANCE

MARRY ME AGAIN: A BILLIONAIRE SECOND CHANCE ROMANCE

LOVE SCARS: BAD BOY'S BRIDE

MERCILESS LOVE: A DARK ROMANCE

RECKLESSLY HIS: A BAD BOY MAFIA ROMANCE

STEPBROTHER CHARMING: A BILLIONAIRE BAD BOY ROMANCE

STEPBROTHER UNSEALED: A BAD BOY MILITARY ROMANCE

Prairie Devils MC Books

OUTLAW KIND OF LOVE

NOMAD KIND OF LOVE

SAVAGE KIND OF LOVE

WICKED KIND OF LOVE

BITTER KIND OF LOVE

Grizzlies MC Books

OUTLAW'S KISS

OUTLAW'S OBSESSION

OUTLAW'S BRIDE

OUTLAW'S VOW

Deadly Pistols MC Books

NEVER LOVE AN OUTLAW

NEVER KISS AN OUTLAW

NEVER HAVE AN OUTLAW'S BABY

NEVER WED AN OUTLAW

Baby Fever Books

BABY FEVER BRIDE

BABY FEVER PROMISE

BABY FEVER SECRETS

Only Pretend Books

FIANCÉ ON PAPER

ONE NIGHT BRIDE

SEXY SAMPLES: MAN ENOUGH

I: Cupcakes for Room 205 (Tabby)

They say a woman knows it's obvious when she's found the one.

Prince Charming isn't subtle.

She remembers every first with Mr. Right. Every second, third, and fourth.

Every beat of her own enchanted heart.

His face, his smell, the mischief dancing in his eyes that makes her all tingly and weak-kneed looking back on their wedding day, and then again many years later through the fog of love.

The lyrical cadence of his voice etches on her brain

forever. His first kiss – the one that *has* to happen with storybook perfection – leaves the heart drumming on infinity shuffle, an echo of sweet nostalgia in her blood.

When I first saw Rex Osborne, there was none of that.

Just the roar of his old truck pulling into our lot. Two doors slamming shut. A half-second glance at him from behind while I hoisted the snow-packed shovel over my shoulder.

Another second spent staring harder. Maybe I thought his shoulders looked a little out of place in this small town.

Too big. Too broad. Too tall. Too *heavy*.

Too much urgency in his step.

Too much man for Split Harbor, and for me.

I heard two distant little voices at his feet, murmuring the happy nothings children do. Then the three of them disappeared inside the lodge.

It lasted all of three seconds before I tucked my head down and went back to work, scraping snow off the path. I only stopped for one more thing.

A growl rumbled in the sky, almost like thunder, totally out of place in frozen dead February.

I still don't know if I imagined it.

But I didn't imagine him.

I didn't know I'd met the man who'd ruin *imagining* for good, who'd tear what I thought I knew to pieces, who'd dynamite my heart, and who'd ground himself in my life's smoking crater.

Rex taught me so many things and showed me many more. Like what's real, what's undeniable, what's worth every shred of passion in two fiery souls.

Rex taught me how to live. How to love. How to hurt.

And then Rex set me free.

* * *

I tuck the shovel into the corner of the porch railings right next to the bucket of rock salt I'll need again first thing in the morning. So far we've only gotten a light dusting of snow, but more is predicted.

No surprises. It's winter. In Michigan.

My cheeks puff as I hold in the heavy sigh burning my lungs, wanting out. It is what it is. This is my home. My livelihood. My future.

I need to be thankful for that. All of it. And I need to be satisfied, too.

I owe Gramps big time. If not for him, Lord knows where I'd be right now. Rather than living in a lodge where people pay good money to rest, relax, and enjoy life, I might've ended up in a foster home.

Shaking off the melancholy that's been weighing heavier and heavier lately, I push open the employee entrance and remove my boots, coat, hat and mittens before sitting down on the bench to change into tennis shoes.

It'll be better when Russ returns, I tell myself. Who'd have guessed a guy could break an ankle so bad he'd need two surgeries by just stepping wrong off a ladder?

One less pair of strong hands. Which also means I'll be shoveling a whole lot more yet this winter.

"Break time's over."

I glance up and crack a smile at my grandfather's words. "Break time?"

The wrinkles around his twinkling blue eyes increase

as he chuckles while walking down the narrow hallway. "I've been looking to hire someone to take over Russ' duties, but –"

I laugh, interrupting him. "Everyone knows you too well, Gramps. Most who've worked for you before aren't willing to do it again."

"Only the lazy ones."

"So, everyone in Northern Michigan?" I can't resist poking fun at my Gramps' impossible standards.

He scowls at me, which only makes me laugh harder. Pushing off the bench, I step closer to him and pat his upper arm. The softness my hand encounters reminds me he's not as big and strong as he once was.

He's run the Grand Pine Lodge for over fifty years. He'll continue until his old heart stops beating. And I'll be right beside him. Probably after, too. This lodge has been in our family since the first building sprung up over a hundred years ago.

Like it or not, I know my destiny. My place. Some days, it's just harder to accept than others.

"I don't mind shoveling the sidewalks. Never have and never will," I tell him. Truth be told, it's partly my fault that Russ broke his ankle. Fixing up the stables was *my* idea. A way to expand the services we offer, and hopefully increase occupancy and revenue. "Wes Owens will still plow. Just as long as Russ comes back by spring so we don't have to hire lawn care, we'll be fine."

Gramps wraps an arm around my shoulder, nodding his thanks. "We make a good team, Tabby-kitten."

"That we do, Pops."

He scowls again, but then we both laugh. He doesn't like being called Pops any more than I like being called

Tabby-kitten. Never have liked nicknames. Tabby is close enough to a nickname all by itself, and it's all I've got. But I do love the old man, despite how ornery he can be sometimes.

"We got a late arrival," he says, kissing my temple.

"Oh? I didn't see a reservation." I saw the man with two kids from a distance while I was busy shoveling, of course, but I don't say anything. Some days, we have more quick stops here looking for directions than proper guests.

"Didn't have one. I put them in room 205. You'll need to take something up for them to eat."

I nod. None of this is unusual. Exceptional guest service in the middle of nowhere is our specialty, and being as small as we are, it's not like we're ever bursting at the seams. However, this time of year, after the holidays and before spring, we can go weeks without a single guest. "How many?"

"Three. I already told Marcy."

"All right." I plant a kiss on his soft and wrinkled cheek. "I'll see to it, no problem. You head on up to bed and I'll lock up after delivering the food." With a grin over my shoulder as I start walking towards the kitchen door, I add, "I'll see you in the morning."

"Not if I see you first."

The joke is almost as old as him, but I still laugh, mainly because he expects it. Life here would be nothing without reflexes, habits, and little rituals. I wait near the kitchen door until after he turns the corner that leads to the back stairs. Then I let out the sigh that was still inside me and push open the door.

Hustling around the large kitchen like it's on fire, Marcy takes a couple single serving milk cartons out of the double-door fridge and sets them on an already full tray. She's been with the lodge as long as I can remember, a wonderful cook. With my baking skills, we make a good team.

I lift the metal lid off the plate on the tray. "Yum, chicken salad."

"I have a sandwich in the fridge for you, too," Marcy says with a smile.

Skipping meals is my specialty. Comes with running the lodge, where there's never enough hours in the day to cover everything. "What would I do without you?"

"Me? Nonsense, Tabby. This place wouldn't run without you," she answers. "Everyone knows it. Including that grumpy old man."

Marcy loves Gramps as much as I do, and works just as hard. "I'll clean after delivering this and then lock up." Lifting the tray off the center island, I say, "Goodnight."

"Sleep tight," she says, removing the apron she wears day and night.

She has dozens of aprons, all handmade. I still don't know when she finds the time to sew them up in her room on the third floor. Both she and Gramps have rooms up there.

In that respect, I'm lucky. I live in the cabin out back – except when I have to evacuate due to a huge group of guests rolling in. Thankfully, it doesn't happen often.

I exit the kitchen and head towards the back service stairway. The large front steps, as well as the small but serviceable elevator, are reserved for guests only. I try to tread carefully. These stairs are known to creak and I don't want to disturb the few guests we have, making my way up them and down the hall to room 205.

There, I shift the tray in order to balance it against me so I can use one hand to knock. Before that happens, the door flies open. A huge hand grabs my arm, pulling me inside the room.

I manage to keep the tray from falling, but when I meet the nasty glare of the man still clutching my arm, I dang near drop it again.

"What the hell do you want and why are you sneaking around in the hallway?"

Holy crap. Guests have rarely dumbfounded me and never scared me. Until now.

I open my mouth, but nothing comes out. Tongue-tied? Since *when?*

"Well?" he snaps before my mind has a chance to force my tongue loose.

I finally take a good look at Mr. Porcupine. My heart skips a beat. If he wasn't so scary demanding, he'd be damn near gorgeous.

"Are those cupcakes?"

"Are they for us?"

The little voices coming from across the room snap me out of my deer-in-headlights mode. My heart slides out of my throat and back down in my chest where it belongs as I turn and see two little boys. Adorable little boys dressed in red and white striped pajamas with sandy-blond hair and big blue eyes.

The same shade of blue as the man still clutching my arm. No man, at least not one with an ounce of sanity, would accost a woman in front of his kids, so I jerk my arm out of his hold and carry the tray to the table in the center of the room.

"Yes, they're cupcakes, and they're yours." My nerves are settling. Teasingly, I add, "But only if you like chocolate."

"We do!" they sing in unison.

Twins. Identical, and with those eyes, the man could never deny parentage. Thankful my mind works again, I turn to their papa, whose scowl could rival Gramps any day of the week. Slowly exhaling my relief, because I know grumpy men far too well, I say, "I *wasn't* sneaking. I was busy bringing you something to eat. Your sons are obviously hungry."

His piercing blue eyes practically burn holes through me, but I hold my own. He's mad, that's a given, but there's something deeper in those eyes. Fear almost.

Odd.

What would scare a man like him? He's over six feet tall, buff, and certainly not a weakling. His jawline looks strong pinched tight, built like it's made for kicking butt and kissing girls stupid. And the rest of him...sweet baby Jesus. The longer I stare, the harder it is believing there's such a bastard stuffed in this Adonis. I rub my arm, hoping it won't bruise tomorrow from my grabby mystery man.

"Can we have one, Daddy?"

"Please?"

I bite my tongue to keep from answering. We've had enough kids at the lodge to teach me a thing or two. Whether I like it or not, it's never my place to get between a guest and their children.

Cagey, like a trapped beast, he walks towards the table,

keeping his eyes on me. I don't move, not even a step when he stops close enough to lift the lid off the plate of sandwiches. I'm not about to let him know he's frightened me, but I do get a whiff of his cologne. That has me biting the inside of my cheek. Damn if he doesn't smell as good as he looks.

Another suspicious look from his haunting eyes breaks the spell.

Clinging to the good sense God gave me, I say, "Again, sir, I wasn't sneaking around. I'm not trying to poison you, either. Whenever guests check in after meal time, we provide them with an evening snack." He doesn't look convinced. "Try it. Simple. Delicious. Yummy."

He doesn't respond, but picks up half a sandwich and takes a bite before nodding to the boys.

You're welcome, jerk, I think to myself. *Some people.*

The boys each take a cupcake and as they peel back the paper holders, I open the two cartons of milk and insert the straws Marcy included on the tray.

Then I pour him a cup of tea, using the hot water provided. "I can make you coffee if you'd prefer. It's instant, but it's not half bad."

"No, this is fine."

He's still grumpy, but his voice has lost some of its growl.

I hand each of the boys a milk carton, who both have pink frosting mustaches by now. "My name's Tabby."

"My name's Adam."

"I'm Chase, and daddy..." The second sweet boy pauses, his eyes going big as he looks at his father.

"Rex," he growls. My sinfully handsome porcupine has a normal name. Small relief.

"Well, I'm happy to meet you, Adam and Chase." I purposefully don't extend my welcome to Grumpy. "I hope you'll have fun here at the Grand Pine Lodge."

"Do you live here?" the one I think is Adam asks.

"Yes, I do, and I work here, too. So, if there's anything you need, just ask."

"Like more cupcakes?" Chase asks hopefully.

My first instinct is to say yes, but I hold back. "That would be up to your father..."

His eyes, as cold as ever, are on me. Not my face, but my sweater. It might be because it's the same color of pink as the frosting on the cupcakes and his sons' faces, but I doubt that.

Chills criss-cross my spine. My poor battered heart beats faster. It's like he can see right through the heavy wool. My nipples tingle, harden, adding to my shame.

Why? I've been hit on by men three times my age and boys alike, but I've never had *this* reaction.

"I think one's enough," he says. "You each eat a sandwich now and drink your milk."

I grab the menu off the tray before my mind, and body, reacts to how kind and gentle he suddenly sounds. "How long will you be staying?"

He picks up the tea and drinks it down before answering. "Just a few days."

"Well, here's the menu for the next three days. You can either have your meals delivered to your room or eat in the dining room. We're small, so the meal times are also listed, however, we can provide sandwiches and other items all day."

"And cupcakes?" Adam beams like the sun.

I can't help but smile. I used to dream of having children as adorable as these two, but it'll never happen. Reality and the roots I've laid down here go deep. I'll have to just enjoy the kids who visit the lodge. There aren't many men out there willing to give up their lives in order to help manage a place in the middle of nowhere. The few who might think they're willing would soon change their minds. This is a twenty-four hour, three-hundred and sixty-five day job, that also includes one very grumpy old man. My life has no place for children.

Besides, this is a small town. Split Harbor's dating pool isn't exactly extensive or quality. One very lucky lady already landed the resident billionaire a couple years ago.

"More cupcakes?" Chase echoes.

Touching the tip of Adam's nose, I say, "Some days it's cookies."

"I love cookies!" Chase yells.

"I like cupcakes more," Adam says.

"Well, then, I guess I'll have to make both, won't I? Cookies and cupcakes. I like staying busy." I wink at them before turning back to their father and hand him the menu. As he takes it, I get another whiff of that amazing cologne mingled with his scent. It's faint, but intoxicating and very good at making heat swirl deep inside me. The sandwich must have done him some good because he's no longer scowling. He's no longer *quite* as scary. His hair is darker than the boys, but I imagine when he was young it was just as sandy blond as Adam and Chase's. He was probably as adorable as they are, too.

"Where are you from?" I'm pulling my mind back where it belongs.

He sets the menu down on the dresser. "We'll be eating in our room, but aren't fussy. Whatever gets brought up will be fine. Along with coffee and milk. The earlier, the better."

I get the hint. It's none of my business where he's from. His clothes, jeans and a flannel shirt, could be worn in the city or country, but his accent reminds me of Russ, who is very proud of being born and raised in Chicagoland.

I should leave, but for some reason, it's hard peeling my eyes off him. I'm intrigued. Curious to know where his wife is, the boys' mother, but can't simply blurt it out.

He's staring back, harder than before, which has my insides tingling again in ways it shouldn't. *Ridiculous.*

"Well, Cupcake," he says slowly. It takes me a second to realize he means *me*. "You going to stand there all night, or let us finish eating in peace?"

Fine, whatever. I deserve that. He is a guest, after all.

Still, I'm irritated. And know I need to leave before saying something that will really piss him off. "I'm going," I say, "but the name's Tabby. I'd appreciate it if you'd –"

"Short for Tabitha?"

"No. Just Tabby." I cringe a little more than I usually do, giving up my nickname masquerading as a name.

He gives me one more solid toe-to-head stare that has me holding by breath before he whips around. "Let me get the door, Cupcake."

Nicknames. They shouldn't irritate me the way they do, but I can't help it.

Not when everyone always assumes Tabby is a nickname. It's the only thing my father ever gave me – whoever he was. One among many boyfriends who came calling on mom. My throat thickens slightly as I glance towards Adam and Chase. Those two boys don't know how lucky they are. Neither does their jackass father. I give them a small wave, walking out the door that's being held open impatiently by daddy's huge hand.

"Goodnight, Rex," I say, simply because he's a guest. A jerk, but a guest nonetheless, and we can't afford to lose customers in the winter. Not even a giant asshole.

He merely shuts the door.

I huff out a breath, and though I'd like to take a moment and lean against the wall to catch my bearings, I need space pronto, so make a beeline for the stairs.

Once I'm in the hallway safely downstairs, I place a hand on the wall, taking a few deep breaths. I've never had a man affect me like Rex. For no apparent reason, too.

It's so perplexing anger mingles with the heat he's left in my blood. Okay, so most women would be intrigued by six feet of mystery and muscle, especially one *that* freakin' sexy. But it doesn't explain why I'm coming undone for a Neanderthal who just wiped his feet on my back.

Annoyed, I push myself off the wall and head for the front desk. There, I move the mouse to wake up the computer and type in the password. The main screen appears.

Rex Osborne. Blue Chevy pick-up. No license plate number listed.

No, of course not. Gramps thinks that's a silly question even though I've warned him it might be important for security. Paid cash for two nights.

I log out and walk to the front door. Tall, dark, and sometimes handsome strangers are nothing new to the lodge. Insta-fascination I really shouldn't be experiencing is.

Maybe it's because our other handsome strangers come here to unwind, relieve the stress in their lives. Not this one. The man upstairs was wound tighter than a drum, and the blue pick-up backed up so it's practically hidden beneath the trees confirms something tickling at the back of my mind since he accused me of sneaking around outside 205.

Rex Osborne is hiding *something*. Or maybe, he's hiding from someone.

Either way, I want to know more. After locking the front door and turning down all the lights, and checking the kitchen, where I also leave a note for Marcy, I put on my coat and leave through the employee entrance. Rather than taking the shoveled pathway to my cabin, I walk around the lodge, to the far end of the parking lot. I'm able to get a better look at his truck from here.

Illinois plates. I knew it.

II: Settling In (Rex)

I stay hidden behind the curtain so she can't see me. She's already looked up at the window twice, as if sensing she was being watched, or she might just be that nosy – something that'll get her into more trouble than she'd ever bargain for.

Cupcake. I'd called her that out of defense, needing to keep my distance. Distance from everything and everyone.

Especially soft spoken girls who look as delicious as their dessert namesake. Her with the scorned looks lodged in her honey-hazel eyes. Her with the dark chocolate hair warning me it'd feel like velvet on my fingers.

Her with the hips, the legs, the ass that's divine, hopelessly hidden behind her Ms. Average outfit.

Shit. I catch myself hard and shake my head, remembering she's one more problem I don't need.

How the fuck did I end up in this predicament? By fucking, that's how. At least at the beginning.

Of all the men in the world, all the one-night stands, I'm the one who's getting royally fucked long after the fun ended. As my anger churns harder and hotter inside my guts, guilt rises to meet it. Cupcake has already walked away from the truck, back around the lodge, so I move away from the window. Stopping near the foot of one of the double beds, I stare at my twin boys

They're sleeping soundly. So innocent, so good, they almost take the edge off old mistakes.

Yeah, they came out of that one-night stand causing the present woes, too. I don't regret that. *Never will.*

It's ever screwing the bitch who bore them I regret. Should've known six years ago when I met her she was more trouble than any man needed. She'd been hot, sexy, and all over me. I'd had a hard week laying custom shingles on the roof of a frigging Senator's mansion.

I was ready to get drunk and wet my dick. We barely made it out of the bar. I fucked her in the front seat of my work truck parked in the alley. Afterwards, we'd gone back inside and partied some more, then we both left without another word.

Typical party at a watering hole on Chicago's rust belt. I never planned on seeing her again. Nine months later, when I was served the papers about submitting a blood sample, I'd long since forgotten her name. Until reading the second page of the court document, where our history was described, vividly.

I'm no deadbeat. I gave a paternity sample, accepted the DNA results, and agreed in court we'd share visitation to Adam and Chase. Limited and supervised visitations for her. Nelia claimed she hadn't known how to get a hold of me before the boys were born. An obvious lie. The name of my construction company, T-Rex Builders, was on the side of every work truck. Any number of people from the bar that night could've told her who I was, how to contact me.

She knew what she was doing from the start. Never attempted to get a hold of me to see the twins she abandoned, just thought I'd hand over child support, and lots of it, on a monthly basis.

She'd been dead wrong.

In more ways than one. Too fucking many to count.

And now she's dead.

Only saving grace about that is Adam and Chase didn't even know who she was. When, if ever, they heard about her death, they wouldn't mourn. Mommy is something they hear in fairy tales, not a fact of life.

Call me a cold-hearted bastard, but it's a small relief. Both that my sons won't suffer her loss, and that she's permanently out of our lives. She wasn't any type of mother to the boys the past five years, nor would she have ever changed. Didn't have it in her.

Raising kids takes heart, and Cornelia Hawkins didn't have a loving bone in her body, or the slightest clue what it took to be a mom.

Hell, Cupcake's already shown more affection towards the boys than Nelia ever did. Tabby, as she prefers to be called – the very reason I'll keep calling her Cupcake – may never know how badly Adam and Chase needed those chocolate treats tonight.

Not only had they been as hungry as me, and that was a damn good sandwich, the boys needed an ounce of kindness. Two weeks of driving around, spending nights in sleazy hotels and eating greasy drive-thru burgers, was taking its toll on all of us.

If Adam hadn't had to pee, and I hadn't pulled off on a side road to give him some privacy, I'd have never seen the faded sign advertising this place.

Grand Pine Lodge: A secluded hidden gem.

That's what the sign said, and that's exactly what we need. Sanctuary. A couple days off the road to wrap my head around what's happened, and what I can do about it next.

Because I'm not spending the rest of my life in jail for murder.

Fucking bitch. I knew what she was doing, but sure as hell hadn't expected this outcome.

Worst part is, I'm not the one who killed her.

I run my hands through my hair, scratching at my scalp. It itches like hell from not being washed good and proper in a couple days. The other hotels were too run down, too caked in dirt, I'd barely had time to run my head through the sink.

This place is old, but it's actually clean. Time for a real shower. Then a good night's sleep. I'll be clearer headed in the morning, able to think things through.

I grab the duffel bag I purchased in some dinky road-side town and head for the bathroom.

The shower helps. Bed's comfortable, too. So I let my

mind wander free while I'm waiting to fall asleep. Even crack a grin as the Cupcake's face forms in my mind. That pink sweater hugged her in all the right places, didn't it? And those eyes...they're not really hazel. I remember more.

A brownish-green with specks of gold that sparked hellfire at times. Especially when I'd asked if she was going to stand there invading our space all night. Her long hair was thick and dark brown, pulled back in a ponytail, making her look even younger. So did the way she hadn't worn makeup. She hadn't needed any. There was a natural beauty to her. A grace, almost. Something I haven't seen in a woman in ages.

Chicago's full of girls with hair as colorful as rainbows and decked in cosmetics. Plenty of them are pretty, some teetering towards beautiful, but there's something about Cupcake's naturalness that takes my mind off everything else. At least briefly.

Or maybe it's her attitude. I'd startled her, frightened her even, but the moment she'd seen the boys, she'd turned friendly and kind. Sweet as the name I've given her. That stirs up more than it ought to. Makes me wish things were different for Chase and Adam.

Hell, I wish that for myself. If Nelia was more like Cupcake, life would be pretty damn good right now. I wouldn't be in this mess. I'd be home, probably with something pink and delicious to come home to.

I like that thought, insane as it is. I drift off imagining the boys enjoying their colorful frosted cupcakes all over again.

* * *

My lungs are on fire, my breathing ragged, coming in gasps that hurt going out as much as the air burns going in. I grab my head as the spinning slows and the faint sunshine coming in the window confirms I'm not in a penthouse apartment, standing over Nelia's dead body.

Sweat pours down my neck and my hands shake as I tell myself it was only a dream. A fucking nightmare that I've already lived through and will continue to. Have to for Adam and Chase.

A knock at the door makes me realize that's why it ended. In the dream, Aiden had knocked on the door. That's not what happened in real life. He'd come at me like the crazy drugged up shit-hole of a man he'd been. I'm not sorry that fucker's dead either. Never will be.

The knock sounds again. Now, wide awake, the idea Cupcake could be outside my door has me tossing aside the covers. I grab a pair of jeans out of the duffel bag. "Coming."

Without bothering to zip or snap the jeans I shove my legs through, I open the door. The gray-haired old man who checked us in last evening stands there with a grimace. I can't tell if it's a frown or a smile.

"Tabby's note said you wanted breakfast early," the man said. "If she made a mistake, I can bring it back later."

"No," I answer. "No mistake. Thanks." I open the door wide enough to take the tray. "The boys are still sleeping, so I'll grab it." They're always starving when they wake up. As he hands me the tray, I say, "Hold on, though, I'll get the one from last night."

I set the tray on the table, find the one from last night, and carry it to the door. The man was hard to read, but knowing I can't afford anymore enemies, I say, "Thanks, the boys enjoyed the cupcakes."

"Tabby will be glad to hear it. I'll give her your compliments. You need something, just push one on the phone. That rings the front desk."

I nod and close the door, then give myself permission to crack a smile. The phone system in the place is as horribly outdated as everything else here. Damned if I care, it's not a dump like some of the other roadside motels we've stayed in the past two weeks. The lodge is clean and well maintained, just old.

The building must date back to the 1950s, maybe earlier. Being the carpenter I am, I'd noticed all that when we'd checked in. The place has solid bones, and with the way it's been kept up, it could stand for another century.

By the time I turn around, still trying to gauge how ancient this place really is, Adam and Chase are up. They're sitting on their bed, scratching their mops of tousled hair. Whether the sound of voices or the smell of food roused them, I have no idea.

"Hungry?"

"Yeahhhh!"

"Shhh," I say, even though it's too late. Their shout has my ears ringing, let alone any poor souls in the rooms next door. "Other people are probably still sleeping. Don't be rude, boys."

"Sorry," they say, once again at the same time.

It's uncanny, but deep down, I love it. They do most everything at the same time. They're like any kids making innocent mistakes as they grow, but they'll never need to apologize for who they are. "It's okay," I say softly. "Come on and eat."

"Are there cupcakes?"

I smile and rub each of their heads before reaching down to remove the cloth covering the tray. "Most people don't have cupcakes for breakf…" My words fade away. Besides three plates covered with domed metal lids, there are cartons of milk, a pot of coffee with a single cup, and three pink frosted cupcakes on the tray.

I can't help but chuckle. "I guess we aren't most people, are we?"

"Nope," the boys say while climbing onto the chairs.

"Are we going home today?" Chase asks.

"No, not today." Not ever is what I really mean.

"Yippie!"

They eat the cupcakes first and I let them. It's no great sin when I feed them right most days. The scrambled eggs, bacon, toast and hash browns fill me up. Damn good. I sit back to drink my coffee while the boys devour their smaller portion of the same breakfast I just had.

It's not long before I'm pouring myself a second cup. Hot and black, just how I like it. A sinking feeling gels the food in my stomach as I watch them eat.

I have to figure out what to do. These two need me. *Will* need me for years to come.

Since freeing them from the penthouse apartment, we've bounced around Illinois, Iowa and Wisconsin, zigzagging from ATM to ATM, drawing out my daily limit. If only I'd had the foresight to up that amount. I have enough money for us to live on for years in the bank, but hadn't thought about upping the amount. Worse, knowing the transactions left a trail anyone could follow, I pitched the card out the window over the side of a bridge and headed for Canada.

What choice did I have – money or demons in hot pursuit?

We could jump in the truck right now and make it to the border in a few hours, but that's just as risky as it was yesterday. I'd have to show my ID to cross the border. I don't know who's watching or what the Chicago press is saying back home.

Hunkering down would be the best bet, let things cool off till I can contact my lawyer. Granted, Justin was a business lawyer, not a criminal one, but he'll know someone who can help.

While the boys are finishing up, I dig the tablet out of my duffel bag and turn it on. I'd bought it along with clothes, duffel bags, and a cart full of other essentials the day after leaving Chicago, using a credit card which I then flushed down the toilet in the men's room of the gas station after using it to fill the truck's tank.

My grandfather's old truck is a gas hog, but reliable. I took it out of the pole shed on his property, where it's been parked since grandpa died ten years ago, and where I left mine. My cousin lives on the farm now, and probably won't go in the shed until summer. Hopefully. If he does, I hope he sees the note I left behind. It simply says I'd borrowed it. John takes the truck out on the roads every summer, just to keep it in running order, so I knew it'd take us wherever we needed to go, about as untraceable as we could get. Which is exactly what we needed and why I threw my phone in the back of a shipping truck with Florida license plates at a gas station.

Fucking-A. What a mess.

After punching in the internet password written on a slip of paper and taped to the front of the phone book on the desk, I search hotels, resorts, and all sorts of other lodging options along the Canadian border for an hour or more. I'm not sure how long it's been, but I do know my options are crap. I only have a couple of grand, tops, in my billfold. Spending three hundred a night isn't feasible. This place, the Grand Pine Lodge, doesn't even have its own website. The price is very reasonable, too.

What I need is a job. Income. Enough money so I can pay our room and board here, saving my cash for when we have to leave. The dollar stretches a bit further over the border, but only if I've got plenty to stretch.

It's far from my biggest worry, too. The Stone Syndicate won't stop looking. They know where Nelia's money came from, and they know who killed Aiden.

They know my fucking name, who my kids are, and every sacred stretch of Chicago soil I ever frequented. We can't stop for long. We *have* to keep moving.

"Dad, there's a horse out there," Adam says, breaking my quiet panic.

"Can we go look at it?" Chase asks.

"Or ride it?" Adam pipes in.

They're getting restless. I've kept them busy getting dressed, combing their hair and brushing their teeth, all on their own, which takes ample time considering they're only five.

"Sure," I say, suppressing a sigh. "Fresh air will do us all good, I suppose." It'll give me time to look around, too, maybe see if there's a back road out of this place. Valuable info I may need if the time to leave comes sooner than I think. "Get your coats on, and don't forget your mittens."

"They're gloves, Dad," Chase corrects.

"Right, don't forget your gloves." I smile. Nelia may

have given them half their genes, but they've got my looks and brains. My focus.

Small blessings. Can't fathom what the hell I'd do right now without them.

It's only a little after seven and the hotel is pin-drop quiet, so I tap my lips with a finger as we walk down the stairs. Their hushed giggles make me shake my head. This is how they've been since we left. Following my commands without questions, acting like the entire thing is one huge adventure.

Technically, it is. Just not the joyous kind they think.

I open the door and close it again behind us as quick as possible. The boys can't hold back their shouts of freedom any longer as they tear across the wide front porch and down the stairs.

Whoever does the shoveling around here must get up early. The porch, steps, and sidewalks are clear from last night's snow, as well as a wide pathway to the barn that's a good hundred yards off to the east side of the lodge. Shoveling that much wouldn't have been easy. A good two inches fell, the wet, heavy kind that makes good snow balls, snow forts, and snowmen. The boys run on toward the barn, stopping to scoop up a handful every now and again.

I scanned the area, looking for signs of trouble, or anything out of the ordinary. Whoever shovels, must not also plow because there aren't any tracks in the parking lot. It's still got my truck and the two other SUVs that were there last night.

Nearly deserted. That'll do fine.

As satisfied as I can be given the circumstances, I follow the boys, catching up with them on the backside of the barn, where they're crouched down looking between the two bottom rails of the fence at the two shaggy looking horses.

"Can we go in there, Dad?" Adam asks.

"No."

Just then a door on the barn near the fence opens and I take a double look at who comes strolling out.

Cupcake. She must love pink. I didn't know they made canvas work coats in that shade. Her hair is in another ponytail and a thick head band covers her ears. Pink again.

My morning wood is back with a vengeance, straining against my denim.

"Well, good morning!" she says to the boys, never once looking at me. "What brings you early risers out here?"

"We saw the horses," Chase says.

"Can we pet them?" Adam asks.

"And ride them?" Chase grins.

"These two are too old to ride anymore," she says softly, "but you can pet them, if it's all right with your father."

The boys look up at me, hope sparking in their eyes. So does she, which makes my heart thud oddly.

It's got to be the stress. I've had women since Nelia, yeah, but always kept them at a distance, far from me and the boys. I'm never getting burned like that again. But fuck, I'm not a monk, and a woman as attractive as Cupcake has the bewitching ability to turn me hard in a heartbeat.

"Can we, Dad?"

I turn to them and nod.

"You'll have to come through the barn." She points to the side of the building. "The door I shoveled a path to."

Testing my hearing, I ask, "You shoveled the path?"

"Yes."

"And the sidewalks?"

"Yes, why?" she cocks her head.

The boys are already running, so I simply say, "No reason."

I'm impressed, and that's got nothing to do with her dick-teasing looks. A woman who bakes and shovels is a certain rarity in this day and age. Then again this isn't the big city.

By the time I get to the door, the boys have shoved it open and darted inside.

"Be careful," she says. "Slow down."

The boys listen, slowing to a brisk walk as they make their way around piles of lumber.

"We're in the middle of a remodeling out here," she says.

I nod, taking it all in.

Big and solid, the barn is what I'd call a clean slate. This is the part of construction work I've always loved. Envisioning the potential, what the final project could look like restored. Unfortunately, I don't get to do it as often as I'd like anymore.

Most of the time, my customers have professional blueprints ready to go for my crew.

Shit, the crew. Just thinking about them twists my lips sourly.

That was one of the two phone calls I'd made before I threw my phone to the wild. To Randy, my construction manager. I told him to cut the men a month's worth of paychecks and shut everything down. It was the best I could do and it still pisses me off, but I had to make a choice. Fast.

A day or two more, and the Syndicate would be all over my company. They'd go after my men for info, hell, their families. I couldn't put more lives in danger. Protecting my boys is enough. More than enough.

The other call had been to Mrs. Potter, the nanny and tutor I'd hired for Chase and Adam in better times. I told her I was taking them out of town on business and would call when we return. I'll cut her a severance check, eventually, but she already screwed me once. *If she'd said no to Nelia that fucked up day she came...*

No. I can't go there again.

Holding in a sigh, I follow the boys, who are following Cupcake, taking my time to examine the space. Whatever helps get my mind off poison. Like the lodge, the barn was built well and it's still solid. Even the floor. By the time I catch up to them through the back door, she's given each of the kids a bucket. A horse eats out of each one, both snorting happily to the boys' delight.

"What type of remodeling project?" I finally ask.

She eyes me critically while continuing to pet one of the big brown horses. I don't blame her, I wasn't friendly last night. After a few tense seconds, I walk over and pet the other horse, acting as if I don't care if she answers or not.

"We're turning it into more of a stable, with a large tack area room, feed storage, and office."

"For these two?" I'm not much of an animal person, but I recognize old when I see it.

"No. We'll keep them, but also bring in more, so we can offer trail rides to guests."

"What are trail rides?"

She laughs at how both boys speak simultaneously, word for word. "Horse rides."

"Yippie!" They both jump, no doubt hoping to be the first happy customers.

Picturing a layout inside the barn, I ask, "How many horses?"

"I'm thinking six," she says, "but it depends on Clayton. He's our neighbor and this will be a partnership of sorts. The man boards horses and always has more than he can exercise on his property. He doesn't have enough acreage for trails, either. I think the guests will like it, and hopefully, we'll both make some money."

It's a solid plan, though I'm not about to say it. I'm also seeing a job for myself. One that won't take long, but could pay the money I need.

"Unfortunately, the remodel is delayed right now."

"Why?" I snap, trying not to show my hand. Not easy.

"Russ broke an ankle and probably won't get back to work for a couple months. He's kinda our jack-of-all-trades around here. He was spearheading this before the accident."

Shitfire, this is too perfect. My mind goes a hundred miles per hour, estimating how long it'll take me to complete the remodel as we stand quiet for a short time.

Then Cupcake glances down at the boys and then back up at me, breaking the silence. "So, not to break up the party, but I've got other chores. Can't let you stay out here, sir. Liability reasons."

I nod. "Fine. Thanks for letting them feed the horses. Boys, what do you say?"

"Can we do it again?"

I give them a look. "Boys..."

"Thank you, Tabby!" They both lower their eyes and I give a satisfied nod.

Cupcake laughs. A soft, airy sound reminding me what kind of trouble I'm in getting too close to this woman. "Adorable. Do you two *always* talk at the same time?" she asks.

"Sometimes," the boys answer shyly.

The sound of more singsong feminine laughter makes me wonder if the boys ever heard such an angelic sound before. *Hell, have I?*

"Just you working in the barn while the help is out – Russ, right?" I ask.

Cupcake nods. "Yes. Well, I fill their water tank and feed them grain every morning and hay every evening," she says while collecting the buckets. "It's easy enough."

"How do you keep the water from freezing?" I wonder aloud.

Her eyes say she still doesn't trust me, yet she answers, "There's a pump house in the far corner of the barn that we keep heated."

Room for improvement. Another opportunity, if they'll bite.

I wave for the boys to follow. They have more questions for her as we walk through the barn. She answers each one while I scan the area again, making mental notes. The old man who checked us in last night said he owns the place, so that's who I need to talk to. Once we exit the barn, she says goodbye and walks towards the back of the lodge, a plastic salt bucket in hand. I keep the boys outside until they've worn off some energy, then lead them inside.

Off the foyer where the large front desk is located, there's a big front room with a TV and a large game of checkers set up on a coffee table. I get the boys settled in first. I haven't let them out of my sight since that night our world caved in. Don't want to now, but must, in order to talk to the old man.

I won't be far, knowing this is the safest place we've been in two weeks, so I leave the room and cross the foyer again. There's a door behind the desk marked OFFICE. Unable to remember what the man said his name was, I scan a magazine on a side table with a subscription label. Morris Danes.

That's right. I've sold multi-million dollar construction jobs, convincing Morris Danes to pay me to remodel his barn should be like taking candy from a baby.

I knock, fully prepared to open the door upon invitation.

Instead, it opens as someone leaves.

Shit.

It's Cupcake. The old man sitting behind her bristles hostility. My shoulders want to sag. If she has anything to do with it, I won't get this job.

GET MAN ENOUGH AT YOUR FAVORITE RETAILER!

Printed in Great Britain
by Amazon